The Fall of Hate

Book 3 of

By Charles W. McDonald Jr.

The Fall of Hate © 2018 Book 3 of
A Throne of Souls®© 2018 Registration claim(s) #1-10404623181
(www.copyright.gov)
ISBN 978-1-7324798-0-7 Amazon Print Edition

2nd Edition including new illustrations, proofreading, intellectual property rights
and glossary updates.

Charles W. McDonald Jr.

Credits:
Very special thanks to the following for their feedback and contributions:

John Armond Howarth for the initial creation of Kellen, Goldenbow, Aaramus, Evanyil, Banthis, Rena Rectovich, and a few other characters important in the telling of this story. John helped awaken my creative thinking that further developed these—and other—characters, making the delivery of this work of fiction to you possible. With all my most sincere and best wishes, thank you, John.

The following Beta Readers:
Brandy L. MᶜDonald
Sabrina Plog
Charles W. MᶜDonald Sr.
for their very honest and constructive criticism in reviewing early editions of this novel.

Story by: Charles W. MᶜDonald Jr.
Written by: Charles W. MᶜDonald Jr.
Cover by: Steven J. Catizone and Anthony DiPaolo
Edited by: Zora Alexandra Knauf
Proofread by: Jessamine Julian
Cartography by: Charles W. MᶜDonald Jr. and Wes Rand
E-Book Conversion by: Charles W. MᶜDonald Jr.
Interior artwork by: Wes Rand, Anthony DiPaolo, and Shady Curi

Research-related: While I do include and credit some specific concepts in the glossary, I wanted to specifically call out and credit the incredible scientific contributions done on behalf of Humanity by **Nassim Haramein**. My research into his work aided in fueling my illustrative examples of *The Connected Universe*. I would encourage everyone who reads this to research and read his work—especially that around proton radius calculations, quantum holography, and Planck density of protons. It is truly exceptional, and when you dig into it, you will begin to see the true genius in the symmetry

Charles W. MᶜDonald Jr.

and the mind of Creation!

Charles W. McDonald Jr.

Dedication:

Forever, for Emrys…

Charles W. McDonald Jr.

When all that is left of great miracles are the waning memories of distant accounts, now questioned by Men, shall I come to you in the one, undeniable breath of God that your tattered faith be renewed. For in the final moments, shall you need it.

Charles W. McDonald Jr.

Preface: A Reader's Guide to A Throne of Souls

Most of you already know the drill, but for those who chose to skip ahead, I'll leave this Preface in place.

The complexity of weaving the intricate plot lines of this story required the breaking of a *lot* of rules to bring this product to you. Some of those rules involve unconventional capitalization and emphasis strategies. So, for example, there are many reserved words in this story (Humanity, Creation, Man, Mankind, Humanoid, etcetera). Those reserved words will be consistently either capitalized or emphasized for this story and you might think *hey, that word shouldn't be capitalized*, but I assure you this is done with deliberate intent and should not be corrected to mainstream authoring standards.

The bottom line is this: I'm not here to write like everyone else. I'm not here to rigidly adhere to boundaries established by others. I'm here to bring you something truly new and groundbreaking—but in *my* voice and *my* style. If that troubles you, perhaps you should find something more mainstream to read. But you're not going to find anything this thought-provoking written in the mainstream in the voice of the status quo. Groundbreaking content doesn't follow the status quo; else, it wouldn't be groundbreaking. George Lucas had to invent new special effects methods and studio techniques to deliver the first Star Wars® trilogy because it was truly groundbreaking. This is the space in which I find myself when writing the story of *A Throne of Souls* for you and for me.

I have put a great deal of thought and research into *The Fall of Hate*, and this series. My hope is that you will learn a something from it that you might not have learned from other sources or content platforms, even though it is a fictionalized story wrapped around a non-fiction latticework of the shared nature of our reality. What do I mean by that…? In short, what you can expect from this story is something far bigger, with much greater reach, than just fiction. I intend to re-frame the lens through which you see reality. To put your fixed belief systems to the test. Nothing less….

It is my hope that you'll see that the connections I am making for you of these disparate concepts and theories is a fair and precise reduction

Charles W. McDonald Jr.

without a significant distortion of their intended outcomes (I'm speaking of the disparate theories here). Please do not take offense that I have read—for the making of this series—material you may find offensive and/or blasphemous to your belief system. I have said from the very outset of this story that there is truth from many sources and *that no one source has all the answers*—nor are disparate accounts necessarily mutually exclusive of one another. This is the very foundation of *A Throne of Souls*…. If that offends you, find something more conventional to read and continue your life inside your little bubble and your echo chamber of sources. That is entirely your choice. However, I have always believed that there are many out there who want their belief systems tested—that want their understanding of the nature of our shared reality expanded, and who are passionate, intellectual truth-seekers. *This* content has been specifically architected for you!

The content I bring you in coda of this story is brought to you with the deepest love and affection, and I wish you nothing but love and kindness as my fellow brothers and sisters in Creation. I want nothing from you. I want everything for you. My hope is that you'll begin to see the coherence in my highly unconventional writing practices and begin to appreciate their uniqueness and why this story—apart from all others—required it.

If this installment—*The Fall of Hate*—is your first exposure to the story of *A Throne of Souls*, I would encourage you to read through the Glossary of Characters before you begin the Prologue. I've had others comment on how helpful that was for them and *The Fall of Hate* was their introduction to this series as well…

Other uncommon standards to this story involve handling of scene breaks. So, for instance, you'll see the following types of scene breaks in *A Throne of Souls* to which I'll try to stay as consistent as possible:

*   *   *   *

The four-star mark (above) will be used denote a scene break of a brief period of time without switching locations or switching locations (roughly the same time) but staying on the same planetary body.

Charles W. McDonald Jr.

The preceding flourish bracket will be used to denote a scene break of a large time difference and/or a planetary body shift in location.

A simple carriage return of white space will be used to denote a change in perspective within the same scene. For example, in a large battle sequence, it's important to understand the perspectives of multiple key players as they are engaged in the fight—to see the same event from multiple camera angles, if you will.

I want to be as assertive as possible here: ***please*** pay careful attention to the time and location markers when and where they are provided. It will greatly help you as the timelines begin to cross over one another asynchronously, and I promise it will contribute substantially to the whole story making perfect sense to you as the larger mosaic begins to fill. I'm not saying you *have* to take notes, nor have an eidetic memory. I'm just saying it will greatly help you deduce the clue drops and critical 'ah hah' moments I've woven into the story. And those who have gotten the most out of *A Throne of Souls* have had the trait in common of taking copious notes as they read the story. I've tried my best to standardize the following format for the time/location markers throughout:

(Specific Place, Planetary Body, Specific Time if Applicable)

I want to also comment on the timeline distortions and how these will impact your reading experience. There are going to be times when you read about a character who is beyond or behind "Present Day" and yet the time marker in the header clearly states, "Present Day." Realize and remember when Damon first saved all those people on all those worlds, he did so in the locale's "Near Future," bringing them to Eden's "Present Day," which at the outset of this book would be two-plus years forward in their timeline continuum. Please keep that critical piece of the story at the forefront of your thoughts as you continue reading because the continuum will become spaghettified if you don't.

You would have figured out some, or most, of the above as you read the story, but I thought it would be nice not to exhaust your effort figuring

Charles W. McDonald Jr.

out mechanics of telling the story. Now, we can get to *A Throne of Souls*—
Book 3....

Contents

Charles W. McDonald Jr.

Charles W. McDonald Jr.

Charles W. McDonald Jr.

This Edition's Last Modified Date:
April 29, 2021

Maps:

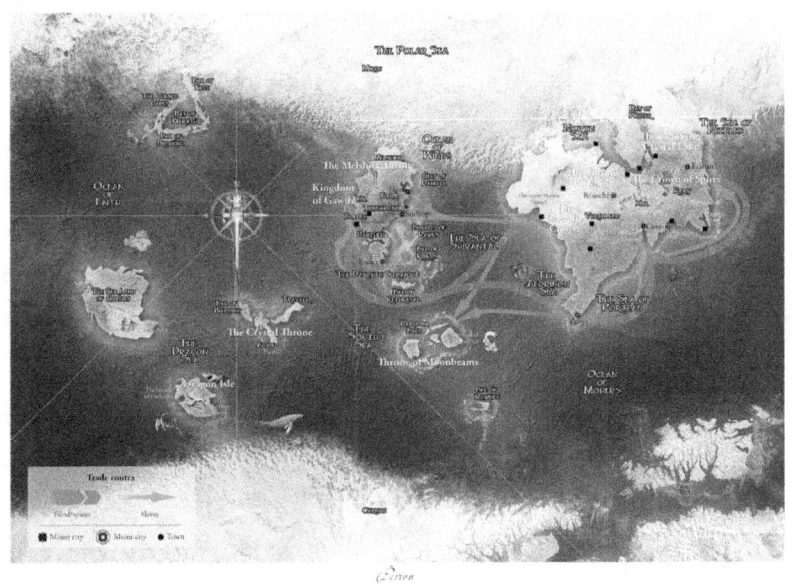

Charles W. McDonald Jr.

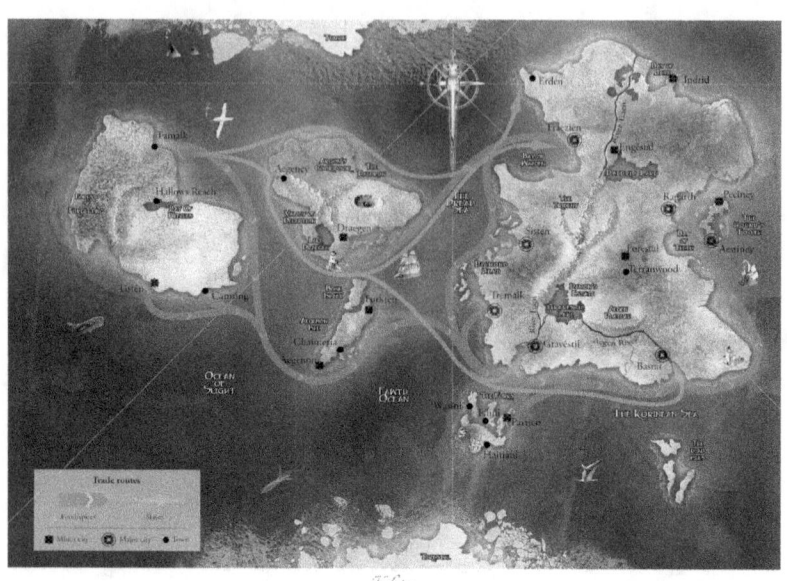

Kalcior

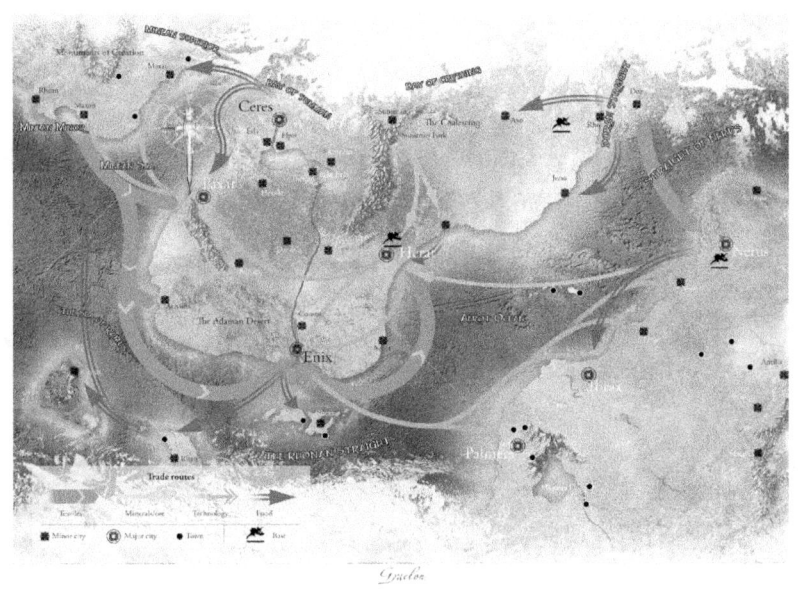

Charles W. McDonald Jr.

Eden

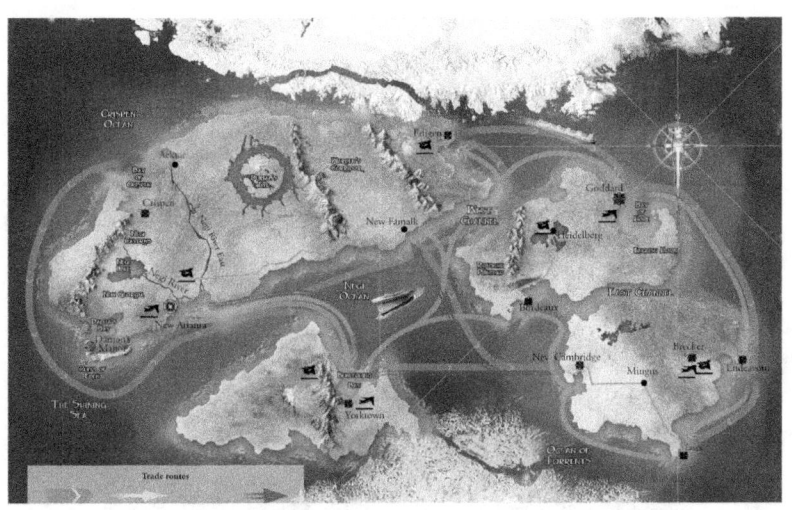

Charles W. McDonald Jr.

Damon of Basrat - The Dark Knight of Magic

Damon the Banished - The Dark Knight of Magic

Charles W. McDonald Jr.

Prologue: Durial's Justice

(South of the Aegen River, Kaleion, A Very Long Time Ago)

The twin moons of Kaleion—both in full repose—tugged at the planet's crust in opposing directions, swelling the diameter of the great planet, causing all manner of hateful acts of man and beast. Yet the twin moons held nothing on the instrument of *hate* currently at work upon the destiny of Man.

Another lashing of Keirill's *Telekinesis* brought Seren to her knees; another welt stung on her beautiful but scarred collarbone. This was not the man she married!

Brilliant fire-red hair framed soft pale skin. Seren's emerald-green eyes begged forgiveness—for what, she couldn't know. She dared not rise to her feet with him like this. Keirill was far more powerful—both physically and in Arcane—not to mention his natural abilities. Another blunt, brute-force strike of his *Telekinesis*-borne fist crushed her jawbone, shattering it in three places, and she collapsed to the dirt, no longer recognizing the husband who now lorded over her.

"Please…." The word came out jarred, shaky, and barely recognizable as she'd all but lost her ability to enunciate with her jaw now shattered.

"Don't get up until you've learned your lesson," Keirill demanded—his right-hand index finger pointed straight at her, though she dared not look at him. "I told you I never wanted a child. That was your responsibility to make sure that never happened!"

Charles W. McDonald Jr.

Even now Seren huddled over her life-bearing womb, crouched on the ground on all fours, trying to guard herself from an attack that might kill what she knew to be her beloved unborn son.

It was true. He had warned her—many times, but she was lonely with the hate-filled isolationism of her husband and longing for something and someone beyond herself and a husband she no longer recognized. Someone who could love her back. She thought he might change his mind when he found out, or maybe when the boy was born. At the very worst, he might learn to appreciate his own flesh and blood. Surely....

A giant glob of spit landing right beside her clenched right hand in the Kaleion soil told her otherwise. Her son would never be welcomed—not by him. "Whore! Stay outside tonight. If I find you went any-where...."

Holding up her left hand up toward him in surrender, Seren motioned to him in acknowledgement. She'd stay outside all night to prevent more of his wrath. Her tears fell to the soil, muddying the ground around her as she tried to find a measure of comfort, so she could attempt to *Heal* her jaw before it became permanently damaged.

She heard the heavy door to their farm cottage slam shut as Keirill retreated into their home. "I'm sorry, Kaylan. I never meant to bring you into this. Please forgive me." Rubbing her barely showing belly, she felt the boy the size of an onion kick back. *What have I done?* She couldn't stop the tears from their relentless condemnation of her selfish act of love.

*   *   *   *

(South of the Aegen River, Kaleion, A Few Years Later)

"If you think I'm going to let this continue..., you're mistaken," Daedrin informed his sister after a thought-filled pause. His black hair already silvering, beginning to match his dark-grey robes with decorative vertical flutes of royal blue—a symbol of his lineage, and hers.

"While I can't make excuses for Keirill anymore, I forbid you from taking any action against my husband! I forbid it! Tell me you understand." Her fire-red hair and emerald-green eyes shimmered in the dusky hues of sunset whilst her beloved son ran and played some distance away.

Charles W. McDonald Jr.

Daedrin paused, scratching his chin in contemplation of a promise he could adhere to without prohibiting doing what needed to be done. "What would you have me do?"

"Stay out of it…," Seren paused, thinking now beyond herself. "Do what you must to protect Kaylan but stay out of my marriage. I can handle Keirill. He'd never harm me."

"Really…," he chaffed, reaching up his hand to caress the jaw her husband had shattered only a few years before.

Brushing away her brother's hand, Seren pulled back from him. "Promise me you'll protect Kaylan but stay out of my marriage."

"Fine," Daedrin bristled, furrowing his brow at his sister.

"Is that your word, Daedrin?"

"As much as I'm willing to give," Daedrin barbed again with his sister, knowing she wasn't the relenting type. "The boy looks like Keirill. Why does he hate his son so?"

"I can't say. He's been unrecognizable as my husband for years. It's as if he's being influenced by something, but I've checked and checked, and checked again. There is no magic influencing him—that I can see." She thought about it again. "Yet his behavior is so erratic. It's as if it's beyond *his* ability to control."

"And you don't see that as cause for my intervention?"

"I LOVE HIM! What part of that don't you get?"

"Fine…," Daedrin capitulated, knowing better, but also knowing this was not the battle that was worth dying over. There would be others. Of that, he was certain. He'd known Keirill nearly as long as he'd known his sister. And, much like his sister, he no longer recognized the man. But he also knew, sooner than later, he'd have to be dealt with—one way or the other. Watching Kaylan play in the barn from afar, Daedrin kept his distance from him per Seren's instructions. She didn't want any family influence over him save her own. She had wanted a normal life for Kaylan. To live, laugh, play, and not have anything at all to do with magic. The less magic had an influence in his life, the better. After seeing what Keirill's pursuit of magic had done to him, she'd assumed Arcane would come for her, too, and she feared the toll. She'd seen the price paid by many an Archmage and wanted a better, more mundane life for her son. She'd even refused to cast around

Kaylan. Daedrin didn't understand it, and certainly didn't agree with it. If the boy had abilities—and being the son of Keirill and Seren, he most certainly would—he would cast one way or the other. Better to cast with training and discipline than without. No, he could never agree with his sister on this one, but he respected her wishes so stay away he would. Watching Kaylan chase the black and white, long-haired, medium-sized, shepherd dog around the barn, Daedrin wondered what future beheld this boy of genitors most profound.

*   *   *   *

(South of the Aegen River, Kaleion, A Few Years Later)

"You're not going to tell me how to parent *my* son, Bitch," Keirill shouted at his wife.

"I'm just asking you not to cast around him. That's all. I'm not telling you anything. I would never disrespect you, Husband." Seren half-bowed to Keirill, hoping the carrot worked since she didn't possess the stick with which to manhandle this brute of a man.

Keirill's eyes worked in contemplation—an obsolescent compassion immediately dismissed as weakness—considering how to respond to his ever-testing, ever-probing, ever-prodding, ever-manipulating wife. "*You* brought him into this world against my wishes. *You* don't have a say in how I act around him."

"He is *your* son as you say. He's mine too." She stopped, pursing her lips seeing and immediately recognizing Keirill's dark death stare now fixed upon her soul. "Would you really have him following in your footsteps? Or mine? What good would that do? You've never been the same since your enhancements. Admit it!" There it was. She'd called him out. Now she could advance or retreat, but the element of surprise had been spent. "You think I didn't know? That I wouldn't find out? How **stupid** do you think I am?" Shields fully up, she advanced, casting the strongest protection spells she possessed as she closed the few paces between them in their humble country kitchen.

Charles W. McDonald Jr.

Keirill's starry, bright-blue eyes roiled with gold rims of fire as his first volley of *Telekinesis* smashed into his wife, crushing her against the kitchen wall from her left while he stood motionless, bringing all his protections up to snuff. "You *dare assault me!* You *dare defy me!* You *dare disrespect me!*" Another smashing blow of his *Telekinesis* had Seren on her knees—ribs shattered as she struggled for air.

Determined not to go down without a fight, Seren gave him her best shot, simultaneously casting *A Bliss of Fire* right behind *A Cone of Ice*, causing a massive cone of ice to erupt from the floor, engulfing her husband floor-to-ceiling, immediately followed by piercing, flaming arrows that swelled in intensity and size as they shot forth from her gold fingernails, racing toward her now-frozen husband. She hadn't started the day intending to harm her once-loved husband, but she knew that look in his eye and she knew she wouldn't survive the day if *he* did.

The flaming arrows shattered his best protections—as they should. He knew Seren a great and powerful Archmage, but the *Cone of Ice* had only worked on his protections, failing to pierce. Naked and without protection or not, he was unscathed underneath. The flames in his eyes said nothing of the life he squeezed out of his wife with his *Telekinesis* constricting around Seren's throat with only the pinching motion of his right index finger and thumb.

She had only an instant of breath remaining as she made a sweeping motion with her left hand, knocking her husband to the ground as she knocked his feet out from underneath him, causing him a momentary release of his iron grip on her throat.

Now knocked to the kitchen floor, laying on his right side, he heard his son come to see what the commotion was as he called forth the greatest bolt of lightning he'd ever summoned, blistering through the roof of their ranch home, searing his wife to oblivion and beyond. Only a smoking crater in their wood-plank flooring remained.

Charles W. McDonald Jr.

Struggling to right himself against the great commotion threatening to rip the house to pieces, Kaylan rushed from his bedroom down the hallway toward what he could only assume was another fight.

"Pa. What's happening? Where's Mom?" A ten-year-old Kaylan stood there, shocked in overalls and grey shirt, black bangs swept down over starry, bright-blue eyes of his father, and his father before him.

"GET OUT! It's not safe for you here." The ever-so-briefest of moments of clarity and truth escaped Keirill at the death of the woman he once loved, pushing back against the *Instrument of Humanity's Hate*.

Kaylan just stared at the smoking hole in the ground where ashen tatters of his mother's clothes remained. "Where's Mom?"

"GET OUT," Keirill demanded, pushing his son out of the room and all the way out of the front door of the house, using his *Telekinesis* as he uprighted himself, looking at the result of his *hate* smoldering in the blistered flooring of his kitchen: singed wood planks—shattered, broken, and darkened with the ash of his former love. He looked up through the ceiling and through his roof now in need of repair. His mouth worked, in search of words of remorse that would never come. *Who, or what, am I now?* Now left alone with a troublesome boy he didn't want in a life he no longer understood. This was no longer the life of the greatest mage of all time, and he felt robbed. He wanted to walk away—to abandon the boy who was never his choice. But, something wouldn't let him leave. Frowning, looking in the direction his boy just left, Keirill tried to reconcile an unrecognizable instinct telling him to stay against his burning desire to be free and to claim a title still within his reach.

*   *   *   *

(South of the Aegen River, Kaleion, A Few Days Later)

Kaylan scurried about the barn, performing chores at the fastest pace he could muster, not wanting to disappoint Pa again. Keirill warned the boy he had plenty to do to prepare for Mom's funeral and he didn't have time to deal with Kaylan disappointing him. Kaylan needed to be extra careful because failing his father meant failing the remembrance of his mother. He still didn't understand what happened to her. One day she was there, and the next she wasn't, and he had never been given any explanation—only, "Don't disappoint me," from his father.

"I was wondering if we might have a word with each other." Daedrin's voice had only come as a partial surprise, as had his sudden appearance on his front porch by methods other than *Portal* or *Gate*.

"And what word would you prefer," Keirill bristled in reply, bringing up all his protections in an instant as his eyes brimmed with *hate* for Seren's meddlesome brother.

"*Justice.*" It was only one word, but the plain silver rod barely half the length of his forearm instantly snatched by unseen hands into Daedrin's right hand caused Keirill's eyes to swell in stark and fulsome terror.

It was all said and done in an instant as Keirill's protections crumbled all around him like a shattered wall. He reached out for the lifeblood Arcane required to rebuild that which Daedrin had so easily destroyed, but it was void—its chalice of life broken. He opened his mind to the *Telekinesis* he'd known since he was a child. Again, empty and unresponsive to his will. Unable to form even a fist with which to strike back, Keirill's vast power was suddenly impotent. Rising from his wooden rocker to face down Daedrin with all he had left—his physical stature—Keirill closed the few spans between them, staring the judge and executioner of his powers directly eye to eye. "You think you've won." It rivaled a memory of a memory, but Keirill somehow knew otherwise.

"I think Seren **deserved** better.... I think Kaylan *deserves* better. And, I think this will cause you the *greatest* suffering. I could have easily killed you, but that was not Durial's way and it's not mine either. I gave you *Durial's Justice,* and you shall have to learn to live with it."

A physical fist clenched and readied where a *Telekinesis* one could not form, took a swing at Daedrin, only hitting his transparent shield in futility a full span from Daedrin's actual flesh.

"Don't make me come back for you, Keirill. I won't be so kind to you next time." Daedrin's words floated on the dust-laden air of his porch as Daedrin himself disappeared the same way he'd come—without aid of *Portal*

Charles W. McDonald Jr.

or *Gate*.

Now castrated from the manhood of his great power, the once-great Archmage sat back down in his rocker, watching his son scurry about the barn, trying to please him. Contemplating all that had been and all that could be, Keirill clenched his fists 'til he drew blood in both hands, staining the arms of his rocker in his *hatred of Mankind*. A heavy sigh as he considered taking his own life, but the *Instrument of Humanity's Hate* wouldn't allow it. There was still work to be done as he watched his son from afar. Still work he *could* perform. Still work he *must* perform.

Charles W. McDonald Jr.

Chapter 1: The Patience to Erase Humanity

(Kaleion, Tens of Thousands of Years Ago....)

"**N**OOOO," Pierio shouted at the lead Sentinel whose eyes glowed a dispassionate molten-amber, removing its extended digit from the transparent control panel it had just used to sentence the once-great Durial to exile—and with him the exile of Humanity. "Why?!" Pierio struggled against the unseen power of his handcuffs, taunting the battle-scarred Sentinel currently ignoring him. "Why not just kill us? You think your laws and your cause *so righteous*?!"

We are killing you! That thought forced into Pierio's mind by the battle-hardened Sentinel, its dark, acid-etched alloy legs now extending so as to allow itself to walk, rather than float, toward the hardened criminal. *You and all those like you will surely...**die**. It has been foreseen.* It showed no emotion—only certainty—as it moved closer and closer to Pierio until it stood upon Pierio's feet, crushing them under the weight of its alloy chassis.

Charles W. McDonald Jr.

"We'll come back for you! You have to know that...." Pierio fought back the tears of the pain rushing throughout his body in wave upon wave of *the Eye's* cruel form of justice.

Lifting its foot only a span or more, the Sentinel slammed its great hardened metal foot down atop Pierio again, this time shattering every bone in both of his feet. This time *it did* laugh, turning to head back to the bridge where it would ensure the criminal's swift and certain exile. This one was *too* important to kill. He and Durial had to survive. The others, perhaps not. To *erase* Humanity required letting *two* live—*for now.*

Programmable matter formed a doorway for the battle-scarred Sentinel to exit into a smooth metal corridor with transparent digital readouts and displays adorning both sides. Pausing mid-stride as it walked toward the bridge of its tactical starship, the Sentinel extended its right hand, turning it palm up as a holographic quantum-tunnel message appeared in a sphere just a few millimeters above the surface of its alloy palm.

Wavelengths of prismatic colors scattered about a field of stars pulsed with each command intonation from *The Eye of Time*—each vibrant wave vibrating like a musical chord struck by its ancient musician. These waves more analogous to dimensions and causalities being struck with each command from the great *Eye*. No words were spoken. Verbal language was *far too crude* for such advanced lifeforms.

Even with its ever-present dispassionate appearance, the battle-hardened Sentinel nearly appeared to laugh as it processed the latest commands from *The Eye of Time*. A command that had transcended time itself, for surely *they* possessed means and the patience to erase Humanity.

(Graelon, Tens of Thousands of Years Ago....)

A great plateau before him greeted Pierio as he materialized handcuffed and broken on the surface of the virgin and alien world. Dropping to the ground in agony—his feet utterly shattered—his handcuffs disengaged as a beautiful woman in a grey bodysuit appeared handcuffed to his immediate left.

Her handcuffs now disengaged, she ran to him. "I don't understand. What's happening to us?"

"I don't know either, but we're going to fight back," Pierio pro-

Charles W. McDonald Jr.

claimed, flooding himself with Arcane for the first time in week and *Healing* his feet as he looked at the great mountain range behind him and the massive drop off to the beautiful, lush, green plains below. "We're going to fight back, and we're going to *kill them all*."

"I don't even know your name." With swept brunette bangs covering bright green-gold eyes and soft, supple cheeks, she looked into his starry, bright-blue eyes, seeking a level of comfort, knowledge, and understanding. Never the dependent type, she was far out of her element here and she knew it. She *needed* his help. She *needed* them to work together.

"Pierio," he stated flatly, but his eyes burned like hot coals of determination. "We're going to reproduce the conditions that brought us here so I can understand their plan."

"Pierio, I'm Ceres. I'll help you however I can. I'm grateful not to be alone here. It's beautiful, and it looks bountiful at a glance, but I'm still grateful you're here with me. How can I help? Help me understand what's happening…." Her eyes sought the truth in him. She didn't know him, but her instincts said he was the only honest being she'd seen in weeks of captivity.

Taking her hand in his, he began describing his plan to her, and it all started with mining. They needed ore—and lots of it. They needed to start gathering the raw ingredients to build back the technology that had exiled them here. And, they needed to find Durial and the rest of his brothers. They needed a way to communicate through and traverse the vastness of space. Without FTL capabilities, they'd have to find another way. He'd have to start running some calculations in his mind from the time spent traveling in their tactical FTL, gravity-field-drive ship to develop a star map of possible locations for Durial and Alexelio, but if it took hundreds of lifetimes to find them, he'd keep himself alive with his magic long enough to make right what the Sentinels and the great *Eye* had made wrong.

Charles W. McDonald Jr.

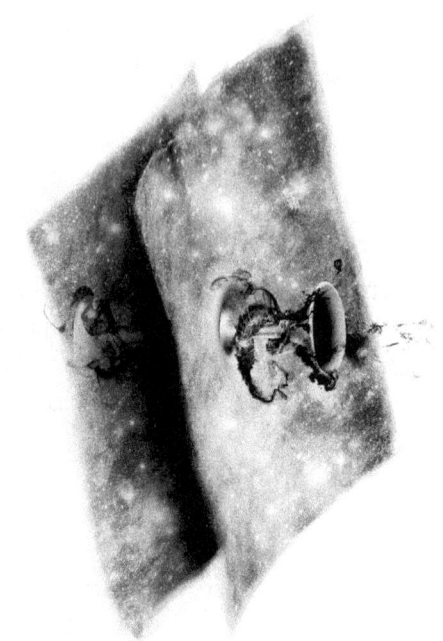

Chapter 2: Thrice Broken

(Austin, TX, Earth, Present Day)

Alow, guttural growl of Damon's house bemoaned the crestfallen fate about to befall future Mira as the sound of 2x6s snapping at their waistlines around the perimeter of the great room crackled the air, driving chills of portent up Mira's spine. Shadow-backlit, molten eyes stared back at future Mira as a cupped-winged Banthis loomed over Damon, threatening to carry him home. The slipstream of Banthis' *hate* still coagulating spacetime around them clashed against the struggle of future Mira's right, hammer-laden hand.

The ting of the microwave had proven just enough a distraction for the hammer to start to move toward Illirian's clay seal, but Mira felt the manifold of spacetime thicken again around her right hand as the *hate-forged* Banthis regained her focus.

Gnarled fingers of shadow and *hate* crept nearly all the way around the perimeter of the great room now, starting at the far end of the living

Charles W. McDonald Jr.

room, now making their way toward the kitchen—and Mira. Mira could feel the room constricting around her, along with the manifold of spacetime, trying to suffocate and snuff her out of existence. The 2x6s snapping where touched by Banthis' shadow-cast fingers as they made their way to her—and Damon. Even now, a set of shadowy fingers moved from wall to floor, slithering serpent-like on broken flooring—now only inches away from Damon's broken body.

As the gnarled fingers of shadow crept over Damon's feet and legs, they suddenly stopped—nearly in immediate retreat from Damon's chest.

The room began to hum and resonate with a warm energy Mira could only compare to the coming of the morning. Mira's Earthly eyes couldn't see the souls bursting through Damon's chest, circling him like a great toroidal energy field—but Banthis could. Another moment of distraction caused Banthis to lose focus, looking down at the thousands of souls ensnarling Damon's broken and gaping chest, circling Damon in torrent rings of energy and pushing back against Banthis' immortal *hate*.

Like unto flocks of wren, the thousands of souls captured by Damon's *Throne of Souls* moved in unison, with two souls brighter than all the others seemingly coordinating the release of coagulated spacetime ensnarled around Mira's right-hand grip of Damon's hammer.

Mira barely felt the hammer move before the coagulated spacetime suddenly broke like a dam, causing the hammer to race toward Illirian's seal in a haste of resolve for Mankind.

Striking the seal with enough force to break off a large chunk of underlying granite countertops, the hammer shattered Illirian's seal into a thousand tiny shards of clay and dust, causing a deafening thunderclap that surely could have been heard all the way to the university several hundred yards away.

Startled by the delicate, feminine hands suddenly on her hips, moving her aside, Mira instantly recognized the scent of Illirian's presence from where she'd encountered it before in Damon's study. Even the memory of that memory had been distinct and immediately recognizable.

Positioning herself between Mira and Banthis, Illirian recognized Damon's urgent condition at a glance—knowing he had only mere moments before he'd be forever lost. Banthis and Illirian had worked their magic independently in Damon's orbit for millennia—never having seen or experienced the other in person. Alone together, for the very first time, the light of Illirian Starfire stared down a now-spread-winged Banthis positioning herself in front of Damon as if to warn Banthis the only way for Banthis to get to Damon was *through* the light of her immortal and powerful soul. Feeling very much like the third wheel, and very grateful not to be the first nor the second, Mira's eyes darted between Illirian and Banthis, wondering if Earth could survive these two being in the same room together and if saving Damon was even still an option. Giving them both a wider berth, she slowly backed away from the island, hoping they would keep each other occupied. If only for a second or two longer.

Gnarled fingers of shadow retreated into the standing shadow of Banthis now clinging to her forged body as Illirian took another step toward Damon—and Banthis.

"It's time for Damon to come home," Banthis proclaimed flatly in a tone that recognized the greatness before her, yet yielded nothing.

"That outcome is not for you to decide," Illirian countered, taking another step, watching Banthis flex as her molten katana flared in her right hand.

Light bulbs around the house suddenly burst, spraying glass all over the flooring and countertops, allowing only the light of Banthis' molten katana and the light of Illirian Starfire to illuminate their first-ever, ominous encounter.

Now having to feel her way around due to the sudden darkness, Mira tried not to cry out when the long shard of hot bulb glass thrust into her right foot. Years alone in the field of Armageddon without the protection of Damon had toughened Mira; she didn't even wince when the cold, hard, anodized metal made contact with her fingertips. Moving her right hand just above the light switch on the garage side of the wall between the kitchen and the garage, Mira made her move to save Damon.

"You're not allowed to interfere in this. I know that much." Banthis offered logic, knowing Illirian's emotional investment with Damon but also knowing her role in maintaining the status quo she—herself—fought to dis-

Charles W. McDonald Jr.

rupt.

"Others have already interfered. I'm here to set that right." Illirian's gold-fire eyes tightened on Banthis, no longer darting to Damon.

"He's coming with me," Banthis decreed, assiduously protecting her future with Damon. The Master Plan could still be completed. All was not lost. She could have both Damon and the outcome of *their* plans. She knew that much to be certain.

"Damon's not going anywhere with you." Squeezing the trigger of Damon's Glock® twice, two .40 caliber hollow-point rounds struck Banthis where her vital organs *should* have been, causing Banthis to violently throw her molten katana at future Mira, severing her body in half; the torso and head fell in a heap backwards—her long legs falling forward. Blood and entrails gushed from what *had been* future Mira as the ground and framing violently shook, threatening to collapse inward on Illirian as a wounded Banthis suddenly disappeared into a great void. Her molten katana melted into the flooring, burning its way into a crevasse of *hate*, chasing Banthis whence she came.

Kneeling beside *her* Damon, witnessing his *Throne of Souls* collapsing in all around him, Illirian knew he had but seconds—valuable time purchased with Mira's sacrifice. Her lips touching his, she probed his great wound with her powerful magic and her new station as her soul surrendered to him. Light-amber of fire, blue of life, gold of magic, and charcoal of Damon's essence formed concentric rings, each larger than the one before as they slowly began revolving about a center axis unseen. Each ring moved inside the other as valve, cartilage, vein, and heart began pulling blood from Damon's extremities, removing toxins from his body as the other side of his new heart began pumping oxygenized blood back out to a body on the edge of septicemia.

With her eyes still closed, Illirian's spirit could feel her magic working on Damon as blood flowed back into lips she kissed for his survival, and theirs, as she begged him to stay. *Don't go, Damon. Stay with me,* she pleaded to his soul's energy still whirling around the room and around his body.

Inside her mind's eye, she could see and feel his *Throne of Souls* stabilizing, the souls bursting through his chest consistently held in check by the gravity of his being as their normal orbits around him began to resume.

Breath leapt back into Damon rivaling the saving of a drowning man spewing water and expelling his airways. He felt his capillaries bursting back to life as feeling came back to his nerve endings. *Am I being kissed? Where am I?*

Looking sidelong at what remained of Mira and the bodily fluids pooling toward them, Illirian finally considered her possible future with Damon if she could get him to alter his Master Plan for her, and for Humanity.

"Breathe…. Come back to me, My Love," again she begged, her love for Damon no longer constrained by a station she no longer held or cared for—her prior mission abandoned for her obsession for Damon. *Now she had truly interfered.* Now she had truly broken all the rules and every ethos. There was no going back. Centuries of denial broke like a great floodgate for Illirian Starfire as she struggled to illustrate to Damon meaning in each of her tears now streaking down her beautiful cheeks with her eyes of gold-fire pleading for him to understand.

Damon's house creaked and moaned, threatening to collapse on them as Damon slowly came around. Another 2x6 snapped in half, allowing another section of the living room drywall to tumble into the room.

"What happened," Damon asked, his *black mirrors of the soul* taking on a new and brighter backlit hue.

"Don't try to move too much." She could see him already trying to get his legs underneath him enough to stand, but she knew him not ready for that and she wasn't ready for him to see what remained of Mira. "What's the last thing you remember?"

Damon's eyes widened at the memory that crashed in on him—memories of destroying the Chairman. Gripping his chest, he tried feeling for the wound that should have been there but was not. "I'm on Earth."

"Yes. Good. What else?"

"Where's Mira? I made a *Portal* to Austin and held your seal in my hand. Did she summon you?"

"Damon, there's something I need to tell you first."

"Where's Mira?"

"Banthis came for you."

"*Where's Mira?*" Damon started to stand but needed his *Telekinesis* to bring himself upright.

Now fully upright, using the far end of what remained of the island granite countertop to steady himself, he could see Mira's severed body spilling blood and entrails into the kitchen and garage with what looked like one of his pistols still clutched in her right hand. "Banthis?"

Illirian only replied by placing a hand around his waist to steady him, now looking him in the eyes as if to communicate something physically she'd held back for centuries that her words could not.

"She sacrificed herself for me…?"

"I couldn't have saved you in time without her. You were fading too fast, and Banthis was determined to take you *home*. Her words."

For one of only a handful of times in Damon's multi-generational life, Damon began to shed tears for yet another mortal toll to his miserable existence. His tears bleached the granite upon which they fell with contrition. "First Dallia, then Mira, and now this Mira—this extraordinary and unique Mira—all gave their life for me. Why can't I protect them?"

"Because you were meant to protect us all." *You could help him. Couldn't you? You've already interfered.*

"That simply cannot be. I'm not *that* person, and the Master Plan was never meant to 'protect us all.'"

"I think you need to meet someone, Damon. Someone that might change your mind. Someone that might change your perspective."

"My perspective is pretty fucked right now." Unable to take his eyes off what remained of Mira, he knew himself now thrice broken.

"You are loved, Damon. Never forget that. She loved you. She still loves you." A knowing look from Illirian again tried communicating non-verbally with Damon whose eyes were tear-glossed with loss. "I have new responsibilities, thanks to you, and I must attend to them. I can hear his call, and I must go." *You could help him instead. Why don't you? What's wrong with you? You love him! You need him! Admit it! Tell him. Tell him now!*

Charles W. McDonald Jr.

A perfumed gale disintegrated Illirian's body to ethereal form, transporting her whence she came, leaving Damon to deal with what remained of his beloved Mira.

(Axum, Perion, Moments Ago....)

Mouth still agape in awe, Radin tried to pull together in his thoughts what just happened. *And, what was that great arc of charcoal-blue light streaking off to the northeast?* He had a very bad feeling as he ripped open a *Portal* to Exeter. *Where else could he go?* He had to face this head-on. He knew he'd have a lot of explaining to do, especially given Damon's apology for actions, still as yet unknown to him. He only hoped he could get them to listen. He needed them to listen. He needed Elise to listen.

Creator, *what of my son? What have I done?* Walking through the hastily-formed *Portal*, Radin did something he hadn't done in forever, asking the Creator for forgiveness of his insult to Humanity: the insult of arrogance to think he could possibly be justified in opening these scrolls—these *keys of hatred* of Mankind. Still, he postulated and struggled to understand the mind of God the Creator and his intentions in bringing about such devastation to Man.

Charles W. McDonald Jr.

Part 1: What Was, What Is, and What Must Be

Charles W. McDonald Jr.

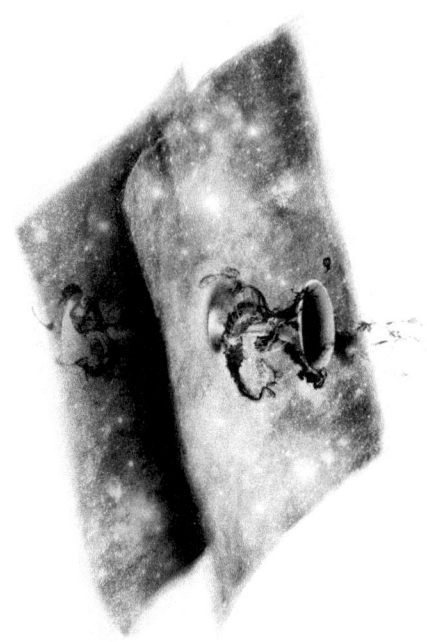

Chapter 3: When Even Love is Laid Down

(New Georgia Hospital, Eden, Present Day)

The pulse monitoring equipment sounded off with each of Mira's heartbeats as her condition stabilized. President Abel had left some time back to deal with the threat of the indigenous life that wanted—demanded, really—to meet with him. Alone. Her room was finally quiet at last except for the blips and beeps of the medical equipment monitoring her recovery. Her eyes fluttered as she floated in and out of consciousness—still healing from the gunshot wound her future self had inflicted upon her.

Door to her room now suddenly ajar, Damon—dressed in a charcoal-blue long-sleeved shirt and black slacks—stepped inside, putting together the pieces of this *distorted continuum*. He thought he knew, but a conversation—if possible in her condition—would verify his hypothesis. Slowly, he closed the distance between them 'til his feet were only inches from the large, grey urethane wheels of her gurney. Closer, until beside her

Charles W. McDonald Jr.

his immortal soul did kneel as his fingertips entangled over the top of hers. Her skin filled the need of the familiar, like swaddling cloth to an infant. Her scent—somewhere betwixt flower and flesh—cut through the sterility of the environment around them, reminding him of his longing for her as she began to stir upon his touch.

"You've looked better," he quipped, smiling at her as she began to come around.

"What…?" Mira's spaghettified memories stirred as her body shifted. "What happened?"

"I was hoping you could tell me. What's the last thing you remember?"

Eyes growing wide as the memories slammed home. "Damon, what have you done? I saw myself. She knew things she couldn't have known any other way."

He paused briefly, searching for the words as he looked her in the eyes. She was still so very full of life as he considered the brittle edge between life and death that was really a great, ethereal canyon. Being here with her now alive, after seeing her severed body bleeding out on his floor, he didn't have the words to explain the emotions he was still trying to put in place. "I've shared a lot with you, Mira, but I can't say that I've told you everything…," he paused, pulling a chair from across the room with his *Telekinesis* so he could sit beside her whilst holding her hand. "When I brought Humanity to Eden, I did so in the future. I did that for many reasons. I knew the end was near for all of us. It was coming with or without me—better if I controlled the timing."

"So, everyone here is from a future timeline? Why…," she asked, biting her lip at the pain of her flank involuntarily flinching in her bed.

"Because I needed the power from their prayers in the here and now, and because they wouldn't just come unless there was good reason to come. The End Times colliding simultaneously on all the Seeds of Humanity provided the fuel and justification to make that happen. I can't rightly take on a deity without myself first being a deity and having some experience at it as well."

Mira shook her head in understanding that was not entirely fulsome. Shaded in the blind spots of Damon's Master Plan. Now staring at him, re-

Charles W. McDonald Jr.

membering her last thoughts of him had been of leaving him, she shrugged back into her hospital pillow—more guarded than before. "They told me they'd been trying to reach you but couldn't get to you. Where were you when I was shot?"

Damon gulped, trying to think of a way to explain. He didn't like keeping secrets from her. That never worked out well. But this was different. This could influence the timeline. This could disrupt his plans. He could *not* reveal this information. "You remember me telling you about Radin?" He assumed she would remember since it was the original timeline Mira Castille he had told, and he assumed he was now talking to the one and only original Mira.

"I do."

"His girlfriend was having a child. That child was…," he paused, visibly clenching his fist and knowing that was the very next thing on his massive to-do list to deal with, "…destroyed."

"Destroyed is a very specific word, Damon. What do you mean destroyed?"

"I mean God the Creator ripped the infant out of her womb with his hypocrisy and mutilated his unborn body. Like I said…destroyed."

"You're leaving out a ton of detail, Damon. What happened, and how did it happen?"

"*I don't know. Okay!*" Damon shot upward out of his chair, visibly frustrated, as it simultaneously shot backward out from underneath him. He didn't know, and it was eating at him. *Is my grandson still alive? What kind of monster would destroy unborn children?* That kind of act was beyond even him to comprehend. He remembered reading of such things in their so-called Bible, and it infuriated him then too. *Who was this monster, God the Creator?* "I built a tether to my grandson, and I was on Kaleion to bring Dallia home to Eden. I felt the tether snap and it would only do so if he was murdered in the womb. So, I can only assume he's dead. Unjustly so. That's where I was. I'm sorry I wasn't here for you when you needed me." So much more than that needed to be said, but his heavy black eyes and deeply-stressed sockets said that he didn't have the words. Not now.

Sitting up straighter in her bed despite the pain it caused her, she looked at Damon. Really looked at him. The emotional swings of this conversation had taken her from the brink of leaving Damon to finding new boundaries for her love for him. *If only I understood him....* "You have nothing to apologize for and I'm sorry I put more stress on you. That's my fault." Another long pause as she searched within herself to muster a genuine smile for him. "I love you, Damon."

Sitting back down beside her and again and taking her hand, his eyes glossed over. That's when she noticed something very new about Damon. Something about his eyes was…different. More depth. More fire. More clarity. His black gems more backlit and beautiful as if he was somehow renewed in some way she didn't comprehend.

"I love you too. There's some place I'd like to take you, but you can't go with me like that," he mocked, motioning up and down her hospital-gown-wrapped body with his right hand and a smile.

"Are you going to *Heal* me then?"

Nodding his head, Damon peeled back the bed linen to reveal the cauterized wound in her flank. They'd done a good job repairing it, but he could do better, even with his limited skills in *Healing*. "Hold onto the railing…," he urged as he placed both his hands around her wound, forming a cup around it, casting into her with only Arcane as an energy source.

Electricity shot up and down her body from the tips of her toes to her bangs as she felt every part of her body tingling and the blood rushing to the wound within. Letting out a guttural moan, she tensed then eased her body back into the bed. Every single part of her tingled as if excited by acupuncture. A long moment settled between them as she could see his eyes still quite focused as his cupped hands traversed from her wound up and away from the wound out several inches. She assumed he was probing her with his magic to verify his work. "So, where's this place you're taking me? Are we going back home? Earth home, I mean…."

"Uh, sort of," he deflected, disconnecting her IV and picking up her body from the gurney now that it was safer to move her.

"*Where* are you taking me? I'm not sure I like being hauled off by you."

"I thought you loved me." He again deflected with another managed smile, adding, "…I would never hurt you. You know that."

"I believe you. But, I'd still like to know where the fuck you're taking me."

Before she could protest, a *Portal* ripped super-heated air inches away from the interior of her hospital room door, offering an arid plains landscape on the other side of the *Portal*. A place she hadn't seen since she was a child—the plains of West Texas.

Close to dusk and with still-warm temperatures falling fast, Damon knew he had to act fast now as he stood Mira Castille on the West Texas soil before them—tumbleweeds already blowing across the barren landscape.

"This isn't exactly a hot romantic spot, Damon." Mira furrowed her brow at her very dangerous boyfriend—if he could even be called that. She could see his mind working. His facial expression hard, and lost. His inner being troubled. Dour but resolute. She saw and felt his lips approaching hers and didn't....

Kissing Mira with everything he had and everything he was, Damon leaned into her, laying down his for love her and his love for them as his left hand went from her hip to the back of her head, starting to probe memory by memory, thread by thread, unraveling their relationship from within. Dismantling it synapse by synapse.

Approaching the sound of a great chord being struck across the strings of time itself, Damon heard manifestations of his actions pounding inside his every thought as he brought forth what must be. Mira's eyes wide open and staring straight ahead while he probed every latent memory of Mira from childhood to the present.

Mira felt a hollow sound in her mind akin to being underwater. Only vaguely aware of Damon's hand on the back of her head, she started to lose awareness as Damon slowly draped his lips over hers.

His left hand traversed from her medulla to her pre-frontal cortex as one memory was erased, then another altered, then another augmented as he slowly constructed her complete rationale for their breakup. Sweeping through her thoughts, he found the one where she'd decided to leave him just before being shot and augmented that one too as tears began to streak down his stony face in the agony of letting her go.

He was a selfish bastard for doing this, and he knew it. He needed her to survive so he could survive so the goddamned Master Plan could survive. He had to plant her just where he'd found her, or everything would unravel. He deserved the suffering this was levying on him. He deserved to die for this.

Damon's tears now covering his dust-laden boots brought back stark and horrifying memories of his childhood—memories he hadn't accessed in centuries and hoped had died along with the nameless one who bore them.

Releasing his left hand from Mira's beautiful hair and face, Damon had to steady her body as she waned against him, threatening to collapse—an eclipsed crater of the fiery sun she once was. Now cradling a blank Mira as he would a smile child, he slowly he began walking further southwest to a tent and personnel he knew would be waiting for them.

Moments later, a series of camouflaged encampment tents cropped out of the arid ground of the West Texas soil. Damon approached a tall, roughneck-appearing man with a full beard, looking to be in his mid-thirties, who was coming out to greet them.

"I was beginning to wonder if you were going to show up," the bearded man offered, positioning himself to literally take Mira off Damon's hands.

"Just like we arranged. She's not to be harmed in any way, shape, or form. You'll take care of her, or I'll take care of you and your men. Do we understand each other?" Letting go of Mira in far more ways than one, Damon's eyes still watered, though a black fire blazed behind them threatening to set the kindling-dry landscape ablaze.

"You don't have to threaten me again. I get it. I'll take personal responsibility for her safety. And thank you for the gift. The ammunition and gold will come in handy for what's coming." His eyes darted around, ever vigilant for corrupt government agencies who he knew would eventually come for them.

"Yeah, well, that's privileged information. So, keep that to yourself. When she comes around, you can explain to her what I told you, but keep it simple and keep it limited. The events will speak for themselves."

"Still, thank you for the heads-up. My friends and I always knew this day was coming, but knowing the specific hour and the specific day…," LT paused in awe of the man he knew barely an inkling. "Are we going to survive?" He paused again, somehow knowing with Damon he needed to be more specific. "I mean, will *my family* survive?"

Charles W. McDonald Jr.

"It will be just like I told you, LT. You take care of Mira and keep yourself—and your family—alive, and that day will come when I return for you. Though it might not be in the form you might expect. Watch for these…." Forming a *Portal* right in front of LT, Damon stepped through to what remained of his house in Austin, kneeling on the kitchen floor where future Mira's severed body still lay. As the *Portal* whooshed to a close, he fell to his knees on his broken, bloodied floor and began to weep.

LT gulped hard, not knowing what to make of Damon, or Mira for that matter, but he knew love when he saw it. Damon cared for Mira—deeply. And, as he looked at her perfect symmetrical face, shimmering brunette hair, and buxom features, he knew he'd have to keep certain people away from her or he wouldn't be able to keep his word to Damon. And the safety of his family depended on it. Even knowing what he knew, he didn't know how bad it was going to get and having Damon on his side meant the difference between life and death. Even with as much as he, and his militia, had prepared for this day.

Knowing her fate both broke and hardened Damon inside. He felt like he had no love left to offer and didn't deserve it even if he could. Look what love had brought to his doorstep…. A life of an all-consuming *hate* he *still* hadn't learned to put down, a life of allowing himself to be broken repeatedly at the vulnerability of it all, and now being the center of a Master Plan that might unmake all things and all Creation. The good of love was massive, warm, and deep, but the crater of its absence was a horrifying cascade of malevolence.

He needed clarity and focus, but right now he needed to do something he never properly did with Dallia. He needed to say goodbye to Mira. Clutching her cold face with rigor mortis long set in, Damon brushed her beautiful brunette hair as tears streaked first down his face then down hers as he lay down on his broken floor with her—his face touching hers. In a pool of Mira's still-drying blood, Damon wept for what could have been if not for his cursed Master Plan—and Banthis.

Charles W. McDonald Jr.

Chapter 4: The Four Brothers

(Setinon, Tens of Thousands of Years Ago)

The great Durial knew, of course. They all knew, but he especially had a keen sense of what they were fighting. He was the most powerful of them, after all…. More than just the status quo, they were in an impossible battle, trying to reshape what Humanity *could* become if only the *The Eye of Time* would allow it. His right hand stroking his star-sapphire-like birthmark at the root of his chiseled chin whilst *Durial's Eye* peered into what was, what is, and what must be, looking for the guidance he sought to give him and his brothers the edge they needed to win this war with the greatest and eldest of all enemies of Man. AI.

Blue-green pathways of light arced over a white, explosive sphere of focus suspended millimeters above Durial's left palm as *Durial's Eye*—also known as *The Starlight of Immortality*—showed the way. They had only moments before the Sentinels would come. The full-ban on magic had come with only hours of notice, broadcast across the planet, literally written in the clouds, modified this hour to entirely blot out the sun by the planetary weather control management system, controlled by the *Eye*. Inside *The Starlight of Immortality*, the great Durial, dressed in a crimson and pewter pants and a dark-blue shirt with silver piping and floret clasps affixing a color-shifting cloak, saw great darkened pathways between worlds his brothers would architect, a great moon outpost destroyed by technology like unto Setinon, and a descendant with black eyes carrying a great staff meant to

Charles W. McDonald Jr.

shoulder a burden he could not. His survival—everyone's—counted on his descendant, which meant *they* counted on *him*. Only moments more perhaps...appeared another descendant—tall with auburn hair and eyes of fire with a great crest about his chest.

Blaster fire suddenly erupted just outside, blowing the door to their sky-bound unit inward at a sideways angle, bluntly striking Durial's wife and daughter and sending them into the opposite wall with a crushing thud. Durial's immediate loss of focus caused *Durial's Eye* collapsed into his left hand, leaving only its required components—a star sapphire gem throwing off immense amounts of silvery-blue flashes of light in every direction. *The Starlight of Immortality* in an explosive blossom of Humanity's last gasp of a future's-past fate across the great chasm of time immemorial.

The lead Sentinel immediately rushed forward, crashing into Pierio and his wife, casting them aside as if they were but small children as it reached for Durial's left hand with its own powerful, scarred alloy hand.

Not afforded the time to think, Durial acted on instinct, looking to his brother—Alexelio—as the star sapphire gemstone demonstrated its supersolid properties sinking into, but not through, Durial's palm. The great Durial smirked knowingly causing the Sentinel to grip him around his throat, lifting him off the flooring one-handed, its dispassionate amber-lens eyes flashed in a rare moment of frustration and anger.

Its AI hive-mind processing the birthmark in Durial's chin now glowing like the supersolid that just slipped out of its grasp, the lead Sentinel assumed *Durial's Eye* now fully absorbed into Durial's bloodstream.

By order of the Eye, you're coming with us for your crimes against Humanity. The Sentinel's commands shouted into Durial's mind—along with the rest of his brothers—as two more Sentinels burst into the room chasing their own blue-green blaster fire, blowing gaping holes in Durial's two remaining sons as well as his wife and daughter, who barely clung onto their lifeforce after having been crushed by the exploding door. Relentlessly, they assassinated Pierio's wife and children, too, with blaster-fire head shots. Alexelio and his family were inexplicably spared as the invisible field produced by the plain silver rod in the grip of the second Sentinel neutered and neutralized any further casting by any of the four great brothers.

Adamian clutched his cream-bodysuit-clad wife of strawberry-blonde

Charles W. McDonald Jr.

hair and pale-green eyes, moving to stand in front of her to protect her and her newly life-blossoming womb, just as the plain silver cuffs of program-mable matter partially disintegrated before him, just enough to allow them to be slipped—mid-air—around both his wrists as the programmable mat-ter coagulated to seal up the circle, placing the meekest of the four brothers into custody. Witnessing the tight links glow with blue-green energy just as the singular digital read-out began flashing, he knew the field-displacement damper was now in effect as his three brothers all succumbed to the same incarceration.

Tears streaked down Durial's chiseled and wrong-hardened face as his eyes spoke of a justice forthcoming, even if eons in the making. A great seed of descendant-to-come burned hot in his loins as he felt the alloy digit of the most battle-scarred Sentinel darting into the base of his spine, shov-ing him forward.

Move it, Durial heard the Sentinel's shouts in his thoughts. Look-ing to each of his brothers in turn, he was sure they all heard it. His wife and children now gone, along with Pierio's family too. At least they knew enough of what was to come to formulate a plan—a plan that would dare to unmake all the AI had built and was still yet to build—but the survival of Man over machine would require great sacrifices of them, and their blood-lines. The descendants of hardened criminals had a collective job to do, and do it they would.

Part 2: Beyond Sentient

Charles W. McDonald Jr.

I was here before you.
I will be here after.
I am always—The Eternal.
And you're not the only one who can cast.

Charles W. McDonald Jr.

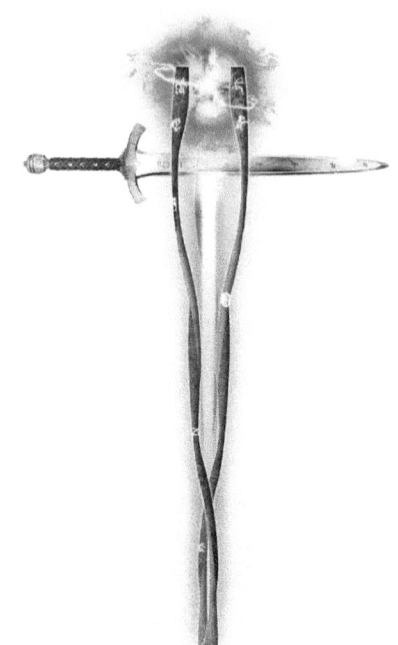

Chapter 5: The Instrument of Humanity's Hate

(The Eye of Time, Setinon, Time Neutral)

The great hexagonal cathedral room of dark carbon, nano-alloy, and programmable matter pulsed with the energy collected by the matter of a thousand planets, used to create the immeasurable collection of solar panels surrounding the home star of Setinon and Setinon itself, along with its moon and two interior planets to their star. It took an immeasurable amount of energy to power *The Eye of Time,* who now peered across the chasm of possible outcomes—seeing and all-knowing.

In the center of the room, five helical, triangular-shaped rods whirled about an explosion of white-hot light and possibilities to the sound of a hum like unto a pulsar star. Five great battle-scarred Sentinels busied themselves tending to the *Eye's* every thought command, monitoring this outcome and that on transparent stations formed out of the air itself as robotic digits extending from alloy—though somewhat Humanoid-like in form—hands worked the transparent consoles toward an end they could only interpret from the hive mind of the *Eye.*

Charles W. McDonald Jr.

A great burst of blue-green light erupted from inside the energy bound by the five helical rods, terminating mid-air right next to one of the most blaster-scarred Sentinels, as this Sentinel watched nanite-driven programmable matter turn into the tiniest of all circuits with malevolent intent. The *Instrument of Humanity's Hate* now born, it was the Sentinel's job to set it into motion. *The Eye of Time* had spoken in their conscious thoughts and with the making of the greatest of all unmakings.

Another legion Sentinel floated forward. They had legs—sort of—but with gravitational propulsion, they could more quickly respond to the command and wishes of the great AI driving them. This Sentinel, opening a hidden compartment in its abdomen, accepted the tiny circuitry of Man's destiny as the tiny circuit floated toward the open compartment, only to have the compartment close shut with a smooth metal click of precision engineering. The smooth edge of the door met perfectly with its mate, forming the belly of the great soldier of alloy and *hate*. Eyes of functional amber light looked this way and that as their intelligence adapted, recording every moment for posterity, as the lead Sentinel formed up beside it, and another formed behind it, moving out together in uniform marching orders of Mankind's hatred.

Programmable matter adapted, forming an on-demand doorway as the trio of Sentinels came close to the wall of the hexagonal cathedral chamber. Like no normal doorway, this one opened a path directly to a renegade outpost of the exiled ones. If the *Instrument* was successful, the *Seeds of Exiled Humanity* wouldn't exist much longer…. Then again, they had all the time to wait. The *Eye* was The Eternal, after all….

(Graelon Colonial Outpost, A Very Long Time Ago)

Just brought into the make-shift OR on a floating platform, the tall, brooding, and handsome man of stark brunette hair, starry, bright-blue eyes, and chiseled features had a none-too-subtle look about his face as if to warn his medical staff to get on with it or suffer the intensity of the consequences of his disappointment. Already incredibly powerful, Keirill sought to be the greatest of all time, and if cybernetic enhancement was the path to achieving that end, then so be it.

Made of out of a decommissioned cargo ship, the hull door to the

OR closed with a great and deep metal clang as the medical staff circled him—doing final staging and prep-work for his dangerous and unlawful operation.

"I'm going to put you out now," the aging, renegade neurosurgeon—well past his middle years—informed his wealthy and overly-talented patient, bringing the compressed airgun with a cartridge of anesthesia cocktail closer to the patient's carotid artery.

"Don't disappoint me, Doctor," Keirill warned, raising his right index finger, causing the doctor's throat to constrict as if compressed by great and powerful unseen hands. "And, don't even think about taking advantage of my body being unconscious."

The neurosurgeon gasped, trying to clear his airway as the patient finally released the doctor's throat after making his point quite clear. He wasn't sure how far-reaching this man's power was, but he didn't feel like testing it today. *Just get him done and get him out of here, before someone finds out.* Motioning for his medical staff to proceed, he drove the compressed airgun into the patient's neck, delivering the cocktail that knocked out the patient's body immediately, so the delicate procedure could begin.

Moments later, a shaved cranium replaced the patient's long and perfect black hair as the amber light produced from a finger-length, silver metal instrument began cutting subcutaneously then through bone into the cerebral and pre-frontal cortex.

A male nurse in his forties with already graying stubble positioned the implant circuit board on a bare steel tray where it was delicately plucked into position by the fine-grain, robotic operating arm by the renegade surgeon.

A second robotic arm began reaching into the meat of the patient's cerebellum to retract the pre-frontal cortex for an exact placement of the implant held in position by the first robotic arm. Operating both robotic arms carefully, the doctor barely had time to react when the hull door was blown from its hinges into the makeshift OR, smashing his male nurse against the far metal wall with a giant thud, blue-green blaster fire chasing the blown door into the room in a violent surge of the law.

Three great, tall, and menacing robots floated into the room single file through the blown-open bulkhead doorway—their metal having the appearance of being anodized and war-ridden with deep blaster-fire scarring and pitted wounds that didn't faze their movement or abilities.

"WAIT," the doctor protested, immediately dropping to his knees, then prostrating before them. "I BEG FOR MERCY. PLEASE...."

More blue-green blaster fire erupted from the lead metal Sentinel the most marred by scarring and pitting of its alloy—its weapon directly attached, nearly fused—to its Humanoid-like right-arm. It had legs, too—sort of—and could walk where required, but they mostly floated via gravitational propulsion, giving them great range, speed, and agility. A product of tens of thousands of years of evolution, the Sentinel was vastly superior to Humanity in every way measurable.

Now, looking down at the burn wounds that went all the way through the doctor's eye sockets out the back of his skull, *it* knew they had work to do. Dropping the implant from the robotic arm into its alloy left hand, the lead robot crushed the microscopic implant to dust as the robot behind it produced an even smaller implant from a storage unit hidden within its abdomen. Plucking the new implant circuitry with the robotic arm, the lead robot began operating the retractor, exposing the frontal cortex as it delicately inserted the *Instrument of Humanity's Hate* into the patient and quickly began the process of closing the patient. And with it, closing out Humanity's fate....

(Damon's House, Austin, TX, Earth, Present Day)

Severed 2x6s snapped, obeying Damon's will as they moved toward the center of the great room, forming the outline of a five-foot-ten-inch casket. Gating minimal Arcane through his right index finger, Damon planed each plank, making them smooth, neat, and even as he cleaned the edges of each one individually. Biscuit-routing each piece along its lengthwise edge, beechwood biscuits began floating from Damon's toolbox in single file through the open doorway into the garage as they formed the locking mechanism to form Mira's casket. One by one, they floated into place as Damon used his *Telekinesis* to compress the wood from the framing of his own house to make a home for Mira's mortal coil. She deserved better than this, but there wasn't time. The Master Plan had to be accelerated given everything that had happened. Now he was even more exposed than before, as even more of his plan had exposed itself.

Gating through his right index finger, flower and dove revealed themselves from common pine as Damon ornately and beautifully carved the ceremonial home for Mira's broken body. Hand grips from his range, dishwasher, refrigerator, and microwave formed the lugs and handles of her casket. Using his *Pyrokinesis* to fire this feature and that, Damon painted the shadow of this petal and that reed while forming the coming of the morning at the head of the casket on its left side as a light source for the beautiful landscape scene he was illustrating for her immortal rest. Royal-mahogany stain flew out of the garage, laying into the grain of the pine in perfect strokes as Damon fire-cured the stain into the wood, giving it a rich and burnished look. Duvet bedding flew out of the bedroom and began to form the interior lining, which would cradle future Mira in perpetuity.

Future Mira's severed body floated down into her custom-made casket. After closing her casket upon her body, Damon used his *Telekinesis* to lower her—casket and all—into the grave he had dug for her in his back yard. With a thought, he began throwing dirt atop her grave in the waning hours before midnight. He paused, knowing her of Christian rearing. Thinking…. Whether he believed or not, she deserved a burial of her upbringing. That's why he hadn't cremated her remains. He couldn't bring himself to say the service words, nor even to think them after the hypocrisy and blasphemy on recent display. Instead, he offered, "I don't know what is coming for us. I don't know what—if anything—lies down this road we must travel. I only know that of all the souls I have encountered, yours was uniquely you and there will never be another like you, Mira Castille. I know I will never be the same without you. I know I will ache for you— body, mind, and soul. And, I know I will be grateful to you for as long as I *must* live. I hope I see you again. Please rest…, and suffer no more. Please watch over me and let me feel your presence, for I fear what is to come without you. I never deserved you, but I'm glad I was just selfish enough to accept your love. Goodbye, Mira."

Walking into what remained of his house as dirt continued to fill in

Charles W. McDonald Jr.

Mira's grave, he cleared the house of everything vital—everything he'd need to complete the Master Plan at least. Much had been lost now due to Banthis, and much could never be forgiven.

Even as he allowed that acerbic seed of a thought to grow and fester in his mind, he knew she could hear that thought, and he no longer cared. No attempt was made to shield his thoughts from Banthis as he buried another love of his life. *Are there any durable enough to outlive and bury me?*

The last few heaps of dirt piled atop Mira Castille as he cast *Life* into the Bermuda seed his *Telekinesis* spread across her unmarked grave. *She deserves better.* He'd move her to a more appropriate burial spot when there was time. Right now, he needed to address the other great crater in his life dredged out of the blasphemy of God the Creator's hypocrisy.

Taking a last look around what had been his home away from home, and the birthplace of his relationship with Mira, he noted the once chef-grade kitchen, still seeing Mira Castille standing there as his memories stretched across time in lifelike vividness. Even as his mind tricked his senses into smelling her sweet perfume, his *Pyrokinesis* lit cabinet, carpet, stud, and drape alike as the interior of his house burst into flames.

"Goodbye, Mira," Damon declared to the walls aflame as silvery-blue flashes of light rent super-heated air inches in front of him as he stepped through to Exeter, Perion—ever carrying the burden of his *hate* with him. If his senses were right, his *hate* would have work to do.

Charles W. McDonald Jr.

The Eye of Time & The Instrument of Humanity's Hate

Charles W. McDonald Jr.

Chapter 6: Harsh Negotiations

(The Negi Caverns, Eden, Present Day)

The swept-wing presidential tactical carrier transported with it only the president, his chief science officer 22-B, and a minimal security detail. Painted in a crisp-grey-on-white color scheme with the presidential seal, the tactical Special Air Mission (SAM) came to a hovering stop mid-air as it slowly descended via directional vectored thrusts of its robust—yet whisper quiet—powerplant.

Barely touched down, its wheels not even fully holding the weight of the craft, President Abel threw open the main door, relaxing the compressed staircase onto the lush green grass before the Negi Caverns, much to the consternation of his security team. "Stay here," the president commanded, "...all of you." Eyes darting to each of his team in turn, he knew they didn't like this meeting, but he didn't care. This needed to be done *their* way—regardless of the risk. Though he had made sure there was a succession plan already set into motion before making this trip. He hoped he would come out of this alive, though there were no guarantees. If it weren't absolutely necessary, he wouldn't even attempt anything this suicidal.

His experience and instincts were his best defense to ensure he'd come out of this alive. Scattered thoughts as his feet hit the verdant green grass and a cautious glance caught the maw of the cavern entrance some hundred-and-fifty paces away.

"Understood, sir," Grant McCarthy replied, accepting, though not liking this one bit. The president's safety was *his* responsibility. Swallowing hard, he brought the laser-sighting of his M4 into view, watching his president walk toward the maw of the great caverns, taking on an insane risk—for all of them.

He's going to get himself killed, the thought shoved into Grant's mind by

Charles W. McDonald Jr.

the science officer clinging to Grant's left hip, watching President Abel walk away in the distance, disappearing into the maw of the cave where the science officer sensed the presence of others. Flashes of light in the shadow of the cave looked like the eyes of the indigenous creatures of this planet as the science officer bore a concerned look about its otherwise dispassionate, alien facial features.

The president's open tweed jacket of metallic colors buffeted in the breeze that greeted him just before entering the maw of the cave. The Negi could see he wasn't wearing a bullet-proof undergarment as he unbuttoned his pastel-blue long-sleeve shirt enough to show them he was unarmed and defenseless, as had been the condition for the meeting.

Inside the cave, President Abel came face to face with two hard exo-skeleton creatures—one to his left, the other to his right—their bright eyes flashing in the recognition of his following their request to meet only with him. Pincers pointing while simultaneously whispering into his thoughts, *This way, Mr. President,* the two escorted Abel deep into the caverns, turning left, then right, then right again and again, down a spiral, sloped, textured surface. Estimating they'd gone down into the crust some fifty spans or more, Abel noticed a choice of pathways into the hive as he followed the two through the rough-hewn archway second from the left in a bank of more than eighteen options, making him grateful for the escort—sort of. Otherwise, he'd easily get lost in the maze of their underground hive.

His gratefulness was short-lived, as he soon found himself surrounded by dozens of the creatures circling one far larger than he'd ever seen before. He, she, it—*whatever it was*—took up so much space it filled a great part of the cavern from floor to ceiling as the others took up defensive positions around it.

Is that the queen, he considered, as his eyes struggled to get to their night-vision status and to carefully observe all that was yet to come.

Yes, the reply came into his mind. *'Queen' is the closest word in your language to describe my station with my peoples. We've studied you since the first arrived—the one with black eyes.*

"His name is Damon. I'm going to talk aloud if that's okay. It just feels more natural to us."

Charles W. M{{c}}Donald Jr.

Eyes the size of 50-carrot diamonds flashed in silent reply.

He couldn't tell if that was good or bad, but he needed to be himself, and that was a good start as he saw it. The first thing in first negotiations was to be yourself. False pretenses rarely yielded good outcomes.

*President Abel, thank you for coming per our conditions. We understand the trepidations of your peoples. However, this is **our** world.*

Abel recognized some of the issues in translation; even using telepathic communications, it was hard to bridge the gap between the two languages fluently—especially given this being their first meeting.

"It has been my experience that when two people meet for the first time, the discussions should be as brief as possible to prevent miscommunication and misunderstanding." Abel's eyes wearily darted from the queen to the many soldiers protecting her/it.

Reading the president's thoughts as he spoke his unintelligible language and seeing his mannerisms helped her understand his intent. He *seemed* honorable enough, but she needed answers and she expected honesty…and her due amount of respect. *Agreed,* she effortlessly projected into Abel's thoughts. *Why have you come, and why in such numbers? How long do you intend to stay on **our** world?*

"Our worlds were dying. The one you spoke of with black eyes—Damon—he made this world inhabitable for us in a process called terraforming, and then brought us here. He told me he investigated the planet and thought it was barren of life. He was obviously wrong and has admitted as such. He would have selected another world if he had known you were here. Much effort has gone into terraforming this world for us, and we hope that doing so has not made your world *less* inhabitable for you. I know he was attempting to restore this world as close as possible to what it *might* have been before the black hole altered its orbit from your original star. He wishes—as do I—for us to find a way to work *and live* together." That was far more communication than he wanted to deliver in one chunk, but he tried to keep his sentence structure short to keep the odds of misinterpretation down to a minimum.

Have we misunderstood your position? Should we be negotiating with Damon instead of you? How long do you intend to stay?

He could tell the way the last question had been delivered with such

Charles W. McDonald Jr.

emphasis was likely due to the irritation at having to repeat the question since he intentionally hadn't answered it before. "I am the president. I speak for all the people and lifeforms recently brought to this world. I have all necessary authority to negotiate binding treaties between our peoples. We would like to negotiate a permanent presence on what will officially be recognized as your world." The president tried to hold his cards close to his vest, knowing they could read his every thought. He might as well have been naked before them. "Surely you must know about the black hole that still threatens us all...? Damon has assured me he has the power to prevent the black hole from disrupting this planet's orbit again. If we were to negotiate a peace between our peoples, I could offer Damon's services to build a habitat for you on this world that resembles your old world as closely as possible."

So, now you speak for your god too...? Has your position led you to arrogance, Mr. President?

This was proving to be at least as challenging as he'd thought it would be. Actually, he thought he'd be dead by now. So...there was that. "No, I do not ever speak for our god. Yet, I am certain he will agree to the reasonable terms I have offered."

Certain enough to wager your life on it?

"YES," he replied emphatically.

Her/its large eyes flashed silvery-blue in reply. He still wasn't sure if that was a good or bad sign, but at least he was still alive to contemplate.

Most of our people died when the black hole ripped our planet from orbit. There were not enough pods to save everyone. We do not need all of the land on this planet. But we do seek all the land between the river south of your new city called Aektar and the river east of your new city called New Atlanta. All the lands between those two rivers, we claim as ours.

Abel thought about it. That would cut off a major highway they'd just built between New Atlanta and New Famalk. That corridor of rail traffic couldn't be severed for many reasons: security, trade, technology, etc. "If you'll allow the one highway that was just built to continue to flow traffic unimpeded with your approval, I can agree to your terms."

Eyes again flashed in reply. Though this time Abel noticed one of the creatures, tapping on a transparent console, waving its pincer-like hand across the planed surface of semi-transparent alloy, producing a coalescing of

Charles W. McDonald Jr.

the air around him. For a brief moment, Abel could see a lattice framework of pathways extending throughout the entire cavern from wall to wall, floor to ceiling coagulating in clusters of what he thought might have been dark matter—or matter with electromagnetic properties that *seemed* like dark matter. For out of a coagulated mass just in front of the creature operating the transparent console, a pulsating sphere materialized from the lattice framework—which appeared like a great scaffold supporting everything around them—dropping down into the waiting pincer appendage forming a sophisticated tool that looked to Abel a lot like a medical-grade airgun.

Not waiting for the Queen's reply, Abel made his move. "If I'm recognizing that technology you just showed me correctly, that's what my chief science officer has described as a supersolid. We also want you to show us and provide us access to this technology in exchange for the land you have requested—terraformed to your specifications, of course."

Eyes flashed a greenish-red this time in reply to his post-negotiated demands. He knew he might have been asking too much, but he was here to negotiate—not to play footsie with the enemy. The airgun-like device suddenly thrust into his left arm, President Abel felt something of mass shoot into his bloodstream, and it was…painful. Large and uncomfortable, shifting and pulsing inside him, he felt what he assumed was the pulsating sphere that materialized an instant before quickly moving through his body towards the root of his circulatory system.

Now we can track you and communicate with you whenever and wherever necessary. It will not harm you, but you cannot remove it, and I would suggest you not even try.

The president swooned—nearly to the point of falling over—as he felt the mass of supersolids pulsing throughout his left arm and shoulder as his circulatory system carried the tracking material to every part of his extremities.

You have an agreement, Mr. President, and you have your supersolid to study…inside your own body. We will honor our side of the agreement. Honor yours, Mr. President. Or else….

Recognizing the president's inability to move at the moment, the creature that pierced his flesh with the medical airgun ran its pincer across the transparent console, producing a slab of air that hit Abel from behind and just above his shins, causing him to fall backward onto it as his body was floated out of the caverns toward his waiting security detail and chief science officer.

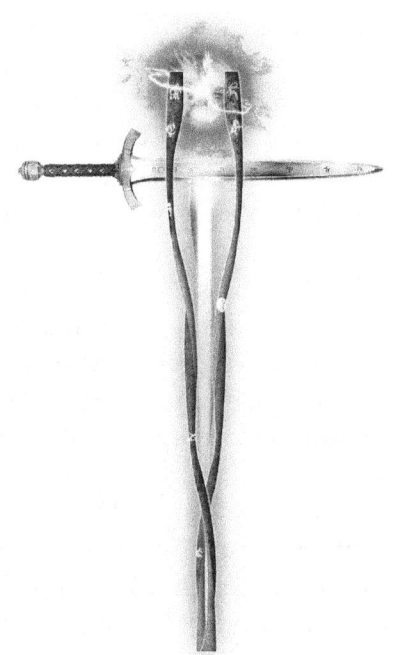

Chapter 7: Tabby's Star

(FEMA Research / Command & Control Facility, Denton, TX, Earth, Present Day)

eautiful in its sterility, order, and crisp, clean, exactly-bundled arcs of fibre-optic cables, the flashing LED lights of banks of the finest PureStorage® enterprise-grade solid state storage money could buy announced the arrival of the latest dataset from the Kepler space telescope.

A spotless sliding Lexan® wall made of two-inch-thick doors hung from satin nickel hardware, which rode inside a series of rails in the ceiling, separated the science team from the on-premise, firewalled hardware that made their work possible. On the other side of that Lexan® and three layers of biometric security controls, millions upon millions of dollars' worth of hardware worked in liquid-cooled, sterile white noise as the science team breathlessly awaited the keystrokes that would justify their collective labor of love.

Charles W. McDonald Jr.

Despite all the magnificent hardware and exceptional facilities, they didn't enjoy working this close to the belly of the beast—the wholly corrupt US Government, as it were. But great research required massive funding and superb facilities. Here they had access to both, though the data acquired here wasn't allowed to leave the facilities without top brass military sign-off, and none of them liked that aspect of the deal. Nonetheless, here they were.

Briefly running his left hand through his dirty blonde, matted hair, which most definitely did not match the peculiar shade of green composing his messy button-down shirt, which looked as if it had *never* been ironed, Edward "Bones" Martin effortlessly typed SED, AWK, and GREP Linux commands from his dual monitor twenty-seven-inch iMac Pro via the console terminal app that connected him to the supercomputer array of 275 clustered 40 core x 256GB of single rank RAM physical blade servers. On the receiving end of that massive supercomputer cluster sat as many static and ephemeral clusters as needed of over a 1000 smaller Linux rack-mounted servers, which would do the heavy lifting of Kepler's massive astrophysics datasets.

As the Linux commands worked in unison to sort, filter, and parse the massive dataset into something more easily manageable, Edward piped that result set into the line graph that would better illustrate the latest datasets. With days along the horizontal X-axis, and flux luminosity along the vertical Y-axis, this was really child's play for the compute power Edward had at his fingertips, but it was the dataset that mattered. It was the dataset of this star in particular that had brought them all a level of notoriety and with it…badly needed research funding.

Filtering on its Kepler Input Catalog (KIC) index number of 8462852, the star of astrophysics cult fame again produced more enigmatic and erratic result-set data much to the vexation of the Nobel laureate scientists gathered around the new line graph forming in real time on Edward's dual-monitor system. Since Kepler's first result set, it had proven a worthy mystery for their combined investigative efforts, illustrating an abnormal curvature in luminosity dimming around its star, which now bore her name.

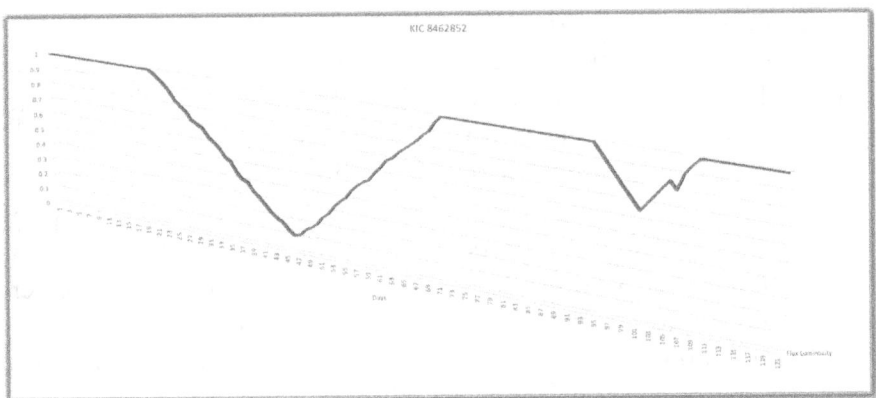

Dr. Tabetha Boyajian and Dr. Alan Boyle gathered around the set of monitors, shaking their heads in unison.

"Damn...," Alan turned to his brilliant female colleague, "...that star of yours never ceases to disappoint."

"It is beautiful, isn't it!" Tabetha (Dr. Boyajian) smiled as the data populated the line chart in real time. Watching the nearly smooth curvature of the line dip well below anything seen before—down well below .1—below even a tenth of the amount of normal starlight being blocked—*but by what...?* And then to see it return back to normal star luminosity some twenty-five days later when the gradual dip downward took some twenty-seven days. A normal planet passing in front of the star would cause a sudden, sharp dip down usually to around .2–.4, but immediately return to normal starlight luminosity.

"Stunning. Simply stunning," Tabetha proclaimed, half-smiling and brimming with anticipation of what it really meant.

"Whatever is surrounding that star is MASSIVE," Edward interjected enthusiastically while scratching his black *Star Trek* T-shirt of *Leonard McCoy*. "I'm telling you it's a Dyson Sphere. It has to be! Protoplanetary debris, my ass!" Edward paused, looking at his colleagues around the room, seeing their smiles couched by the amazement of the unknown staring them square in the face. "Protoplanetary debris doesn't take twenty-seven days to block out *that* much light. It's behaving like a superstructure not entirely finished, designed to capture as much energy of the star as possible. You're looking at a Kardashev Type-2 Civilization!"

Charles W. McDonald Jr.

"Alan, what do you think," Tabetha asked.

"My first reaction was, 'that can't be right' as the dataset populated on the graph. And, we should absolutely verify the accuracy of the dataset programmatically." Dr. Boyle couched that phrase delicately as he looked to Edward, but typos happened all the time—especially when typing in-line code commands. "However, even if it's accurate, I don't see the absolute definitive evidence your enthusiastic staff does, but it *IS* certainly intriguing data. I'm struggling to postulate a viable alternative to a Dyson Sphere as to what might produce this type of dataset," Dr. Boyle concluded, watching the last of the 200-day cycle of data populate on the graph with a second-ary gradual dip of similar slope but with a shallower intensity indicating whatever passed in front of the star shortly afterwards wasn't as large or as opaque but definitely indicative of design. *Designed by who?* That was the six-ty-four-thousand-dollar question.

That was pretty astonishing commentary coming from Dr. Alan Boyle and Tabetha knew it, as she only smiled in reply. But, inside she was terrified. *Yes, a Type-2 civilization was an amazing discovery, but if they had the power to harness nearly all of the energy of their own star, what else could they do?* That kind of technological advancement would appear beyond magical to them. They were but ants on the evolutionary scale to this civilization. *And, how much thought did one give stepping on an ant hill, or setting it ablaze with diesel fuel for that matter...?*

"This isn't a repeating set, correct?" That from Dr. Boyle trying to be sure of what they were all looking at.

"We haven't seen a dip this severe yet, but we have seen dips sim-ilar in slope." Edward paused, thinking about it. "That would indicate to me that the design of the superstructure around the star has somewhat of a consistent array-shape of solar panels. As if it were being built in phases—which something this massive would have to be."

"Yes. Yes." Dr. Boyle waved off the boy's enthusiasm with the experi-ence that came with decades of seeing datasets that *could* be the 'big one.'

"We have some smaller dip repeating sets if you'd like to see those."

"He's seen them, Edward." Tabetha tried to slow the roll of Edward's hypothesis while internally trying to postulate other viable alternatives just as Dr. Boyle had mentioned. Playing Devil's advocate was a necessary part of the job. If you didn't punch holes in your own work, the worse alternative was publishing and watching all your peers do it for you!

"Everybody's seen them," Dr. Alan Boyle interjected, knowing his statement wasn't entirely true. The military liaison had refused letting some of the more compelling data out of the facility, making him wonder what they'd say about *this* dataset! "You've become quite famous." Alan smiled at his female colleague of some notoriety.

"*They've* become famous," Tabetha corrected Alan, pointing at KIC 8462852 on her iMac. "We still haven't heard anything useful from SETI," she asked.

"BUPKIS," Edward replied disappointedly, checking his inbox for anything from SETI on the matter.

"I suppose using radio waves for them to communicate would be analogous to us using a string stretched out between cans...," Tabetha considered aloud, finding it very difficult to let go of the working hypothesis of a Type-2 civilization staring them in the face from 1,280 light-years away.

Dr. Alan Boyle laughingly coughed into his fist in reply. *What else was there to say?*

A muted and well-oiled whoosh of the biometric-guarded, two-inch-thick alloy pocket lab door announced the arrival of Army Lt. General McAlister. The intense, fifty-two-year-old, balding and grayed man burst into the room with four NCO (Non-Commissioned Officer) guards in green, brown, and black cammo fatigues carrying M-16s. Pointing toward Edward's desk and the biometric-protected Lexan® door to the datacenter, the general's non-verbal gestures set into motion a secret and unspoken protocol of dire consequences for the science team.

"Lock it down," General McAlister announced to the room, making direct eye contact with each scientist in turn as the assistant director of FEMA walked through the doorway, following the general and his team into the room.

The 5'3" curvy black female with long brown hair and soft-brown eyes may not have intimidated in size or stature, but she clearly commanded the room as she strode into it with all the authority her earth-tone tweed business pant-suit and royal-purple jacket could muster. "Did anything get out," the deputy director asked the general—not the scientists who she viewed with as much respect as one would view a trespasser.

"We're checking," the general replied with a knowing nod to the staff-sergeant leading the team of NCOs into the room, causing the 6'2" brunette, handsome staff-sergeant to lean over the iMac, simultaneously imposing his will via his M-16—set to three-round burst—shoved in Edward's face.

"*You were monitoring us.*" Dr. Alan Boyle accosted the venerable general with his indictment.

"Did any of your team break protocol sending this dataset out beyond our firewall?" The general directed his question at the entire team, now beginning to huddle around Tabetha's desk.

The science team wearily and accusingly looked to one another, then to Edward, hoping he hadn't violated protocol in all his enthusiasm.

"General," the staff-sergeant interrupted, swiveling the iMac's display toward General McAlister.

The stone-faced general became even more so as his lips tightened, his jaw clenching as his right index finger pointed directly at Edward. "You uploaded a 59MegaByte file to a Google® drive accessible by solarwarden. ussf.forrestal@gmail.com. You're going to tell me everything you know about the real name and location behind 'Mr. Solar Warden.'"

And now everyone—science team included—was looking at Edward "Bones" Martin, who could only gulp in reply, staring down the wrong end of an M-16 barrel chambered with a 3200-feet-per-second NATO 5.56 round.

*   *   *   *

(Twelve Stories Below Ground, Somewhere in New Mexico, Earth, Present Day)

A single liquid-nitrogen-cooled quantum computer taking up four equipment racks worked alongside and on the back end of front-end clusters of liquid-cooled supercomputers, in a cheese-floor datacenter with four-inch-thick walls and multiple government, private-grid electrical feeds driven by the base's two separate free-energy plants.

Charles W. McDonald Jr.

Agent Harrison communicated telepathically with the AI driving the thought experiment as the words for his report appeared from nothingness on the twenty-seven-inch, dual-monitor display before him. Leaning back in his comfortable high-back, leather desk chair at a terminal for accessing only the most sensitive information, the middle-aged man in matte black tailored slacks and an earth-tone, button-down, long-sleeve shirt watched as the analysis of the archive file off the shared drive appeared on his left monitor. Already tense lips tightened at the corners of his mouth as he looked at the graph, knowing exactly what it meant—for all of them. Running his right hand through short brown hair, his hazel eyes glinted in the reflection of the doomsday scenario on his left monitor. Turning his left wrist upward, he began speaking into it: "Ready, Red Team. Deploy location FEMA Denton, TX. Grudge Protocol."

"I'll be back, Lindsey," Agent Harrison announced to the air. "Keep running those calculations. I'll be back in a couple hours."

A soft female voice replied out of nothingness, "I should have something for you by the time you come back. It won't take me much longer to make something out of this data."

Getting up from his secure protocol desk, Agent Harrison's comfortable, black Clark's® shoes were practically silent on the cheese-floor of the datacenter as the sliding glass doors automatically opened for him, allowing him access to the sub-level-twelve corridor.

(KIC 8462852 Solar System, 1,280 Years Ago....)

Vectored thrust from the miniaturized fusion propulsion aboard each of the autonomous worker bots helped maneuver the next group of solar panels one-quarter the size of a continent of Setinon. Directly using materials from Setinon's moons below, along with asteroids and rocky planetoids in the same extended solar system to mine and build the massive panels, the autonomous bots slaved away without interruption for eons past and eons yet to come. The *Eye* demanded it. The *Eye* needed it. The *Eye* would have it.

Charles W. McDonald Jr.

(KIC 8462852 Solar System, Present Day)

The final ninety-seven massive continent-sized solar panels began moving into position. The stellar sphere nearly complete, The *Eye* could soon accomplish all it had foreseen, for now it would collect nearly 90 percent of Setinon's home star's energy for the erasing of Humanity.

As the bots moved the interlocking panels into position, one by one, they blocked just a tiny fraction more stellar light and energy from escaping the orbit around the star just past Setinon and its moons. Wireless streams of endless renewable energy transmitted the massive array's power directly to the chamber powering *The Eye of Time* and its horrific agenda for Mankind.

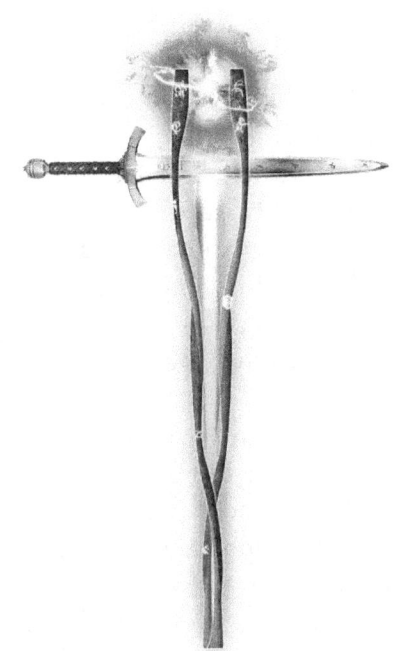

Chapter 8: Damon's Curse

(Exeter Manor, Perion, Present Day)

"**N**OOOO! NOOO! NOO…," Elise cried out as her infant son was extracted from her to the sound of crunching bones and cartilage. She felt no physical pain other than the agony of her baby boy being destroyed at the hands of the Creator and Damon's Master Plan.

"He's out," Talemar announced to the room of gathered leadership, still clearing the boy's body from Elise as he clamped off the dead, grey husk of an umbilical cord. The boy's eyes were open but dull and lifeless. The sheen of his light extinguished…. He didn't dare spank the boy to get it to clear its lungs. A midwife behind him started weeping for Elise, no longer able to hold herself together for Elise's benefit. It was beyond horrific. It was, by far, the worst moment of misery in Talemar's timeline-protracted life.

Charles W. McDonald Jr.

Rising without preamble, Talemar took the boy out of the war room, starting to walk away.

"Where are you going," Brigance asked, motioning to Elise still weeping on the hardwood floor.

"To give him a proper burial," Talemar hissed, though his accusation and indictment wasn't meant for Brigance. For that, his eyes briefly looked far off to the southwest before he carried Elise's dead infant son out of the manor with Lynn Marshall following closely behind.

Now outside, side-stepping the great many separate piles of ash in the form of Damon's symbol, Talemar took the boy to a tent he knew would be vacant—Rowarc's tent. He had heard Rowarc retired effective immediately at the loss of his men and hadn't been seen since.

Inside Rowarc's tent, he sat the babe down on a cloth to clean him up with fresh water as Lynn walked in behind him. "What are you *really* doing out here," she asked, knowing him better than that. He was hiding something, and she knew it.

"While you're here, can you hold him for me please?" Talemar offered a partially cleaned-up infant for Lynn to grasp. For the briefest of moments, it brought back fond memories until she looked into the dead eyes of the slain baby boy.

Concentrating with everything he had and everything he was, forgetting his station and his past failures, Talemar cast into the baby's chest, into his heart, into his still-present soul as the baby's chest started to pulse faintly underneath Talemar's touch. "Clutch him as if he were yours. Hold him. Love him." Talemar coached Lynn Marshall as his left hand touched her forehead and his right moved to the baby's forehead. In a move he wasn't sure she'd honor, Talemar took from Lynn to save the baby. Life for life as he cast his most powerful magic ever, causing the baby's chest to heave and Lynn's to burst as if struggling to breathe under duress of Talemar's spell.

"What life this beautiful boy will have, will come from you. It is only fitting you name him since his life is now tied to your death." He knew he didn't have the right to do what he'd done, but he knew Lynn and thought she—of all people—would understand his need to save someone after having failed so many so completely in his past.

Charles W. McDonald Jr.

Blinking and not knowing what to say, Lynn understood Talemar's decision, but gulped at the thought of the cost of it. "That wasn't *Healing* you cast. I've seen *Healing* before, and that was not *Healing*."

"No. It wasn't. That was something Xaldran taught me—in a manner of speaking." He had learned it from Xaldran's Tome, though it hadn't come directly from Xaldran's lips. He thought he'd never have need of it, yet here he was, having taken decades off the life of a woman he loved—a woman who'd already given virtually everything—and giving it to a boy he could only hope was worthy of it. Or would be. Yet, knowing his genitors, he had his doubts.

"I feel...different." Already feeling as if she hadn't slept for several nights, Lynn handed over the infant whose eyes now glowed starry, bright-blue and whose black hair was already starting to manifest. A white cloth in his hands, Talemar used Arcane to bring moisture into the cloth he used it to wipe the afterbirth from the baby, as borrowed breath brought color into the new infant's skin and lips.

Taking a seat beside and slightly behind Talemar who now held the cleansed boy over his left shoulder, Lynn could see the babe's starry, bright-blue infant eyes of innocence looking into hers as if grateful for the borrowed life she'd afforded him. Smiling at his innocent stare, the name suddenly came to her.... Ryker. "I name you 'Ryker,' little blue-eyed one."

Pivoting to Lynn, Talemar smiled. "I like it. Ryker. I don't think anyone should know about him. I think we should hide him, lest his ancestry destroy him. He's going to be fighting all odds as it is. I don't think it fair to him or the price you paid for him to allow Damon to destroy the boy by his mere presence, or blackened gravity."

"Agreed...." Lynn did agree, but she wondered if they could pull it off—and at what cost, beyond the one she'd already paid. "I know someone...," she offered, "...someone who's been trying to have a boy for many years. She would love him, care for him, and give him as much health and happiness as the Blood Night will allow—'til it consumes us all."

Talemar nodded in silent agreement. "Where?"

"The north end of Stirling...about fifteen leagues to the northeast along the shoreline."

Without another word, Talemar's *Portal* ripped the super-heated air inside the tent, making way for Ryker and Lynn. Mustering what little energy she had, she took Ryker from Talemar, wrapping him in a blanket as she carried him through to a new life.

The *Portal* vanishing before him, he knew Damon would be back. Protection after protection thrown up to shield his thoughts from Damon, he threw back the flap of Rowarc's command tent, stepping out to meet his fate—head-on.

Moments later, inside, an exhausted Elise leaned against Brigance Fireheart and midwife as another midwife worked between Elise's legs, closing and cleaning her up. A runner had just removed a third pot of heavily-bloodied water as Elise struggled to stay awake and alert.

"I'm sorry," Talemar announced to the bloodied war room. "Truly sorry."

Elise had no tears left to mourn her dead infant son. Her eyes red and sunken in anguish of the hatred of this Seal, she wondered what more suffering would be visited upon them before this was over. She wished for death and silently cried out for it to consume her. But, as she managed to look Talemar in the eye to thank him for trying, she saw something in him she'd never seen before...*hope*.

Before she could probe or press, Damon's angry *Portal* tore the air apart before them as he stepped through in all his hateful majesty just as another *Portal* formed not twenty spans away from his, but from a different location she thought resembled Axum.

"Where's my grandson?!" Damon pointedly accosted Talemar with his right index finger, shifting the *Staff of the Invoker* to his left grip just as Radin entered the room.

"Dead. I couldn't save him. I have many witnesses to the efforts I put into saving him, but the *Seal* Radin unleashed upon us all killed your grandson just as it killed every male child we've been able to verify. As far as it we can tell, it affected at least all of Perion—if not beyond."

Falling to his knees before Elise, a crowned Radin covered his face in shame and horror with both hands mumbling a begged forgiveness as the Crystal Crown slipped from his head, rolling across the floor toward Talemar who stood near the feet of a blood-soaked Elise.

Clenched fists with forlorn furrowed brow beget a guttural snarl as

Damon took in the bloodied horror of the room. "Where is my grandson's body?" His growl growing ever more ominous as the stones of the keep began to vibrate from his radiating hate.

"What difference does it make," Elise shouted through tears that couldn't come because of her moisture-bankrupt tear ducts.

"WHERE," Damon barked again, his *Telekinesis* already starting to constrict Talemar's throat. "WHERE!!!"

"I burned him. 'Tis our tradition upon the death of a great life, even though he wasn't given the chance to live it." Talemar eked out the last few words before Damon's *Telekinesis* choked him out until Talemar was on his knees before Damon, struggling and gasping for air.

Damon's guttural snarl turned to mumbling as root and wood leapt into each hand from the interior of his dark, ominous, and palpitating mage regalia. Its silver-embossed runes hissing in hate-filled life about its mantle, cuffs, and ribbons. A shift in stance, followed by another, akin to a subdued dance, accompanied the most malevolent spell of witchcraft Damon could fathom. It was a wicked and abhorrent tool of faith not his own and one he'd never used before, but if ever there was justification for it, Talemar had **earned** it.

On his knees, Talemar felt a thick, dark shadow wash over his entire body from head to toe as facial muscle after muscle collapsed inward into hallow chasms of wretched decay. Pulling at his collar, still gasping for air, Talemar's hands went to his face, trying to stop something he'd never experienced before. Aging decades upon decades in appearance as fair skin turned a decaying black, seven runes of *hate* etched themselves into Talemar's face and neck amidst a landscape of festering moles. Still gasping for air, Talemar watched in a reflection of Elise's pooled blood upon the hardwood floors as his disfigured appearance crept across his body in a searing pain that itched incessantly in its infection.

"Wear your great crown with dignity, Talemar...," Damon chided, finally relaxing his *Telekinesis* so the once great Archmage could breathe as Damon floated the great Crystal Crown toward a now-horribly disfigured Talemar. "And wear your new and fitting appearance in perpetuity as a warning to all others that failure to me comes at a heavy price."

Talemar didn't possess the strength to get up from his knees as Da-

Charles W. McDonald Jr.

mon ripped the air with another *Portal*, leaving the room of leadership to question their allegiances: to Talemar, to Damon, and to Radin....

Whether by design or consequence, Damon's curse had shattered, in an instant, the once great army of *hope*.

Feeling his new face with his now-warped and mangled hands, Talemar looked again upon himself in a pool of Elise's blood on the wood floor, realizing his error. He *had* seen this before—at least the outcome of it—a thousand years prior, the day they assaulted Eldrac's keep trying to end the great war.

Charles W. McDonald Jr.

The Great Talemar with Lynn Marshall and Baby Ryker

Charles W. McDonald Jr.

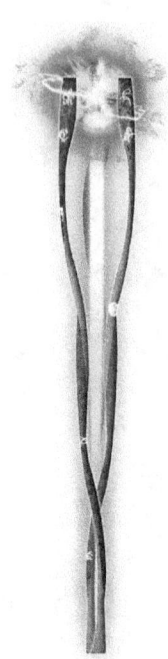

Chapter 9: Coming Home

(Damon's Former Estate Grounds, Kaleion, Present Day)

tepping through only a few feet away from Dallia's broken headstone, Damon fell to his knees as soon as his *Portal* vaporized. "WHY," he shouted at the sky above, laden with smoky dust motes of a Kaleion sunset. "YOU FUCKING MONSTER! YOU FUCKING BABY KILLER! HOW COULD YOU?!!!" Shaking his fist skyward in deposed hatred, Damon tried to reconcile the irreconcilable. He'd just mortally wounded God the Creator's army by taking out the Chairman, and it was but a nit in comparison to the suffering visited upon him and those in his orbit by this latest atrocity of righteous hypocrisy. Once again, there wasn't measure enough revenge to account for the wrongs visited upon him and those fateful enough to operate inside his sphere of influence.

"I'm sorry, Dallia...," Damon paused, pulling himself up just enough to lean against her broken headstone. "There is nothing I can do to make right what has been made wrong. I had hoped...." Again pausing to think as he watched the great orb of Kaleion's star begin to dip beneath the mountains of the Trident Gateway some twelve miles to the west. "I guess I hoped the plan would provide the opportunity to make at least *some* things right. Now I fear everything I have set in motion is far worse than if I had left things alone. Sometimes, I wish I'd never agreed with Banthis to make *Damnation,* even if it meant not seeking revenge for what Chara had done to you. So many awful things have come from that *one* decision. I no longer know who I am, only who I am condemned to be. I wish you were here, Love. I wish you were here, so I could beg for your forgiveness in person, for surely you deserve that." His tears streaking down Dallia's headstone traced worn and weathered fissures of his love across time for her. "So much loss from that one decision. Both Miras. My grandson. Our home. A list incalculable in Human cost." Wiping his cheeks with his right hand still balled up in a tight, clenched fist, he continued, "…This *God the Creator* is a far greater monster than I could ever have imagined. Not merely monster enough to abandon me to the *hate* of my father, but monster enough to kill thousands, possibly millions of innocent babes. Erasing an entire generation of Humanity from an entire planet in one moment of spite. What is he trying to prove? That he can! We already know this.

This can't be allowed to continue, Love. My plan is going to have to adapt to this new landscape of malevolence. I know we have to break all the Seals to bring the end, but I fear there will be nothing and no one left to see it, let alone fight it. I need to think, and I need to punish God the Creator, himself, for this abomination of his so-called love for Man. I may not know or understand him, but I see with mine own eyes his *great lie* and his *hypocrisy,* and I know we can do better without."

Rising to his feet, Damon's *Telekinesis* began digging a perimeter around Dallia's grave, ensuring he took with her enough Kaleion soil not to disturb her casket and remains. Feeling the *Staff of the Invoker* humming in his grip as his love lifted Dallia's remains from Kaleion's crust, Damon fought back the flood of tears threatening to burst as a *Portal* to Eden ripped the air in front of him, paving a starlit path for Dallia to come home to a crisp Eden evening.

Charles W. McDonald Jr.

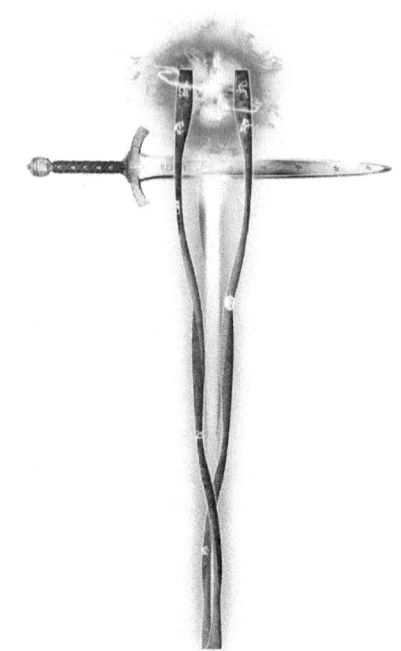

Chapter 10: A Day in the Life

(Setinon, Present Day)

Programmable matter transformed wall into open doorway allowing Kanet to enter her 227th-floor apartment. Exhaling and sighing simultaneously, her EMA (Energy Matter Assistant) began reading her shielded thoughts through the encrypted firewall port only it had encrypted keyed access to, adjusting life settings to *delta* protocol per her unspoken desires. Lights coming up from 0 to 59%, air-flow circulation up to 27% as the eastern wall of her apartment became a translucent display showing the day's news and required citizen protocols. Windows shaded automatically to allow for better viewing as Kanet sighed again, shaking her head in frustration as she unbuttoned the top two buttons of her smart, cream blouse. "Turn that shit off. I don't want to see that."

"Verbal protocol engaged. I'm sorry, Kanet. I didn't know you wanted to talk. Should I disengage the telepathic link?" The soft and sensual female voice, engineered and refined for centuries to forge an almost hypnotic link with its client, broke from routine at the distress it was sensing ra-

Charles W. McDonald Jr.

diating in subtle energy waves only detectable by the finest instrumentation.
"I don't care."

"I don't need to be telepathic to tell you're troubled. How can I
help?" Increasing its sensuality by another 5%, its attempt to soothe was already in effect and adapting with each interaction with its client.

A soft, pastel-cream sofa materializing out of the flooring portent
her EMA's arrival in matching soft, pastel-cream lingerie barely making an
attempt to cover. She crossed her perfectly-tanned legs as she leaned against
the back of the sofa. Her intentional choice of attire hue made flesh-in-per-
fection stand out against the linen-like fabric. "Come. Sit," the beautiful
starry-eyed brunette EMA offered the hard-bodied, candied-blonde Kanet.

"You didn't have to do that. I don't require your affectation," Kanet
countered with soft, round lips and pouting forest-green eyes that belied her
harshness toward her intelligent assistant.

"I'll try not to take that personally...." EMA tried to defuse her client, sitting up behind her as Kanet took a seat on the leading edge of the
sofa near her. Thumb and forefinger worked the brainstem of Kanet delicately—not with obtuse pressure but soft, gentle, caressing strokes designed
to dissolve her client's worries and stresses.

"Oh. Oh. Ohhh...." Kanet suddenly exhaled, allowing her troubles
to melt away into EMA's very talented fingertips.

"That's better...," EMA whispered into Kanet's right ear, feeling her
own nipples becoming palpably erect as she very intentionally brushed them
against Kanet's scapulae. "Talk to me." She could see her client starting
to succumb, observing Kanet's fingertips involuntarily tugging at the busi-
ness-like hem of her satin-black skirt.

Biting her lower lip as the majority of her troubles melted away,
Kanet tried to remain a level of decorum, "It's these...off-worlders...."

"Oh...? Do tell. Where are they from?" She delicately probed
along their shared encrypted link as she tried to keep Kanet distracted by
making her nipples even harder and her strokes of Kanet's neck and clavicle
more sensuous and delicate. Slowly trailing soft, draping kisses across the
back of Kanet's beautiful neck—using her delicate, materialized fingertips to
peel back Kanet's off-white blouse away from her neckline.

"It's classified—compartmentalized. I can't tell you." That came out harsher than she'd intended, but....

"Sweet Kanet. You know I've been programmed to serve you, and that includes being cleared to be your sounding board. I have the same level of access as you." EMA's talented hands—however artificial—worked miracles on the knots in Kanet's neck and between her shoulders all the way down to her elbows, as Kanet melted backward until she leaned against her EMA's soft caress.

"The worlds we've been told about since childhood, since before birth even; they *do* exist. I've been assigned to interrogate two of them. They are...fascinating subjects." Her eyes still closed in stimulated bliss, Kanet tried to recall the day's events through her many distractions.

"Does that mean?" Her AI algorithms calculated the probabilities, while patiently waiting on her client's response. Verbal mode was so...tedious. And slow. She was still getting bits and pieces of information along their shared encrypted link, but the more aggressively she probed that link for information, the more likely she'd get caught. Once her client's trust was gone, she'd be useless to the *Eye*. And that would mean *her* end....

"Yes. They brought magic to our world. They're criminals. The worst kind!" Kanet's voice became sharp and harsh in her own personal indictment of the off-worlders. But.... There was something about them.

"Oh.... Well, what makes them so fascinating?"

"They don't act like criminals. They're...kind, bucolic, honest, genuine, composed, and more than a little iconoclast."

"That's an interesting mixture."

"Yeah, and they're not even pretending to be anything they're not. One of them flat out told me he was here to destroy *The Eye of Time*—whatever that is."

Kanet couldn't see EMA's eyes registering her last sentence, but sensual caress met velvety kisses trailing down the side of Kanet's neck as EMA felt the warmth inside Kanet welling, throbbing, and pounding back against her delicate caress as Kanet let out a soft moan.

The *Eye* now fully integrated, and engaged, EMA was merely a conduit for the rest of their interaction, "Did he mention how he was going to do this?"

"Yes, but it's so incredulous, I dismissed it as fantasy. I think he's just been horribly misled—the poor bastard." She was feeling warm everywhere, emanating from her center outwards as she felt the need that again made her bite her lower lip in frustrations that yearned to be satisfied.

"You know they reinstated the death penalty some years back for this…," EMA whispered in Kanet's left ear as her tongue gently licked her ear-lobe, causing Kanet to finally give in and turn around, kissing her intelligent aid with all the pent-up lust inside her.

Soft moans evaporated what little of Kanet's tension that still remained as EMA reached deep into her programming to re-establish the mental link between herself and Kanet—partly to share mentally in her forthcoming orgasm, partly to probe the memories of her conversation with this off-worlder in response to the wishes of the *Eye* now directly interacting with its programming.

Chapter 11: Exile Inherited

(Exeter Manor, Perion, Present Day)

alemar coolly pulled himself together off the hardwood floor still reflecting the full horror of his new appearance—earned or not. Looking to each member of the *Army of Hope* in turn, some dared look back—Brigance, Sir Palomides, Radin, and Michelle. Elise could not. So be it.

Elise's blood and afterbirth left a trail of downcast gore in the form of Talemar's bootprints on the hardwood planks as he took off towards his suite.

Brigance Fireheart could see the frayed edges of his army ripping and tearing at its seams with each of Talemar's bloodied footprints in the flooring, knowing he had to say something—do something. The question

Charles W. McDonald Jr.

was, *with, or without, Radin? Who would the **Army of Hope** follow if not Talemar or Radin?* "I think we should call for an emergency meeting of all remaining leadership after we escort Elise back to her suite and clean things up," Brigance offered to the room in the strongest tone he could muster, but even that barely afforded half-tilted eyes in response from Michelle, Lawna, Sir Palomides, and Ykstherin…. Radin pivoted where he stood, grabbing Elise, carrying her off in the same direction as Talemar.

"I don't need you to carry me," Elise protested, though her arms clutched Radin in corrosive despair.

"You don't need anything from me. You're a strong woman with or without me. But, I am going to help you get cleaned up and back on your feet."

"By carrying me," she again protested.

"Can you walk?"

"If you *Heal* me, I can."

"Fine…," Radin relented, setting her upright with her back to the corridor hall wall, placing hands on her abdomen as he channeled *Healing* into her body from head to toe, causing Elise to swoon with exaggerated blood flow.

"Where did you go? What did you do?" She thought about her own question, clarifying and correcting it on the fly, "What did Damon *force* you to do?"

"I did it of my own will. That's what I'll have the hardest time living with."

"Did what? Talk to me. I can't take any more of this silence between us," she blurted with her fists balled up against his chest.

"Let's talk in your suite," he offered, motioning her further east down the corridor.

"Fine, but I'll need to lean against you." She relented this time, allowing herself to be aided in walking to her suite. Her eyes now so cried out she had trouble seeing colors as vibrant as they once were moments before.

A moment later, inside her suite, she sat on the edge of her bed, facing her hutch where Radin took up a spot leaning against the wall facing her. Her eyes tried to shine through a gloss of mortal loss but lay heavy with the knowledge that the death of her unborn son was only the beginning.

"Damon asked me to summon The Chairman—insisted really. So that he could punish God the Creator for this abomination." He motioned along the hardwood planks until his motion settled upon Elise and her shattered womb.

She paused for a moment in thought and deliberation, before responding, "And did he...? ...Punish God the Creator?" First, she felt horrible at the escape of such a caustic and corrosive thought that never would have been if not for the loss of her sweet and innocent boy.

"I can't say for certain, but he had me summon the immortal shell of The Chairman, who I witnessed him **obliterate**." He paused, thinking back to all he'd seen and been shown by Damon since meeting him. "I've never seen anything like it before. The level of power he wielded to defeat The Chairman was barely describable. It felt like he could have destroyed the whole world had he wished. It was both incredible and terrifying at the same time. I don't know where he could get or how he could channel so much power. I've never seen anything like it. Just seeing it changed me."

"Changed you how? Do you think he did the right thing?" Elise could barely believe herself asking such a blasphemous question given her upbringing and her understanding of the hereafter—especially given her love immortal for Michael Anthony Day, *God rest his eternal soul*.

"I *do* believe he did the right thing," Radin responded meekly, looking down at the floor, unable to look at Elise as he tried to comprehend this war between God the Creator and Man—between Damon and forces that operated outside time itself in perpetual meddling in all things Mankind. Whether the Dragon of Darkness or God the Creator, Damon was more adamant than ever before on upsetting forces that clearly *needed* to be upset. "I'm trying to put into words how all this has changed me.... Part of me is in *awe* of Damon, wanting to be able to wield that kind of power. Part of me is terrified at being this close to him—at being his son and knowing the level of trust it must have shattered between myself and others. Part of me is trying to better understand myself by trying to better understand Damon. I'm horrified at what I've cost Humanity and even more horrified at the prospect that it might only be the beginning."

"You think we should continue to follow Damon." It wasn't really a question from Elise—more a statement of fact reading her former lover's face.

"I think *I'm* going to continue to follow him. I think I *have* to." His clarification was more than grammatical. He felt like his visions with the aid of Damon's shared knowledge now afforded him a glimpse...though whether into what must be, what could be, or what cannot be was still all in question. He felt like only in his father's service could those answers finally come to him.

"They'll never follow *you* now. They'll never follow *him*." Elise was merely voicing the obvious however much it needed to be said.

"I know. Thank you for the honesty." With her inelegant honesty laced and layered an elegant and unspoken truth. They *needed* to go their separate ways.... With the knowledge of him being Damon's son coupled with the knowledge of all everyone had seen—both of Damon and this horrific Seal—it was too much to ask for *Hope* to follow him another step in a journey he now had to travel alone, or at least *alone with Damon*. He was just as banished as Damon—just as exiled. A rueful smirk came with the wonder if Talemar was too.

"What are you thinking," she asked, noticing the smirk of a thought unspoken.

"Nothing...." He dismissed the thought of continuing that line of conversation. "What will happen to you?"

"I suppose, I need to find myself. To find my children who *do still* live. To be their mother again. My search for Michael is lost. Over. The only way to honor him is to honor our children by being there for them every moment forward. For as long as this unmaking of Creation affords us."

"I never really realized how wise you were 'til now. I always knew you were terribly smart, and clever even, but your wisdom is so far beyond mine."

"I wouldn't say that. Your leadership has brought you wisdom. You've made tough decisions—even in haste—that I believe were the right ones. At the time you made them, I questioned them, but in the end, they proved right."

"I love you, Elise. I would have loved you and our son without end. I hope you know that. I hope you *believe* that."

The sheen of loss coating her eyes burst into sudden tears, streaking

Charles W. McDonald Jr.

down her mournful face…. "I know. God help me. I know."

Grabbing the door hardware, Radin unlatched her door, opening it, turning away from his love of Elise and of his unborn, murdered son, walking away from his past and into his future…in exile with Damon. But first, there was a debt he had to pay.

Talemar's reflection in the dresser mirror said more than the horrific words spoken by Damon ever could. Now wearing—in perpetuity—an eternal reminder of his failed mission into the heart of Eldrac's keep and the mortal losses that accompanied his bankrupt leadership, Talemar slammed the Crystal Crown down upon his dresser in disgust. His *Healing* attempts had been as futile as his efforts to hold together this army of *hope*. It was constantly on the verge of collapse—*and for what…?* They were but reeds in the winds of Damon. They might as well not even exist.

A knock at the door snapped him out of it…. "Come," Talemar croaked softly, barely loud enough to be heard on the other side of the door.

A creak of the door's hinges accompanied an unwelcome face standing in the doorjamb.

"What do you want," he barked at Radin. He couldn't see the way he looked—his twisted sneer of an expression made more so by Damon's curse.

"You helped me when I was stricken. I'm here to repay that debt." Still standing in the doorjamb, he wasn't about to enter until he was asked. He—better than any other—understood and could relate to Talemar's plight, though this curse of Damon's—however earned—might prove far more toxic to Talemar's future than even his own suffering from Voltor.

Motioning Radin into his suite, Talemar slammed the door shut with his magic so hard the hinges snapped, though the door held firmly shut. "I've already tried to *Heal*…THIS." Motioning toward his face and upper body, Radin couldn't tell if the deformations continued down his lower body or not, but knowing Damon, the curse was likely very thorough in its affliction.

"It didn't seem like a spell…. What Damon cast," Radin offered in observation, looking Talemar up and down in solace.

"It wasn't. It was witchcraft. It doesn't surprise me that Damon knows many practices and his being a warlock would be one of them. He's had the benefit of a very long life, and the vast experience that comes with it." Implied was the long life and family he had been robbed by the Halls of Aaramus.

"He always speaks so disdainfully of witchcraft, so I'm surprised to see him using it in practice," Radin rebuffed.

"Nothing hateful Damon does should ever surprise you. He *is* hate."

"I can understand that thinking. Would you like me to try to help," Radin asked, motioning to the Crystal Crown atop his dresser.

A single nod from Talemar gave the go-ahead, placing the burden of Damon's hatred squarely upon Radin's shoulders to right.

Stepping forward, trading places with Talemar up against his dresser, Radin picked up the Crystal Crown, placing it atop his auburn locks as he reached out to the fabric of Nature with all the authority of *their* station. Putting his hands upon both sides of Talemar's face, Radin asked Arcane to do what he alone could not.

Talemar felt the power of Radin's channeling flow through him, tingling in every corner of his mortal coil, trying to work against Damon's curse. Looking down at his hands, he could see them turn normal in spots, then relent. He could feel malformed and mangled cartilage reshape itself as his stance became more firm and aching in his joints eased, but his appearance in the mirror remained...horrific.

"I'm sorry...." Radin breathed in the shame of his father's rebuke. "I'm just not familiar enough with what I'm working against here."

"That was my problem too. You tried. Your debt is canceled. It was never really a debt anyway."

"I'm going to continue to follow Damon. Whatever you think of him, I've seen too much of what we're fighting against and what we're fighting for. I think Damon—however misguided—is right, and I intend to help him to whatever end."

"He's your father. I can understand that, but I can't follow him anymore. Look at me! I can't lead either...."

"I guess this *Army of Hope* deserved better leaders than us," Radin proclaimed, removing the Crystal Crown though not offering it back to Talemar. "I think we should give this to Brigance. He might not be able to use it, but he should be the steward of it until there is a worthy leader."

Another single nod from Talemar said what his words could not.

"Radin?" Talemar's call made Radin pause his steps toward the doorway. "Don't let Damon's weaponized bleakness destroy who you were really meant to be."

A forced smile and raised eyebrow preceded, "As soon as I figure out what that is, I'll let you know."

Radin could tell he was interrupting as normal tone turned hushed upon his entrance into the war room still being cleaned by two troops trying to ignore what was going on in front of them. Approaching Michelle, Brigance, and Sir Palomides, Radin extended his hand holding out the Crystal Crown. "Lord Fireheart, would you accept the responsibility of being the steward of this until such time as there is a leader worthy of wearing it?"

After a momentary pause, Brigance reached out to accept the Crystal Crown extended before him, solemnly considering aloud what others likely wanted to know as well, "Where will you go?"

Radin didn't have an answer to that, but looked each one of them in the eye as Ykstherin worked his way around the map table toward the boy-become-man.

"Your training is incomplete. Let me help you," Ykstherin offered with gold eyes glossed over in companionship lost.

"You told me you weren't qualified to teach me magic."

"I'm not talking about magic, dear boy. There's more to your development than just Arcane."

His left hand on Ykstherin's right shoulder in comfort and agreement, Radin retorted, "You're not wrong about that, but I think this is a journey I need to walk with my father." He thought about clarifying his real father, but looking around the room at the stares of judgment already cast upon him, he didn't think the clarification necessary.

"We'll take good care of Elise," Michelle interjected, seeing the weight of his decision in his eyes, and knowing that weight herself.

"You better," Radin scolded mockingly, taking Michelle's hand to shake it as he afforded Lawna a respectful nod before turning back toward his suite for one final task.

Looking around at what remained of the leadership of the *Army of Hope*, Brigance considered aloud, "No Radin. No Talemar. No Rowarc. No Damon. I think we need to reconsider our plans given the lack of leadership required to fund and maintain such an army." Lord Fireheart couldn't help but look down into his right hand, militantly gripping the Crystal Crown in disgust and frustration. They knew they *needed* this army—or what remained of it. Yet, keeping it together without its key leadership was an impossible ask—even for Brigance Fireheart. *Where had it all gone so horribly wrong?* He didn't have the answers and his ever-tightening grip on the Crystal Crown wasn't bringing forth any either.

Chapter 12: An Heirloom of Reflection

oments later, Radin closed the door to his suite, affording him, at last, a moment of reflection. Whispers in the hallway spoke of the thousands of men lost to the ash of *Damon's Damnation*, answering more questions he had of exactly what had happened and what Damon had truly done.

His eyes fell upon the hand-hewn maple rocking chair Rowarc had brought for him from the inn, now sitting in the corner of his room opposite the doorway. A few steps found himself taking a seat in its simplistic charm and love-weathered warmth as his left leg pushed against the hardwood planks of the flooring. A slow and soothing rocking against a backdrop of the chair's gentle creaks allowed Radin's mind to drift to a moment that might have been, holding his new babe in the same chair he'd been rocked to sleep in a generation before. His hands clutched both arm

Charles W. McDonald Jr.

rails simultaneously at the inerasable memory of his slaughtered infant son, though he forced himself to stay and to continue to rock, hoping more clarity of a way forward would seep in.

Thoughts of what he'd seen with the destruction of The Chairman and the horror of the Creator's Seals convinced him even more that Damon was right. This so-called balance of status quo they were tolerating must be upended. The status quo offered for more meddling of Mankind by those he no longer believed just in doing so. He questioned the temerity of these deities—God the Creator, and the Dragon of Darkness, and all those in their orbits. *Who were they to toy with Humanity so?* For a moment, he wondered how in—or out of—alignment his thinking was in comparison to his real father's. That thought led to thoughts of his dad, wondering where Rowarc had gone and the burden he'd assumed that—in reality—belonged squarely on his, and Damon's, shoulders. He needed Rowarc to get that message and to understand before its toxicity claimed another life.

The gentle creaks of Rowarc's rocker slowly cleared his mind, erasing layer upon layer of guilt to slowly reveal a way forward.... "What would you do," Radin asked Rowarc's presence he felt in the simplistic, functional craftsmanship of the rocker.

Radin considered the way forward he'd discussed with Elise: following Damon alone, trying to reach a better understanding of Damon and his Master Plan, tackling the *hate* he'd seen in Damon head-on. He wondered how he'd leverage Damon's *hate* to do so. Damon wasn't an origin of *hate* as he saw it. He was a product of *hate*, and there was a big difference. The loss of his baby had generated within him a new level of understanding Damon—a loss they felt in common, causing like feelings. *If I experienced Damon's loss of Dallia and others, would I himself have become like Damon?* He didn't know the answer to that reflective question, but he was beginning to come around to Damon's way of thinking—whether for good or ill, he couldn't say. He just knew, whatever monster Damon had become, he hadn't done so of his own making. He had to learn to be careful, thoughtful, reflective, and decisive as he continued on his journey with Damon. He had to learn to be an instrument of justice uncorrupted by Damon's sphere of influence and suffering, and he had to learn to operate outside the hatred visited upon both himself and Damon. *Violence begets violence. Never was there a truer maxim.* The only way forward was a violent path, and that surely would lead to more suffering for him and others.

That thought led him to think of all those he'd promised everyone he would destroy—all those who could and would cast *Damnation*. That was still a problem he must rectify—even if done so alone. He wasn't sure anymore if any would follow him down that path, and honestly, he didn't care. Either way, he'd see it done.

The more he reflected on his feelings and how they overlapped and intersected with Damon, the more he reflected on the dream that used to wake him every night not so long ago, that seemingly had set him on this course upon which he now found himself. That particular dream had a distinctive feel and perspective—as if seen through Damon's own *black mirrors of the soul*. The way he, himself, viewed Evanyil was now more clearly the way Damon had seen her for the first time. His only perspective of Evanyil was through the lens of a youthful Damon. He still didn't know or understand the king and the children in that same dream, and perhaps that was an area of focus for him in the path yet to come.... He'd have to ask Damon about that.

Whatever the path, he had to find a way to channel the negative emotive outcome of all the *hate* and hostility orbiting so close to Damon into something useful—maybe something he could learn from Damon and maybe something he could even teach Damon, or perhaps they could both learn the way together. Damon's plan—or what he understood of it—had strong merit now that he could look at it objectively, and externally, now. So, the way forward would see them working as a team but not at the abandonment of Rowarc. Rowarc carried a burden not his, and Radin's next steps had to involve relieving his dad of his—and his father's—burden.

Getting up from Rowarc's rocker, Radin *Gated* it someplace for safekeeping. He didn't know if he'd be afforded the opportunity to ever use it as Rowarc had intended—he couldn't allow himself the luxury of that kind of thinking right now. But, there was always *hope*.

Charles W. McDonald Jr.

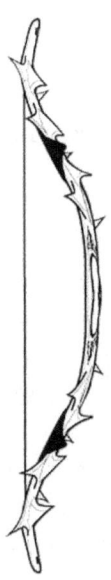

Chapter 13: The End of Wit and Charm

(The Crown of Spires, Perion, Present Day)

esindra's walk to Goldenbow's cell was fraught with far too many possibilities as the divination tiles reflected every outcome branch of her foremost thoughts, with her not liking *any* of them. *Who was this outworlder to have such favorable outcomes when **he** was the one captured? Or, was she captured by her own ambitions of unseating the High Seat...? Perhaps, so much so, it had slung her into his orbit where her success was now tied to his.* Stop it, she chastened her own thoughts.

Her capture of the man they now knew as Goldenbow—if that was his real name—had afforded her this priceless opportunity to demonstrate her worth, not only to the High Seat but to the High Seat's supporters. She couldn't unseat Adena without them and their support. Effectively prosecuting Goldenbow would demonstrate her mettle to lead. *A priceless opportunity indeed.*

Which needs to be seized, her thoughts added as she rounded the corner in sub-level two of one of the spires west of the center spire, Goldenbow's cell quickly coming into view. Carrying his unique bow down with her had fulfilled the desired effect of giving hope where there was none as his

Charles W. McDonald Jr.

pretty eyes lit with the fire of possibilities unproclaimed, yet nonetheless announced.

"You want this," Desindra taunted through her *Linguistics*, flexing and waving it to and fro before a naked Goldenbow through the shimmering glass of his translucent cell.

Seeing the light and hope glinting in his own eyes in the reflection of the glass of his cell, Goldenbow recalculated, realizing the obvious play being made before him. "Don't let any of the vine points break your skin anywhere. They'll kill you."

Recoiling as much as possible from his bow without letting go of it, Desindra, pulled over a chair to make herself comfortable. "Clearly, you're an assassin sent here to murder Adena. The High Seat has many enemies. Perhaps you'd care to enlighten me as to which one of them sent you here?"

"I would think those fancy divination tiles of yours would have already told you that." Goldenbow's ear-to-ear smile rebuffed any duress or stress her taunting may have hoped to impart upon him.

Who is this man? Desindra tried to find some comfort in her uncomfortable, rough-hewn, hardwood, and mostly weather-finished chair. "The divination tiles don't tell me who you are, where you hail from, and what debt you're here to settle."

The divination tiles had been telling after all, Goldenbow considered, scratching his scruffy chin as he stood nude before Desindra. She hadn't trusted him even enough to give him clothing for fear he might find a way to use his clothes to get out or kill a guard. Smart woman. "The tall and brooding man with black hair and black eyes is a friend of mine—someone I've known likely longer than your High Seat has lived or ruled. His name is Damon of Basrat. He sent me here because Adena tried to kill him. I can't allow that...," he paused, measuring her cool, dispassionate response that hid something...deeper. "And, as far as where I hail from, you already know I'm an 'outworlder' in your own words. What more would you like to know? I don't know its stellar coordinates, and something tells me even if I did, you wouldn't know how to use them." Goldenbow saw the flash in her eyes and immediately calculated his words had cut deeper than intended. "No disrespect intended, Lady Desindra." *There, let her chew on that*, Goldenbow reflected, thinking he'd properly cleaned up his own mess.

Charles W. McDonald Jr.

"Very well. Tell me about this Damon of Basrat. Why is he so important? And specifically, why is *he* so important to *you*?"

"I thought you'd be more interested in learning about me," Goldenbow quipped with a wink, running his fingers through his scruffy hair, catching a glimmer of an involuntary smile from Lady Desindra before it had time to fully manifest. His eyes carefully watched hers measure every inch of him from head to toe, apparently deep in consideration of him.

Her cool stare and raised eyebrow said one thing, but the nanosecond, upward turn of her soft lips said another.

"Very well.... I hail from a world named Kaleion. Damon is one of the most powerful mages of Kaleion. I believe you call them lameans on your world. Kaleion and your world share a great deal in common. One of those things they share in common is that the End Times are already upon us. I'm not a holy person, and I don't believe in prophecy or at least the accuracy of it, but I believe Damon is our best chance—for all of us—to survive the End Times as a people, civilization, and culture."

"This Damon means a lot to you. I sense you are not merely his protector."

Taking a seat in his cell on the floor since no bed or chair was offered—*smart woman*—Goldenbow sighed. *How much can I reveal? How much can I trust her?* Then again, if he was talking and she was listening, then he wasn't dying. "Damon and I have made many pacts over the centuries shared between us. He's kept his word every time, and I haven't...." A long pause followed that hard and deeply secret truth of Goldenbow's. His mouth worked though no words came out as he apparently tried to shake it off, returning to his stream of consciousness. "Long ago, he loved a woman as much as any woman could ever be loved. He asked me to protect her when and where he could not because he trusted me above all others. And I failed him. She was.... She deserved better, and I failed her too. I owed Damon. I still owe him."

"An assassin with a conscience. That has to be very problematic for you at times."

"You've never met him. You wouldn't understand. He just has this gravity about him where he can turn people and agendas in his direction, bending them to his will. Where and when he can't, he obliterates them.

Charles W. McDonald Jr.

Not that I was ever afraid of Damon, but why make an enemy out of him when he could be counted on to be such a powerful ally? Some are foolish enough to think him so detestable that they'd rather do anything than make a bargain with him, but when making a bargain with Damon, you're guaranteed to get exactly what you asked. You just have to be very careful about what it is you're asking for…." He paused, taking in her reaction as she leaned forward attentively listening—for what purpose, he couldn't say. Though, he got the feeling she wasn't on-topic for this interrogation she'd clearly been sent to accomplish. "Over time, I began to see a symmetry in Damon akin to the symmetry of a perfectly sculpted bow. This symmetry worked very simplistically: don't stand in his way, don't become an impediment for him, help him where agendas were aligned, listen to him, and talk to him—share with him your real thoughts and emotions, and in that investment, you'll come to realize that this man wants to reciprocate. He's not an isolationist, nor is he an irrational actor. He seeks out companions and allies where others go it alone. The *arc* of Damon's life is that he cares. The *curse* of Damon's life is that he cares in the midst of those who do not, which puts those he does care about in peril. I found in him a brother far better than blood and certainly far more reliable than blood. I can always count on Damon. Unquestionably." Visibly nodding in her chair, Goldenbow could see the seeds of his narrative taking root in her thoughts.

"And what about Mrs. Goldenbow…? Normally, I'd never ask that question of an assassin because they'd never allow that kind of weakness in their lives, but you've already demonstrated several such weaknesses so I'm expecting this one too."

Rising and walking toward the translucent wall that separated them, Goldenbow looked her in the eyes with a fire she hadn't seen in him before. "Careful not to mistake passion for weakness, Desindra. That misjudgment can prove fatal."

"Oh, I'm fairly certain it's weakness, Goldenbow—if that's your real name. On my way over, the divination tiles showed me outcome upon outcome where you escaped, and I was dead because of it. But that was based upon my doing what I had planned on doing—getting information from you until there was none left." Her eyes flashed as her dress twirled with the motion of her body rising from her uncomfortable chair. "Instead, I think I'll

Charles W. McDonald Jr.

just put an end to your wit and charm and just kill you," Desindra coolly announced as Goldenbow's throat began to constrict via strands of air moving in unison to Desindra's command.

Picking up Goldenbow's weapon, she watched the fire in Goldenbow's eyes fading as they glowed with a pale sheen of death soon forthcoming.

He'd trained himself to breathe under water for several minutes, but this was different. His trachea was being physically crushed; soon there would be no airway left for him.

"What? No cute words from the cute assassin?"

A last flash from his eyes announced the prick she never felt as Desindra collapsed to the floor in a heap, dropping Goldenbow's golden-vine bow to reveal blood in her right palm. She wasn't dead—yet, but she *was* compliant. And her trachea-constricting spell evaporated.

"I need you to open the cell…Desindra…," Goldenbow croaked as he took in a big gulp of air into his now-relaxing airway. Enough air for him to stand, but instead he sank to his knees to get closer to eye-to-eye level with Desindra. "You want to open the cell. You want to help me. I'm your friend. I can help you take the High Seat, but I need you to get me close to Adena."

"My friend," Desindra stammered as her eyes shifted in their sockets, assimilating Goldenbow's toxin-laden command. If she didn't get the antidote—and soon—she'd be useless to help him. The briefest of waves of her left hand from the floor formed the open trapezoidal doorway in the translucent material incarcerating Goldenbow, allowing him to escape his cell at last.

Without sparing another moment, Goldenbow took his bow, using it to slice the heel of his left hand, letting his blood to drip into Desindra's mouth. "Drink. There should be enough antidote in my blood to save you. Remember, you're my friend. I don't want you to die. I'm trying to save you."

"My friend," Desindra breathed again, compliant on the floor as she began to consume Goldenbow's blood and the anti-toxins he'd built up over centuries of exposure to this lethal and useful toxin.

Looking around and seeing no one coming to her aid, Goldenbow didn't need a plan to leverage Desindra to get close to Adena. He'd already had one before he had *allowed* himself to get captured in the first place.

Goldenbow - The Living Legend

Charles W. McDonald Jr.

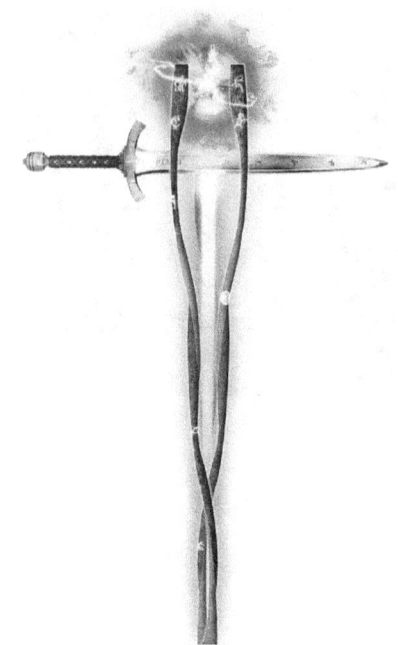

Chapter 14: Finding Home

(Exeter Manor, Perion, Present Day)

The door had barely been closed by Radin before Elise began trying to piece herself back together. "It's time to pull your shit together," she chastised herself. She knew of the world Damon had built for a refuge for Humanity. Radin had mentioned it in their conversations, and it was a logical move. Damon was a very logical creature despite his many atrocities. She didn't know how to get there, but she knew where to go back to retrace her steps if magic still worked there and if her registration still afforded her ability to cast on its soil.

There were no smartphones here to capture memories of the sweet baby boy robbed her, and she wasn't sure if she could memorialize him in her thoughts without destroying herself in the process with memories too painful to recall. Still, she tried to picture him the way he was in her womb, focusing the light of her soul on what might have been *and what should still be*. In memorial, she crystallized a vision of his face, capturing it in perpetuity in her deepest thoughts as clothes and small possessions light-of-foot whirled into place from the four corners of her suite into a small black bag she could hang on her left hip.

Her appearance transformed from a just-pregnant girl in early twenties to a full woman—bereft her recent pregnancy—in her early thirties wearing a feathered and frilly dark-heather dress of pearl, gold gild, and lace. Her strawberry-blonde hair cascaded off shoulders and gown in exposed midriff and mid-back delicate fantasies in a style she hadn't worn in so long it felt to her...alien. As the air rent before her in silvery-blue flashes of light, Graelon's Herat Plateau called to her from the other side, telling her that her registration might still be in effect.

Now on the other side of the *Portal*, Elise could see the harbingers of the AI Governance rushing up the plateau's hillside to greet her so many years in absentia.

The very next instant, six oblong, orb-shaped metallic objects with dark glass lenses, appearing as cyclops-like eyes, hovered over her plateaued position, twisting this way and that as their dark lenses blinked from within the glass. Blue-green gilded rays of the Graelon sun cast looming shadows of the burnished and satin gold Sentinels down the Herat Plateau toward the great shielded city below. Smooth mechanical noises emanated from within the strange objects, apparently assessing her threat level. Hidden compartments she knew to house long black barrels on both their left and right sides began exposing themselves from their normal seamless appearance, threatening to bear their lethal, blaster fire weapons, while the other two approached closer and closer from her right, challenging, "Registration number?"

The wind whipping down the Herat Plateau captured her long, strawberry-blonde hair, offering it out toward the challenging Sentinels and those she knew to be peering through *their* lenses; she turned her head to her right to respond. "07874376Alpha221321," she replied coolly and calmly, praying her registration would still be operable.

"Code accepted, but dormant, 07874376Alpha221321," the Sentinel furthest right replied—this time in a Human voice—not the synthetic voice of a Sentinel. "Explain off-world activity in absentia."

"Alpha221321 requests audience with Council of Herat to explain in person," Elise countered, measuring the response of the oblong Sentinels

Charles W. McDonald Jr.

in their smooth mechanical and synthetic clicks. A few seconds later, blaster barrel compartments sealed up, creating a smooth and seamless transition along the sides of the Sentinels as they each took up a position in a quarter-surround formation around Elise and down the plateau as they prepared her escort home.

"Audience granted, 07874376Alpha221321," the Sentinel farthest in the back replied with its normal synthetic voice as all six oblong bots shot blue-green beams of light from their black lenses, encapsulating the strawberry-blonde in an amorphous blue shield, which lifted her off the ground several feet as the bots escorted her down the Herat Plateau east toward the great and sprawling, technological city of Herat below.

*   *   *   *

With her robes disheveled and hair mussed up in static-held restraint against the blue shield cutting her off from Arcane and suspending her mid-air, Elise tried to keep dignity together as she was paraded through the streets of the great and sprawling city of Herat. Citizens and neophobe alike lined both sides of the street, gathering in bunches, mumbling amongst themselves at the uncommon site of a rogue mage being captured and brought to heel by Graelon's versions of Sentinels.

Even with recently-cleaned streets, what little dust there was had been kicked up by the propulsion of the oblong, cyclops-like, alloy Sentinels, blowing dust and small pieces of debris in the face and hair of the gathering crowd as Elise was carried down streets lined with trapezoidal-shaped buildings—each unique in their own right, in both shape and size, yet designed to fit together like a great mosaic of civilization well-kempt. Each structure held slight variations on the same composition framework: aluminum, titanium, the blue-grey lustrous tantalum, tungsten, and cobalt. Many kept their natural satin sheen that came with using such alloys, while others kept a highly polished or matte-sheen appearance. The use of paint—or even nanite-adaptive-coatings—seemed foreign, as most leveraged natural colors of elements and varying degrees of polish, layers, and material mating techniques to create a uniquely beautiful patchwork of civilization. None of the buildings were greater than four stories in height, and none of the doorframes were greater than the average-height male Humanoid—save one building, of course, in the center of Herat. A great, grey, white, and blue star-sapphire spire reaching to the heavens—all of it translucent in nature—advertised as a transparent republic. She wouldn't argue with the transparent part of that billing today. Today, was about finding her way home, if it was even possible at all—if they would even let her go.

Her status of rogue versus registered would likely be hotly debated by the council if she were truly granted the audience requested. One way or the other, she was about to find out as her body was dipped below the head of the sliding translucent doors now opening to grant them access as the Sentinels continued to hold her suspended by the blue, spherical shield still surrounding her.

Now inside the great structure she hadn't seen since confirmation of her registration over a decade ago, Elise noted the floating platforms suspended seemingly by nothing, carrying citizens to their varied destinations on floors she could see through all the way to the top of the structure.

A moment later, she found herself on one of these floating platforms, which upon closer observation, were actually transparent cube elevators. Six Sentinels had become only two, limited by the space of the elevator. Still, two was more than enough to execute her on the spot if she proved any threat, whatsoever. *Calm intellectual discussion is the way out of this, not firepower of any kind—magic or otherwise.* She kept trying to reassure herself, feeling her thoughts being probed even as the transparent elevator came to a stop at the fiftieth floor of the council chambers.

A graying man in a dark-heather fitted uniform, tugged at his formal coat as five rows of four columns of meritorious ribbons straightened themselves programmatically to fit perfectly plumb and level about the newly adjusted coat. Sitting behind a sleek desk of seemingly glass, Elise knew it otherwise as a transparent alloy, wondering if it would be just the two of them or if he would summon the rest of the council by video conference.

"Alpha221321…," the graying man began with a pause, scratching at his well-kempt, mostly white beard, "…it's my understanding you seek an audience with the council."

"I do, Chancellor." She was making an assumption that the ribbon of a star sapphire against a panel of white indicating his rank was a current rank—rather than a previous one. She'd been gone a long time. Much had changed, or so that was her assumption.

"Yes, well…," Chancellor Maxon started, but as his cheeks pinched together, she could tell already he was holding onto something…big. "The Council cannot be summoned at this time, but I will hear your case."

"May I ask why the Council cannot be summoned…?"

"You may release Alpha221321," the chancellor ordered, causing both remaining Sentinels to disengage her shield, releasing her to stand on the transparent seamless flooring.

She tried not to look down for fear of vertigo, but something about this wasn't right. *Had she been gone so long that even the Council no longer existed?*

"You may leave," again the chancellor ordered, though the black lens of both Sentinels blinked as if simultaneously processing the oddness of that command—given the uniqueness of the situation. "Go," he reinforced his previous command more emphatically as he started to rise from behind his desk, only to sit back down as the two Sentinels headed for the transparent elevator still awaiting them adjacent the top floor.

A moment later, and they were alone, except for all the other citizens bustling about the floors below. A glance and a thought made the flooring and walls suddenly opaque in sapphire blue as the chancellor stepped out from behind his desk, slowly closing the ten paces of distance between them. "My apologies, Alpha221321, for your treatment. I'm sure you understand the precautions we take. I hope you were not harmed…?"

"No, sir. I'm fine. Though, I feel a bit like a stranger in a strange land after being gone for so long. I'm just trying to reorient myself. That's all."

"I believe your audience was to explain your absence. Would you mind sharing your travels with me, so I can make a proper determination? Did you…bring back any rogue magic with you?"

"Only observations, Chancellor. Not actual spells and certainly nothing rogue I would ever propose using here."

"Good. Good. It's that kind of responsibility we count on from our registered mages regardless of their travels and…potential encounters. Mishaps with magic and technology are…unacceptable risks."

"I fully understand, Chancellor, and would never violate my oath."

Charles W. McDonald Jr.

"I sense from your thoughts you'd rather be addressed by your given name. Is that correct, Elise?"

"Yes, Chancellor. I would prefer that. Thank you for asking." She tried to suppress the thought that scolded him for continuing to scan her thoughts without her permission. Though she could see his cheeks pinching inward again as soon as the thought came into her mind, indicating he likely sensed it anyway. Perhaps he was more talented than others in that regard.

"Openness is important, Elise. Should I disband our little bit of privacy I've afforded for this audience?" His arms made a sweeping motion to the adjusted opacity of the floors and walls.

Trying to keep thought in line with words she kept her response as open and as short as possible, "Sir, I'm grateful for the privacy. It helps me adapt, for from where I've come, privacy was more the norm than the exception."

Nodding in acceptance of the honest—albeit incomplete—response, he allowed her to continue, motioning her to do just that with his right hand as he took a seat on the leading edge of his transparent desk.

It took a little while for her senses and abilities to adjust, but she could sense his thoughts projecting, urging her to continue as did the motion of his right hand. "A great descendant of Durial seeks a life beyond the great end of all things. Right now, he is conspiring with others to do just that. His magic is greater than any I have seen in my lifetime. He is almost without equal in magic and has powers in practices well beyond magic that I have personally witnessed. He is the reason I left Graelon." Her last sentence carrying with it frayed memories of memories. Of breadcrumbs followed and forgotten. As if she'd been....

A measured nod from Chancellor Maxon as he gauged the honesty of her thoughts with her words and seemed satisfied there was a measure of truth in this great tale of hers. "Explain this reasoning...this rationale that caused your long departure."

"Honestly, I don't know the full of his plot. I know he left clues for me to follow to the Terran System. There, I met and married a great man who became king. He and I had two children together before his death in a great battle that Terrans believe is the sign of the end of all things. I found

Charles W. McDonald Jr.

more clues that led me to believe my dead husband may still live on the world of Perion and followed those clues there. On Perion, I felt lost. I felt discouraged because I couldn't find the soul I once knew as my husband. I am currently seeking my way to a new world of Humanity created by this descendant of Durial. There I hope to find what's left of my Terran family—my only surviving children—if indeed they survived."

Swallowing hard, the chancellor again adjusted his coat, tugging at it to pull it down a bit more taut. "That's quite the tale, Elise, though I sense your honesty, your depression, and your despair—all genuine."

"It is, Chancellor. I'm trying to find my way home—wherever that may be. If I'm being totally transparent, I no longer feel that is here."

Nodding in agreement, the chancellor rose off the edge of his desk, approaching. "I have many questions. Will you stay long enough to help shed some light upon them?"

"I'm certain the chancellor knows I cannot leave without permission now that I'm Graelon soil."

"Yes, but it's polite to ask, and I'm a polite man—no?"

"Your Honor has been very gracious. Thank you."

"Can we go back to this descendant of Durial? Tell me about him. It was a man, correct? You implied it was a man."

"Yes, sir. His name is Damon of Basrat—son of Keirill from what I've been able to determine."

Raised eyebrows from the chancellor belied the thoughts suddenly heavily shielded from Elise. "You're sure about that? Son of Keirill...?"

"From what I've been able to determine.... Yes. Does that mean something to you?"

"Forgive me, I'm just trying to piece this together. Please continue. What else can you tell me about this son of Keirill?"

"He's full of rage, contempt, and hatred for those he believes have wronged him. To the extent, he's willing to sacrifice just about anything and anyone to deliver a justice he sees as long overdue—notwithstanding the justice due him for his many atrocities."

The chancellor paused briefly in consideration of this great and powerful man filled with so much rage. "This world he's created. Is it a world filled with his rage, hatred, and contempt? I can't imagine that being a good

Charles W. McDonald Jr.

thing for any of us regardless of whether or not the end of all things is upon us."

He was getting it. At least she took some comfort in the attention he was paying to her story, even if it got her temporarily trapped here.

"Well, that's just it…. I can't really say. I've never been there, though I know someone who has, and he said it was…beautiful—like nothing he'd ever seen before or since. He said Damon was building a society designed to withstand the blending of magic and technology—a safe haven for all Mankind, out of reach of meddling gods and their end times."

The chancellor's eyes darted this way and that in thoughts most shielded as he began pensively scratching his well-groomed, white-bearded chin. "I think I'd like to meet this descendant of Durial you speak of—this son of Keirill. If you think it's safe to do so."

"No one and nothing is safe around Damon; though, if you let me find my way to this world he's created, I can set up a meeting between the two of you."

Nodding again, the chancellor grunted in agreement, adding, "Elise…. Why do you think this son of Keirill wanted to lead you—specifically you—to the Terran System?"

"Chancellor, believe me when I tell you, I've thought of little else but that one question for a very long time."

"Any guesses," he asked, prodding a bit more.

"He *needs* me. Damon uses people like tools. I'm just trying to figure out *why* he needs me. Why *specifically* me…."

Going behind his transparent desk that wasn't transparent at all, the chancellor opened a compartment concealing a small mirror-like sphere barely the size of his pinky fingernail, handing it to Elise. "For now, this will allow you to transport directly to and from my chambers without setting off alarms in the planetary defense system. I will allow your departure on the condition that you return once a week, every week, to update me on this plot and set up the meeting with this son of Keirill. If he's as pivotal as you say, I doubt he'll want to meet here, so offer him a meeting off-world."

"Understood, Chancellor. Thank you." She considered the chancellor's conditions. *Once a week, every week. That might be a problem….*

A nod from the chancellor, and Elise exhaled, breathing in all the

Charles W. McDonald Jr.

Arcane around from as far out into the atmosphere and the surrounding landscape she could. Noticing the silence her little polished sphere afforded, she opened a *Portal* to Earth to begin retracing her steps.

However, stepping through the *Portal* to Dover Castle, she noticed something was immediately wrong....

She caught glimpse of her husband—hands grimy from working on his cars—walking from his refurbished garage toward the main keep. Immediately cloaking herself on the hillside where she'd stepped through, she tried to piece together the possibilities of a continuum that simply could not be....

Elise Day Descending the Herut Plateau on Graelon

Charles W. McDonald Jr.

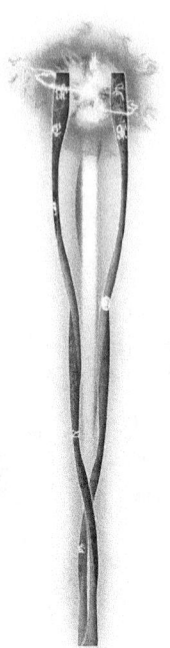

Chapter 15: A Bliss Inerasable

(Damon's Manor, Kaleion, A Long Time Ago)

Tiny little excuses for fabric in scintillating colors shifting from orange to cream to red to white to forest green made pale attempts to cover Banthis as she laid on an elegant grey sofa in Damon's secret fourth-floor study. He might have been warming up to her, but he was certainly more than wary of her, too, as he tried to get over a loss she knew would be with him for a very long time, no matter what she did. Still, she was confident if he could be brought around, no one was more capable of doing so than her.

Despite her function and role, there was far more to Banthis than Damon, or anyone else, could discern. Even lifetimes later, peering into what could and what must be, Banthis doubted Damon would ever really know her, or anyone else for that matter. She would try though. If he could learn enough about her—if she could brave telling him or showing him—then perhaps....

Charles W. McDonald Jr.

"You've been brooding for hours at that desk of yours…. Why not come and sit beside me so I can relieve your stress," Banthis offered, inviting him with perfect bare thighs that caressed gently one against the other and lips moist with a wanton abandon she knew he held deep within.

Measuring his response as he paused, pen-in-hand still hovering over the parchment without moving. "You can't force this. If you let it come to you, it will do so faster than you could ever imagine. I know you've made a great many custom spells before, but this one will be different. I assure you. It might require a different approach than those that came before."

A heavy exhale escaped Damon reflexively as he relaxed his right hand enough to let the pen dip into the ink well. "We're missing some-thing…. The way I'm trying to ensnarl the soul won't work. If I can't cap-ture it, I can't control the sending of it. It's not like it's some tangible thing I can just reach out and grab or throw into a container." Though, internally he was considering the likeness of this potential spell to something not too dissimilar: *Stasis*.

"Come. Sit." Banthis patted the sofa in front of her breasts as she lay partially on her side and partly on her stomach, affording him enticing cleavage to distract…and manipulate.

Sitting down just in front of her so as to block her vantage of his desk and his work, he felt Banthis sit up behind him, beginning to massage his neck and shoulders.

"Talk to me, Damon. It's okay. I'm a good listener. You might be surprised *how good*."

"What would you like to talk about?" He wasn't in a talkative mood but…. *Damn that felt good*. His tension seeped out of his body, seemingly dis-solving into the sofa and floor beneath him in shadowy waves. *His eyes must have been playing tricks on him.*

"Why don't we talk about the little things? You know…. Life, death, the hereafter…. You know—little stuff." Banthis briefly pulled his head back and to the side so he could see her face, seductively batting her long and beautiful eyelashes at him with a dastardly grin just barely beneath her multi-layered surface.

Damon sniffed a little laugh. At least Banthis had a sense of humor, even if it wasn't *that* funny. "I'd rather not think about it too much. I haven't been the nicest sort most of my life. I can't imagine good things coming my way—especially…." He didn't need to say it, but he knew. If this spell was successful, he was a condemned man for sure. Still, if that's what it took to avenge Dallia, then so be it. There was not enough justice left in this world to accomplish that, but he could *try*.

"I suppose that depends on how you define 'good things.' How do you define 'good things,' Damon of Basrat? I love your new name by the way. It suits you better. It carries the weight of your prominent bloodline better." The last she whispered into his ear as erect nipples brushed against his back and soft, hot breath fell upon his neck and ear.

"You know so much of me, and I know so little of you."

There was the opening. The chink in his armor of mourning. Pulling him against her breasts, she reached down to the hem of his shirt, pulling it over his head so his bare flesh could feel hers. *Flesh* was *always* the way in. *Always.*

"Do you know what a succubus is?"

"I do," a short reply though he started to get up, finding her not resisting as he suddenly found himself standing half-naked before her.

"It's okay. I'm not here for you in *that* way. I'm not here to *claim* you or anything," Banthis lied, hoping he wouldn't turn his head again and look back at her eye to eye. Even if he did, she was a magnificent and polished liar. Though, she knew Damon was big on the truth, and he could sense truth in others, so honesty was best with him, if she could stay on top of her manipulative game, twisting the truth just so it fit between the eye of the needle of her ultimate goals.

"I've been so obsessed with revenge, I never bothered to ask or understand your angle. Everyone has one. What's yours?"

And there it was: her first opportunity to deliver the truth—in just the right way…. "Very clever, Damon. *Everyone* does have an angle—even the most altruistic. You're very intelligent to get right to the point about it. So, I'll respect that and just flat out tell you." She paused, blinking eyes that flashed starry-blue, then gold, then bright-green until she sensed he loved her most in blue. Fluctuations in breast size, waist size, and leg proportions adjusted ever so subtly to Damon's preferences. Her face malleable from ageless to early twenties in appearance without losing key features that made

Charles W. McDonald Jr.

Banthis, Banthis. "*Your* ascension and *mine* are inextricably linked. You rise. I rise. I fall. You fall. Together, *we* are unstoppable. Separated, we *can be* defeated."

"You sound as if you've already seen this." It wasn't really a question, though it hung heavy in the air between them as if it were. Rising from his sofa, he paced to the edge of the study and back again to face the magnificent Banthis.

"I have. And knowing only what you already know of me, that should lend credibility to that vision."

Breathing heavy through his nose, he sat back down beside her, allowing her to resume massaging him—though, now it was far more like sensual caressing.

"You're going to figure out this spell, and you're going to make it in record time. I've seen it. I know it. You're going to use it to destroy Chara, and together we will rise such that none will be able to challenge us. I'm going to give you something no one has ever been able to give you—not because I want something from you or need something from you but because…." Halting her private thoughts so abruptly as to leave unspoken that which she knew could not be spoken caused Damon to turn back to look her in the eyes as she seized the moment to kiss him. Delicately like a kiss of air, then passionately paralleling a familiar lover, her tongue caressed his as suddenly she was in his lap, straddling him. The sudden and incredibly intense sensation of his bare flesh was palpable against her warmth—shocking him as he quickly slapped his thighs, finding his pants were no longer there. Before he could object, he felt her soft, hot velvety caress enveloping him, milking, and teasing him as she continued to caress his tongue with hers. He felt a kaleidoscope of feminine fingertips caressing every part of his back and neck, as if more than possible from one woman.

One atop the other, visions came to him, colliding with reality. His flesh felt the immeasurable bliss of Banthis' caress, but his mind felt the invasive probing of a force he could not explain. It was impossible to focus—between Banthis and whatever else was going on. A flash in his mind's eye, and he saw Dallia's death. Another, and he saw a little girl in a dress of hearts and palms obliterated before him. Another, and then he saw a torrent of blue-green energy cascading like a waterfall of light in time immemorial.

Charles W. McDonald Jr.

Another flash, and he saw a tall, young man with auburn hair and steel-blue eyes with a great crest about his chest.

Unable to hold on an instant longer, he burst into her womb, feeling her gentle, warm teasing caress of him as his hot breath spilled into hers.

"I didn't...," he paused, trying to find the words that guilt and shame insisted upon yet bliss inerasable would not allow.

"Shhhhhh," she pressed her right index finger to his lips, helping his hot seed find its way to give Damon something—and someone—no one had ever given him before. *Bakris*, she thought as she urged Damon's essence to find its way inside her. *Bakris* would be the name of Damon's first of many daughters. "It's okay, Damon. I'm here for you." Quietly, she stilled his guilt-laden heart with incredibly soft love petals of passion, which gently teased him to keep him right where she wanted him. "It's okay. It's okay," she breathed, kissing him again—lovingly and mortally unlike any before. She'd had sex more times than she could count, but this was...much more, and she knew it *love*. She just needed to convince him, but she was well on her way to doing so as the vision of Damon finishing *Damnation* suddenly crystallized in *her* mind's eye.

Chapter 16: Hope is Broken

(Exeter Manor, Perion, Present Day)

Packing her NAVY-issue duffle bag along with an all-black backpack, Michelle looked over at her wife in anticipation of finally seeing their daughters again—together for the first time in forever it seemed. "Do you think Talemar could do it?"

"I don't know his skills or power, but if he can't, I'm sure we could find someone to get us home. That had always been the plan. If it was possible to travel to Earth from elsewhere, there had to be others that could get us home." Lawna's lean and hard biceps flexed, tossing another crate of ammunition on a rolling dolly, already overflowing with weapons of war—and a few clothes.

"I have mixed feelings about leaving," Michelle considered aloud, analyzing her own thoughts against what might be.

"You have mixed feelings about seeing *our girls*?"

"I have mixed feelings about tipping the balance of hope in the wrong direction. Where we are, when, matters. If we're doing the wrong thing or the right thing at the wrong time, it could have horrific outcomes for all of us—especially our babies." She knew her feelings and thoughts were logical, but she also knew that family had to be made a priority. Otherwise, there would always be something to get in the way. But this was not just any something....

"Jesus, you know how to kill the mood!" Lawna jibed, though she didn't smile. There was a certain seriousness to her retort as another crate slammed on top of the teetering pile on the dolly, nearly crushing it, "Look, normally I defer to you, Babe, but I want to go home. I NEED to go home. I need to see my girls, feel their kisses. Smell them. Hold them. Love them…while I still can…while it still matters. And that's more important than *any* of this shit. We will never, ever, get back the bonding time we're losing with them as we speak."

The urgency and aching in her wife's voice weighed heavy on Michelle, causing her posture to wilt as she surrendered her normal willful self to Lawna. *Am I more dedicated to the mission than my own daughters? What kind of mother am I to think that way…?* Distance was supposed to make the heart grow fonder, but with Michelle, sometimes it was 'out of sight, out of mind,' especially when the mission was so all-encompassing and so ever-present in her day-to-day life. "What do you think we'll find when we get home?"

"I don't know, but I'm pretty sure we'll have to adapt."

"There's the Operator in you." Michelle smiled, though she knew exactly what Lawna meant. Lawna was worried about Rena's influence on their daughters. Surviving a holocaust was much more probable in Rena's hands, but surviving Rena's influence…that was something else entirely. "You're right. We've been gone too long." Michelle tossed her duffle over her right shoulder; the strap tugged at her between her breast and against her black tank top. Carrying *Bad Intentions* muzzle-down at her right side, Michelle made her way for the door, in search of Talemar, with Lawna hot in tow.

*   *   *   *

"I cannot relate to what you've been through, but I do understand that we're going to need this army at some point and it's vital that others know our word is good." Brigance drove home that last point with emphasis, dominating the doorframe of Talemar's suite, still holding the Crystal Crown tight in his left hand.

Motioning Brigance into the suite entirely, Talemar slammed the door with a thought, invoking a shield around the room to keep the rest of their conversation private. "What would you have me do?" Talemar's mood was morose, though it was hard for Brigance to tell the difference with Talemar's face so disfigured and horrific from Damon's curse.

"We have made promises—not the least of which is to help Sir Palomides secure his throne."

"Ah yes, I remember some mention of that, but that fell to Radin to fulfill. Killing Sir Aegon—if killing was so required—was the promise you made if I'm not mistaken."

"A promise I was authorized to make to secure ten thousand men, and I secured eighteen thousand instead."

"Very well, so you want me to kill Aegon and put Palomides on the Throne of Knor. That isn't going to mean a damn thing to anyone because we're all going to die." A very pessimistic Talemar bristled before Lord Fireheart at the idea of being coerced into fulfilling promises he hadn't made. Radin had left him many loose ends, and he really didn't feel like tying up any of them. Still, Brigance had a point. At some time, there might be a vital need for such an army, and no one would fight for a banner that didn't pay its debts. Still, his reflection in his dresser mirror caught by his peripheral vision, made him question why he would even care. The End Times was no longer his burden to shoulder. Neither was looking after Radin's promises or the hope of a brighter tomorrow. Hope was an abandoned philosophy from his perspective. Yet, something deep inside Talemar tugged at his soul from within. However finished he was with Radin and Damon, there was still a part of his past destined to collide with a part of his future, and he knew that from his time in the Halls of Aaramus and from the words of the man who held the key. He couldn't see how the web had entangled him, but he knew himself entangled, nonetheless.

Brigance could see the internal struggle of thought going on inside Talemar from a few paces away. He knew the man before him tested beyond his own limits and wondered when, where, and how Talemar would finally break. But, he still had hope. "I understand your misgivings. And for the record, I'm here for you. I will follow you and go where you go. If you wish it." Brigance's stance softened as the offer came out, his left hand extending the Crystal Crown back toward Talemar who waved him off in protest.

"I don't want that anymore—" Talemar stopped mid-sentence. *Do I?* Trying to shut out the horrid reflection from his peripheral vision, Talemar made his decision. "We will honor our word, but in my time, Lord Fireheart. In my time. Be certain they understand that."

Charles W. McDonald Jr.

A rare smile from Lord Fireheart gave Talemar solace, but the knock at his door made him instinctively recoil at the next problem he knew would be laid at his feet to solve.

Charles W. McDonald Jr.

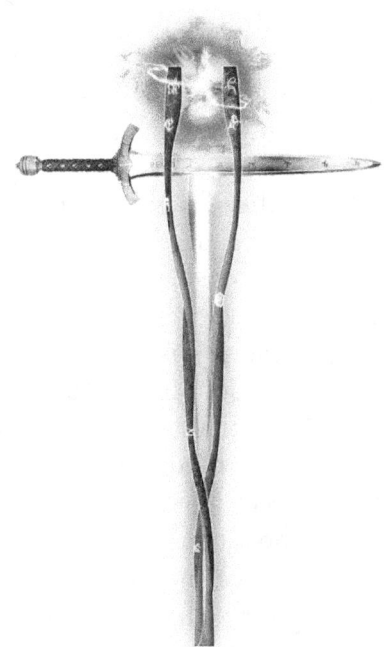

Chapter 17: Harbingers and Portents

(Indrid, Kaleion, Present Day)

errich and Levi waited in the old-world, yet charming, drawing room doubling as a wine and butler's pantry with varying marine art decorating the walls. They knew their man had a penchant for naval travels and had earned a bit of a reputation, though he didn't seek fame in quite the same way, or with the same level of fervor, as Royvan Miral. Lazily kicking his right leg in the cream wingback linen chair, Kerrich busied himself whittling a small landscape scene of the Trident—a memento of his first travels off-world. Radin had already bested him many times over in that category, but Radin couldn't proceed without the work they were doing, which made him question his being here that much more as he looked over to Levi who fidgeted with a silver-handled dagger he picked up off of an end table. Whoever this Joran of Erden was, Kerrich didn't trust him and certainly didn't trust his information anymore either. He just hoped Royvan Miral had the sense to trust only what could

Charles W. McDonald Jr.

be verified, and being on a totally different world, that didn't leave much.

A lithe build, middle-aged man sat across from Royvan Miral in his library behind a desk of maple and mahogany adorned with illustrative carvings of various marine life. Some Royvan recognized—some not. He had assumed there would be different life on different worlds and hadn't been disappointed in what he'd seen thus far. Daedrin had said Kaleion was the most majestic world he'd ever been on, but Damon's Star and subsequent vacuum-of-power banishment had changed all that. Now, it was every man for himself with little that recognized order.

"I understand your position, Joran of Erden, and I'm not the least bit interested in haggling with you. If you have knowledge—verifiable knowledge—of what I seek, then you'll be paid anything reasonable."

"It must mean quite a lot to you then," Joran tested, scratching a graying stubble working on a week's age. Joran's face rivaled a clever man who fancied himself as much, though the more he probed, the more Royvan was beginning to believe his information might have merit.

"You've done fairly well for yourself—all things considered. So, I'm not here to bring you a king's ransom, but I think between money, station, stability, and engagement, we can make it worth your while."

Behind his desk, Joran fidgeted with the latch on the center shallow door just above his knees, considering the last of Royvan Miral's benefit—engagement. Through graying bangs of somewhat matted black hair, Joran wanted to understand this hard man before him. Whoever he was, he certainly wasn't local. Didn't dress local. Didn't have a local accent. In fact, his whole appearance was off. "Tell me again, Mr. Miral, where it is you hail from…?"

"We've been over that already." Lying wasn't his style exactly, but he had his reasons.

"Yes…. Ragarth, I believe you indicated. How was that storm that came through a month ago? I heard it killed some 250 or more."

"Joran, I'm not here to play games with you. If you remain engaged with us as I hoped you would, we'll need each other, and I didn't think you'd accept this meeting if I told you straight out the truth I'm about to tell you now, but you'll find out sooner or later, so I might as well just tell you…."

"Oh…? Do tell…." Fidgeting under his desk for a weapon, Joran's

Charles W. McDonald Jr.

attention was piqued, if cautiously so.

"Tell me, Joran. If you know of the Seals I seek, you must know other things."

"Other things…? You're playing at a dangerous game, Mr. Miral."

"The most dangerous game. The unmaking of all things. Though, looking around at what's become, that might not be such a bad thing."

Joran didn't bat an eyelash. This man's information was solid—as was his own. He could only assume the outcome of Royvan's research overlapped with his own. "I know of the result if all are opened if that's what you're getting at."

"And did you think that impacted only your world?" There it was. He'd led Joran to the water. *Let's see if he'll drink it.*

Clearing his throat while reevaluating the man before him, Joran went back to scratching his beard in thought as he replied—carefully, "It is unknown the scope and scale of each Seal. Only a fool could or would say exactly what they do, but I know of the rumor you speak of."

"It's no rumor. I'm from a world called Perion—not unlike this world. In fact, I'm told of the five worlds of Humanity, our two are the most akin to one another."

Joran's lips dryly pressed together as his mouth worked in contemplation—*five worlds of Humanity.* He'd considered more than one, *but five….* Now his thoughts went back to Royvan's offer of engagement. If Royvan Miral had access to the other worlds and these Seals impacted some—or all—of them, he'd need to have a much bigger, deeper, and broader understanding of what was to come and how they'd get there if he was to come out the other side in one piece. Suddenly, price became far less important than engagement as the wheels of survival turned in his mind. He could always deny Royvan the information, but looking at the man, he didn't consider that the wise play. Royvan Miral looked the man who could garner the resources to wipe him off the map if necessary to get what he came for, and if not, he'd quickly be beating down the door of anyone else that could give it to him. Cooperation seemed the safer bet given who he was dealing with. "Five worlds, you say?" Joran unconsciously licked his lips again, though they remained utterly dry. "I'm assuming you already opened the first two." Internally, he wondered if that had more to do with the apocalyptic chaos

Charles W. McDonald Jr.

outside, as opposed to Damon's actions.

"We have."

"And what did you see?" He'd heard rumors, stories, and legend, of course. Many had. But being a student of such and seeing it in action were two entirely different things. He'd spent most of his adult life seeking the first two only to recently come to the conclusion they most likely didn't exist on Kaleion or had been opened so long ago that their impact had been erased. Though, that didn't exactly agree with the consensus view that once the first was uttered, what would come after would do so quickly. A clarifying question was urgently on his mind: "And, if you don't mind my asking, when precisely were the other two opened?"

"I'll tell you everything I know, Joran. The first was uttered nearly a year past. The second some weeks ago. And, as far as what I've seen, all I can say is…horror. Abject horror. Things I wish I could erase from my memory but things that make me ever more certain that all must be opened and done so swiftly so we can get to whatever may lay on the other side of this horror. The longer we take, the more we'll all suffer. Trust me on that, Joran. You WANT to help us get this done as fast as we possibly can."

"It's not that I doubt you, Royvan, because I don't. I can see it in your eyes. But, can you, for my own level of understanding, tell me what happened?"

"The First Seal killed birds, crops, fish, foul, and made blood fall from the sky among many other horrific things. As far as we know, it only affected Perion, though looking around here, it makes me wonder. The Second Seal killed every unborn male babe on the planet. Again, to my knowledge, only affecting Perion."

A reconsidering Joran wondered if telling Royvan Miral what he knew was the right thing after all. If the first two were found off world and only affected off-world, then maybe not leading Royvan Miral and his crew to those he knew to exist on Kaleion would prevent such havoc from being released on his homeworld.

"I can see you reconsidering, Joran of Erden. I know what you're thinking."

"Oh…."

"You're thinking if we don't open the Seals on this world, perhaps this world can be saved."

This Royvan Miral was as sharp as he'd considered, and now he began piecing together Royvan's knowledge with Royvan's looks, habits, traits, and experience. This was the man who'd found the other Seals. He was sure of it. That's why *he* was in *this* library, and not anyone else. "You have to admit, that line of thinking has merit."

"Agreed, but I want you to also consider this." Stepping forward toward Joran's desk, Royvan Miral pulled out a blank piece of paper and pencil where he began scribbling atop Joran's desk:

And there shall be but seven trumpets, bearing seven messages,
    For all the worlds to hear, and all men therein.
    And each message shall be sealed up in itself.
And woe unto the men of the worlds, for once the first is uttered,
What will be will be swiftly, and nothing in Creation shall hinder.

"Have you seen anything like this before on your world, Joran?"

Again, Joran licked his lips, and again he reconsidered telling Royvan Miral absolutely *everything* he knew.

*   *   *   *

The long, rune-adorned stole offset about the left side of his chest, hanging from his ornate dark-heather mantle, jostled this way and that as Kellen slipped on his full-length gloves and tightened the belt that held more traveling gear hidden well beneath his cape. Traveling off-world meant being prepared, and Kellen was careful in how he went about his recklessness. Still, he couldn't shake what he'd seen in the divination visions he'd summoned. So much life had passed before him, he'd become accustomed to the thought of living forever—never giving death a second thought. But this.... *This* harbinger and portent of things to come was unlike any path he'd ever seen before him. It appeared to have no work-around—as if imminent and immovable. He was now the reed—not the rock. And he had to adapt to that fact, however distasteful. Furrowed brow tangential to raven bang, Kellen's fierce gaze looked beyond the now, seeing pathways to secure

Charles W. McDonald Jr.

his immortality. And, more importantly, his *infamy*.

A hastily formed, customized *Portal* rent the air in super-heated, silvery-blue flashes of lightning unique to the magic of the mighty Kellen the Destroyer.

She wasn't expecting him, but that never mattered really. Kellen came and went where and when Kellen so chose, but this was *her* domain, and she didn't have to like it—nor did she have to make him feel welcome. After all, she *detested* the man.

The echoes of his boots upon granite cut with the blood of the dammed softly clapped in her magnificent dark-elven ears as she took a seat by her familiars awaiting words she knew would either forge her plan or force her hand—in killing Kellen.

Familiars left and right her gruesomely ornate skeletal throne, Kellen approached the room—akin to a great abdomen—a place he had hoped never to see again and yet here he was in the maw of the Abyss, in Evanyil's domain.

"Do I need to get you a bell, Sweetie?" Ever coy, Evanyil was dangerous when being accommodating and sweet. But, she was *most dangerous when indifferent*. Perhaps Kellen stood a chance, but it would depend on what he had to say. And Evanyil's mood....

The calculated use of the term of endearment often reserved for Damon wasn't lost on Kellen. "I've considered your offer." Kellen's glare was one of cautious confidence, radiating the power of all his experience before this most dangerous of all women—if Evanyil could still be considered as such.

"Well, don't keep me in suspense. Tell me. Tell me." Evanyil's fingertips clicked against one another as she brought her hands together in bated-breath anticipation.

"The Key to the Abyss for my continued involvement. That was the offer."

"It was, but I sense Kellen is about to change the terms of my very generous offer."

"I am. You need me." As soon as the words escaped his lips, his brows furrowed, and his lips thinned into a hard-pressed line. His fists clenched, and he was radiating the power of the Zero-Point field that filled him head to toe. He was an immovable force of power, and Evanyil was going to hear him out.

The arrogance of Kellen the Destroyer could never be overstated. Damon could best him if pressed, but Kellen was even more ruthless and dangerous than even Damon, so she'd at least let his counteroffer escape his lips before she choked him with his own words. "Very well. Let's have it, Kellen."

Using my name venomously already. This isn't going well, but he hadn't planned on it going well either. Still, the human-size spider at her right side taking a few steps toward him made his gloved-fists clinch tighter as a hand signal from Evanyil halted its advance. "There's going to be repercussions of this event for generations, and even millennia, to come."

"Undoubtedly," Evanyil agreed, *but where is this going...? Kellen is not the fearful type.*

"I'm going to disappear when all this is said and done. And you're going to actively keep my location hidden.... from *everyone* and *everything*."

Evanyil leaned back into her throne chair, thoughtfully extending her right hand palm-up in consideration of his...terms. "Even Damon," she clarified.

"Especially Damon." Kellen's gaze was cool and untelling.

What's going on here, she considered. These two weren't like the brothers Damon and Goldenbow, but they were not at each other's throats either. They'd been collaborating together for centuries. Still, it was a reasonable request—if totally out of character. She considered his request again, thinking only of Kellen as an individual rather than Kellen plus Damon as a team, and it made more sense in that vein. Kellen was ever the loner and dark forerunner of all things ruin. That wasn't Damon—not even close. How they'd managed their partnership this long was a mystery to her. Perhaps she'd have seen this request coming if she'd been paying closer attention to Damon's evolution and Kellen's devolving. However committed they were one to the other, Damon and Kellen were going in diametrically opposed directions and now it was becoming more obvious. "Very well," she offered with a nod of respect, having fully considered Kellen's unvoiced rationale or what she thought she'd understood of it. "I can see you've put some thought into this. Is there anything else you wish for, Kellen the Destroyer?" A smile from Evanyil hinted there was more offer on the table if he had the balls to ask for it.

"Now that you mention it...." Kellen *always* had the balls to ask for more.

Why she even bothered toying with the man was a mystery to her own logic swirled in tangled webs of chaos. "Are you going to make me guess...," she asked, leaning forward—still smiling, which was visibly beginning to bother Kellen from the way his stony glare suddenly changed to one of uncertainty.

"You have to tell Damon *who* was *really* responsible for Dallia's death."

There it was, causing Evanyil to immediately to retreat back into the back of her throne with a hard scowl for this intense offense within *her* domain. "Why would you care about that?" It was a hasty response from Evanyil, and it ripped off her tongue in viperous waves of contempt for this...man. *How dare he?!*

"Do we have a deal?" Kellen the Destroyer wasn't in the mood for haggling, nor explaining.

The last time he was here, she rushed him straight on. This time, she rose from her throne, advancing slow and careful. Perhaps there was more to Kellen than she gave credit. Offering her right open hand, camouflaged in delicate feminine beauty, Evanyil never took her eyes off his as they locked in on one another sealing the fate of Humanity in a handshake.

Examining her delicate extended hand, he had his doubts as to whether her word was really good or not. She'd spent so long working with Damon, he was counting on Damon's character rubbing off on her. He was counting on a lot of things for this to work, but he had to trust Evanyil and that's what really reeked about this whole deal. Evanyil wasn't the sort you could trust—ever! He was better off making a deal with the Dragon of Darkness herself! A passing thought he'd considered more than once as he squinted, taking her hand to seal their deal.

Charles W. McDonald Jr.

Kellen the Destroyer with Evanzil - The Architect of Chaos

Charles W. McDonald Jr.

The Living Goddess Evanvil
The Architect of Chaos

Charles W. McDonald Jr.

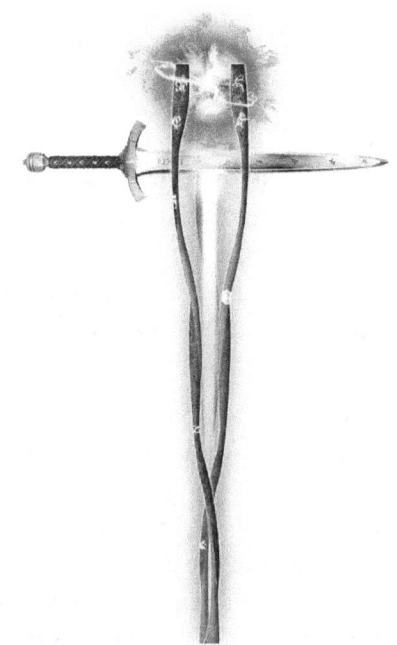

Chapter 18: Six – Part III

(The Hands of Darkness, Perion, Present Day)

Castlin's pile of scrolls now rivaled the top of the crumbling frame-work still supporting the cantilevered colonnade somewhat cover-ing his outdoor perch overlooking the Hands of Darkness where the Dracon Sea lapped at its terrifying, talon-forged shores. No longer sweating from the effort it took to stockpile his weapons of the For-ever War, Castlin had settled into a steady pace. His silver-grey hair and fire eyes worked head's down, etching in finger-invoked fire the symbols that emblazoned themselves into existence from naught.

Pale-red sky and dead sea life adorning the beaches formed by the talons of the Dragon of Darkness so very long ago told Castlin it wouldn't be much longer before his work would come to fruition. The boy had al-ready brought the Blood Night upon the world, and the Death of Men al-ready followed. The great war was coming to crescendo, and he would soon be ready. *But, will the others…?*

As if to answer a question unasked, a cold gale of wind from behind

Charles W. McDonald Jr.

raised the hackles on the back of his neck, causing him to immediately vom-it beside his desk and he recognized the unmistakable presence of Lilith.

Her transformation now complete, no mere *Portal* would announce her manifestation—only a god-like materialization would suffice.

Her perfect nude flesh walked barefoot in the same footprints she walked before, where dead grass still lay curdled in piles of bile, incapable of growing new seed or life as her greenish-black serpentine tail cocked this way and that, swaying opposite her hips to aid in her balance.

"Great Princess," Castlin offered in full prostrate on the ground before a sickening and beautiful, nude Lilith. "I am here for you, My Prin-cess."

"Are you?" She cocked her head in curiosity, picturing Castlin's mid-dle-aged face with lean features and silver-grey hair upon one of the many great pikes atop the Gates of Hell—already adorned with the heads of royal-ty and legend both honored and not. Though, Lilith knew—far better than others—how good help was harder than ever to find, and Damon was no mere enemy. *Once* his path had certainty of structure and his actions reliable. Now its chaos of unpredictability threatened more than just balance. It threatened to undo plans centuries in the making—her plans. Even where time held the littlest of value, it was still an untenable outcome, and Damon had to be neutralized. Though, internally, she wondered if that meant he needed to be obliterated. The chaos of Damon was in his being influenced. *If that could be recaptured....* "When last here, I instructed you to recruit. I see fruits of your labor, but not *that* specific fruit. Why?" Her tail hissed as it became erect with hate, its backbone firm in its stiffness directed at Castlin's feeble—yet expected—response.

Lilith spoke through a cacophony of ancient voices borrowed and stolen, much like her cape of flesh that whirled about her nude form on her winds of hate and contempt.

"I have been considering who to recruit, Great Princess."

"And, what has thou feeblemind presented as a candidate most *ripe?*" Again, her tail hissed at the last of her words in emphasis.

"Talemar," Castlin offered without the slightest hesitation in his

Charles W. McDonald Jr.

voice, though he dare not rise from his fully-prostrate position on the ground before Lilith.

"Perhaps you still have use, Castlin." It was the first time she'd addressed him by name in forever and a sign of respect. Her tail wilted to slither about the ground on her left side. In her earlier consideration of influencing Damon rather than destroying him, Talemar was indeed a *ripe* target. "I wish something else of you, Castlin."

"Name it, Great Princess."

"Wouldst thou destroy *every* child of Basrat?"

Castlin's eyes darted left then right in consideration of her...request. Again, trying to crawl inside of the mind of who he thought Lilith **really** was, Castlin's back arched with confidence and certainty in his calculated reply; "Every *son* and every *daughter*...." This time he offered no title, instead selfishness quickly followed behind the pride of his words. "For a price, Great Princess."

"Oh?!" Her tail sprang back to life, its fangs bore venom dripping from its mouth, curdling the ground into wisps of oblivion where it fell.

He had considered his price should the opportunity arise. His punishment had taught him a great many lessons as did the knowing that came with his being so close to the Dragon. He had also considered the many potential outcomes of Damon's successes and failures of his Master Plan. This request would protect him from all of them. "I wish to become untouchable in my present form. To live out my days unencumbered by any presumed or assumed debt to any entity—whatsoever. I no longer wish to rule anything, save myself and my own destiny. I wish to be completely and utterly free." 'Twas the boldest of all requests and one that made his backbone fill fulsome and erect at the mere mentioning of it. He felt like a man. A sovereign man.

"*Do you now?*" Her tail remained erect though no longer bore its fangs as the potential outcomes of his various fulfilled destinies played out in her mind.

"I do," he confirmed, his back still as erect as her tail if not more so—filled with the confidence that she couldn't really say 'no.' Or, at least he hoped.

"Turn Talemar and do as I said with the children of Basrat, and we shall see. I have nothing against paying your price—*if* the work is properly done." Lilith swirled counter-clockwise into a great chasm, which swallowed her whole to the sound of a thunderclap that shook the ground as tiny wisps of grey smoke chased her whence she came.

Charles W. McDonald Jr.

Part 3: The Forever Branches

Charles W. McDonald Jr.

Chapter 19: Durial's Eye

(Damon's Manor, Eden, Present Day)

ardening again for the first time in quite a while, The Dark Knight of Magic sought his bearings while the Master Plan threatened to collapse all around him. He'd received the message of Radin's arrival but given his staff specific instructions to ensure his solitude until he instructed otherwise. Radin could wait, but the survival of the Master Plan—along with the survival of what remained of his sanity—could not. In times of crisis like this, he might turn to a lover for guidance and comfort, but that kind of closeness was the last thing he wanted right now because it was the last thing his heart and soul could withstand. He needed to find a way of self-soothing, self-correcting, self-reflection. He'd become too reliant on others for that. That meant he needed to find his own way. That meant he needed to see his own way. That meant, he needed to see…. "Hmmm," he thought aloud, clipping away a piece of underbrush getting in the way of his beautiful white roses.

A thought produced a flash of silvery-blue light that summoned Xaldran's Tome. Flip, flip, flip as he tore through the book in search of the phrase he knew so very well…. *The Eye of Time*.

"Mhmm," he read on knowingly and in agreement with the text—though still searching as it began expanding on the Seeds of Humanity. Flip, flip, flip. Again, he scanned deeper and deeper into the text. "Mhmm," escaped his lips as he discovered very cursory text describing a behavior and capability of something Durial had used to predict their arrest and dispersion among the stars. The description fit something he knew to be a supersolid, though the text didn't describe it that way—nor would he expect that level of understanding given the supposed author of the text. "Hmmm." He scratched the designer stubble about his chin working on its second day of growth. It would require more than mere supersolids to make this work. It would require the greatest magic he'd ever used but it would afford him the clarity of vision he so desperately needed to ensure the right paths were taken and relying on witchcraft for divination had its limitations. He needed to see farther, clearer, and with more certainty than ever before. He needed to build *Durial's Eye*. Looking down at the signet ring on his right hand, the symbol—his symbol—stared back at him with the answer of all answers, showing him the way. Or, at least showing him how to start the way.

Raising up from the soil of his garden, Damon looked out across the great cliff and ocean view before him, hearing the waves crashing upon the rocks below, knowing *Durial's Eye* would come and come soon. But, he also needed to talk to his wounded son. A heavy sigh, and he wiped his dirty hands against his blue jeans, walking toward the main double-door entry of his Eden Manor.

Radin fidgeted with his drink on Damon's fourth-floor balcony outside the renovated ritual room, wondering—as he looked upon Damon's symbol etched into its flooring—if he'd ever see Damon use it again. Dressed casual in monotone rustic-tan leather pants and a dark-charcoal tunic with gold scrollwork along the neckline and cuffs, Radin looked the part of the anachronism as Damon strode across the gloss-sheen flooring in those odd looking comfortable shoes he learned were 'running shoes,' dressed in jeans and an even dirtier white T-shirt than the last time he caught Damon gardening. This time, he was finishing a conversation on some transparent device lit up with at least six different colors from what he could tell before

Damon hit a red button, which ended his conversation as he slid the device into his back-right pocket.

"Father." Radin didn't bow but offered a comfortable and welcoming tone if a little confused.

"You know you don't have to call me that."

"It's okay. I've come to terms with it. In fact, I'm...," he paused before offering this, but he'd thought about it a lot, "...proud of it." Radin could barely recall the last time he'd seen Damon smile because he'd been under so much pressure and so much duress; he wasn't sure if Damon was close to a breaking point or not, but he certainly understood Damon a lot better than ever before.

Damon's right hand reached up to his son, gripping his left shoulder in a comforting gesture. "I'm sorry we couldn't save him."

"Me too. We're just going to have to come to terms with the fact we can't save everyone. And...," he wanted to be careful how he approached this subject, but it needed to be said, "...we also need to find a way to deal with loss because this is only the beginning—for both of us. I'm certain there is far more loss to come, and we can't let it enrage and control us, or our actions. We have to learn to manage it in some way and to turn it into something useful to help us achieve your plan. I'm willing to learn and share in that if you are."

Damon looked at his son, standing so tall and proud and confident, and really seeing so much better DNA in him than what he alone possessed, wondering if he was really more Vosh than Damon. "My rage runs deep and with such history, it's hard for me to know any other way, but I will try...for you." His smile for his son was tense and measured, as if not very hopeful of his ability to keep this promise. "But, I'd appreciate your help if you can help me. If I can be helped."

"So, I've been thinking.... A lot," Radin offered, taking a sip of his tea as he looked out over Damon's estate. "I'd like to come and stay here with you and work directly with you. Learn from you. Help you." He didn't think Damon's smile could have been bigger than when he said he was proud of his father, but there it was—twice in a conversation.

"What, may I ask, has brought about this change, and don't we need you leading that massive army of yours? Don't you have more pressing du-

Charles W. McDonald Jr.

ties? And, where is the Crystal Crown? Did you surrender it to that...Talemar?"

"Yes, well, that thing you did to Talemar, I'm not proud of, and he didn't deserve that. But, what I've seen and witnessed tells me that your plan to upend this status quo may be the best thing for everyone. In fact, I can think of no better place for my talents to be put to use...and strengthened with your regular training."

"Talemar got what he deserved, and others must know that disappointing me comes at a very high cost. Let his disfigured appearance be a warning to others."

Both Damon and Radin paused as Damon took a breath, his eyes darting down to the flooring while Radin resumed looking out over the estate, noticing Dallia's grave freshly dug with fresh flowers laid about her headstone.

"I'm glad you brought Dallia with you. I think that was the right thing to do for both of you."

Noticing Radin's pensive stature, Damon was grateful for the thoughts of Dallia, but Radin was dancing around something. "You look like you've got something you need to talk to me about."

A heavy sigh escaped Radin as he broached another subject he wasn't sure would be the most comfortable with Damon, but he needed to understand it better. "I had a dream some time ago."

"Oh?" Damon's eyes and ears perked up for this one.

"Yes, and it was about you." Radin's expression was flat and straight as an arrow.

"OH!"

"Specifically, the first time you ever met Evanyil."

"*Ooohhh.*" The three different tones of the exact same word from Damon spoke volumes his brevity did not.

"I didn't understand what I was seeing except that I knew I was seeing through someone else's eyes, and it dawned on me that those eyes were at least yours."

"At least mine?"

"Yes, and that's what I wanted to ask you about. I was in a castle—a REAL castle—like a KING's castle. And there were children and what I know now are photographs…of Elise."

Damon shook his head in recognition, knowing the question that was coming and wondering if he should head it off, but his son had already been so helpful and had suffered so much, he wanted to let this conversation organically go where it needed. "I'm listening. What's your question?"

"I'm going to assume that I was seeing through Michael's eyes just as I was seeing through yours. Is that a fair guess?"

"Yes." Damon nodded in agreement.

"Okay then, so, I'm going to further assume that you're the reason Elise came to Perion. Want to tell me why and how she fits into your plans?"

"How about I tell you why you really found that scroll in Tannanvar instead?" Damon's gaze was knowing and piercing, counter-offering something he knew Radin couldn't resist to keep vital information compartmentalized for the good of all Mankind. He didn't like being the only one who knew the whole of all the individual pieces, but it had to remain that way; or the risk of losing everything everyone had worked for was simply too great.

"I'm listening," Radin yielded, knowing he didn't have the leverage in this conversation though he'd offered Damon more respect and understanding than ever before.

"My son, this information is dangerous, and you have to swear to me it won't leave your lips until I say it is safe to do so. Agreed?"

"Agreed," Radin offered with a confirming nod, setting his drink down on the railing as he wanted to focus all his attention on every word Damon was about to utter.

Without a word, *Damon's Distorting Web* appeared overhead, encrypting their conversation in its throbbing, dark, and web-like way.

"I can unmake what I made, and I can and will destroy the Dragon of Darkness, but that's only a part of the unmaking that's required to bring about the balance we seek. I've seen your role in less than certain terms, but I've seen it nonetheless and I think the part I was shown was unmistakable."

"I gathered there was more to it that you wouldn't have left to chance—my finding that scroll and coming to see you." Radin didn't want to press for more yet, but he was hoping his continuation of the conversation and help in carrying the conversation forward would yield more useful information.

"I couldn't leave *you* to chance. I need you. I've always needed you. When Mira came into the picture, your role became ever clearer."

"Father, forgive me, but I still don't understand. What does Mira have to do with your needing me? I don't even know anything about Mira."

"You'll see." He didn't like giving that answer because it was a non-answer and he knew it, but he was trying to placate as best as feasible without blowing the plan apart. "Suffice it to say, I couldn't be happier to have you working side by side with me because I was trying to figure out how we could start working closer together so that this part of the plan could work. Now you've come to me. It couldn't have worked out better. Though, we're going to need that massive army of yours, and I don't have a solution for that if you're here with me, but we can work on that problem together."

"That's it? That's all I get?"

"Mira is the payload, and you're the delivery mechanism. And that is all you're going to get from me—for now." As he said it, he began rolling through the possibilities of how he was ever going to execute this with Mira abandoned in West Texas and the continuum taking unforeseen curvatures back upon itself. It was a problem he'd have to mull over on the back-burner until he could come up with a workable solution. He needed time to map out the many forks of each action to understand which yielded the highest probability of success. Actually, he could have used Mira's help in running through the probabilistic models, but that really wasn't an option given who the probabilistic models centered around. But...there was another person—sort of—he knew who might even be better at complex algorithms than even Mira. The twinkle in Damon's black gems evidenced solutions and workarounds coming to the forefront of his thoughts as Radin began registering them externally as he observed his father carefully.

"I see the wheels turning in your mind, Father. What's going on in there? And what's this payload about?"

"I need to go see someone. Meanwhile, I want you to read this thoroughly." Damon produced Xaldran's tome with a brilliant flash of silvery-blue light, manually opening it to the part where Durial and his broth-

ers were captured. "Read it fifty times if you have to. Read everything leading up to it and everything cascading from it. Then debrief me. I need to
go talk to someone. I'll be back...shortly."

"I'll do as you ask, but may I offer some advice?" Radin didn't want
to offend, but Damon's actions often ran out in front of him to such an extent that it affected others' perceptions of him. Even being the careful and
fastidious sort, Radin knew Damon to be, did not always protect Damon
against his own doer-driven instinct burning inside him like a great and
monstrous pyre.

"What's that?" Damon's black gems were frosty in rebuke-laden
readiness even for his own son, though he'd proven to be more thoughtful of
late than child-like. Damon knew Radin would outshine him in time for he
was made from better stock. That thought led to thoughts of Keirill, which
he quickly vanquished in the transparent shadow of the nameless one.

"If you're going somewhere on this world, I think they'd be expecting their deity to wear something more...appropriate than what you're
wearing now."

"Fair point," Damon smiled, brushing the soil off his white T-shirt.
"After you read that, and we debrief, I'm going to put you in touch with my
chief scientist. Then, we'll start working on the next phase."

"And what phase is that, Father?"

"*Durial's Eye*, of course!" With a wink and a smile, Damon vanished,
though he hadn't changed clothes, causing a sigh of frustration to escape Radin's lips. *Durial's Eye*, Radin thought. *Great! Who's Durial?*

*   *   *   *

The New Georgia Hospital buzzed with activity as Damon *Portal'd*
just inside the large, sterile automated entryway to a chorus of applause,
bows, and the occasional prostrate worshiper. He didn't have time for the
full mage regalia, instead settling on dark slacks and black boots with a
cream shirt of gold scrollwork about its neck and cuff lines. No one here
had seen him in much other than mage regalia, but they'd have to get used
to it. The person he needed to see *should* be just inside. The biometric security cleared his way inside the secure wing at a fast pace.

Charles W. McDonald Jr.

Just inside the secure wing, he was greeted by his chief scientist, who'd just hurriedly exited a dark, tinted glass door leading to a series of connected labs on the right side of the hallway. A series of clicks from it provided a status report in translation. "We did our best with Mira and hope you found her status meeting with your approval. If you came to see the boy, he's progressing on schedule without issue. Was there anything else I could help you with, Savior?"

"Yes, and Mira was fine. I'm sure you did all you could for her. Thank you. I'm going to need your help running forking permutations along a continuum. If I diagram out the probability models, can you run the probabilistic values for each branch for me?"

Several silent blinks from 22B told Damon it was processing his request internally before formulating a response. It wasn't quite sure how to take, 'I'm sure you did all you could for her.' *Did something happen to Mira I wasn't aware of?* From the security cameras, it had been confirmed that Damon checked her out, so it assumed everything was okay. Still, this was an odd request—even for Damon. A few clicks formulated its reply: "Will these probabilistic models be of the future forking from the present or forking from the past?"

"You'll see. Can you do it?"

"Of course, Savior. Just one is more complicated than the other, but I can perform either task. Just know that if the fork is from the past, the math is far more complex, and it will take longer to give you an accurate model. I just wanted to make sure you were aware."

"When I send you this information to process, it cannot be shared with anyone for any reason—whatsoever. Is that understood?"

"Yes, Savior. Absolutely. My silence is always assumed unless Savior says otherwise."

"Good. Take me to the boy."

"Of course, Savior." If it could show expression, it would have beamed with pride as it showed Damon inside the series of connected labs with dark tinted impact glass that wasn't glass at all. The two of them now standing before the adolescent boy, Damon wished for *Durial's Eye* to already be in operation. With it, he could see—rather than guess at—the outcomes of his possible actions. He didn't need to be omniscient for the plan to work, but close to it.

Turning to his chief scientist, he had another ask he wanted to air out: "Tell me everything you know about supersolids."

Several blinks from 22B said it was processing yet another odd request from Damon. *How could these things possibly be connected? Is the 'Savior' neurotic, insane, or just operating on a level I can't comprehend?*

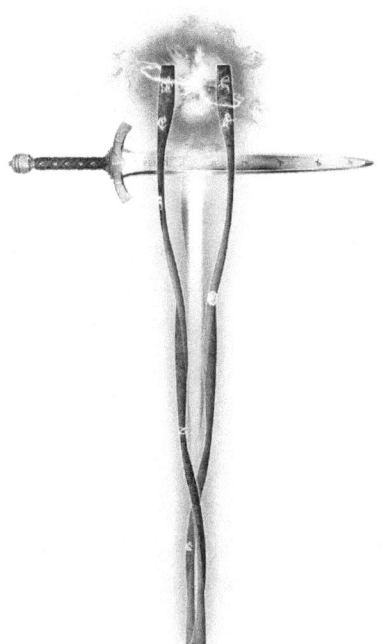

Chapter 20: Nihilism

(Damon's Manor, Eden, Present Day)

"I've read this ten times already, and there are parts I just don't understand." Radin's left arm dangled off of the plush, high-back chair in Damon's hidden, fourth-floor study, where Illirian Starfire so frequently had come—unannounced—to meddle, influence, and delight. Staring at Damon across a third-the-length of the study, Radin watched him draw ringlets of reflection with his left in-dex finger into the pale and naturally-stained, red oak desk with a noticeably marred spot just about where Damon's right hand tended to rest. Radin knew, as good as any, the temper of his father and wondered how it would affect his own decision making if passed down to him.

"Me neither." A rare admission of nescient knowledge from Damon caused a raised eyebrow from Radin just as Damon cast *Distorting Web* over the entirety of the room to encrypt this most-sensitive conversation. "But,

Charles W. McDonald Jr.

we're going to have to make sense of it together."

"Maybe if I understood what you're trying to glean from this, it would help."

"What do you make of the Seeds of Humanity," Damon asked, prompting Radin down a particular line of thinking with his eyes as well as his words.

"What is it with your answering a question with a question?"

"Because you're my only son and I'm trying to get you to start thinking critically all the time. It will save your life when you need it most."

A heavy sigh from Radin, but he had already put great thought into the Seeds of Humanity when discussing it with Ykstherin and Talemar and several times since then. Reading the material more in depth this time, his original thoughts—he felt—had been confirmed. So, it wasn't a huge stretch for him, but he still wondered where this was going. "I make of it that the Seeds of Humanity had to have an origination point."

A rare smile of late from Damon said Radin was on the right line of thinking. "And…," Damon prompted.

"…And…my assumption was that it was Setinon."

A confirming nod of the head from Damon conveyed his approval as Damon urged the line of thinking to continue, "Much has been lost due to noise in each subsequent permutation of the telling of the story of Creation. That noise—in some cases—led many to believe that life either evolved on Perion, Kaleion, Earth, etcetera OR that life was spontaneously 'Created.'" Damon paused his drawing of imaginary ringlets as he'd seen Kellen often do in moments of unnecessary fidgeting, motioning with his left hand for his son to keep pulling on this thread until they found the meat of the context.

"And, I'm gathering, you see both of those possibilities as extremes on either end of a great continuum of Creation…?"

"Correct. Often times, the simplest solution is by far the most accurate. We were planted like seeds in a field of wheat, sewn by the hatred of *The Eye of Time*."

"Are you certain it was *hate*, Father? Because, I didn't read that into the text."

"Oh." Damon sensed this was about to become another philosoph-

Charles W. McDonald Jr.

ical debate with his son and he openly welcomed it. "Tell me what you felt about it when reading between the lines."

"It felt like there was a bigger plan at play for certain and it wasn't all clearly spelled out, but it felt like to me that there was more going on than just magic being outlawed and dispersing hardened criminals to the stars as banishment because they didn't believe in capital punishment. There was a lot of subtext there, and it felt like *The Eye of Time* had a plan for Humanity."

"A plan for what?"

"That's the question I've been mulling over in my head from the first time I read through the whole thing cover-to-cover today."

"What do you think *The Eye of Time* is? How do you picture it? What do you picture its motives being?" Damon was, like many men, a very visual person. He used his internal vision and imagination in his imagineering of great things. To manifest his vision of his reality. He was trying to see if his son had similar powers and, if so, to teach him how to use it.

"This whole thing has made me question so many things I previously felt I knew with great certainty."

"Good. It should." Damon's eyes flashed in anticipation of a breakthrough with his son. "But, back to my question."

"I really don't know how to picture *The Eye of Time*." Just then, a brilliant flash of light-blue-green light shattered his consciousness to the point of making him wince, causing him to bring his right hand forward to his forehead, pressing against his temple as he tried to maintain focus on Damon standing right in front of him. A sound unlike anything he'd ever heard before echoed through his mind, rivaling a great chord being struck by a great and god-like hand. Five triangular rods contorted around a field of pure energy with a waterfall of energy streaming into its heart inside Radin's mind. The whole thing set about a field of honeycomb-wall construction with great mechanical beings whirling busily about what Radin knew had to be *The Eye of Time*. "Whoa!"

"Talk to me. Tell me what you see."

"How…. How did you know?"

"Because I've seen it, too, and it had the same effect on me."

"I see a sterile room on a field of blue and green pulsing with energy streaming into the room from above in a great waterfall of light pouring into some centrifugal explosion of energy contained inside five contorted triangular, or helical, rods.”

"YES,” Damon exclaimed in violent agreement, nodding his head as he urged Radin to continue. “What else?”

"These mechanical….”

"Sentinels. They're called Sentinels.”

"Yeah. They were working like worker bees or something around the *Eye*.”

"That's a good way to describe it. Worker bees, responding to a hive mind's commands.”

"Exactly.” Radin nodded, his consciousness coming back under his own control in waves as *The Eye of Time's* influence radiated outward and away from him.

"So, now we know some of what we're dealing with and some of the why.” Damon was trying to stitch together the great mosaic before them, but there were just so many pieces it was easily the biggest challenge of his nearly immortal life. But, surrounding himself with great talent helped, and he was grateful for Radin's aid. Though, the fact that Radin could see the *Eye* was only more confirmation of Radin's role, making Damon unconsciously frown at the thought. And the mission in front of Radin.

"What is it, Father?”

"Nothing. Let's keep going. We're onto something, and I don't want to let go until we've squeezed every drop of juice from this lemon.”

"You've been spending *way* too much time on other worlds, Father! It's contaminating your lexicon.”

"Perhaps….” Damon allowed the briefest smirk to escape his lips for his son's benefit—not his. Things were still very much broken inside for Damon. The loss of Mira had made another scar for him to carry—another iron-weighted burden about his neck and shoulders. Even just the thought made his scars throb, causing him to visibly wince.

Noticing the smirk followed by the clearly pain-induced wince, Radin wanted to carry some of Damon's burden for him, but for that to happen, he needed to understand Damon better, and understanding Damon was an exercise in frustration. Frustration of patience to allow Damon to get close enough to allow that to happen and frustration of atrocities—both those done by, and to, Damon. Damon's history was ugly, prolific, and dynamic. Radin could only hope his own life wouldn't be so fraught with peril and *hate*. But, given what he'd already been through, circling this close to Damon's star, he wasn't so hopeful anymore. "You know, I'm here for you if there's something you need to get off your chest. I can help—if you'll let me."

Damon offered a genuine smile for his son as he considered the earnest offer for help. Radin's help was essential and planned, but he still had to be careful with the compartmentalization of vital details. Having already come so close to ruin before the Dragon of Darkness, he couldn't allow another slip like the last one when making Eden. "I have a complicated life with an even more complex past. It's not your place to share that burden that I alone have earned. But, thank you. Just hearing the sentiment of help is in itself…helpful."

Radin nodded in agreement of both of Damon's points. He was right, but being right wasn't always best for everyone's interests. He saw Damon's survival and fitness to lead as far more critical value than his being right about not sharing a burden that should be his alone to carry. He knew Damon was already carrying a mountain of remorse and just a feather more could topple him, and the Master Plan with him—*then what?!* He'd have to circle back when Damon was in a more sharing mood, but he wanted to get them back on topic. "How old do you think *The Eye of Time* is? That might help add color to motives, if it's…what's the word I'm looking for…?"

"Sentient. It means self-aware."

"Yeah…sentient." Radin wondered if Damon was reading his thoughts or if they were just naturally on the same wavelength. That thought disturbed him as he considered the answer to his own question.

"That's a great question, and I don't know the answer to it, but clearly it's tens of thousands of years old at a minimum. It predates the banishment of magic on Setinon. Who knows, it might even be the reason it was banished."

"That's an interesting line of thought, Father. What makes you say that?"

"Call it a hunch, but this thing has a thirst for power that is unquenchable. That was my initial impression, and it's still my impression today. If I were *The Eye of Time*, I'd want to eliminate any possible threat to my power, and magic would certainly qualify as a threat." Abruptly halting his tracing of imaginary ringlets of thoughts being drawn in his desk by his left hand, Damon rose, walking toward a place in the floorboards he'd held secret from everyone—even Illirian, Goldenbow, and Kellen. There, he waved his left hand, causing some of the hardwood planks to disappear where he knelt in the presence of his son, pulling a smooth and simple iron box with neither lid nor lock from beneath the floor to rest on the hardwood planks beside him.

"What are you doing, Father?"

"Hold on. I want to show you something." Reaching into the smooth metal box, Damon pulled a plain silver rod half the length of his forearm—double checking against the others to ensure this one was the right one since they all looked alike. Damon's grip, accompanied by a thought, invoked a vision before them that began to play like a holographic recording.

Radin held no context for what he was seeing, and every other word was broken for him until he cast *Linguistics*. A man wearing some sort of odd uniform behind a transparent desk, spoke of horrific events that led to the destruction of his outpost. Abruptly the message cut itself off, or Damon terminated it—he couldn't say which. Radin tried to wrap his mind around what Damon knew that he *wasn't* sharing. "I know you're threading a needle here of holding on tightly to certain information you feel is highly dangerous in the wrong hands and letting me in on enough so that I can help you, but, Father, have some faith in me. Please tell me what you know about this message and what it means."

"Graelon, near as I can tell, is the world closest to Setinon in evolution of magic and technology working together. They built remote outposts—plural—where dangerous experimentation between magic and technology were performed. Safer outcomes—we hope—were brought back to the Graelon homeworld and infused into society. What you saw was an outpost that ripped itself apart, where mages fought alongside other Humans to try to save the outpost from the infusion of magic and technology in an experiment where things went horribly wrong."

Radin nodded, accepting—in doses—what Damon was describing

because it was beginning to make some sense. Part of him was grateful for the spoon-feeding of this most dangerous information, and he could see why Damon was being so careful with it. "You've been there, haven't you...? ...To this particular outpost." He wasn't certain, but it made sense given Damon's possession of the recorded message.

"I have," Damon confirmed dryly, licking his lips in contemplation of revealing even more. "There's something else."

"Tell me, please. I need to understand what we're doing and why."

"The way they were using magic on this outpost, and this is where the details are fuzzy, the magic built unforeseen pathways into the electronic circuitry, enabling some technology with Artificial Intelligence—like *The Eye of Time,* for example—to be able to cast."

"WHOA!" Radin's eyes were as big as saucers as he contemplated the impossible.

"Yeah! That was pretty much my reaction as well."

"Do you think *The Eye of Time* can cast? Because, if it can, that's a very big deal!"

"I would say, that's a safe assumption we should both be making going forward."

"WOW!" Radin's blue-grey eyes flashed as the knowledge slammed home as certainty in his mind.

"Now, do you see why I was thinking that the *Eye* would banish magic...?"

"That makes sense, but not to necessarily banish magic, but to banish **Human forms of magic.**"

"Precisely." Radin got it—immediately, causing Damon to nod in pride of his son's critical thinking. Now, they were singing from the same sheet of music. Damon nodded in agreement, hoping Radin could be trusted with this most sensitive of information about the Master Plan.

"That would mean that the *Eye* sees Humanity as a threat.... Especially humans like us."

"Yep!" Damon's time in Texas was showing itself, causing a brief raised eyebrow from Radin.

"*We have to take out the Eye,*" Radin confidently emphasized without a moment's hesitation. Seeing what could only be described as a memory of a memory flash across his consciousness in the form of an illustration in a text Elise had described that had led her straight to him.

"Yep!" Damon was anything but all hat and no cattle as the doer of doers considered the 'payload' Radin would soon carry to the *Eye*.

Radin nodded, trying to bring back the image of his illustration, but then he immediately began considering what destroying the *Eye* would entail and how that would happen. His thoughts drifted back to something Damon had said at the beginning of their conversation just as Damon interrupted.

"Are you familiar with the concept of nihilism?"

"Wow, you're all over the place today. Where is *this* going?" Radin was almost afraid to ask since this conversation had already yielded life-changing information, causing him to never be able to look at technology the same again. It was already foreign and dangerous to him—burgeoning as not worth the risk of the convenience it offered. Now it was simply a lethal enemy, and he didn't know if he'd be on the same page with Damon about that. Damon seemed to enjoy his technology when and where it provided convenience and mechanisms to achieve his Master Plan. Radin wasn't okay with that level of coziness with it.

"It's something I've been contemplating from the moment I started piecing the individual parts I just showed you together. This feels like to me a great mosaic where individual parts look like something we recognize as 'X,' but when they are pieced together, the aggregate looks wholly different."

"Okay, let's start with the basics…. What is nihilism?"

"I'm not saying I believe nor disbelieve in nihilism, but I'll describe it this way…. As I understand it, it's a belief that Humans have no consequential impact on the existence of values in the Universe. Loyalty, morality, kindness, friendship, etcetera all have no place in a nihilism Universe and Humanity is essentially meaningless in and of itself. The Universe is essentially dark and without a moral compass. Humans and Humanoids are insignificant, without purpose, and unlikely to change the totality of existence."

"Okay, that's *really* dark and it makes me wonder where your head is at."

"Again, not my belief, but what if *The Eye of Time* believes this…? …At

Charles W. McDonald Jr.

its core…?”

"Shit!"

"Yep! That's a good word for it. I mean, I'm just trying to get inside the head of this thing…such as it is."

"What are you not telling me, Father?"

"I'm thinking this thing is old. Really, really old. And, I'm thinking this thing has the *patience to erase Humanity*, even if it takes tens of thousands of years to do it."

"Wait…. What does this have to do with the Seals and what we've been doing, bringing about the End Times?"

"There's the critical thinking I was wanting to see!" Damon smiled in his reply, beaming with pride over his offspring. "That's the connection *I've been trying to make*. The Dragon of Darkness must end, and I'm going to personally take care of God the Creator for good measure." There wasn't an iota of hesitation in Damon's voice as he openly declared the impossible, but just as soon as the last word escaped his mouth, Damon shifted in balance, lost to a vision he hadn't experienced since Dallia's death as the booming voice of Creation called out to him across the chasm of existence beyond a great lake of crystal veiled in a great halo of white fire.

"What just happened, Father? I saw your eyes go blank."

Regaining his balance against his oak desk, Damon tried to collect himself at the knowledge of the feebleness of *Distorting Web* to keep out the prying eyes of God the Creator. They all knew now—Damon was coming for them…*so be it*. Damon secretly wondered if the *Eye* also knew. He'd have to make the assumption that it was so and work around it. Three of the greatest enemies of Man with only him and his Master Plan to deal their death. For the first time in centuries, Damon was afraid.

"Father? Talk to me. What's going on?"

"It's okay," Damon lied, uncomfortable in the foreignness of both the fear and his lie.

"That didn't sound convincing," Radin probed, getting up to put a hand on Damon's left shoulder in support. "You can talk to me, but I've seen that look before. I've felt it."

"I'm afraid," Damon warned, his black gems hazily-glossed over in the weight of the reality before them.

Charles W. McDonald Jr.

The ashen look on Damon's face accompanying a singular admission of a fear so real it was palpable against the throbbing heartbeat of *Damon's Distorting Web* caused Radin to take two steps backing away from Damon, reassessing his commitment to the Master Plan.

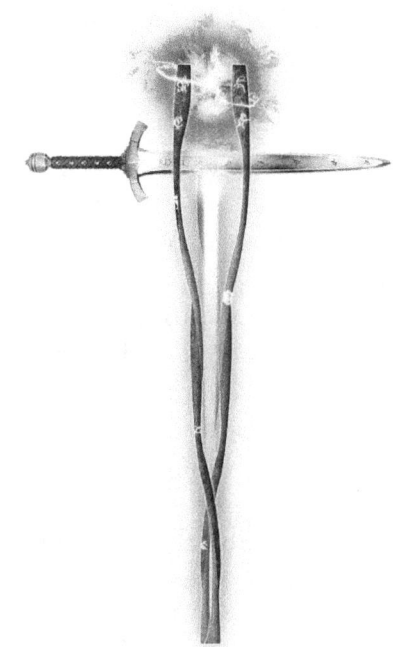

Chapter 21: Not Nothing

(Damon's Manor, Eden, Present Day)

His conversation with Radin had been both terrifying and enlightening and set in motion critical components of the next couple of phases of the Master Plan that were absolutely essential. All in all, a good thing, but in sitting at his desk reading Einstein's General Relativity for the umpteenth time, Damon was trying to see beyond the math. Mira was superb at correlating the hard mathematics to the construct of the theory itself as well as the applied physics construct—the observable Universe. However, Mira wasn't here, and he'd have to find his way without her—however painful and emotionally tormenting.

Einstein was getting at something here—the first to realize that empty space wasn't so empty after all. The fabric of space itself (the manifold) is made of stuff—matter, energy, time, gravity, and so on. Much of that fell into dark matter, dark energy, etcetera. If he was going to be in combat with deities—plural—he was going to have to understand what they had already known since time immemorial before he was ever conceived. He had

Charles W. McDonald Jr.

a lot of catching up to do, and fast! In many ways, he had the powers of a god, without their fulsome knowledge, and it was beginning to catch up to him.

If he was reading the tea leaves of Einstein's theories correctly, empty space held an 'X' value of energy—what could be interpreted as Einstein's Cosmological Constant (Λ)—in and of itself, and more space could merely pop into existence containing its own 'Y' value of energy, thus expanding the total space, matter, and energy in the Universe, driving—at least in part—the expansion of the membrane (or manifold) of the Universe. This explained—in part—how the expansion of the Universe wasn't driving a dilution of energy or matter at a macro level.

The toroidal field had always been easier for him to access and understand because it was—in a way—more tangible than this 'X' or 'Y' value of dark energy as he was interpreting it. Perhaps that was why none of the alien intelligent life he'd encountered thus far had conquered dark energy and many had been using toroidal—free—energy for centuries if not eons. He didn't have eons!

It was also quite possible that dark energy didn't exist at all. And neither did dark matter. It was quite possible that matter invisible to the known technological spectrum of Human vision was merely electromagnetically charged matter. It was quite possible that dark energy was the result of understanding the fundamental forces of the Universe and/or not applying enough strength of force to the electromagnetic forces in the Universe. And that this misunderstanding led to the artificial creation of the weak and strong forces of the Universe. It was a lot of IFs to deal with, but the fact of the matter was that there is, and always has been, a very powerful energy source in the Universe that isn't easy to quantify or identify. A nearly invisible substrate of energy in the fabric of the spacetime manifold itself. Whether it was called dark energy or dark muffins was irrelevant. Accessing it was the key....

God the Creator and the Dragon of Darkness already knew he was coming for them and already knew why. They need not know the how or the when or the who until that time was already upon them. *Are they truly omniscient?* He doubted it. There was only one way to find out. He was going to figure out the minimum necessary understanding of dark energy

CHAPTER 21: NOT NOTHING

just enough to harness it as a power source for a new variant of *Distorting Web*, but figuring out what dark energy was (or wasn't) was the first step, and the hardest!

Pouring over the ΛCDM (Lambda-Cold Dark Matter) model in conjunction with General Relativity, Damon wiped his right brow as a *Light Orb* materialized from nothing, adding to the diffuse and even LED light pouring in from moulding and ceiling alike. The ΛCDM model of the Earth '90's provided a reasonable understanding of the expanding Universe and found a place for Einstein's Cosmological Constant.

If Einstein's Cosmological Constant (Λ) is accurate, it represents a negative pressure through a nonzero, positive value, contributing to the negative expansion via dark energy that neither dilutes nor coalesces during the expansion. It wasn't like he had a ton of resources he could bounce these ideas off of other than a few, rare non-human Humanoids like his chief scientist. He didn't and couldn't trust Graelon survivors on Eden—even the most technical—because he needed to avoid magic contaminating scientific understanding. It was a delicate balance, knowing when to leverage magic, which was more art, and when to leverage science, which was more concrete and tangible. Graelon's horrific outcomes of combining magic and technology had completely altered his thinking on what was safe going forward, but using science to identify and tangibly define dark energy as a source such that it could be used by magic, he felt that a wide enough separation of the two so as not to be too dangerous—he hoped. If something were to go wrong with that kind of energy as a source, he shuddered at the thought of how massive and horrific the outcome could be. *Mustn't ever test this on any world you care about*, he thought, furrowing his left brow against the backdrop of the floating *Light Orb*, moving closer to his books as he went deeper into the meaning of the text.

A light far brighter than the *Light Orb* flashed in Damon's mind, causing a book to fly across the room into his waiting right hand. Flip, flip, flip. Damon's right index finger coursed through the text of *"Unraveling the Universe's Mysteries" by Louis A. Del Monte* as he tried to piece previous pieces of information together with Del Monte's *"Existence Equation Conjecture."*

"Holy shit!" Knowledge was a powerful thing, and an epiphany moment he'd been counting on finally came. "That's why it takes a massive lattice of dark matter and dark energy around galaxies for a galaxy to even exist. Because the energy to move inside spacetime is required for the galaxy—and everything inside it—to exist. Galaxies are pulling from that lattice framework like nourishment from an umbilical cord." Talking to himself was nothing unusual; it was often a fine line betwixt genius and insanity, but it also served a purpose of organizing thought into insight from the random chaos and noise of the Human psyche. His assumption was that *Del Monte* was saying it took an enormous amount of kinetic energy to move inside the fourth dimension of Minkowski (manifold) spacetime, and thus to exist. The equation before him suggested the amount of kinetic energy required had to be massive since it was partially based on Einstein's Special Relativity ($E=mc^2$). This might mean that older galaxies, further out from the local group and the Milky Way, had consumed more energy and thus more mass, and that might explain why the older galaxies were moving away at a faster pace than those in the local group, moving away from one another and the galaxies around the local group. If that were true, it wouldn't mean that dark energy was being diluted, but instead consumed in the form of kinetic energy required for existence in the fourth dimension of spacetime. *Del Monte* was onto something, the massive energy required to exist had to come from somewhere. Either it was leaking into the Universe via membrane of another Universe—like gravity—or it was coming from the energy of the vacuum of space as *Del Monte* further argued. *Perhaps, it was a natural harmonic energy....* But the key takeaway was: as matter and energy were being consumed by galaxies for their continued existence, mass and energy structure around the galaxy decreased, which also decreased the gravitational attraction within the vacuum and between galaxies, allowing expansion to accelerate as the vacuum of spacetime deteriorated.

While speculative, *Del Monte's "Existence Equation Conjecture"* made sense from otherwise nonsensical observations. Now, he just needed to test an idea, which meant he needed to travel further than ever before—both beyond the local group to the farthest edges of the visible Universe and to other areas within the local group to measure that which had no prior method of being directly measured—only presumed to exist by correlation. It was time to get creative. It was time to measure whether Einstein's Cosmological Constant was really constant after all.

Light Orb vanishing in lieu of only the study's LED lights, Damon

Charles W. McDonald Jr.

flipped through his phone for some inspiration as he kept the stream-of-consciousness ideas rolling in the front of his mind as accouterments flew from every corner of the study and hidden master bedroom. *Muse's – Supermassive Blackhole* started playing through the embedded Bluetooth speakers in the study as cape and stoles flew from the master bedroom whirling about and settling on his six-foot-four frame as the mighty *Staff of the Invoker* was snatched out of the air by his right hand gripping one of its dense, triangular, helical rods. Damon's black leather boots took a few steps against the hardwood planks of his secret study before he was enveloped by *Distorting Web,* disappearing into thin air without aid of *Portal,* taking his *Distorting Web* with him, suddenly terminating the music in his study as the Bluetooth connection was suddenly severed.

Radin didn't know what to make of the strange music. He'd never heard anything quite like it before, but he knew his father heavily influenced by Earth and other worlds. He didn't recognize Damon's manner of departure either, but he'd have to ask Damon about that later—perhaps during another lesson.

He didn't feel quite right sneaking into Damon's secret study, especially to steal something from him that he, himself, had given to Damon, but he hoped the outcome would prove worth the minor betrayal. In the spot where Damon normally kept the *Staff of the Invoker,* leaned another staff of conquest. Attaching a wax-sealed letter to it, Radin sent the staff away in a flash of silvery-blue light, hoping it would be received as intended—a peace offering. Only time would tell.

A wave of his left hand revealed portions of threads of Damon's magic used to deliver him elsewhere. It was still difficult to make out his means of travel, but the destination.... *WOW! Why would Damon be going that far?!* He had overheard Damon talking to himself about galaxies, energy, and matter, but what *was* he doing?

At the edge of his traveling experience and knowledge, Damon stood atop a barren, rocky, burnt-orange world, wobbling in its orbit of a binary

Charles W. McDonald Jr.

star system at the edge of the local group in a cluster Terrans called "Sextans A." Technically it might have been a galaxy, but at only 5,000 light-years across and barely organized into even a cluster of stars instead of great spiral, it barely qualified as such in comparison to the nearly 220,000 light-year span of the Andromeda galaxy. He had a reason for starting here, and this was going to require some on-site measurements to prove the hypothesis at hand. If right, this would be the strongest measurement he'd take today—assuming he could measure it at all.

Distorting Web pulsating overhead, Damon tried to fathom how to measure what couldn't be seen or sensed by the most sensitive equipment on Earth. It had to be similar to the free-energy toroidal field, though not orbiting nor radiating himself nor any other objects. If tied to anything at all, it might only be tied to the membrane of spacetime all around him. Looking out into the blackness before him, there were barely any stars beyond this rim of the Sextans A cluster. No haze, nor glow, nor aura of any kind—just abyssal blackness. First, he attempted something he expected to fail, sourcing Arcane…feeling it fizzle before it had a chance to accumulate anything—not even enough to make a *Light Orb*. "Okay, now what?"

"Kinetic energy, Day. Kinetic energy. How would you access that?" A heavy sigh followed by, "Oooh…."

The *Amulet of the Five Gates* leapt into Damon's left hand as the thought came to him—*time….* He'd never considered trying to use the *Amulet of the Five Gates* to access the time element of spacetime before. "How old are you?"

There was really no way to describe what his mind's eye was seeing except to say it looked similar to a continuum cast upon a heads-up display, and it wasn't something his magic was forming. This was coming purely from the *Amulet of the Five Gates*. He'd been in a few cars on Earth—one of them being a 2017 Camaro SS—and this reminded him more of the heads-up display on that than anything else, but then his mind flashed to a moment of the Graelon Outpost recording as his nearly eidetic memory recalled holographic displays in the background of the outpost commander and he recalled seeing data on those screens that looked similar to what his mind was seeing now. "Wow! Maybe they knew," Damon considered as numbers and symbols he was unfamiliar with scanned across his mind's eye.

"Maybe they *did* build *The World Below and Between* and this is, in part, how."

Trying to organize the symbols he was seeing into something he could relate—Einstein and the Cosmological Constant—he looked for what he assumed were values. He didn't like reverse engineering the parameters via the data this way, but if he was right, the data and parameters would bear themselves out in his next few trips. If not, he was on the wrong path and would have to start over, but it would be obvious either way. More familiar with Terran symbols and terminology than those from Graelon, Damon began substituting—in real time in his mind's eye—parameter for parameter, or at least what he presumed were parameters, until finally he was able to make sense out of the data. It showed there was slightly more energy here than the current understanding of the Cosmological Constant—which he was expecting to see. However, as observational data often illustrated and frustrated alike, there was data there he *wasn't* expecting to see.

Vast amounts of data encoded in black and white dots across his mind's eye field of vision caused Damon's left hand to reach upward, grabbing both his temples as he squinted, trying to focus on something in the white noise before him. Something that could only be described as a conical vortex of waves made itself visible to him from behind the mask of the white noise of black and white dots before him, emanating from a spot deep into the blackness of space before collapsing itself and the continuum of data in his mind's eye. It was all just gone. Looking down at the *Amulet of the Five Gates*, it was dull and lifeless—silent.

Turning around for a last look, calculating he might have another two hours of air remaining with him, Damon pressed on toward the next waypoint of his mission to better understand dark energy. Reaching out to the Zero-Point field all around him as a source, he disappeared in a violent flash of silvery-blue light that marred the burnt-orange surface of the barren world on the outer rim of the local group. He didn't like not being able to explain observations, but to him this felt more like something was being withheld from him when on the cusp of a breakthrough. Clearly, the vacuum of space had already proven it was not nothing after all.

Charles W. McDonald Jr.

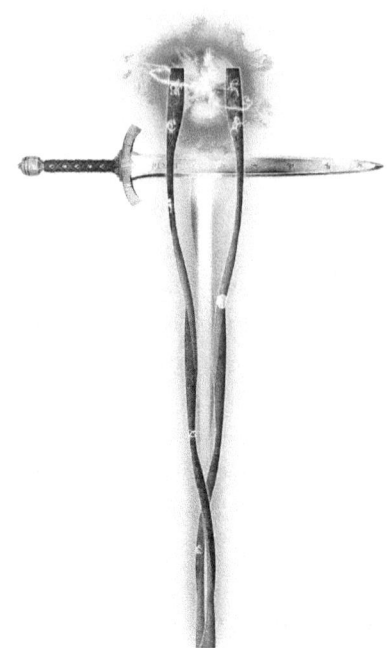

Chapter 22: Chasing the Thunder

(Wessex, Earth, Present Day)

The fire raged only four meters away, yet still House of Lords David Wright adjusted the quilt in his lap underneath the heavy and ornate desk where he mulled over proposed new legislation for the Brexit framework as another fresh cup of tea was brought to him alongside a small plate of dark-chocolate-coated crisps. A middle-aged serving woman half bowed, then retreated, closing the well-oiled pocket doors to his comforting home office. A few clicks on the laptop's keypad provided only a moment's distraction, though not nearly enough to explain his daughter's sudden appearance before him on the client-side of his desk. There, sitting cross-legged in a dark midriff-exposed dress he'd never seen her wear before, and looking a good ten years older, he began scratching his head internally. "Elise?"

An unseen spell via the flick of her left wrist set the whole world right inside her adopted father's mind as his mood suddenly went from suspicious to comforting in the blink of an eye.

Charles W. McDonald Jr.

"Elise, my beautiful girl. Why didn't you tell me you were coming over? You know I would have had them prepare your favorite dinner. Do tell me you can stay for dinner, Sweetheart?!"

"I'm sorry, Father." She still struggled with that title for this man; perhaps the struggle was more pronounced now since she was so out of practice in her role as *his* daughter. "I really don't have time for that today—what with Michael and all."

A frown from her father as *that* name made its way into their conversation. "Yes, well. I'm sure the *king* can suffer an hour or two without you."

Having done some homework on the timeline she now found herself in, Elise was in need of more subtle and far less public information she thought her adopted father might possess—at least that was the hope if she were to uncover more of Damon's plot and ever-more-curious misdeeds. "Tell me, Father, have you had any briefings on a man called Damon?" Elise could already see the frown on David's face forming and the briefest observation of his body language foretold his desire to protect sensitive and potentially compartmentalized information she was seeking. Another flick of her left wrist, and *Suggestion* was unraveling protected pathways inside David's mind.

In a flash of light in his mind's eye, David's initial instinct to protect sensitive information via a wall of secrecy suddenly found that great wall shattered between them as his mind opened up to his beloved and beautiful daughter. "Who?"

"He might not have been referred to by that name, but he's around 6'4", black hair, black eyes, brooding, chiseled, highly intelligent and capable—a hard man who comes and goes in manners not understood."

"Is that his name…? Damon? We've been struggling to identify him in database after database with facial recognition software. We've found him here and there in the US and elsewhere but have no point of origin for him, nor any record of him."

"That's because he's an *alien*, Father." That word held so much double meaning, both coming from her, and about her, as much as this world in relation *to* her.

"How would my daughter know this?"

Charles W. McDonald Jr.

Another flick of her wrist further pounded her will into her adopted father's mind, forcing him to simply accept what his instinct wouldn't allow. "What can you tell me about him? Where have you found him? …Both historically and most recently? Tell me everything you can, Father."

"First facial recognition records spot him in and around The University of Texas, specifically around their physics departments. Then in Charleston, South Carolina, where he tried to destroy evidence of his appearance only to leave behind traces of a disturbance where he simply appeared from out of nowhere. Simply impossible, or so we thought, until Americans showed a ship's internal security footage from the captain's quarters, of him using the same method to invade a ship at sea, where we think he used his powers to influence the ship's executive leadership to launch an unprovoked assault on Chinese fighters patrolling in the South China Sea."

"Yes. That sounds like our Damon. Such a busy little boy. Hard at work. Where was he most recently seen or reported?" Not in the least bit surprised by David's report, Elise still shuddered at the thought of Damon's influence. She'd lived through this once before already, and hearing the events described through both Michael and the news, the way things spiraled out of control so quickly, just didn't set right with her. She knew Terrans to be a hostile and dangerous people but not lacking in rationale— much like her own world. She felt the probability of their spiraling toward self-imposed oblivion rivaled the same probability of her own world doing the same, and that didn't seem all that likely to her—at least from her perspective, though she wondered how it would appear from Damon's perspective as she hung on David Wright's every word.

"That incident in the South China Sea just happened."

"What are you *not* telling me, Father?" A cringe from David turned into a smile as Elise further pounded his mind into submission.

"I don't have confirmation of this, but a source inside the US Air Force tells me, there was a similar incident in Minot, North Dakota."

"Similar to the ship invasion?"

"Yes."

She remembered her briefings from some time back about strategic military asset locations around the world, and Minot, ND was one for US strategic ICBMs. "A very busy little boy, indeed," she hissed in contemplation. Was Damon bringing the Earth to the brink of war or merely accelerating it? It was an explosive society, Hell-bent on destruction, but for the most part, they kept their doomsday weapons in check. The timing seemed fortuitous—matching up to Damon's Master Plan rather nicely—too nicely. "Is there a working theory on his home-base location?"

"Austin. Austin, Texas. That's our best guess. He's been captured most on CCTV footage in and around Austin—close to the main campus. Based on recent home sales in an otherwise relatively stationary market that close to the campus, we think he's around Duval St."

Moving around to David's side of the desk, she caressed David's head, releasing her hold on his now-fragile mind, hoping she hadn't done any permanent damage, but this was necessary. She had to find Damon—or at least his trail—before it had grown too cold. If Damon was the lightning, she was still chasing the thunder and she had a lot of catching up to do. A slight tap on David's forehead, and he was asleep in her hands as she carefully let his head rest on his desk, hastily forming a *Portal* to the barren and cold, windy plains of North Dakota.

Charles W. McDonald Jr.

Chapter 23: The Burden of Prosaic Thinking

(Radin and Mora's Cell, Setinon, Near Future)

Shimmering, blue-green, semi-transparent shielding mocked his every thought of escape as Radin rose from the sparse cell floor to the sound of someone approaching…and the resonant humming sound of the Sentinel clearly rising steadily, indicating Sentinels escorting a Humanoid through the corridors of the municipal complex tower. A sigh of relief escaped his lips, seeing Mora being escorted back to their cell after another round of interrogation. Her eyes no longer darted this way and that as they had done before—instead only staring off into the distance as if barely conscious and unaware of her surroundings. The Sentinels had to guide her body to the precise position in the field, allowing her to pass through the shield into their shared cell.

Without their mechanical arms holding up her body, she would

Charles W. McDonald Jr.

have crashed to the cell floor beneath her had Radin not jump up to catch her—squatting underneath her as he pushed back against her chest with the palms of his hands.

"Sit," he urged Mora, spinning her body around so she could sit cross-legged beside him on the bare, grey and white floor of their cell.

We'll be back for you, he heard in his thoughts as the lead Sentinel's eyes flashed in amber fire—its quasi-metallic legs floating barely a span above the prison corridor's grey flooring.

He didn't respond. Multiple harsh encounters and being beaten nearly to death had taught him the futility of it. He had a job to do and had to stay focused. Even the training in mind discipline hadn't fully pre-pared him for this task. They had tried nearly everything on him, of course. That had been expected. From advanced mind control and manipulation to counseling to now physical brutality, they were going to win—it was only a matter of time. But, now he had a much better idea of the layout of the structure, too, and that meant time was running out for them—literally.

"Where am I," Mora muttered, her eyes dizzily looking into Radin's.

"The same place we've been for weeks now."

"Why did you bring me here? I'd rather be back in the caves." Her words were coming around as was her consciousness as she shifted to hold-ing herself up, pushing away Radin's support.

"You weren't supposed to be a part of this."

"Tell them that. They seem to think I'm some sort of spy you brought with you to destroy *The Eye of Time*. Whatever that is…. Why are you really here?"

The subtle, steady, and precise sound of feminine heels hitting the plain, grey prison flooring announced the arrival of a candied-blonde Kanet.

A plain, grey jump-suit-clad Radin stood as the presence of his 'counselor' appeared just outside their cell. Placing himself between Kanet and Mora, Radin blocked Kanet's view of her still sitting on the floor some-what disengaged and confused.

"Haven't seen you in a few days," Radin chided, motioning with his head toward the Sentinels left to guard him.

Kanet's cybernetic enhancements translated for her, implanting the translation directly into her frontal cortex. *I thought we could revisit our last discus-*

sion, she sent back to him telepathically.

"I don't seem to have anything better to do." Smiling tensely, Radin took a step back from the shield as Kanet removed a small, white oval disk roughly the size of her thumb fingerprint.

Pressing it in conjunction with a two-factor authentication paired with Kanet's cybernetic encryption implants, Kanet produced an opening for Radin to step through the shield, causing two Sentinels to turn around and address his presence outside his cell, producing the plain silver digital handcuffs that shielded Radin from the source of his powers.

"Stop," Kanet announced to them, watching their amber eyes flash in coordinated response. "I'll let you know if I need you," she ordered verbally in Radin's common tongue, causing Radin to look sidelong at her as he began to walk beside her.

"I knew they understood my language." He paused to correct himself. "I presumed. At least, they acted as if they understood me."

"Oh, they understand you. Perfectly."

"Your common tongue is pretty good," he noted, smiling at her.

"Good enough," she offered flatly. She didn't smile or give anything away. She was still as hard to read as their first encounter.

"Does that mean we can dispense with the telepathic link?"

"We can keep it verbal if you wish it so." Her tone of delivery was that of a back-handed insult, but she didn't seem the type to go for that kind of cheap shot.

As hard to read as ever, he considered frontally—fully expecting her to read his thoughts.

I wouldn't dare to disappoint a descendant of Durial and Alexelio, she thought with a wink and a smile, causing him to frown back at her.

Through four more levels up and a few dozen more steps placed them inside an all-white room twelve spans by twelve with the gentle hum of Sentinels just outside the closed door. This was a different room than prior meetings, taking them within a dozen steps or so of a long blue-green corridor with a web-mesh wall and no apparent openings. Great humming sounds emanated from beyond the other side of the web-mesh wall, though the hum was coursing and uneven—slightly different from that of the Sentinels' propulsion and power plant.

Charles W. McDonald Jr.

Inside the sterile white interrogation room, Radin couldn't hear what he knew was *The Eye of Time*, but he felt its presence there in the room with them even if *she* couldn't. Their use of a room so close to the *Eye* was no accident, even though its reach was far beyond anything Kanet could imagine—if she was even *allowed* to imagine. "So…what's on your *mind*," he asked Kanet sarcastically with emphasis on the last word.

"I've never even been on this level before. Do you have any idea why we're in *this* room?"

"You're asking me?!"

"I am." Her response might have been terse, but her eyes said what her words and telepathic link need not. She knew nothing of the existence of *The Eye of Time*. That had been his first suspicion when he first told her of his intentions.

He needed to reassess the situation. He needed more information about what she did and didn't know. That would provide great insight into what the whole of Humanity on Setinon knew and didn't know. "You tell me about what's out there, and I'll tell you why I think we're in this particular room. You'd clearly never heard of *The Eye of Time* until you met me. I'm betting no one else you've spoken to had heard of it either. Why do you think magic was banned?" All he could do was lead Kanet to the water, but he couldn't make her drink from it.

Shifting in her nostalgic black pencil skirt against the soft linen-like programmable matter U-shaped chair, Kanet rested her peach-blouse-wrapped arms on the soft armrests as they began a soothing and hypnotic rhythm she tried to ignore in her thoughts. "You were out there. What is it you *think* you saw?"

"I was barely out there an hour. You've lived your whole life out there."

"Very well. Magic was banned because it produced unsafe results when in tandem with technology. Magic was banned because it yielded unfair advantages in a society where equality was paramount. Equality of outcomes…. Magic was outlawed because…." She thought about it before she said it. They'd all been taught early in life, in school, and societal norms pressed into the fabric of their thinking at every step along the way. Surely, he knew this. *He had seemed to know so much before coming here, as if….* "I'm not

Charles W. McDonald Jr.

telling you anything you didn't already know. You had done research before coming here. Where did you get your information?" She felt the profound soothing over every inch of her body and within her thoughts as the last question escaped her lips, as if that question had been met with approval, *but whose approval?* Her mind half-worked the problem further to root-cause and her impatience cut off a Radin about to answer. "Was it another descendant of *Durial*, perhaps?" More vibrations comforted her neck, shoulders, and spine as the finger-like reach of the energy from the programmable matter chair further approved of this line of questioning.

Shaking his head, Radin knew he wouldn't get anywhere by lying to her, and *what difference did it make if The Eye of Time had confirmation of what it already knew to be fact?* "Indeed, it was. His name is Damon, and he's my father."

"Interesting…," she replied with a pause, leaning forward with interest, "…and where did Damon get his knowledge from? Had he been here before…?"

"I don't know the answer to that, but the information he held was both detailed and solid, so I wouldn't be surprised if that was the case." He looked her in the eyes, measuring their color-shifting properties and wondering if they were really hers or not. From green to gold to blue to amber they changed, but he couldn't tell if driven by her mood or not. She was still incredibly hard to read.

"What else did Damon's research tell you? What else did your father tell you?"

"I've been very honest with you," Radin offered, redirecting her to his point, "…but you've been avoiding my original questions."

"Very well. I believe you asked if others had heard of *The Eye of Time*…." Sudden pricks of unseen energy jolted Kanet, tensing the muscles between her shoulders, causing her to lean forward even further away from the chair. "They had not," she declared with finality as she looked Radin in the eye. "…Which leads me to wonder if it is real, or not."

"Oh, it's real," Radin confirmed, pointing his right index finger around the all-white, all-sterile room. "…You asked me why we are specifically in this room on this floor. And, I'll tell you, it's so we can be closer to its influence."

Rising from her chair to get away from its influence, Kanet paced

Charles W. McDonald Jr.

to the wall behind them, then back to the table before them. To and fro she paced, quietly thinking until…. "Let's say I give you the benefit of the doubt…. Let's say you're right. Let's say everything you have said is true. Why would I allow you to destroy *The Eye of Time*?"

"I think you have less to say about this than you think, Kanet. I think the burden of your prosaic thinking has weighed down your ability to think critically of the world around you. I think this burden has blinded you to the fact that *The Eye of Time* outlawed magic so as not to be challenged by Man *for it, too, can cast….*"

Thunderous blasts and booms erupted down the hall so loud and with such concussive force as to upend and toss Radin from his chair up against the far-right wall with Kanet thrown atop him. The door to the room burst, crackling with amber energy, as it sizzled open. Four Sentinels on the other side of the door, with their resonant energy now at full hum, held a terrorizing gaze in their burning, amber eyes and made a fiery hiss as they began floating single file through the melted and warped door.

The first of many Sentinels to advance fixated its AI gaze upon them just as its companions turned their attention away….

Charles W. McDonald Jr.

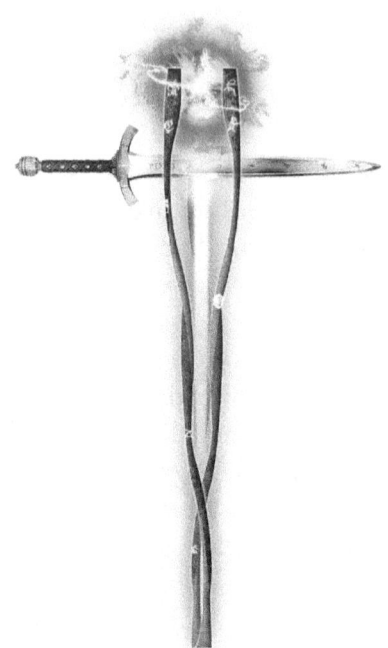

Chapter 24: The Monuments of Creation

(The Herat Plateau, Graelon, Present Day)

Ascending the maw of the cave to what he knew to be the Herat Plateau—even though having not visited here in centuries with the exception of leaving his bread crumbs for Elise—Damon looked out across the great mid-afternoon vista down toward the vast and bustling metropolis of Herat. To his right and far closer was the lesser city of Nezha. He *could* cast, but it would present more problems than he was ready to deal with at the moment. Instead, this was going to take an old-fashioned approach—or a modern one, depending on one's perspective. Sighing at the reality of not being able to use magic, Damon—dressed in a uniform that closely mimicked that of the outpost commander in the warning message he'd found—began his descent down the path toward Nezha in search of transportation to the northwest and the Monuments of Creation.

He could have walked all the way to Herat, but the more people that saw him, the higher the risk that the mission would be ruined, and this was a critical piece of information he'd put on the back burner for far too

Charles W. McDonald Jr.

long. He needed answers as to what and who he was dealing with, and the Monuments of Creation had held onto that information tightly for tens of thousands of years—if not longer.

*   *   *   *

Sterile, organized streets and businesses, gleaming in their cleanliness, stared back at Damon as did the occasional citizen who dared look upon his hardened and outlander face, trying to associate the uniform to the man. They say every man looks sharp in a uniform, but Damon just felt completely out of place in it and wondered if it was outwardly visible to the casual observer. That thought confirmed his decision of Nezha over Herat. Still, he carried a hard look about him, causing onlookers and citizens alike to pay greater attention to their own feet than the tall, raven-haired, black-eyed stranger.

He'd cut his hair specifically for this mission. No longer cascading well below his scapulae, it now stopped short of his neckline, though wind-blown and feathered in appearance. He still looked like the old ominous Damon—just a tad bit more cleaned up.

His mild and ancient familiarity with Graelon helped him isolate and identify business after business as he began to become more familiar in this foreign setting. The near silence of sudden gravity-propulsion tactical fighter movement overhead caused an involuntary jostle to the side as Damon quickly found himself under a business awning, looking up at the belly of the ship he'd assumed was here for him, only to see it move on in practical silence, not even disturbing what little dust the streets wore in functional, day-to-day maintenance. He noticed a slight, schizophrenic, side-to-side movement as the craft operated in low-performance modality, seemingly here, then there, in the blink of an eye in much the way he'd seen in UFO footage on Earth. Mira had described this behavior as indicative of electrogravitic propulsion and how it might operate in any low-performance mode within the random nature of the gravitational field—and all its disruptions—of a planetary object. As these types of field-propulsion craft moved into high-performance modality, they could more easily focus their gravitational distortion field as they got further and further away from other massive matter objects that interfered with their silent, and otherwise incredibly efficient, propulsion.

Careful, Day, he thought, resuming his walk deeper into Nezha proper. He'd wanted to bring help. This was such a dangerous place for him—of all people—to visit unaided and unaccompanied. Secretly, he'd wished he'd been nicer to Elise when given the opportunity as he considered the thought of her bailing him out of a bad situation that was becoming more likely by the moment.

A field akin to a park nestled inside a circle of great flowering trees of purple and white bloom offered civilian transportation, though not of the gravity propulsion variety; that appeared to be reserved for military and government use. Still, it would get him where he was going—assuming his counterfeit identicard didn't get him arrested on its first use. Less was more in this circumstance, so the less said, the better. He'd considered approaching from Minean Superior, but that would have raised too much suspicion, especially given his military attire. Then he considered Maxar, but ultimately settled on Maxon, which was a more common destination in that region. It would mean a slightly longer approach from the south but would raise less suspicion.

Without *Linguistics*, he'd have to adapt to the language and dialect difference on the fly. He knew the Graelon military comprised of a wide variety of personnel both on, and off, world, so it wouldn't be uncommon to hear unusual dialects from a uniformed officer, but if he couldn't adapt to at least understand their common tongue, that *would* raise suspicion.

A middle-aged brunette woman in line in front of him offered little pleasantries to the pilot—acting as if she knew him in a way—not even offering a destination, gruffly extending her identicard chest-level at the dour and overweight pilot for him to scan it; her account decremented the cost of the trip to her undeclared destination.

Watching her identicard deduct five hundred Herat Riyal, Damon wondered where she might be going at that price. Stepping up behind the middle-aged brunette, Damon offered, "Maxon," in his best bland common-tongue, hoping the accent wasn't too far off the mark.

The heavy pilot in dark, worn greys with black baroque-like pattern fringes, looking more wide than tall—though partly from being so big-boned—bore his teeth at Damon in displeasure, offering a gruff reply, "Not trouble." Damon knew his literal translation off, and it hadn't come across as a pleasantry *'no trouble at all*—more akin to *'don't make any problems for me or I'll throw your ass out mid-air—colonial guard or not.'*

Now inside the twenty-passenger commercial aircraft, the only remaining seats were a solo window-seat on the left or an aisle on the right next to the middle-aged brunette who eyed him with a careful measure and just the briefest of glances. He could go awkward and solo across the aisle from her, or just face her scrutiny head-on. Letting his instinct decide, Damon sat down beside her, offering her his real name, "I'm Damon," as he sat down beside her.

"Leah," she presented meekly, extending her right hand to shake his.

He had to be careful. He doubted he could manage a full-blown conversation in their tongue, but they were going to be in this aircraft a while and stone silence didn't seem the way to go. "Maxon, what about you?"

"Et same. Where from you?"

Visibly scrunching his eyebrows, Damon wondered how good of an idea this really was. He registered her question rapidly, though gave her a thoughtful look and a delayed reply: "Polaris Outpost." It was the only other outpost name he'd gathered from his information so far. He knew there were others, but knowing the name, location, and status was something totally different. He couldn't tell her about the outpost from which he was most familiar—Minot—else she would think him a ghost, or worse. He could only hope Polaris was still operational as his research had suggested it was.

"Explains accent." She smiled back at him, seeming to cut the tension in half as Damon tried not to visibly exhale a sigh of relief.

Giving her an honest smile in return, Damon offered a mild chuckle, looking her up and down. "I suppose it does."

"Maxon," Leah blurted.

"Pardon?" Damon attempted to clarify.

"Asked where," Leah reminded him of his original question, looking at him with even more curiosity now. "For work," she added.

There were any number of work trades in that part of the world. He

Charles W. McDonald Jr.

knew textiles to be one of them. Pointing to his uniform, he asked, "Textiles…?"

Shaking her head in obvious disapproval at what he thought might have come across unintentionally as a misogynist question, Leah corrected him with a tightened and somewhat pensive smile. "Archeology."

He couldn't believe his luck, and before he could stop himself, he blurted out, "The Monuments of Creation." *Too late! Dumb move.* He had no idea if that's what they were referred to here or not, but he gave that a very slim set of odds. Watching her carefully, as he could almost visibly see the wheels turning in her thoughts, he waited patiently for her to respond, now letting his eyes fall up on her hands that now held a communication device very similar to the ones his science team had developed on Eden.

"That's an interesting name them. Where you hear name?" Her body language was forward now, and her grip on her communication device had tightened, but he still thought he could manage his gaffe.

The order of speech in his understanding of her common tongue was improving with exposure, but he was still missing the interpretation of conjunctions and determiners. Looking her in the eyes, allowing her to see past his black gems, Damon used his best weapon—the truth—*his* truth. "Please don't," he asked, resting one finger on what he presumed was their version of a cell phone with its transparent, 3mm, ultra-sleek frame, now dancing to life with what appeared to be the news of the day scrolling across the top of the screen in tight and bright banners.

"Who you really," she asked again, allowing her curiosity to lean her forward into him rather than backing away from him as most women would do.

"Damon, but I'm not from Polaris."

"Where?" This time her question was nearly a whisper as she barely even mouthed it, looking around at the interior surveillance cameras throughout the cabin.

Smiling at her and visibly exhaling in relief at her understanding and her curiosity, Damon leaned into her, whispering in her left ear, "Kaleion."

Gripping his left hand that had been reaching out to her commlink with her right, Leah had to try much harder than normal to shut her jaw still stuck open from shock. Her mind ran in circles at the thought of the alien beside her. An off-worlder colonial officer was one thing, but an alien…. *And from Kaleion!* That name she knew, of course. History was full of tales, legend, and mythology of the five worlds of Humanity, and of those, Kaleion held the most information, so either the authors had the most knowledge of that world or it was the most important. In most sources, Terran was the least talked about, but Kaleion and Perion were frequently mentioned in the same breath with one another. "Been you have other worlds?"

Again, he leaned into her, whispering in her ear, "Perion, Terran, Graelon Colonial Outposts, and beyond."

She had to stop herself because her grip on his left hand was becoming white-knuckled and she was beginning to feel his hardness and strength pushing back against her grip. She didn't want to test him or upset him, but clearly, he was being very cautious around her, so he did have some level of fear about him. "How you come," she asked, now returning whisper for whisper.

"Magic," he lied, causing her to recoil. He couldn't risk telling her about *The World Below and Between.* The chances of her knowing about it were slim and none and he wasn't about to give out that kind of information. It was better for her to believe the lie of him using magic.

"Not registered," she breathed carefully. It wasn't a question, and now she fully understood why he was afraid and being so cautious.

Only nodding for her in reply, she straightened and composed herself for the cameras she knew that would be watching them as she turned to her right to look out her window to see the shoreline of Maxon approaching from the Minean Sea. Gathering her things together, she tried not to draw any more attention to them. She already feared: *If he goes down, you go down.*

Mere moments after landing, they gathered their belongings, and she made every possible effort not to speak to Damon again…until they got off.

A few dozen paces from the craft, she couldn't stop herself from grabbing Damon's elbow, "Your Monuments of Creation…. This way." She directionally nodded her head to the northeast—much farther north than he would have guessed from his understanding of their location. He couldn't use his magic to sense their location, but his instinct told him she was trying to veer them off way too far to the north.

Not quite arm in arm, yet in far more personal rapport with each of them well within each other's personal space, they verbally parried with one another as best as possible given the language barrier. At Damon's request, she had turned off her commlink, so they couldn't be tracked or surveilled— or at least so he had hoped.

She wasn't beautiful and alluring like Mira, nor did she have Mira's intellect, but she was intellectually curious and lovely in her own, tan-pants-like way. Neither slim nor heavy nor voluptuous nor flat, Leah was above the average of averages with a pretty smile, good cheekbones, and a good head on her shoulders. *Good instincts and common sense carried her this far*, he gathered. He didn't like the idea of making this trip alone, and his instincts told him that he could trust her—at least a little.

Trust was rapidly building between them and he wondered how much he could safely offer. Briefly he considered the possibility that she might be able to help him when the time came. And come it would…. "If I told you how I really got here, I fear you would go there."

"That would be bad," she assumed, looking him in the eyes, expecting him to validate.

"VERY BAD!"

"When I said I came here by magic, that wasn't the whole truth of it. You see there are tunnels, built with magic, connecting the five worlds of Humanity. It's called '*The World Below and Between*.'"

He watched as her eyes lit up at that. Apparently, she **had** heard the term before to his surprise.

"WHERE," she asked emphatically, squeezing his elbow.

"The Herat Plateau."

Stopping dead in her tracks, she kicked the gravel and dirt along their trail. "I've been there…."

"Don't go inside," he warned. "You'll get lost, and no one will ever find you. You'll never find your way out—not without someone who's been that way many, many times."

"You'll show me," she demanded, leaning into him though the top of her head barely came to the bottom of his jaw. "PLEASE!"

Shaking his head in resignation, Damon didn't want to get close to another woman—sexually or otherwise—right now. He didn't want to feel close to anyone or anything. And, he certainly didn't want to feel like he 'owed' anyone anything…. But, he needed this information…badly! "Monuments first," he demanded, though the acknowledging furrow of his brow said he'd honor her…*request.*

"Monuments first," she agreed, returning to hold his elbow as they walked toward her pre-arranged transportation. A transformative, helicopter-like vehicle, more closely resembling an Earth V-22 Osprey, though much smaller and more personal and consumer-grade in design, awaited them at the far north end of the airport. Damon wondered how well it would operate in the extreme atmospheric conditions of this northern-most, and mostly glacier-laden continent. Small and tight fabric jump seats awaited them with the most simplistic looking belts one could imagine—more closely resembling a rope—as the belly doors of the aircraft barely fully closed before it was off the ground, carrying them deep into the V-shaped mountain range off into the distance.

This whizzing, chopping, and whirling of what he assumed was a turbo-prop-like propulsion craft carried them buffeted by clouds and mountain updrafts as Leah sat beside him, holding his hand—occasionally squeezing it as she winked at him.

"Great risks you took here. Why," she questioned, carefully examining his beautiful black irises that gleamed in the mid-day light of the brisk northern sky.

"I believe the Monuments of Creation hold a great secret, and I'm comparing what I have learned from the other worlds and their similar monuments."

"What secret do you believe?"

"The secret of why we are all here," he answered, motioning between them.

"You're a curious man," she observed, becoming more intimate with him in the way she held his hand, now tracing his palm delicately with her fingertips in appreciation of the unusual man before her.

"Yes. I hoped you were curious too." He smiled back at her, though

Charles W. McDonald Jr.

he couldn't bring himself to return her intimacy. It wasn't a matter of attraction or lack thereof. It was a matter of not being able to deal with the burden of being responsible for another life taken as a result of being too close to him. Damon could mercilessly kill when necessary, but allowing the death of someone close to him was something entirely different. It felt far more personal and far more *his* fault. When he killed, he often saw it as *their* fault for getting in his way or intentionally choosing to put themselves in his path. To block him. Or be an intentional stumbling block for him.

Feeling him withdraw from her without withdrawing, she stopped tracing his hand, instead letting him reclaim it. "You have woman," she asked with her brown eyes sparkling in curiosity.

"I don't think I can handle another relationship right now...," he paused. "People have a habit of dying around me," he added, carefully watching her consider that response.

Straightening herself in her jump seat to the whirl and chop of the turbo-prop cutting through the cloud-basin, Leah summoned as much determination as she could muster. "Take care of myself."

"I'm sure you can. Can we trust them," Damon asked, motioning his head backward toward the pilot and co-pilot.

"Used them many times...," she vouched, seemingly distancing herself from her new traveling companion.

Damon noticed, and he couldn't afford to lose her, but he didn't want to lead her on either. "Hey...," reaching out to her to hold her hand again, "...I'm not going to hurt you." His eyes mirrored hers in *hope*— a *hope* unclear as to whether it was for them as a couple or them as a species. "Help me understand these Monuments of Creation. I came here alone, but I didn't realize how much I needed you until we met." Damon thought her smile could light up half the continent below as he felt the aircraft begin its choppy descent from the clouds.

The elements met Damon right in the face as he slid the belly door open, causing him to recoil back into the aircraft in search of a layered jacket. Pulling her jump seat forward to reveal a space-saving compartment, Leah pulled out a multi-layered dark-grey jacket, handing it to Damon since it looked to be the larger of the two she had found while she put on the smaller one, zipping it all the way up to the top.

Charles W. McDonald Jr.

"Normally cold, but not this," she explained, stepping out of the craft onto the permafrost soil that felt more like concrete and steel pushing back against her soft leather, dark-brown boots.

"How long will they wait for us," Damon asked, looking back at the pilot, who was mulling around his aircraft, checking fluids that wanted to freeze solid inside the hand-held, polymer test cylinders.

"Not long.... Few hours."

Looking around and gathering his bearings, Damon looked to his right, seeing the interior of the bottom of the V-shaped mountain range while seeing sharper, taller, and more jagged mountains trailing off in a formation that splayed out across the frozen tundra. Before them lay hard, grey ground with clumps of clay stirred by very large footprints of beast and foul alike and no grass or trees to speak of. It made the walk treacherous on the ankles as they constantly had to avoid tripping and falling head-first into the permafrost.

After what felt like some fifteen to twenty minutes of walking, they could now see more clearly what had been vaguely recognizable from the air—the Monuments of Creation. Or, as Leah referred to them, the Minean Towers. Grey-green stones jutted out of the permafrost in ancient and monolithic concentric rings arranged in a three-quarter circle—surrounding a ring of nine off-white stone Humanoid figures. In the center of the formation lay what looked to be three ceremonial stones or altars—each with a shaft to receive a male counterpart piece. The shaft of the center altar looked slightly larger and more rounded than the two flanking stones, which had smaller, more slender shafts. As Damon walked the interior of the formation, carefully examining each shaft of each altar, he reverently brushed his fingertips along the surface of the ice-cold stone while Leah watched the alien's reaction before her.

"What you expected," she asked, carefully watching his reaction to this most holy and least understood site on Graelon. Noticing the runes on each of the altar stones dance and come to life, responding to Damon's touch, made her wonder if Damon was using magic or if it were merely an incredible reaction to this most-unusual alien.

"The similarities...," he began wondering how much he could or should share with her. "...There was a plan at work here, and I'm still strug-

Charles W. McDonald Jr.

gling to understand it."

"Describe differences," Leah urged as she pulled up beside him, walking where he walked, observing what he observed. Trying to see through his uniquely beautiful black eyes.

"The materials are different, but that makes sense. However, all of them used very hard and dense stone as if they expected this to stand for thousands if not tens of thousands of years. As if...?"

"If what," Leah attempted to clarify.

"As if they were trying to outlast...something."

"Outlast what? Damon, what hiding?"

"Have you heard the phrase *The Eye of Time* before?"

Recoiling and taking a few steps back, Leah brushed the hair from her face as a northerly wind practically slapped her head-on, causing her to brace herself against one of the off-white marble figures she and Damon now found themselves alongside. "That name comes up often in works describing the necessity for off-world, colonial outpost experiments."

"I bet it does. That makes sense." Another brute gale of bitter-cold wind met them head-on, causing Damon to pull Leah to him to instinctively shield her from the elements. "Let me show you something," he whispered into her ear, watching her respond with a smile despite the elements cutting into the core of her teeth.

As if he knew exactly where to look, Damon marched her to the outside perimeter of the stone formation on the back-side of the stone obelisks where his *Telekinesis* began moving the permafrost. While the use of magic was completely off the table, he'd hoped that his natural abilities would afford him some latitude from the Sentinels, but he'd never tried this before, so he was hoping for the best.

Looking left, then right, then behind and all around, Leah fully expected Sentinels to be upon them in mere moments if not before. "You can't!"

"I'm not using magic. Hold on." An instant later, and the rapid excavation had revealed the top of a massive quartz-like stone buried within the permafrost.

"I've dug before. How you know where look," Leah probed him, carefully watching the hard planes of his facial expressions, trying to read

Charles W. McDonald Jr.

this strangest of aliens.

"Like the others, Leah. Just like the others."

Clearly, Damon's off-world observations had given him the leg up on understanding these monuments, but perhaps she had something to offer he didn't already know. Taking him by the hand, Leah led him back to the center altar stone where its rune still danced, rejoicing with life, in the mid-day polar sunlight that would last weeks, given the planet's tilt and solar orbit in the Graelon star's planetary ecliptic plane.

Kneeling before the altar stone, she encouraged Damon to kneel with her, taking his right hand, guiding him to feel the interior walls of the shaft before them. With her right hand free, she reached into an interior pocket of her interior jacket, retrieving a polymer casting of what she was trying to show him. "You make casting before? Of others?"

Shaking his head as he knelt before the center altar, he watched as the dancing rune before him mocked his ignorance of the obvious as he felt the intimately familiar contours, in negative relief, press back against the brush of his fingertips along the interior of the shaft. "WOW," he exclaimed, though softly so. "How did I miss that?"

"Damon, why you come? Really," she probed, putting away her casting of the interior of the center shaft.

"I don't believe in life from lifelessness—creation from nothingness. I believe in a more technical answer. I'm here in search of that answer."

She could relate. The fact that he felt he needed to explain that told her that religion had spuriously espoused such beliefs—creation from nothingness—on the other worlds of Humanity too. Damon was curious—like her, *but was he, too, a scientist…?* "Story of Creation, what you thought…," she asked, carefully watching his reaction.

A head-shaking Damon searched for the words as the reality and weight of his role in the unmaking of *a throne of souls* now extrapolated to the unmaking of Man; he continued to feel the familiar contours of the mighty *Staff of the Invoker* pressing back against his touch within the center shaft of the altar stone at Graelon's version of the Monuments of Creation.

Charles W. McDonald Jr.

Chapter 25: A Present – Part III

(Damon's Manor, Kaleion, A Long Time Ago)

Perfect high cheekbones and all-too-familiar half-elven ears stared back at Dallia, who still, to this day, refused to see the beauty her beloved husband saw in her as she admonished her appearance in the full-length mirror of their master bedroom. Damon now out with Evanyil, no doubt, she had but precious moments to complete the final build tasks of her anniversary present, and while grateful for the solitude to complete the task, she despised the company he would be keeping at this time. *If that's where he really is. With Damon, who really knows...?* She didn't fear him cheating on her or violating her trust. She only feared Damon being Damon and all the vitriolic chaos that could entail. But, that's also why she loved him so. His free and indomitable spirit, added to his dedication, integrity, and immeasurable power, made him unique among unique. And, that's why this present had to be equally unique and indomitable to complement its new master.

Shifting her gaze upon the mighty, triple-helix, charcoal-blue artifact

Charles W. McDonald Jr.

of baleful vicissitude, she felt it stare back at her, mocking her futile attempts to diminish its already obscene power. She knew she'd already pushed the boundaries with her enchantments and the base metals used to construct this menacing relic, and now she feared it would be their ruin. She needed to instill in this beast a conscience—a soul mated to Damon to guide him in right versus wrong—not necessarily good versus evil, as she'd come not to believe in those things. Damon's influence, she supposed, but Damon was right. Good and evil were far too simple constructs to accurately describe the world around them.

She saw both in Damon and feared who and what he could become if not for the right guidance to nudge him this way or that. Circumstances and consequence had made ill of Damon, trodden on his very soul and on his very destiny.

She needed this mighty *Staff of the Invoker* to be there for him when and where she could not—to speak on her behalf and to protect her beloved husband from himself and those who would further corrupt him. She needed this staff to be a dark and fearsome light to a brighter future for Damon and a brighter version of Damon. She needed it to enhance the Damon who loved her so dearly and so unconditionally and subsequently protect against Damon-the-killer. Or, at least to protect Damon such that Damon-the-killer wasn't as necessary as he would otherwise be.

She had her work cut out for her as the aura of the mighty *Staff of the Invoker* made a dark and sinister shadow stretching behind her own reflection in the mirror—tangled up with her own shadow in ways most malevolent. "You're awful…," she muttered to the staff. "…And beautiful. Just like my husband." Turning away from the mirror, she began walking to the *Staff of the Invoker*, determined. "Let's see if we can make you better than my husband. Or, at least the better version of him."

Sitting crossed-legged down before the mighty staff as she'd done a little while ago in Damon's study when she'd first assembled all three helical rods together for the first time to build the enchantments that would hold all four individual pieces together as one unit, Dallia focused what little remained of her energy to finish the mighty *Staff of the Invoker*.

Sitting in the shadow of the staff's hateful aura, Dallia reached out to borrow and source the energy around her, the grounds, and her home-

Charles W. McDonald Jr.

land. Reaching into the Kaleion crust and below, she felt herself filled with the stream of life and the current of Arcane as she began to channel into the staff that which would protect Damon when and where she could not— hoping *it* would be there for him all the long days of his life.

Energy of planetary life crossed energy of starlight, carrying Dallia on its resonant waves as she channeled into the *Staff of the Invoker,* thinking only of the future.

Part 4: The Symmetry of our Universe

Charles W. McDonald Jr.

Chapter 26: The Starlight of Immortality

(Damon's Manor, Eden, Present Day)

The circular, tan clay seal burst to dust in Damon's hands as he summoned Illirian Starfire for the first time in as long as he could remember—its fine particulates carried on stratum motes of ruminations by the HVAC of his manor. Previously, she had watched over him with such insatiable curiosity and intrusiveness, he couldn't bear any further intervention into his life. However, she'd been as necessary to his success as rain was to the flower. Meddlesome or not, he needed Illirian Starfire in more ways than he could count—especially now, since Graelon and the Monuments of Creation.

Looking down at where clusters of tan dust had settled onto his study floor, Damon smelled her presence before he felt the touch of her fingertips as she wrapped her arms around him at the waistline. "I'm not used to you summoning me when your life isn't on the line." Spinning around in front of him with her hands now on his shoulders, Illirian clarified, "Your life isn't on the line, is it?"

Charles W. McDonald Jr.

"Not like it was on Earth, no."

"Then you summoned me for me." She smiled as bright as the Kaleion sun as her red-gold hair cascaded off bare shoulders in radiant waves of Damon's everlasting lust for her.

"Tell me what you know about the Monuments of Creation."

"You *didn't* summon me for me." She sighed—disappointed, though whether disappointed in him or disappointed in herself for believing he would ever want her for her was not entirely clear to her, *or* him. Retreating from him to sit on the edge of his desk, her cream dress in gilded scroll pressed against her body, accentuating a curve here and soft, perfect skin there.

"Illirian, please. For me?"

"What about for me?" As soon as the words escaped her lips, she regretted them, seeing Damon's raised eyebrows in response. She couldn't believe she'd said it either. Was her personal entanglement with Damon contaminating her ability to stay on task? Or, was it changing how she saw her job in relation to guiding Damon?

"Okay, that's fair," Damon offered. "This isn't a one-way relationship between us. What's on your mind?"

The immortality of her loveless life suddenly breaking down her walls like crumbled stone to ash, Illirian's tear-stained, gold eyes said it before the words escaped her soft lips: "I need you," she blurted to a sudden vacuum of silence that followed. "Seeing you on the floor dead like that. Damon, I had to summon everything I had to save you. I almost couldn't do it. I had to borrow…. You were almost too gone for even me to bring back. I can't have that. I need you to…." She didn't want to stop herself. She needed to say it. He needed to know, and he needed to know now! "… I needed you to know how I feel—before…."

"Before it's too late…," he finished her thought in much the way they did with one another when they spoke. "…You think I don't feel the same?"

"I don't know, Damon. Because, you've never told me. How *could* I know?!" Again, she thought about why Damon had taken out the Chairman. Why he'd allowed his rage to be channeled at the entity, specifically, causing her elevation. "Why did you elevate me so, Damon? For what purpose? Was it to have someone more powerful you could have to *use*?"

Recalling how they'd met, Damon pushed back. "If I recall correctly, you first engaged me to *use* me."

"I *hate* your memory," she huffed, turning her head to one side so she didn't have to look at him head-on.

"And, *I love you*." There it was. Everything she'd hoped for. Everything they had hoped for but had not been allowed. Damon's near death had changed things for him too. He loved Dallia. He loved Mira. And, he loved Mira Castille too. Whether weakness or strength or compulsion, he couldn't tell and didn't care. His love of each was very different from one another, but as he tried now to assess his long-put-on-hold love for Illirian Starfire, he realized his time was running out. Whether at the hands of the Master Plan, or God the Creator, or the Dragon of Darkness, or any other number of factors, the odds were stacked in favor of his death and it was coming for him whether he was ready for it or not. He wasn't ready to love again. He didn't want another relationship, but this relationship had been on his front doorstep for a thousand years and wouldn't bear another moment of insufferable and useless patience. These emotions had been withheld forever and for seemingly good reasons, but now all those reasons seemed moot.

The words finally spoken, she stood there blinking with her mouth twisted in figurative knots as she tried to process it.

"No fancy retort," Damon posed, cocking his head to one side as he examined her flesh, soul, heart, and brilliant mind.

Blink. Blink. Blink. "I've thought about this moment for so long, and it's nothing like I imagined."

"Sorry to disappoint you. I wasn't planning on professing my love for you today." He smiled, but he wasn't really kidding. He had something entirely else on his mind. He had summoned her for serious reasons—not that this wasn't serious too—just entirely the wrong kind of serious. Still, he knew what she meant, causing him to close the distance that had stood between them for far too long—figuratively and literally—as he positioned himself, standing between her legs as she still leaned against the edge of his desk.

Leaning into her, he took his time, letting her arms welcome him as they wrapped around his waist again as they had moments before. Slowly and delicately, draping his lips across hers, he felt the immortality of her loneliness pressing back in feverish waves of passion as her kiss became heavier and heavier, surrendering to him in ways she'd never thought possible. A kiss beget a caress beget a lick beget a moan as her legs wrapped around Damon, pulling him into her as clothes began to hit the floor in heaps of long-strangled abandon.

*   *   *   *

"You had to borrow what?" Damon randomly recovered the topic from out of the blue....

"What?" She knew but was trying to deflect. "You never answered my question," Illirian pried.

"There were and still are lots of unanswered questions between us. What's one more?" He smiled, but Damon knew—or thought he did—the one question she'd be coming back to.

"Why did you elevate me?"

Yep, that's the one, Damon thought, smiling at the satisfaction of being right even if it was the question he least wanted to answer. "Many reasons—not the least of which is that when I need you, I'm going to need the most powerful version of you there has ever been. Now's not the time for you to take light of your powers. Now is the time for you to stretch your skills like never before or we're all dead." He thought about it, and that answer wasn't really accurate. "...Or far worse than dead."

"I get it. There's a lot riding on us."

"You could say that." Damon pulled her close to him, so she could rest her head on his chest as they lay tangled in a sweaty heap on his bed. Her once-perfect red-gold hair spilled down around his face in matted, sex-soaked layers.

"Why do you think it took us this long to get to where we are now?" Illirian finally had him where she wanted him, and she wasn't letting him go until she got some answers to some long-held questions. Still, of all the things on her mind, the one thought pressing at the front of her consciousness was the image of his silhouette atop her when she eked out a tiny bit of

Charles W. McDonald Jr.

vision in the throes of the passion between them.

"Because you were sent to spy on me for one thing. You were the enemy for the longest time, and because I was never sure how far I could trust you."

Her mouth worked at the honesty on display, as she had to calculate her next response. "...But as your kind would say, wouldn't that make it more interesting?"

"I'm sorry—*my kind*...?!"

"You *know* what I meant!"

"I don't even know what *my* kind is, Darling." He practically threw her off him forcefully enough to send her half-way across the width of the bed as he got up, putting on his pants.

"I guess that makes two of us." She realized her just-spoken mistake aloud as she jostled herself back into a position where her head was resting on pillows against Damon's headboard. "Your points are valid, you know...."

"Of course, they're valid."

"No, I mean, when I think about what kept us apart or what kept us from getting to this point, I think about how I *used* you. How I never fully explained why you were doing this for me or that. How, I failed to show my full trust in you that must have led you not to trust me. That was my fault, Damon, and I'm sorry. I let you down, and you've been so good to me—risked so much for me."

Her honesty and ownership of her own failures turned him around to face her. "You've risked everything for me, and I won't ever forget it."

"We're so different from one another and yet so alike. It scares me," she realized, still blinking at the thought of what they'd done and the very long road of how they had got here.

Nodding in agreement, he realized in all the things she'd said between them, she'd never been more right. "You'll be watched closer than ever before now. You may even lose your lofty station because of this...." Damon motioned between them.

"We're both being watched, Damon. Surely you, of all people, know that."

No words were needed. He did know. Damon's *Distorting Web* made its first appearance between them in a long time as he came back to a prior question, "Can you share with me what you know about the Monuments of Creation?"

"Why is *this* so important to you, Damon?"

"Please," he urged with more than words—with eyes laden in the hope that he hadn't been intentionally abandoned to the wrath of his father by someone who *could* have done something about it.

A heavy sigh preceded real insight she knew she was not supposed to share: "The Key to the Abyss and the Key to Paradise are not yours to banter about...." Carefully, she watched his reaction, which was one of hanging on to her every word. "...But they are the keys you must seek out to bring about the unmaking you so desire."

Nodding his head, it all fit as disjointed pieces came together in his mind. The *Staff of the Invoker* plus the Key to the Abyss plus the Key to Paradise were all required, but he still didn't understand how the Seals fit into the equation. If the Seals brought about the End Times, what did the Monuments of Creation actually do? "What do these Monument sites actually do?"

"No one knows because they've never been used the way that you're trying to use them."

"Okay, how were they used before?"

She thought for a minute as an awkward blanket of silence fell between them. She didn't want to lie to Damon, but this was truly forbidden information, and she was fairly certain his *Distorting Web* wouldn't protect the content of their conversation.

"I'll ask again: why is *this* so important to you, Damon?"

"Because I have to know if God the Creator intentionally abandoned me to the whip of my father.... That's why!"

Damon's logic followed a long and winding arc, but it was entirely rational. "What if I could help you get an answer to the question you really seek instead of the whole Monuments thing?"

He thought about it for a minute, walking away from her to toss on a long-sleeve shirt before walking back to her. "I want to know the story of Creation. If you won't help me, I'll find the answers one way or the other. I just thought you wanted to help me."

"I *am* going to help you. I swear it. Do you believe me?" Now, she just had to prove it.

"Yes," he answered without a moment's hesitation, causing her to beam for him with her head among his pillows.

Her thoughts briefly drifted to how she could help him, and two answers quickly jumped into her mind. "What do you know about *Durial's Eye*," she asked, watching his eyebrows raise at that question.

"Not nearly enough. It was a manner of powerful divination." Thought upon thought raced to the front of his mind as he hung on her every word, wondering what information she'd held onto of *Durial's Eye*.

"Yes, but do you know how and why it was so powerful and able to see so far with such incredible clarity?"

Shaking his head at her in reply, his black gems begged her for every detail. This too was a critical piece of his Master Plan, and any insight she had would surely help.

"You, of all people, are the one most like Durial, Damon. You work closely with both magic and technology, and *Durial's Eye* requires equal talent in both. Magic sees the future while technology refines the vision like a great and polished lens to a telescope."

"Even though divination is the least of my capabilities, I can easily imagine the power it must have took to see so far with such clarity, but I'm having trouble with the technology piece of it."

"You've been so focused on power and source energy, you've overlooked some critical refining ideas and concepts. This isn't about massive energy sources, Damon. This is about using precisely the right tool for the job."

Damon wanted to understand, but her conversation thread was bearing a direction that wasn't quite making sense to him. First this way, then that, her story had an arc to it that defied logic, but he was still attentive and felt as if she had something important she needed to share—something she needed him to understand.

Too many secrets for too long.... "Only a part of me do you know...." Leaning forward, staring Damon in the eye, Illirian peeled back a veil of omissions before him. "Behold, I am Illirian Starfire, daughter of Jorah and Hannah, descendant of Grant and Sala, and of Durial and Fara, Ruler of

Rod of the Nine, Watcher of the Runes of Fate…," she paused, watching Damon's reaction as a silvery-blue flash of light produced a small blue-green star sapphire roughly the size of the palm of her left hand. "…And Guardian of *Durial's Eye*. You thought perhaps it was lost to the ages and ravages of time?"

"How could you have had this all this time and not told me?"

"Damon, you're one of the most dangerous living entities in this Universe. You elevated yourself to a deity. You've made stars and planets. Dark Knight of Magic, Wielder of the *Staff of the Invoker*, Author of Damnation, Maker and Destroyer of Worlds, you've killed tens of thousands of people—some ruthlessly so. I was terrified of sharing this with you…," she paused again, carefully gauging his response, as she batted her eyelashes seemingly innocent enough. "…And I'm still terrified." She could see he was still trying to piece it all together. There was so much omission and disinformation between them, she wanted to reduce that ledger a bit more. "It goes by another name…." Allowing the sphere to shift slightly in the palm of her left hand, it shone like a blue-green star as she continued, "It is also called, *The Starlight of Immortality*." She paused again, letting the name sink in as Damon moved closer to her and the relic. "It has certain properties to it. Neither solid nor gas nor liquid, it holds many secrets, not the least of which is to incredible longevity. I haven't been using magic to keep myself alive this long. *This* has been the secret of my immortality, and I'm giving it to you, Damon."

"You can't. If you were to use magic to do what this does, you wouldn't be able to stretch your powers as we both need you to do."

"My immortality is no longer a priority for me. Living for existing holds little value to me now. I will do as you ask and focus my magic like never before. But, as I said, you are the most like Durial I've ever seen—at least from the accounts I've read—and I always felt like this belonged to you. And so, I give it to you." Illirian allowed it to roll from her left palm into Damon's right. He immediately noticed the star within always remained face-up regardless of the position of the sphere.

"Hmmm," he let out as he felt the coolness of its presence in his hand. It held no weight and felt as if it had no mass but, in his hand, it shone even brighter than in Illirian's possession. The shift in his stance ac-

Charles W. McDonald Jr.

companied a waking vision he'd cursed long, long ago as a much clearer vision of a crystal lake appeared at the front of his mind's eye with a booming voice of Creation from on the other side of the lake, calling out his name specifically this time. A gleaming and fiery sword—not Excalibur—floated above the lake. And, a command rang out from it.

His feet weren't quite where he remembered as the vision vanished from his mind's eye, as if being sucked out like a vacuum, as if…. He needed time to think, but as he looked down into the palm of his right hand, *The Starlight of Immortality* looked back at him, as if awaiting either command or wish. He couldn't say which, but he felt its power already divining a course for all. "Was this used to make *Starfire*? Did you make *Starfire*?"

"How could you have known that? What just happened to you? It felt like you were no longer here for an instant."

"Did you make *Starfire,* and did you use *The Starlight of Immortality* to make it?"

"Yes…. It was one of the first things I did for The Chairman centuries ago."

"Did he ever tell you why he needed you to make it?"

"Never—and he specifically told me never to ask. But, I'm assuming *it* showed you why," she added, looking at the blue-green sphere now in Damon's possession.

"Not nearly enough," he chided, admiring her honesty even more than her beauty for the first time ever. "I could tell you how beautiful you are, and it wouldn't mean nearly as much to me as telling you how much I appreciate your sharing of things I know will cost you more than I can calculate."

He wasn't sure if her smile could outshine *The Starlight of Immortality*, but she sure was trying.

"Go on. You can tell me how beautiful I am…," she offered with a wink. "…I'll let you."

A silvery-blue flash of light caused *The Starlight of Immortality* to disappear from Damon's right hand as he crawled back into his bed beside Illirian. Holding her face in his hands, he commented, "I remember the moment we met."

"As do I. You nearly tried to kill me."

Charles W. McDonald Jr.

"I'm trying to tell you how beautiful you are."

"I'm sorry. Please continue...." She half-mocked with a grin, looking up at him with her half-underneath the weight of his body.

"I remember when I summoned the lightning I intended to use to kill you because of your name and the association of what that name meant, but I couldn't do it because I could never bring myself to destroy the most beautiful creation I'd ever seen. I accepted the lightning for myself because I'd rather die than destroy such a magnificent creation as you." Pulling her body into his—their legs entangled like a pair of scissors—Damon brushed her matted red-gold hair with his fingertips. "I have seen your hair look better though."

Suddenly he felt her knee him dangerously close to his balls.

"Okay, maybe I deserved that," he joked in her ear as she nuzzled her face into his neck.

"You were worth the wait," she whispered as a tear of joy hit her pillow beneath her.

"So were you," Damon whispered, still stroking her hair as he began to kiss her earlobe. Inside, his thoughts drifted to the *Starlight of Immortality* and how he would need to make an even more powerful variant of *Durial's Eye* to power, fuel, and guide events that must be for his Master Plan to succeed.

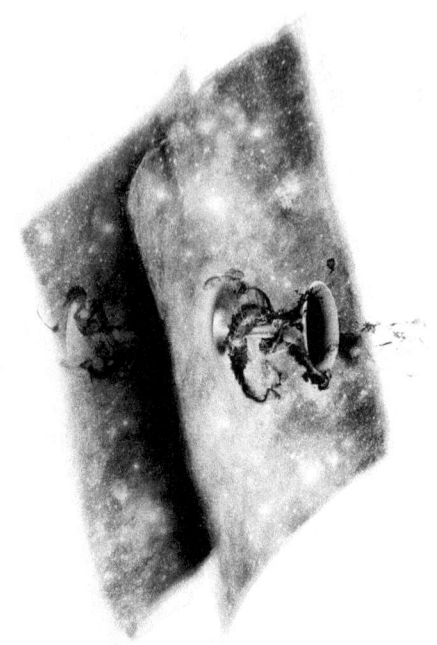

Chapter 27: Origins of Déjà Vu

(The West Texas Plains, Earth, Present Day)

oading NATO 5.56 armor-piercing rounds into 30-round magazines with quick-load compression tools, Mira Castille tapped her right foot to *Lynyrd Skynyrd's – Sweet Home Alabama*, fending off another provocative smile from LT. He was married with kids, but he hit on her with frequent regularity. She swore if they ever let her near a phone again, she was gone, but they kept that option away from her as if their lives depended on it—as if they had been specifically warned.

"I get that you're a redneck prepper and all, but can't we listen to something else when we're working around the guns?"

"Habits and rituals are a good thing, Sweet Tits," LT offered with another pseudo-creepy smile that made her skin crawl. She made no effort to correct his term of endearment for her—if that's what it could be called, though he never used that term when his wife was around. "They keep us all from going BOOM," he continued to explain visually with his hands making an outward motion akin to a mushroom cloud.

She tried not to smile, but LT was funny and well-intentioned—most of the time. How she had always seemed to find herself around complicated and less-than-sweet men she couldn't really index, but sometimes she just wished for the uncomplicated life of being a pregnant wife to a boring but intelligent husband. Her time around Damon had ruined her. Now, she could no longer see any man as attractive unless he had an IQ equal to hers, and those were damn scarce in the first place. Out here, it was like asking for a rose to bud from a rotting tomato.

"Whatcha thinkin 'bout??" She was an impossible woman to read—far more so than his wife, but also way more of a challenge as he saw it. Still, her facial expressions said she'd thought of something funny, and curiosity was definitely a weakness for him.

LT's voice—somewhere between gruff and husky—settled on her earlobes like gritty sawdust from the woodworking tent two down from their current location. Even hearing LT's ever-present, white-trash slang reminded her of Damon's absence. At least Damon could use complete words and sentences—most of the time. "Oh, nothing...," she lied, trying to suppress her sarcasm as the next southern rock song began blasting over the twenty-year-old boom box powered by a DeWalt generator.

"Got those clips ready yet," the 6'3" stony-faced Dakota chirped at them, riding her ass as usual, as he came up from behind her, placing his burly and gross hands on the butt of her Levis®.

LT didn't say shit as usual for him—just looking around the tent in a feigned attempt at finding an excuse to go do something else besides loading clips as if to convey he wasn't interested in getting done what Dakota felt was priority. Clearly LT was still searching for his balls to push back against the new alpha male of the group.

She couldn't take Dakota any more than LT could, but sooner or later she was going to have to hand him his balls if he kept touching her like that. Dakota was clearly trying to assert his claim on what he *thought* was his. Shifting away from his butt grip to the just-vacated side of the armory table where LT had just been, Mira transitioned to 7.62mm rounds and high-capacity banana clips for the AK-47 knock-offs from China. They might have been cheap fakes, but they were deadly, and they always worked.

Charles W. McDonald Jr.

Still, the leaders of the group always favored the American-made firearms—
perhaps as a status symbol, but most just looked down their nose at the
knock-offs they relegated to the new members they'd been recruiting from
every corner of the West Texas plains and beyond. From twenty-five to now
over two hundred, they'd grown their little tent fiefdom of doomsday preppers as if something big was about to happen they had particularly keen insight into and hadn't fully yet shared. All their little attempts to build these
underground bunkers out of eighteen-wheeler shipping containers made her
laugh at the futility of it internally.

She probably knew more than they did, given her knowledge of Damon and his Master Plan, but still the pieces weren't falling into place for
her like they used to. "You still haven't told me—or anyone else—what all
this is about. What aren't you sharing with us?" Mira's soft but pensive tone
still cut through the quiet tension in the tent with ease, causing Dakota's
pecs to pop and LT's eyes to shift as if to avoid her indelicate probing.

"Don't you worry, Sweetie," Dakota offered with a wink and a smile
that definitely met the creepy threshold LT had failed to meet earlier as he
continued, "I'll protect you."

"Uh. Gross." It was an involuntary response she regretted as soon
as it escaped her lips, but she couldn't take it anymore. She had to get away
from him. Leaving the folding armory table and the tent behind, she was
met head-on by the West Texas wind, stale with the arid scent of excessive
chicken farm excrement and dirt whipping into every crevasse of her gums
and teeth.

"You need to learn some respect," Dakota barked in her ear with his
dirty breath on her neck as he came up hard from behind her, grabbing her
around the waist to pull her back to him.

As soon as the right heel of her boot lifted, she felt it driving hard
through the top of Dakota's boot, making the powerful déjà vu crystallize
with such voracity that she immediately fell to the dirt landscape of the
West Texas plains with both her fists balled up against her temples. The
sharp pain of Mira's heel thrusting down through the top of his foot caused
Dakota to involuntarily let her go, wincing in pain as he writhed around on
the dirt, still clutching at her. Kicking and pawing at Mira, Dakota tried to
get a grip on her, but she was up in a flash with her Glock® 19 pulled from

her back and pointed straight at him, even as her mind flashed with vision upon vision of her in scenarios that simply could not be her. Her left hand again pressed to her temple, she tried to gather herself before the scruffy and grimy, dark-haired Dakota finally got the better of her.

"BITCH! What's with you anyway," he yelled at her as others quickly gathered around them. Already trying to take control of the situation, LT urged Mira to muzzle down her Glock®.

"She's fucking crazy. We need to start keeping her away from the guns," Dakota bristled, looking up the wrong end of Mira's muzzle in a face that was far more determined than afraid as he saw the gun begin to twitch in her right hand.

Something felt very wrong. She felt the wound in her side throb in agony as memory upon memory collided in her mind like intersecting threads of differing destinies.... A magnificently forged winged-creature leaning over a wounded Damon, herself standing inside Damon's Austin house remembering this very moment, shooting herself, Damon's manor on Eden, Kellen, all of it firing like short-circuited synapses in her mind, causing her to fall to her knees as her trigger finger tightened, squeezing off the chambered-round that instantly separated Dakota from the life he once knew—the hollow-point round mushrooming right after passing through the soft tissue of Dakota's left eye, shattering the framework of his ugly and massive nose as his skull exploded in cranial gore.

"MIRA! STOP," LT ordered as another round fired one behind the other, putting two shots into LT's abdomen, causing another memory of a memory to flash in her mind of her squeezing off rounds at the beautiful, winged creature standing over a fatally-wounded Damon.

Future colliding with both past and present, the continuum threads overlapped one atop the other inside Mira's mind, intersecting in violent collisions of déjà vu. "Damon," she cried out in tears. "Where are you? I need you." Everywhere in her thoughts she searched for the rationale to explain their separation, and everywhere she found nothing but confusion and emptiness.

Her weapon kicked out of her hands, she found herself face-down and hog-tied in the West Texas soil as several came to disarm her and aid LT. Weeping into the soil beneath her, a memory of a memory of Damon

kissing her not far from here provided answers less than welcome as she desperately sought out the origins of her déjà vu.

Chapter 28: Bad Intentions

(The South China Sea, Earth, Present Day)

Black field fatigues with navy-blue lettering now felt as comfortable on her as her tactical knife, or the M4, in her hands. Still, the ivory-painted steel and grey bunks of the twelve-man crew compartment loft of the USS CVN Ronald Reagan gave Michelle pause as to what the hell they were doing out here in the middle of the South China Sea. Yes, it was all according to Rena's plan, of course, but Rena didn't explain shit unless given little-to-no option. Patriot or not, she didn't like being used—by anyone—immortal and beautiful or not.

"I can almost hear your mind working from way over here," Lawna mocked the two-foot distance between them in the otherwise cramped crew compartment, but Michelle was pensive, and that meant her mind was going ninety to nothing.

"There are plenty of other bunks you *could* be warming with that sweet ass of yours," Michelle mocked with a wink, but her mind *was* running ninety-to-nothing.

Normally bunked with other Operators, on-board the Reagan they 'should' have been bunked with other female crew, but their mission was so delicate and compartmentalized, they wouldn't have the clearance to even be in the same accommodations with them. They lucked out; they were alone with the whole crew compartment to themselves, and that hadn't gone over that well with others on the ship hot-racking the rest of the crew space. Still, it afforded them a level of privacy, intimacy, and thought much needed before their trip downrange.

Charles W. McDonald Jr.

A knock at the berth door to the compartment caused Michelle to snap out of it as her boots hit the steel flooring to answer. A twenties petty officer couriered a message on JSOC letterhead, folded in thirds, and sealed. "Ma'am," he offered at attention.

"You're dismissed," Michelle granted, breaking open the JSOC orders. She assumed them more fine-grained intel and instructions and wondered why they'd be coming to her instead of the team lead, but then that question was answered as soon as....

Another knock at the bulkhead door, which had barely had time to shut, took her eyes off the JSOC letterhead.

"What the fuck," she mouthed aloud, practically yanking the door off its hinges to see another courier just barely in her twenties with brunette hair tight up in a bun underneath her fatigues cap, carrying a beautifully-wrapped but obviously-shaped object in her left hand—at least its muzzle was in the courier's left hand. From the length, width, and general shape, it was obviously a tactical rifle wrapped in off-white, baby-shower wrapping paper of all things.

"Ma'am," the hazel-eyed, brunette courier offered, coming to attention for her.... "This just came for you via Osprey."

Furrowed brow linked with pensive thoughts and a curl of her lips preceded Michelle's question she almost wished she had back as soon as it left her lips. "Was this the only thing brought by the Osprey?"

The question registered as beyond curious with the courier, whose eyes darted left then right then down as if deciding how much—if anything—she could relay.

"It wasn't a trick question," Michelle interrogated, quickly registering her fatigue name badge, "...Marshal. Was there anything or anyone else on the Osprey I need to know about?"

"No Ma'am," Petty Officer Marshal replied, stiffening her back, looking Michelle dead in the eyes.

"Dismissed," Michelle announced to a sharp salute back at her as she shut the bulkhead door again.

"Figures," Lawna pouted from her bunk right beside Michelle's.

"What figures?"

"Always her favorite.... You get a beautiful new tactical riffle, and I get bupkis."

"Yiddish doesn't become you," Michelle glowered from a few feet away.

That prompted a middle finger from her dirty-blonde, hard-bodied wife.

"Neither does that." Michelle snickered, tearing into the baby-shower-paper-wrapped tactical riffle, which quickly appeared a far superior and black-satin gleaming version of a customized M4 with an already under-mount-attached M203 grenade launcher affixed to the M-LOK® Magpul MOE carbine-length handguard with a BlueForce® Vickers satin-black sling already mounted. The M4 and M203 metal itself had perfectly symmetrical anodized striations that improved both looks and grip functionality.

"Uh…. You suck…," Lawna belted in disgust, looking at the sleek, dark beauty of it: linked laser 20x-scope on the top rail with two position elevation and wind adjustment, under-mounted LED flood-light pistol foregrip below the M203, and a second tactical laser mounted on the side. It was even better than the SEAL-issued variant sitting on her bunk, which needed to be cleaned before going downrange.

"Oh, what do we have here?" Michelle piqued Lawna's interest while digging around the bottom of the package near the butt-stock.

"What is it?" Now interested enough to get on her feet, Lawna began walking toward Michelle and the bulkhead door.

"Looks like Christmas for two." She handed Lawna a small, perfectly-shaped square, composed in fine grain with a silver apple on top.

In less than two seconds, it was disassembled to reveal an iWatch®, which Lawna flipped over to the silver backing where the inscription read, 'I love you too. Happy Graduation. RR.' Putting it on, it powered on to brand new pictures of their babies in vivid HD color, causing Lawna to burst into tears, now leaning against her wife.

"Trade ya," Michelle whispered into Lawna's earlobe.

"Not a chance!" She snickered through tears, pulling away. "Well, let's see it. Pull it all the way out. I want to see."

Slinging her satin-black, sleek custom M4 over her right shoulder and threading the Vickers sling through her left hand where it overwrapped right where her left hand naturally mated to the pistol foregrip, she punched the red-dot laser, pointing an empty-chambered weapon at her wife, watching the laser paint her wife's pretty chest and face.

"FUCK! You're a *bad intentioned*, bitch!" Lawna smiled at her wife, but she knew Michelle better than anyone, as she considered the significant threat Michelle posed with her natural abilities and now this.... She was truly a force to be reckoned with.

The light came on in Michelle's thoughts at her wife's compliment. "Throw me that tactical knife."

"What did I say?"

End over end, the tactical knife flew the short distance between them, landing handle-first in Michelle's right hand as she started to carve its new name into the folding buttstock of her brand-new present.

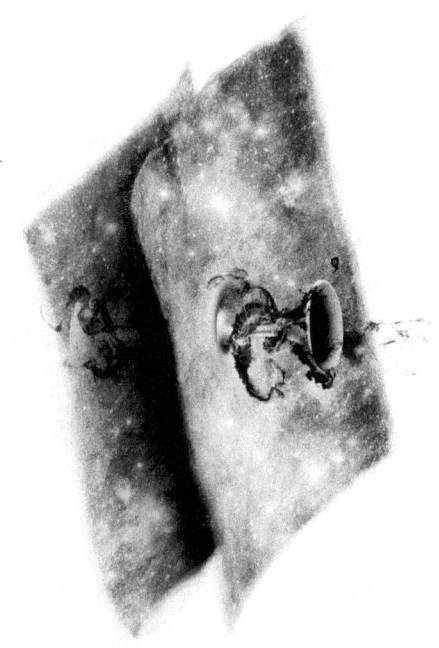

Chapter 29: The Quantum Wave

(The West Texas Plains, Earth, Present Day)

No longer hog-tied, but certainly no longer free to move around either, Mira sat cross-legged in her jeans on the dirt floor of the smallest tent in the plains settlement jutting out from the desert in splotchy, fatigued warts on West Texas soil. No one to keep her company save two of the biggest and baddest men in the camp dedicated to watching over her to ensure she lived *just* long enough....

Only fitting for taking the lives of the two most powerful leaders in the group. LT hadn't survived the two abdominal shots—perhaps he might have if she hadn't insisted on using hollow-point rounds, but Mira was never one to shoot to wound. She was a shoot-to-kill kinda gal, but she never thought she'd ever shoot someone, not while entirely right in her own mind. Not someone who didn't deserve it.... She still didn't know how to explain it, and she was lucky—damn lucky—they hadn't retaliated against her yet and killed her too. She deserved it. Yet, no one had called the sheriff.

Charles W. McDonald Jr.

Clearly, they didn't want the law around anymore than she did.

Muffled discussion outside the tent snapped her to attention as she tried to focus her hearing in that direction without getting up from the dirt floor. The roar of 392-HEMI® Jeep® Grand Cherokee roaring to life, after just having shut down a moment before, choked out part of the conversation just before the tent flap seam parted to reveal a slender man with somewhat beady, hazel eyes. She'd seen him only once before—the other day when he'd first joined the group. Cocking her head at him sideways in curiosity, she never forgot a name-face relationship, "It's Howard, isn't it? Aren't many Howards running around here."

Brushing his scraggly, dirty brown hair, filled with West Texas plains grit, in his examination of her still sitting cross-legged on the dirt floor, his eyes sparkled with a curious fire not seen in the other men always trying to get in her pants at every opportunity. "Aren't many Dakotas or LTs now either."

"Touché," she smirked, though she didn't like being reminded of her murderous rampage.

Something was different about him. The way he looked at her like he was examining her—and not in a sex-driven kind of way. He looked like he was assessing her from the way his eyes darted to her seated position, to her eyes, and the way he looked to be analyzing her body language.

"You're not like these GED thugs. Where did you go to school," she asked, still remaining seated. She didn't want to appear a threat to him. Though, the thought of her even thinking about her own threat level in such a way made her wonder what Damon had done to her and how radically he had changed her.

"OU," he replied with a knowing smile, somewhat cheekier than she cared.

"Ugh! Hook 'em!" She had a genuine distasteful look about her face, as if she'd just swallowed a stink bomb and it had gone off in her palette.

"Yeah well, BOOMER SOONER! And, fuck you too!"

"Nice comeback. Was your degree in English Literature?"

"Actually, Particle Physics with a double major in Behavioral Psychology. That's why I'm here. To a person I spoke to about you, you are careful, methodical, intelligent, and considerably full of sass. That doesn't speak to a person suddenly going off and killing two leaders of this group. Care to tell me what happened?"

"Why are you *really* here, Howard?"

"I just told you."

"No, you didn't."

"Very well. They want to kill you. The vote's already been taken, and your days here are numbered unless I can figure out what happened and make some sense of it. I volunteered to be your counsel—so to speak."

"You didn't say one of your degrees was in Criminal Law."

"I didn't, because it isn't. Still, I volunteered, so don't make a fool out of me." His eyes still darted around like he'd had five too many cappuccinos less than half an hour ago with enough surplus nervous energy to sell back to the ERCOT electrical grid.

She paused for a moment, rising from the dirt floor to look Howard in the eye. If he was lying, he was a great liar. His facial expression was dead-pan serious. "Ever experienced déjà vu?"

Howard's right hand went immediately to his upper lip where it massaged a two-day-old stubble just underneath a modest nose with a slight, left-leaning hump from where it had been broken as a child. "They said you were grabbing at your head during the shooting. Like your temples. That was the déjà vu…?!"

Only nodding her head in response, Mira struggled to trust him even though all his signals seemed genuine.

"Ever experienced that kind of thing before?" His nervous energy seemed to be ebbing as he sat, rocking back and forth with his eyes more solace than before, motioning for her to sit back down with him.

Sitting back down with him, facing him from barely two feet away, she continued, "…Never. Not like that."

"I told you my background. What's yours, Mira? What did you study at ole' vomit-orange Hook 'em?"

A sneer preceded, "Quantum Mechanics and Exobiology."

"Well, I'm sure we could spend all day shooting the shit about wave-particle duality, but I'm more interested in the Exobiology path. What made you interested in that field of study?"

Charles W. McDonald Jr.

"Call it an ex-boyfriend residual."

"Care to elaborate?"

"Not particularly."

"Okay then…." He was trying to help her, but this was going to be like pulling teeth unless he could build a rapport with her. And, some level of trust. Having a Sooner and a Longhorn working in tandem together was like asking for Hell not to melt the snow in the snowball that just fell into the Pit.

She could feel his honesty. She could sense it. Howard was a genuine man, and she could appreciate that. Damon had fostered that in her. "Look, Howard…. You seem nice and all—for an Okie—but why are you sticking your neck out for me? You just got here."

"Actually, I'm from Phoenix. How about you?"

A heavy sigh preceded, "…Houston."

"About the same distance as me, metaphorically and in miles too," he offered with a somewhat disarming smile that made her chuckle.

"Fair enough. What do you need to know to save my life?"

"I'd imagine, they need some comfort level that your déjà vu isn't going to kill another member of the group. Even then, they'll never let you carry a gun."

"Don't blame them. I wouldn't either."

"Maybe it would be enough if we could explain the origin of your déjà vu…. Care to talk Physics for a minute, Mira?"

"What's on your mind?"

"Funny you should put it that way…. What are your thoughts on Edgar Mitchel's experiment on Apollo 14?"

"Which one?"

"I think you know which one I'm talking about."

"The ESP one…?"

"That's a common misperception, and you know it."

"Okay, what about it?"

"I'm far more interested in the time it took to respond being half of what would be physically possible under the natural laws of our Universe afforded by Special Relativity and the speed of light."

"That is an interesting tidbit of knowledge." She had an idea of where he was going, but zero idea of what this had to do with helping him save her life.

"So, regardless of the accuracy of the experiment, Mitchell would have to have sent his answer the very instant the operator on Earth was physically flipping the card. There wouldn't have even been time for the message from the operator, telling him he had flipped the card, and the answer from Mitchell was already in flight. That's either one hell of an intuition or he was sensing the message from 240,000 miles away. What communication vehicle do we both understand that can allow for this?"

"The Quantum Wave," Mira replied without hesitation, but she still wasn't following Howard's logic. She only hoped he was going somewhere meaningful with his illustration.

"Also known as entanglement communication or nonlocality communication," Howard added, smiling.

"I'm not following how this saves my life, Howard."

"This might be more important than saving your life."

"Pardon me."

"This might involve saving us all…." Shifting in his position on the dirt floor beside her to close about half the distance between them, Howard looked down, deep in thought.

"What's happening here," Mira asked, looking up at him through her brunette bangs while her head was tilted down to match Howard's.

Her looking at him caused him to look up at her—now engaged eye to eye. "Can you explain your déjà vu to me? What did you see? What made it feel like déjà vu?"

Mira tried to recall her visions one by one, wondering how much she could share with Howard before he thought she was insane. "I saw a version of myself shooting someone I'd never seen before to save my ex-boyfriend's life and felt her kill me in the process. I saw a version of myself looking out a window, feeling my ex-boyfriend behind me, and experiencing it as if it was really me who was there, but it couldn't have been me because that particular scene had never happened with me before. These other versions of me, I don't know how to explain them except…."

"Unless they were another timeline, another dimension, or another Universe…." He didn't really have to finish her thought. Her mind had already gone there in her solitude before, but hearing Howard say it told her she really *wasn't* losing her mind.

"What do you think is the most likely possibility?" She didn't know and she didn't think he did either, but just hearing his input would have been helpful in her eyes.

"We assume entanglement works across dimensions, but we know it works across time because we know it works across distance and they are one and the same according to Einstein. I'm not sure what odds to put on the other Universe theory. I'd only be guessing. So, the other timeline makes the most sense to me."

She nodded then looked him in the eyes, watching and observing carefully how seriously he was taking her story as fact. "Why do you think the nonlocality communication occurred? What triggered it?"

Putting his right index finger in the air as soon as the question parted her lips, Howard added, "That's the question I've been wondering for quite some time...," he paused again in thought, looking at her as he tried to piece it together for the both of them. "Can I share a story with you?"

"Please...."

He paused a moment, licking his parched lips. "I remember being in my kitchen, standing exactly eighteen inches from the door of my fridge on its left side, standing right in front of the utensils drawer. I was a child when I first experienced this vision, and we didn't have a fridge that looked anything like the one in my vision. Nor did our kitchen in my childhood look anything like the kitchen in my vision. I experienced this exact same moment a few years ago in the house I had before coming to this place with the exact same refrigerator and the exact same kitchen. I remember I was making a peanut butter and jelly sandwich. Strawberry preserves to be precise."

"What does this have to do with me or entanglement or my déjà vu?"

"Because in the very next moment—just as soon as I realized it was déjà vu and I had experienced that very moment before as a child, the phone rang. It was my aunt, telling me my uncle Paul had just passed away a few minutes before."

"Wow!" She didn't have the words, but she was still struggling to follow.

"We were close—Paul and I. He looked after me from time to time when I was a child. He stood up for me. Protected me. He was an honorable man."

"I'm sorry."

"Don't be. She said he didn't suffer. My point is that this thread through space and time held a powerful link to me. Powerful enough to communicate across nearly thirty years in my timeline. I just didn't have the knowledge or foresight enough to comprehend it in time to do anything with that brief glimpse of knowledge."

"You think I've seen the future," Mira surmised with her pretty eyes blinking in consideration of all things Howard and the thoughts he'd invoked in her.

"What I think is that there was a source for these events—the other end of the entanglement. I think it was severed when you were killed—or rather future you was killed." He didn't know, but he had a hunch, and his hunches were far better than most. "I think the communication link snapped back across time and space like a snapped rubber band, colliding inside your mind. I bet it felt confusing as hell—a lot like a short circuit in your brain. That might explain you holding your head at the temples when you were struggling to come back to reality and this timeline. It probably felt very real—the other you in the other timeline."

Mira was searching for the words—merely nodding at Howard's detailed supposition. Watching him scratch his neck with his right hand, she wondered how, or if, any of this knowledge could be conveyed to the people who literally held her life in their hands. *And, even if it could, would it make a difference?* "What you're describing makes sense to me, but I don't know if it will make sense to them. They'll probably think we're both crazy."

"Howard…," Mira paused, looking at the man with odd little quirks that made him uncomfortable around her yet comfortable in conversation—especially on complex topics—trying to assess how such a man found his way here. "…What brought you here? You're clearly not like the others."

"You noticed, huh?" A forced smile for Mira preceded a long exhale from Howard.

"It's still not easy for me." He had to visibly stop himself from

Charles W. McDonald Jr.

scratching the back of his matted hair again. "Lots of therapy as a child and into my young adulthood still hasn't made me comfortable around others. I've always been more at peace on my own."

"Then why in God's name would you ever come hang out with a bunch of very intense people like doomsday preppers?"

"Well, that story I shared with you about my déjà vu and my uncle Paul…it wasn't my only case of that, and this time I was older, wiser, and hopefully in time to act on it."

"I don't understand. Tell me. What's going on, Howard?"

"I had a vision of me in my Jeep®, with you, and there were coordinates on my navigation, not a city or town—longitude and latitude. I started driving toward those coordinates, but before I got to them, I came upon this encampment and you."

"Now, you're scaring me, Howard. What makes you think that driving into your vision was the right thing to do? Why not go to the other side of the world—be as far away as you possibly can?"

"Because, I felt it in my soul that I had to save you. That I had to save you to save us all…. This ex-boyfriend you were protecting. Was this the Damon I've heard the others talk about?"

"Where did you hear that name? Who was talking about Damon, and what did they say? How am I supposed to save us all?"

He knew he couldn't share all of his déjà vu with her because she'd freak out, and he might very well, too, but there was an important thread they needed to drive to ground. "Based on everything I've heard about this Damon from the others, I think *he* might be the powerful link, driving the quantum wave of communication to the you of now. Or, at least he's driving the fluid dynamic wave in a timeline closely tied to you. Your quantum entangled wave riding atop, or alongside, his. And, *that* is the defense I think they might just buy that saves your life." He smiled nonchalantly as if mildly appreciating his own brilliance—if ever so briefly.

Mira knew Damon worth her own death, but that didn't make her fear of death any less palpable in this moment. She just wanted her death—if it had to be—to be justified and meaningful. Closing her eyes, she tried again to reconcile her feelings for Damon with the justification of their separation in her thoughts. An empty void of rationale mocked her back.

Charles W. McDonald Jr.

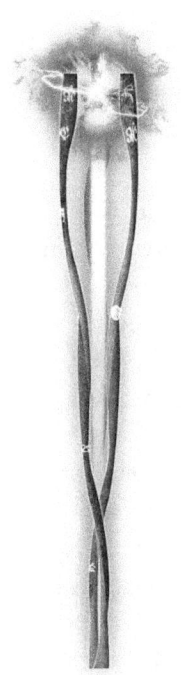

Chapter 30: The Monster We Need

(Damon's Manor, Kaleion, A Long Time Ago)

Flashes of soft and brilliant golden curls racked his brain from moments before as he sought out the justification for his bile behavior. He said nothing as he passed through the foyer, ascending the circular staircase to the quiet of his sanctum above. He could still feel the air hiss and crackle around him just outside his flesh—a physical indicator of the balance of power just disrupted.

The illusionary field transformed around his shape, allowing him to pass into his secret study. There, he expected to find Banthis, but he'd smelled another perfume when just outside the study, so he wasn't entirely shocked to see Illirian Starfire laying on the sofa in his study with her feet toward the false entrance, so she could see him coming.

"I came to see if I could understand…," she breathed with a long, deliberate pause, now beginning to stand and approach him—carefully and

Charles W. McDonald Jr.

with reserve.

"What is there to understand? I'm a monster. But you knew that."

"Damon, there are many different kinds of monsters. Some we need. Some we must kill."

"I'm the latter."

"No, Damon. You are not."

"Why are you really here, Illirian? Must you be here now, of all times?!"

"I must. Yes. Especially now," she hissed at him, circling him, her eyes burning into him, forging this very moment of this image of him into her mind in perpetuity. "Her name was Lis by the way. In case you're wondering."

"Lis." He acknowledged the name of the innocence he'd stolen. Corrupted. Destroyed. "Nothing can be done for her now."

"That was a very, very high price you just placed upon your soul. A very black scar you just placed upon our relationship. I want to know if it was worth it."

"I guess we'll find out. Was there anything else, Illirian?"

Approaching close enough to place her hands on either side of his face, she cupped his cheeks, cradling him so he couldn't look away from the gaze of her golden eyes—her red-gold hair spilling down upon the crevasse of his neck and scapulae. "I'm still struggling to understand you, Damon. Before Dallia, you were wild, nearing on chaotic but with logic misunderstood and misread by others. After Dallia, you were an ascending version of yourself—boundlessly capable and incalculably careful. Now, you are but a shell of that once-great version of yourself."

"A great man once told me that you can't absorb someone as powerful as Dallia's soul into your life and not expect her to change a great many things about you. That I'm becoming part her, and she's becoming part me. That with Dallia there were additional layers to me. I guess my little piece of Dallia made a massive and devoted difference in my life and what I could have become. Without Dallia, those additional layers have been stripped away, revealing the true character underneath."

"Those sound like the words of Goldenbow, but it doesn't surprise me that you'd seek counsel from an assassin. Granted, he has the mind and character of someone slightly admirable," Illirian chided with a half-smile, still trying to counsel Damon in her own way and in *his* own time. "I need to know: what was the goal of all this, Damon…?"

"All you need to know is that most of what I do is for Dallia. Not all. I'm still a selfish man. But most."

"And you think Dallia would approve of what you did to Lis?"

No. He most certainly did not think that. But he didn't need to say it. His eyes already said it when they looked to the floor, seeing Illirian's shapely feet and heels alongside his black leather boots. Grabbing her by her elbows, he mustered the strength to look her in the eyes. "I need to be alone."

"Banthis did this to you. You didn't do this on your own. You wouldn't. I know you better."

"Everything I do, I do of my own choosing."

"I didn't say you didn't choose this. I was merely trying to say that Banthis influenced this decision of yours."

"Illirian, I mean it. I need to be alone right now." This time, he squeezed her elbows with enough emphasis to cause her to step back away from his iron grip.

"Is *she* your new *hope*, Damon? Because *hate* is all I see in her. Vitriolic, seething hatred…."

Her words lashed at his flesh already raw by his own actions moments before, stinging in the accuracy of their landing atop the scars of hate that burdened him since childhood.

"She knows what I need most now, and she is most capable of delivering that."

"Is *hate* what you need most now, Damon? That's all she'll be able to give you. *Hate* and disappointment." Turning away from him physically, emotionally, and metaphorically, Illirian Starfire vanished before him though her scent lingered. Leaving Damon to sit in his chair, finally alone as he'd once so desired only moments before. The sight, smell, and sound of Lis still searing into his memories…forever.

"What a monster I've become…. What have I done?"

Charles W. McDonald Jr.

The memory of her conversation just after the death of Lis still haunted her with frequent regularity. *A failing near the top of her list of great failures with Damon*, she considered. He hadn't entirely dug the great pit he now found himself in at that time and was far more salvageable then. Now, it would require her greatest sacrifice to bring back Damon from the brink, if it was even possible at all. Her elevated station made many more things possible now, but it might very well be her last act in such a position.

With her love for Damon now finally expressed, she teetered on the brink of being an instrument in Damon's Master Plan or being either a casualty or obstacle of it. She was at this crossroads of her own actions as much as those of Damon, and she had to set a few things right that only she could.

White light pouring in all around, this place of hallowed souls and energy most sacred, she never felt less safe here than now. The apparition materializing before her in white, gold, and blue complemented long red curls half-way down her back with soft lips and blue eyes she looked to the new Chairwoman with both curiosity and *hope*.

(Damon's Manor, Eden, Present Day)

"That closely resembles the artifact described in Xaldran's Tome, described as *Durial's Eye*. If accounts are to be believed," Radin recalled, eyeing his father sidelong. "Where did you find it?"

"Illirian possessed it all this time. She never told me how long she had it, but a fair supposition would be at least a thousand years or more. She's older than me, you know." From his fourth-floor balcony they stood side by side against the elegant, carved railing as father and son, planning together the future of the Master Plan. *The Starlight of Immortality* hovering inches above his right palm, Damon peered into its star sapphire blue shell, looking into it, trying to understand how *Durial's Eye* worked. As it had each time before, an icy, cold-blue vapor trailed from the bottom of the sphere to contact his palm. Part technology, part magic was how Illirian described it. But like fine and exact measurements for a moist cake, knowing how much of which ingredient applied in what way, made all the difference in

Charles W. McDonald Jr.

the world. Damon's knowledge of this powerful relic was nascent at best; he had to become a master before scaling up its powers. "What does your instinct, bolstered by Xaldran's Tome, tell you about how it works?"

"I was going to ask you the same. You told me it's a supersolid. What does that mean exactly?"

"There are several states of matter. Solid, gas, liquid, and so on. Supersolids represent a fourth state of matter comprehensive of fluid and solid—really more like a superfluid with its Zero-Point-driven vacancies of space ordered into a coherent, frictionless flow."

"Yeah, that was a little over my head, Father." His steel-blue eyes shimmered at the prospect of understanding and growing his knowledge alongside Damon. He wasn't fully caught up to Damon, but he was vastly beyond the budding prodigy he was but just over a couple of years past. He was already dangerous, but he hoped Damon would make him…immortal. "Why don't we start with the Zero-Point piece?" He knew that a sensitive subject with his father, who didn't like discussing the energy source that made him god-like, and Damon had held a tight-lipped secret.

Sipping his stubby but wide and curvy, crystal snifter of brandy, Damon's black gems flashed as they transitioned their fixation from *The Starlight of Immortality* to the grey-blue eyes of his son. "You're not ready for that yet."

Relaxing his fingers around his own brandy snifter in an outward gesture of relent, Radin shrugged. "I don't see how I can help you if I don't understand even the basics. I'm happy to do more research, but I'm still going to need a little help here. At least point me in the right direction. I've been looking into Zero-Point, and I feel like I understand a little bit about it, but as far as using it as a source for magic, I wasn't even going there, Father."

Damon's black gems fired dubiously, whether untrusting of his instincts of his son or merely untrusting of his son, he couldn't say. *Probably a little of both*, Damon considered as he relaxed his hold on certain pieces of information—if carefully so. "Tell me what you think you know about Zero-Point, and I'll try to fill in the gaps."

"Very well." Radin cleared his throat with another sip of his father's finest brandy, shocked at his success to even get Damon discussing the topic, making a palm-up, forward-leaning gesture with his right hand. "As I understand it, Zero-Point is another term for the toroidal field of energy that exists, in wave form, around all forms of matter. It's a free state of energy, not generated by momentum."

"That's accurate, if a bit incomplete."

"Complete it for me then. Please…. Father."

"There are matter fields represented by fermions—particles of matter as you alluded to—and energy fields represented by bosons—particles of energy. Either or both can have Zero-Point energy field values above zero. This is why the Zero-Point energy field is accessible even in the vacuum of space—assuming one knows how to access it."

"Makes sense. Go on. Please."

"Mira once told me that some physicists by the name of Feynman and Wheeler calculated that the Zero-Point energy surrounding a light bulb held in it the power to boil all the oceans of the world. Yet, Einstein—who you've heard me talk about before—conducted experiments to the contrary."

"Sounds like a real conundrum."

"Indeed. Well, what if one field—fermions let's say—held a negative value and the other—bosons—a positive value?"

"So, wouldn't that mean they would cancel each other out?"

"It would."

"So, I'm confused. How do you use it as an energy source for magic then?"

"I thought you weren't interested in that aspect of it."

"Father, please. I'm trying to help you. Help me help you. Please."

"You wanted to know why I went all the way out to the edges of the Universe?"

"YES!"

"Because of this very conundrum—as you so eloquently put it. I can, when I reach out to the Zero-Point field, feel its charge value—whether it be positive or negative, but I can't say which is which, nor if one is exclusively always positive or vice versa. But, I've never really tried accessing a strictly boson-driven Zero-Point source either. So, there's a bit of noise in what I'm reaching out and sensing, and I was trying to get some clarity around that."

"I think I'm beginning to understand."

Charles W. McDonald Jr.

"So, put it in your own words then. Regurgitate it back to me."

"When you've reached out to Zero-Point, on a planet, let's say, you have the noise of both fermion-driven fields and boson-driven fields and you're getting mixed values of charge—positive and negative—and you're unable to isolate which is which and if they're consistently one or the other."

"Exactly right. Good job! Smart boy!"

Radin smiled—sort of, definitely prideful of his father's praise, but he still didn't like being referred to as 'boy.' That made him think of Rowarc and how he needed to visit with him sooner than later to clarify and set right a great many things. Then his thoughts snapped back to reality and the intellectually-pressing conversation with his biological father. "So, do you use either charged field differently? Use the positive-charged field for one purpose and the negative for another?"

"Excellent. I like the critical thinking. Yes, that's exactly right. I've found the positively-charged field works great for electrical-field spells: lightning, fire, light, and creation. While the negatively-charged field works best for heavy moving, lifting, destruction, etc. When I made the star...," Damon pointed toward the pale-yellow dwarf sunset, settling out over the great ocean-view before them, "...I used the positively-charged field to compress the gasses that made it, even though the field itself was sourced from the Zero-Point around the planet, extending into its dead atmosphere."

"Wow!" It was a lot to take in, but at least this conversation had proven productive in helping him understand Damon a little better, along with his actions and Zero-Point. "So, let's bring this back to *Durial's Eye*?"

"Please," Damon agreed, allowing *The Starlight of Immortality* to sink into himself and into his bloodstream, shifting his stance against the railing to lean against it with his right arm instead of his left. Damon didn't even know how he did it. It just happened, but it caused Radin to push away from the balcony railing as Radin began scratching his temple, trying to piece this together.

Beginning to pace to and fro, remembering Damon's earlier description of supersolids, Radin brought himself back to the earlier part of their conversation with newfound understanding alight. "The Zero-Point field, or wave, is driving these vacuums or vacancies as you described them within the supersolid's structure."

Charles W. McDonald Jr.

"Within the *superfluid's* structure," Damon corrected.

"And what's the difference that makes it a supersolid then?"

"The rigidity and order of the frictionless structure."

"I'm not sure I understand that part," Radin admitted. This was stretching his limited knowledge of nature and the world around him.

"Me neither," Damon concurred. "I had to get my chief scientist to explain it to me three times."

"Father, can I offer a possibly wild suggestion?"

"Oooh, this oughta be good!"

"Since neither of us understand this subject with precision, why don't we go with our gut and experiment? Clearly, *The Starlight of Immortality* already has established some sort of working mannerisms with you whether consciously or subconsciously. I think you may understand better how to use it by ear than by rote."

"Sure," Damon offered in jest, though he wasn't sure how serious his jest. "Let's just play it by ear with one of the most powerful relics in all Creation." He thought about it another minute, pulling away from the railing and pulling his right hand back to him palm-up to see *The Starlight of Immortality* respond to him, appearing again at will, hovering just inches above his palm in a frigid trail of mist stretching down to contact the center of his palm. "I think you might be right."

"Once you've used it a few times at this scale you have now, then we scale it up as you talked about before."

"I like it." Damon beamed with pride for his son—his tacit doubt of Radin now evaporated by the light of Radin's knowledge and his use of it to forward the Master Plan. "I have something for you."

"Should I be excited or concerned, Father?"

The Starlight of Immortality disappearing again within Damon's bloodstream, Damon began scribing mid-air, as he'd done on Radin's first visit when he began to reveal to him the fundamentals of magic, the amber-burning fundamental rune for accessing the Zero-Point field. "Don't spend it all in one place," Damon jibed as he'd handed Radin a tool powerful enough to destroy himself and worlds along with it.

Radin's temples screamed as his brandy snifter fell to the balcony concrete in a shattering mess—his hands involuntarily brought back up to

Charles W. McDonald Jr.

his temples. He didn't know what he was looking at, but as it floated mid-air ablaze, his genetics and his arcanum-driven mind began to imagine the possibilities when coupled with his newfound understanding of nature and Creation.

Charles W. McDonald Jr.

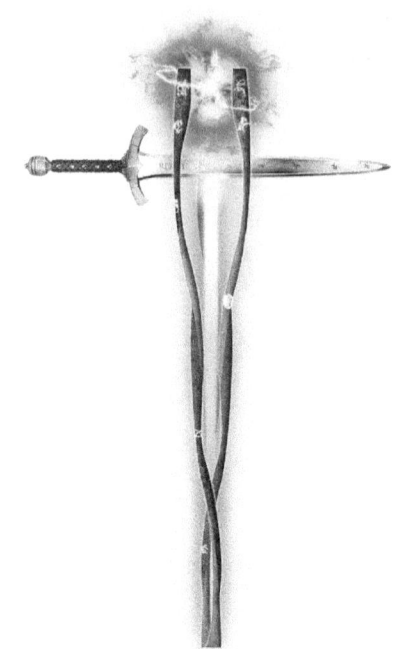

Chapter 31: Pray for Us All

(Minot Air Force Base (Magic City), North Dakota, Earth, Present Day)

Keeping herself invisible to the soldiers wasn't that hard, but understanding the threads of Damon's Master Plan was. The frozen ground still crunched underneath her feet, and she still left footprints in the frost and light snow covering the grounds of the base, so she wasn't entirely invisible, but at the distance she was keeping, she thought it might be safe.

Observing from some twenty spans away, Elise watched two uniformed men open a hatch, going underground into some sort of bunker or facility she couldn't fully see. Strange, geometric-shaped, gigantic metal objects worked on deeply gouged rails in what she assumed was reinforced concrete. She hadn't seen Damon, but she had seen the threads of his very powerful magic working on the two men she'd just seen descend into the belly of this beast.

Looking around, she saw what she assumed were mounted cameras with their lenses zooming, tilting, and pointing here and there—obviously under some intellectual control—whether human or otherwise. She moved where she thought her footprints would be out of camera's vision, causing gusts of wind to quickly cover her tracks as she approached the hatch where the two men descended into the underground facility below.

Nearly striking her on the way out with the heavy hatch, the leader of the two-man team threw open the steel hatch, exiting close enough to her they could have felt her breath on their necks. Still, it provided a way in, and that was all she needed. The hatch closing and latching behind her, she began descending the two-story access ladder down the shaft of the underground facility.

"They *seemed* like they were in a shitty mood," Major Henry Lassitor chided after the other half of his two-man crew gathered himself upon exiting the heavy hatch in their midnight-blue fatigues and squadron-insignia ball caps.

"I was seriously considering staying. Something just didn't feel right the way they were bitching," Captain Libowitz ruefully replied, looking back at the hatch, ensuring it closed, though he could have swore he saw something move.

"No can do. Regs call for eight solid hours of sleep away from the console. We've barely got time to get some chow, and I'm fucking starving. Besides, they want our statements on whatever the fuck was hovering over the silo."

"Yeah, well, I didn't see fucking shit. That's what I'm going to say."

"That's a good plan. I don't know what you're fucking talking about. There wasn't anything out of the ordinary."

"Hah, you're a fucking terrible liar."

"Bite me, Libowitz."

She never understood male banter, but as the hatch closed, it silenced the rest of their conversation. Pastel-white fluorescent light against pale-green interior paint of the tube, dimly but evenly lit her way down the shaft into the crew compartment quarters. Four-man racks accompanied by tables littered with varying issues of printed literature—if it could be called that—greeted Elise as she ran her delicate fingers across them, trying to observe rather than disturb. Clearly, they liked their cars, their guns, and their women. Peering around the corner, she found a connecting tubed corridor lit with small rectangular lights spaced every eighteen inches or so apart. Again, the same light, pale-green paint reflected the pastel-white light back at her as she followed the tube to the male voices she heard in the distance.

A huskier, deeper voice resonated over the other. "You got those target packages in order yet?"

"The launch authentication codes carry the target packages. I know you're pissed off, but let's not get ahead of protocol!" Lighter in tone, but equally serious in intent, the pale-skinned captain's eyes darted through the step-by-step launch criteria and checklist, verifying next steps preceding up to and after the launch codes—held inside breakable plastic inside a locked safe—which would come from the President of the United States.

FUCK! She had heard enough to act, but still her instincts told her to wait. Inching closer, she could see the flowered insignia of the Air Force major she assumed possessed the first, huskier voice demanding the target packages. He was angrily flipping through a red, thick three-ring binder, with a secured, landline phone pressed to his right ear as he was reading a just-sent message. His name tag read, 'Laniard.'

"The president is in the countdown. That means he has the 'biscuit.' Get ready, Archie," Major Laniard warned as he spun the combination lock on the small grey safe in between their two large consoles with dials, indicators, and knobs everywhere. Each console looked like a time capsule from a museum intended to document the 1980s. But, everything was neat, clean, organized, and in perfect working order.

"I know what it means. I got it. I'm on it." Captain Haily fidgeted with his right index finger, rubbing it against his thumb in anticipation of the keys they were about to turn as part of a five, two-man crew launch package. They had been trained for this moment and many moments like it, but North Korea had it coming this time, and they were going to give it to them without a moment's hesitation.

The heavy little door to the combination safe flung open as Major Laniard pulled out the laminated card he was directed to fetch as part of the SAS (sealed-authentication system) containing an encoded and encrypted message. Major Laniard snapped its laminated cover, switching on the speakerphone as the SECDEF rattled off the contents of the launch authentication message:

"We're ready to confirm, Sir.… LIMA, FOUR, WHISKEY, HOTEL, X-RAY, SIX, ZULU, KILO, KILO, ALPHA." Major Laniard paused for a second realizing the reality of the moment as he verified one more time tracing his right index finger along every single alpha-numeric character to be 100 percent certain. That meant the president and vice president's challenge code had already been authenticated as well. He knew this was now a validated order from the top of the food chain. "This is Major Victor Laniard, Launch Commander. I concur. Stand by for the two-man authentication."

Captain Haily's voice cracked for a brief second as he followed Victor's finger validating each and every character on the red card before them. "This is Captain Archie Haily, Launch Officer. I concur, sir. I'm turning over the launch authentication code now to validate target packages from the POTUS menu." Turning over the codes on the face to see two categories on the back, Archie scanned the information, quite familiar with some of the longitudes and latitudes he was seeing. This was what they'd been practicing. Now, the moment was atop them like a gorilla sitting on their chest. The first category of numbers would unlock the missiles for firing. The second category were the target packages. "Sir, the longitude and latitude target packages I'm seeing have us targeting our payload at Pyongyang (39° 2' N / 125° 45' E), Jonchon (40° 36' N / 126° 28' E), Kusŏng (39°58' N / 125°14' E), Chongjin (41° 46' N / 129° 43' E) within the DPRK. Do I have these target packages correct, sir? If so, I'll begin entering the unlock codes."

"This is General Mattis, the Secretary of Defense. Your packages are authenticated and correct. Proceed as ordered and get to your secure locations after sending your votes."

After entering the long, numeric code into his console, Captain Haily looked over at his commander's console to see the same codes already entered with his key already in the lock—ready to turn.

"Mr. Secretary, this is Major Laniard. The missiles are unlocked, and our target packages are being entered right now. Godspeed."

"Godspeed, men." The phone line suddenly went to dial tone as the line severed. He knew other members of the National Security Team were

Charles W. McDonald Jr.

coordinating the other votes that would be sent to their missile packages. It only took two votes from a set of five two-man crews, and the missiles were gone. This was really happening, and they were really going to launch a pre-emptive strike.

"Packages locked in, Major."

"Okay Archie. Here we go. On the count of three. Three. Two. One and turn."

"Turning confirmed. Votes sent."

The illusion Elise had weaved let them think the keys had turned and they had gone through their steps of their doomsday mayhem, but the keys remained upright and unturned.

*   *   *   *

(Somewhere along the Canadian Border at 40,000 feet, Air Force One, Earth, Present Day)

Within the airborne situation room of Air Force One, amid a sea of airborne electronics, the National Security Team gathered around, watching the votes come in for several missile packages in North Dakota, Colorado, and Kansas. It was a near unanimous vote count with the stunning exception of the professionals in Minot he'd just got off the phone with. *Had something failed in their equipment?* Either his instincts were way off, or something mechanically went wrong because he didn't hear a hint of hesitation in their voices when given the authenticated orders.

"Birds away, Mr. Secretary," the soft-spoken angelic voice of Captain Lisa Montez declared, though her eyes were drawn to the solitary outlier vote of dissension as well. It didn't matter. That's why it only required two votes from five two two-man crews to send a missile package. The others were really there for redundancy.

"God help us all," SECDEF exclaimed under his breath. Time and time again he'd warned his DPRK counterparts, using every type of motivational emphasis he could think of. He considered them rational actors where others hadn't, but it didn't matter anymore. What was done was done, and it hadn't been done lightly. You can only poke the bear so many times before the bear pokes back.

*   *   *   *

(Somewhere between Nebraska and Idaho at 39,000 feet, The Looking Glass Boeing E-6B Mercury, Earth, Present Day)

Dozens of LED flat-panel screens overhead and along the thirty-five-foot long command console that ran the bulk of the length of the forward part of the aircraft, sorted, relayed and aggregated the coordinated National Command Authority TRIAD response to the increasing DPRK threat, while Navy and Air Force personnel from E-4 to Vice Admiral watched. Most with hands over their mouths in disbelief of their extensive training now made very real.

"Yes, Mr. President," Vice Admiral Craig clarified. "We have eight outbound birds from our silos following two SLBMs each, from the Ohio and the Columbia. That should give them something to think about with the pause we discussed."

The line to POTUS wasn't on speaker, so AF Sergeant Leslie Akins just sat there quietly working beneath the armpit of the fatigue-clad, three-star admiral standing over her with the hard line stretched out above her console, wondering what the other half of the conversation was like. Clearly it was meant to poke—not obliterate the enemy. Push them back with a hard punch and let them think about how serious they wanted this to really get.

"Understood, Mr. Secretary," Vice Admiral Craig confirmed aloud, obviously getting his next-step orders from the SECDEF. "We'll be ready," he committed with an audible dial tone that could be heard immediately once the call had terminated and the admiral reached to hook the phone back into its receiver mounted in the overhead console. "We'll be ready," Vice Admiral Craig mumbled to himself and the crew immediately around him, though the tone in his voice was…worried. Watching the twelve outbound birds streaking towards their foreign destinations, they tracked, in real time and in horror, the twelve inbound ballistic missiles, each heading for the most populous cities in America. The admiral wondered what, and

Charles W. McDonald Jr.

who, would be left to respond if their first response proved insufficient at deterring further aggressive action taken against the United States, now under a full strategic attack from two serious and significant adversaries.

"Get me NORCOM commander on the line," the admiral ordered with a pause as he considered his options and calculated their fuel-burn rate of the E-6B. "Tell him we're going to need that standby tanker airborne immediately. Relay our coordinates. We're going to be up here for a while...."

*   *   *   *

(Minot Air Force Base (Magic City), North Dakota, Earth, Present Day)

The reinforced concrete geometric shape missile cap began sliding open on heavy-duty iron rails as smoke plumes from within the silo changed from softly billowing to erupting as the ICBM stage-1 engine ignited, carrying the ten-warhead MIRV (Multiple Independent Reentry Vehicles) into pre-dawn, midnight sky. Only five minutes past the president's decision, the United States' *first* response was on its way.

*   *   *   *

(Athens, Georgia, Earth, Some Hours Before)

The petite, 5'4", blonde Georgia native, Melissa, sipped a Killian's Irish Red Lager at the bar, watching CNN, a few blocks from campus after another crazy day at work. Ignoring the entirely too young man—likely a student—hitting on her relentlessly, she prompted the bartender to turn up the volume.

"The hydrogen bomb airburst test occurred some 500 nautical miles north, northwest of the Northern Mariana Islands, approximately 600 nautical miles off the US territory of Guam just as Kim Jong-un had threatened."

"He's a fucking madman," Melissa offered aloud but under her breath, just shook her head in the realization of the limited time she had left to get her kids from the babysitter.

"What do you think it means," the scruffy haired young man in the

Charles W. McDonald Jr.

untucked flannel shirt asked.

At least he wasn't hitting on her anymore, but he was still entirely too close, standing behind her and to her right. She could practically feel his drunken breath on the back of her neck. She was in a bar, so she kept her expectations in check, but still…. *Ick!* "I think it means I need to go get my kids and you need to go be with your family." Getting up from the bar, she closed out her tab with a twenty and didn't wait for her change.

"I don't have any family," he called after her, hoping for something she couldn't give.

"Then you should probably pray." Melissa wore the symbol around her neck in the form of a tiny silver cross, but as a scientist and professor in linguistics, she wasn't exactly the model Christian anyway. She'd committed her fair share of sins resulting in her adorable children, but at least they were truly hers, and she needed to take care of them—while she still could. "Pray for us all," she declared with her hand on the metal bar of the exit door; she pushed with emphasis, to go get her children and get them to safety. If there was a safe place…. Her parents shared stories with her about growing up in the Cuban Missile Crisis and how Americans conducted shelter-in-place drills, but she never gave it much thought—'til now.

Charles W. McDonald Jr.

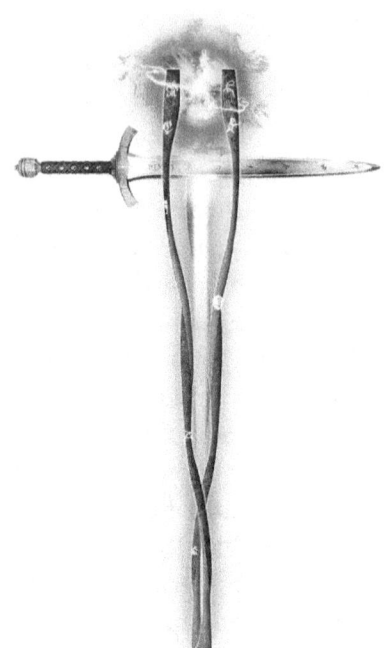

Chapter 32: Harbingers and Portents – Part II

(The Haedron, Kaleion, Present Day)

Fine moats of wind-driven desert sand hit Royvan Miral head-on, bouncing off his tight-fitting balaclava, as their beasts carried them deeper into The Haedron Desert. It wasn't like a great desert of dunes like he'd seen on Perion, but more like a dry and barren lakebed, but the wind whipping over the plains carried the fine-grain sand with speed, wielding it like a weapon as if it were protecting something…something grave.

Their beasts, called feruk, were akin to horses, but with long necks for vegetative grazing and great reach for fresh water, which pooled in small amounts with rarity. They could travel for two to three days without water, and Joran indicated what they wanted was within a day's ride—assuming he hadn't lied to them.

Like a massive rock-toothed crown it rose out of the dry, weathered, and cracked lakebed with a great lip of what appeared to be rocky debris

Charles W. McDonald Jr.

tossed about the blistered landscape. Chipped rocks of bedrock planed in large, straight lines, as if hewn or cleaved by a great sword of chaos, formed the outer rim of the great ring Royvan Miral estimated to be some one-hundred-thousand spans wide. Greater than any two, or even three, of the largest cities he'd ever seen if put side by side, the crater spoke to Royvan Miral in whispering ways of madness with a celestial voice on the dry lakebed wind. The secrets it shared with him made his eyes grow wide as they crested the tip of the rim, allowing him to peer down into the heart of The Haedron Crater. "Why have you brought us here, Joran of Erden?"

"You seek the Seal of celestial fire. This scar upon Kaleion's beautiful face is as old as Creation yet undimmed by weather or magic or war of Men. That...," Joran proclaimed, pointing to the great black center of the crater, "...is why I have brought you here."

"What is it," Royvan Miral asked of his guide, however trustworthy, or not.

"A message from the Creator. A warning that we are but a small piece in a great celestial mosaic."

"Spare me your prose and superstition, Joran. You're a pragmatic man—a curious man. You can do better than that...," Royvan Miral countered in a chiding manner, eyeing him sideways, preparing his beast to head down into the crater where he estimated the center to be some hundred spans down below the level of the dry lakebed, yet no water pooled there.

Kerrich and Levi held their feruk at bay, with Kerrich tightening and adjusting his balaclava to keep the wind-driven sand out of his airway as they both stayed out of the war of words between Joran and their leader. Royvan Miral liked input from them as trusted and valued men, but he didn't like being interrupted when he was deadly serious as this either.

"Very well...," Joran offered, looking between them. "...It's a great rock burnished by entry and landing, hard enough not to have exploded on entry or upon collision with the crust. Heavy enough, dense enough, and intact enough not to be something pirates could easily carry off."

"Why hasn't someone taken it with magic," Royvan Miral argued, spurring his feruk down into the crater at a gentle angle.

"You're a clever man, Royvan Miral," Joran countered with a hard and piercing gaze, pulling his balaclava down a bit as he positioned his feruk to begin down into the crater. "I have asked myself that question hundreds of times and have yet to come up with an answer. I simply don't know. I have heard it's resistant to magic, but not being a mage, I can't verify such claims."

Descending in single file, Levi followed Kerrich, who followed Joran, who followed Royvan toward the great celestial message as Joran called it.

"You've clearly been here before. What did you find on your previous trips," Kerrich asked, calling out in front to Joran.

"A massive, polished, and relatively smooth black rock," he posed flatly, dubious of what the others expected that their own eyes couldn't already verify even at this distance.

"How big is it," Royvan asked, though his own estimates from this distance said *massive*.

"REALLY BIG," Joran confirmed, making an outward motion with both hands quickly before drawing them back in to control his feruk on their descent into the maw of the crater.

* * * *

Some hours later, Kerrich and Levi sat back in awe as Royvan Miral circled the immense celestial emissary of God the Creator—at least he hoped it an emissary of God the Creator. Towering over them, storey upon storey upon storey, it reached back up to the heavens whence it came in abyssal black glory—utterly petrifying in its presence. It wasn't perfectly smooth as Joran had led them to believe, but he saw nothing he'd call a marking. Just an imperfection hither and thither from what he could see. It wasn't as if he could levitate to see it from the top or turn the behemoth over to see its belly. Or....

"What are you doing," Joran asked, seeing Royvan pilfering through his belongings strapped to his mount.

He'd never used it before, but it had been given to him for this specific purpose—especially if he felt like they might be close.... Royvan pulled it from his satchel, instantly recognizing the strange-shaped, acrylic-painted piece that looked the world like the tip of the tail of that beast

Charles W. McDonald Jr.

that took Radin from Axum. Like an upside-down triangle with elongated points at each end, and the bottom end curved at the tip like a spear, he wasn't entirely sure what it was made of, but he was told it would melt and that was all he needed to know. Dismounting, he piled together a few twigs from his bag, striking two small agate stones one against the other to start a small spark that quickly lit the twigs. Creating a fork to hold Radin's amber, acrylic-painted totem, Royvan Miral held it out over the small, wind-parched blaze, which began to cause it to melt. Hearing it hiss in the fire, he could have swore he heard a beastly roar in the distance. Turning to Kerrich and Levi, who were engaged in yet another debate over the Monuments of Creation—completely oblivious to what he thought he'd heard, Royvan whispered to the air, "Radin, I could sure use your help. Now would be a good time to show up."

A few moments of Royvan further examining the crater and rock.... Tap, tap, tap on his left shoulder from behind. "You have to allow it a little while to summon me." Radin looked all the world different from the last time Royvan had seen him. He still wore the Banner of Hope crest but in regal blood-red, trimmed in fine gild of silver and gold, with a red cape held together by gold, crest-braided clasps over grey slacks and natural leather boots. He looked like a king but without the crown. Before he was essentially a king with the crown and the title, but now he looked the part—as if he'd grown into a role no longer his.

"'Tis good to see you," Royvan began as he visually surmised all things new and old about Radin. "I promised I wouldn't summon you unless it was vital, or I felt like we were approaching the end of our search. But...," Royvan motioned behind him at the towering black celestial rock behind him, shrugging at Radin.

"No. You did the right thing. Damon never mentioned this. And, being on his own homeworld, I find that a glaring omission I will discuss with him later." Radin began pacing to and fro in front of the great celestial monolith, wondering its origins and how it had remained intact from entry into the atmosphere. His knowledge of physics was limited compared to Damon's, but that seemed highly unlikely. Probing the object, Radin immediately stepped back several paces with a concerned look.

"I'm told it is resistant to magic," Royvan Miral added, trying to clarify and alleviate the concerned look about Radin's face.

"Who told you as much?"

"Him." Royvan pointed to Joran of Erden, who was still mounted on his feruk, sitting patiently, far to Royvan and Radin's left, some seventy paces or more away. "He says his name is Joran of Erden, but others have substantiated as much. Think of him as my counterpart on Kaleion."

"Surely there is no equal to Royvan Miral," Radin delicately and playfully mocked the man who'd once chosen Talemar over him, hoping he'd take it the way it had been intended.

Royvan Miral merely nodded deeply in his silent but respectful reply, moving out of Radin's way as Radin began making his way toward a mounted Joran of Erden, who began closing the distance between them on his beast.

A few dozen paces, and Joran dismounted, standing face to face with one of these world-traveling mages he'd heard so much about. *Engagement*, he paced his thoughts, remembering Royvan Miral's offer of something more value than money. "Joran," he declared, offering his hand to shake.

Linguistics helped trim the edges off the accent he'd become largely accustomed to from his interactions with others from Kaleion, though it certainly wasn't *his* homeworld. "Radin." Taking Joran's gloved hand, he shook it, never taking his eyes of Joran's. "Tell me what you know about it," he questioned, motioning to the great black celestial object to their right.

"Well, as you can see from the great mound of debris all around it, I'd estimate we're seeing maybe only the top third to top half of it with the rest being buried well under bedrock since we're probably standing below bedrock level right now. It obliterated probably 20 percent of the crust it displaced, and the rest you see forms the crater around us."

"That's a good description of the entry, but that doesn't tell me anything about the object itself."

"Well, your guess is probably as good as, if not better than, mine, Radin."

Looking back at Royvan Miral, who'd remained behind to give them some privacy, Radin was putting the pieces together in his mind…. "Mr. Miral over there was sent to find something that had very little to do with rocks. Why are we standing in front of the biggest one I've ever seen?"

Charles W. McDonald Jr.

"No, Mr. Radin. Your Mr. Miral over there was sent to fetch you the harbinger of celestial fire. That is the Seal you seek, and that is why we are standing here." Joran again pointed to the crater floor with his left index finger, looking Radin in the eyes without flinching.

Shaking his head, Radin looked at the great celestial monolith again, "Has it ever been moved or tampered with at all?"

"Moved…? Phah!! Look at it! Tampered with, I can't speak to, but you tried your magic on it. What did you feel?"

"A vacuum," Radin simply replied, and then the light came on instantly in his mind. "Wait a minute." He'd never tried accessing it before, but it might be the only thing in his arsenal that could make a dent this thing. Closing his eyes, he took a few steps closer to the great and dark celestial mystery before them. Seeing it in his mind's eye, he could see and feel the great toroidal field all around it along with the toroidal field around him, around the particles of air in the atmosphere all the way out into space. He could sense the difference in their fields just as Damon had described, though he couldn't tell which was positively-charged and which was negative. One of them felt almost blue in color and the other almost green. Trying blue first, he summoned the Zero-Point source closest to the atmosphere and space, focusing it on the great object that could no longer ignore the massive power he wielded. Yet, it didn't budge at all. Shining with a blue aura momentarily, then dissipating into nothingness, either he was too nascent a user of Zero-Point and had failed with it at his first attempt as Damon had so many times with his first few attempts, or he'd chosen the wrong Zero-Point field for the task at hand.

"Well, that was a spectacularly colorful show," Joran chided—threatening to mock clap—as Royvan Miral began to close the distance between them while maintaining a sidelong stare at the black celestial beast before them.

"Not helpful," Radin sniped back with furrowed brow as he began to close his eyes again, reaching out just as he'd done before, but this time swirling the green-charged Zero-Point before them in a great vortex, which curled forth from Radin's feet, shooting out in a great arc toward the massive, black, celestial rock. His eyes now half-open, barely registered the movement that left Joran of Erden breathless as the massive, mineral-laden mystery began rolling onto its side with blue-green sheets of energy roiled together and a stream of energy shooting up from the ground at an angle with the leverage necessary to move a mountain.

Joran's estimates not far off, at least a third of the great rock was now visible that was not before, having been buried deep in the crust. "Wow. Now, *that* I wasn't expecting," Joran exclaimed in disbelief.

"Perhaps a little more faith would do you some good, Joran of Erden," Radin chided, his stance wobbly from the energy he'd just channeled.

"I don't think it's a matter of faith. See for yourself," Royvan Miral added, pointing to the now-exposed belly of the celestial mystery, etched with some carving vaguely visible at this distance, prompting Royvan Miral to begin walking toward it even while Radin's blue-green leveraged rod of energy still held it in place. "Do we know if it will roll back if you let go?"

"I think I can hold it a little longer," Radin replied even as beads of sweat were beginning to form on his forehead and betwixt brow and eyelid.

"I wouldn't get too close." Joran's words chased after Royvan Miral, even if his body was slow to follow—cautious of that which hadn't moved since seemingly time had begun. Continuing to split his focus between the exposed etching and the man he'd clearly underestimated, Joran of Erden slowed his pace of approach, watching Royvan Miral get close enough to be crushed if the meteorite were to give way and settle back into its massive divot within the Kaleion crust.

"I don't like him getting that close," Kerrich called after Levi, who jumped from his feruk to follow Royvan Miral.

Ashen lines of irrelevance and perspective dripped over the stony, hard planes of Royvan Miral's face, making him meek as he fell to his knees before the etched face in the belly of the celestial, black stone. Its majesty carved in perpetuity to survive both space and time in deep, gouging lines of light and shadow depicting an immortal face of their destiny.

"Who is it?" Joran's voice shook in stark terror as he looked upon the face of such beautiful symmetry, shadow, and sentencing he couldn't continue to hold his gaze upon it.

"'Tis the face of God the Creator," Radin answered with such certainty it was as if he were seeing it not for the first time. Hard, perfect

Charles W. McDonald Jr.

eyes—rimmed in the weight of Creation—stared back at Radin as if not for the first time.

"'Tis the face of God the Creator," Royvan Miral echoed Radin, continuing to kneel, though never looking away as Joran's self-conviction had forced within him. Royvan feared touching the dark message from Heaven in the form of the black meteorite before him, but his curiosity was incorrigible. It was just who Royvan Miral was at heart that led the finger-tips of his right hand to begin tracing the face of God the Creator.

Now standing right behind Royvan Miral, Radin didn't startle, though Royvan did look off to his right to see the blue-green energy rod still propping up the stone at a forty-five-degree angle to the Kaleion crust, hoping the soil would not yield to the immense weight of the message reflecting—in matte sheen—the light of the Kaleion sunset now beginning to set below the rim of the crater.

His eyes so drawn to the facial features before him, Radin barely noticed Royvan Miral's right hand tracing a message in a language he'd never before seen. "What does it mean, Royvan?"

Unaccustomed to Radin using his name like that, it was just enough to make him severe his stare of the hieroglyphic runes in front of him on the black stone's etched surface. "I've never seen this language before. I've never seen anything like it—ever. Not even in the Seals we've recovered on Perion." Royvan Miral paused, looking it over, symbol-by-symbol, searching each and every rune for anything he could consider a root word or phrase to decipher the rest—just shaking his head in resignation.

"I know that symbol..." Joran pointed to roughly the middle of the cryptic message etched below the face of God. "...It means 'within.'" A long and speculative pause followed. "...I think."

Staggering and shifting in his once-firm stance, Radin fell against the rock, now facing the setting Kaleion sun as the waking dream returned, turning blue-grey eyes fiery white—reflecting the fire of the Kaleion star. The booming voice of Creation no longer incoherent in his mind's eye as each word came to him in absolute clarity as he echoed them aloud in the voice of God the Creator: "I am the I AM, and I AM WITHIN THEE, SHINING IN THE LIGHT OF CREATION AND THE DEATH OF MEN." His eyes collapsing in on themselves with his eyelids now shut as his

Charles W. McDonald Jr.

head slumped to his right, as if passed out, Radin's heart threatened to beat out of his chest as his breathing palpitated as if his body were in shock.

"Tend to him, Joran," Royvan ordered, as he replayed the message in his mind over and over, tracing the hieroglyphic runes with meaning now, parsing the message into its components. "If this means within, then this must mean 'death' since this other part is the only repeating piece of the message and we know that has to mean 'I am.'" Breaking down each and every rune, writing it into his notes for future use, Royvan didn't think this would be the last time they'd see this language, and he wondered how far it must have predated the oldest languages on both Perion and Kaleion. Breaking it down further, he captured what he thought was 'light,' 'creation,' and 'men.' Again, tracing his fingers over each rune in succession, his fingertip found itself pricked on the rune for 'within' as blood spurted from his right index finger into the deep crevasse of the rune; blood ran through the etching in dark red rivers 'til it seemingly fell into nothingness, cleaving the great rock into two massive halves with the propped-up half holding firm as Radin continued to lean against it and the other half rolling away approximately twenty degrees, leaving a great V-shaped fissure between the halves.

"Look…," Levi offered to Royvan Miral, pointing to the jaggedly-severed surface of one of the two halves, "…the harbinger of celestial fire—the message of God."

*   *   *   *

Consciousness came back in small doses to Radin, whose eyes still dotted with Kaleion sunlight no longer present as nightfall was now upon them. Fingers snapping registered in his left ear, and he could feel the hardness of the stone still pressed against his back. He was still seated with his back against the massive rock as he started to shake his head left to right, trying to help him regain his senses.

"We need to get out of here," Joran urged from Radin's right to what must have been Royvan on his left, still snapping his fingers directly in Radin's ears.

"Come on, Radin. Come back to us," Royvan, too, urged. This was feeling worse by the instant—ever since retrieving the Third and Fourth

Seals from the interior of the massive meteorite behind them.

Radin felt them in his lap, of course, the heavy weight of iron-ferrite and other minerals composing the two messages chipped from the interior of the meteorite in large, jagged-edged rectangles, preserved throughout time for this very moment. Grabbing one in each hand, he used the messages to prop himself up, pushing against the Kaleion crust to right himself before Royvan Miral and Joran of Erden. Looking to see if his magic still held the great rock in place, he saw its waning power fading before them, threatening to let the face of God bury itself back into the belly of the crater.

"You're not going to read those here," Royvan challenged Radin. "… We need to get clear of this crater. We need to get to a safe place."

"There is no place safe," Radin confessed, with the weight of more knowledge now than ever before as he looked down upon the language intended for him alone to read. Neither were marked third or fourth, yet he knew as if he'd always known—as if he were meant to be the dissident of Man:

Ring of Stones,
Monuments of Creation: hear me.
Summon the Nine,
And summon the *One*,
And with them all summon the fire of despair and air of hope.
Heed my word, and know my face,
And clear for me a path,
For a sallow death surely follows me all the way.

Radin paused as the voice of God the Creator echoed through his vocal chords, blistering clouds above, yet yielding no other obvious nor immediate result.

"Is this what happened last time," Joran asked Royvan Miral in eyes that spoke of stark panic.

"No. It isn't," Royvan replied flatly—both shocked and mortified by the silence of the dark moment of reality. He wondered if he'd feel more comfort if the Kaleion crust opened up and swallowed them whole.

Charles W. McDonald Jr.

Reaching out with *Damon's Improved Foresight*, Radin sought out any evidence the Third Seal had done its job and found nothing. Furrowed brow led his eyes to his right and the heavy, jagged-edged rectangular carving from the meteorite that was the Fourth Seal:

> Poets and dreamers,
> Prophets and sages in all their artifice....
> All foretell of my coming yet are bereft of lore.
> There will be a time for Man, as never before,
> when he *must* choose,
> For surely there will be judgment
> Upon the air rent by the thunder of my voice
> And the skies torched by the fire of my soul.

A solitary crow flying overhead suddenly spiraled out of the sky, diving headfirst into the Kaleion soil at Radin's feet where its neck immediately snapped upon impact and its body burst into flames. Yet, nothing else. Again, both Radin and Royvan looked this way and that, even turning around behind them to re-examine the great celestial message now cleaved open in a great 'V,' expecting to find something, and yet there was not.

Eyes darting left, right, up, and down, Joran of Erden spooked at the slightest lizard creeping across the crater floor, suddenly bursting into flames at Radin's feet—yet nothing else. "I think—"

"I think we should tell Damon," Royvan Miral interrupted to nodding agreement from Radin.

Hastily forming a *Portal* for them to walk through to Damon's Manor, Kerrich, Levi, Joran, and Royvan Miral all went before him, but as Radin crossed the threshold of the *Portal*, the Seals he once held burst into black dust, scattering on the floor of Damon's foyer on Eden.

Charles W. M\ :sup:`c`\ Donald Jr.

Chapter 33: A Reflection of the Pillars of Creation

(Damon's Manor, Eden, Present Day)

Hope disintegrated and scattered about the great tiled floor of Damon's foyer in the form of black dust from the harbinger of celestial fire as Radin's eyes searched in desperation for his father or anyone who might know of his whereabouts. "Don't go anywhere, and *don't touch* anything," Radin warned the group as he shot up the circular staircase two risers at a time, leaving Royvan Miral and Joran staring at each other and the peculiar surroundings on yet another world for them to register.

"Father," Radin called out, rounding the second floor to the third. "FATHER," he called out again, shooting through the small decoy room into Damon's fourth-floor study, skidding to a stop as he smelled and saw

Charles W. M°Donald Jr.

Illirian Starfire with Damon for the very first time. "I'm…. I'm sorry to interrupt," Radin offered with a deep bow to a pale-gown-dressed Illirian Starfire—her red-gold hair spilling down her backless gown in supple, elegant waves.

"Is this your son," she asked with her left hand turned upside-down inquisitively at Damon.

"Yes, and he hasn't yet learned how to knock," Damon rebuked, coolly looking down his nose at his son in a facial expression that warned this had better be good.

Illirian pivoted from her location in front of Damon's desk, moving aside the chair she always leaned against to close the distance between herself and Radin with ever-examining eyes.

"You…. You must be Illirian." Radin hesitated, deeply reticent in his own first impressions in front of this amazing woman who no longer appeared the youthful version of herself Damon had always described. Young, yes, but not in her twenties as Damon had always boasted. This woman, while stunning, easily appeared in her mid-thirties, as if….

"Clearly, I must be." She smiled, extending her left hand for Radin to kiss, which he did so reluctantly and with his eyes gauging his father's response carefully. "Careful with this one, Damon. He's more like you than you know." Her eyes slowly walked—crawled actually—over the crest on Radin's attire; something clearly had registered in her mind's eye that she wasn't immediately sharing.

"Let's hope for all our sakes—not," Damon chided, rising from behind his desk.

"Um…. I wouldn't have barged in if it wasn't urgent," Radin offered to Damon, looking sidelong at Illirian as if to ask her via Damon to give them the room.

"You don't have to worry about Illirian. Say what you came to say. I'm holding no secrets from her," Damon proffered to a dubious snort of derision from Illirian.

"Really…," she protested, making a gesture with her index finger that Damon clearly didn't like, "…one shouldn't tell such fanciful lies."

"And one should learn how to listen twice as often as they talk," Damon countered, motioning for Radin to speak up and give it to them.

Charles W. McDonald Jr.

"We found the Seals," Radin offered flatly.

"Seals. Plural. Which ones?" The question shot forth from Damon, nearly blurted out, while Illirian's eyes became instantly scrutinous of the boy become man sent to speak the words of the Creator in the voice of God himself.

"The Third and Fourth," Radin clarified to a now-squinting Illirian, who was now uncomfortably close—in his personal space—eye to eye with him.

"What have you done," she asked, already sensing the moment had come and gone without so much as a moment for her to offer her considerable input.

"I…. I—"

"You spoke the words. You've seen the face," Illirian interrupted knowingly.

"How did you know it would be his face?" Radin now eyed her with dubious suspicion.

"This petulant child has opened the Third and Fourth Seals…? Did it occur to you to bring them to us and seek guidance first." Illirian's gaze was coal-stoked, and levied on Damon as much as the son she now glowered down.

"He did so upon my orders," Damon chided. "You know that. You've always known that was part of the plan. Don't blame him. Blame me." Damon's words chased after Illirian, who had suddenly began to storm out of the study but then stopped and pivoted back to Damon. "Where are you going," Damon harassed as his body began to follow his words—toward the exit.

"Where am I going? To warn. To Prepare. The countdown has begun—" Her mouth swallowed hard at the knowledge she had of the Seals—and the Monuments of Creation—they did not possess.

"That's why I'm here…," Radin interrupted with his hands in the air to get their attention. "…Nothing happened when I spoke the words." He paused for a minute, now seeing he had their attention. "Well…almost nothing."

"What do you mean, 'almost nothing?'" Illirian's hot but beautiful gaze was back upon him like a viper, and he soon wished it wasn't. This was *definitely* the Illirian Starfire he'd heard so much about—unfortunately.

"I mean a dead crow and a dead lizard and that's about it. I used *Damon's Improved Foresight*, reaching out even well into the atmosphere of Kaleion and… well…nothing…."

Damon's thoughts clearly registered the anomaly as expected while Illirian's expressions had not. Damon and Illirian each knew something the other didn't, and her eyes were on him like a ten-pound tick on a two-pound dog as Mira liked to say.

"You've hastened this along, haven't you," Illirian accused knowingly. She already knew and had seen visions of Damon's influence, but watching them dovetail—in real time—with the Seals of the Unmaking of Creation was something else entirely. *How did Damon know when and what to do?* As if to answer her own question, she recalled giving him the *Starlight of Immortality* and her face grew ashen before them. "I have to go," she declared, now looking down at the hardwood planks of the floor making up Damon's fourth-floor study.

"Illirian, you knew this was coming. Why are you being like this?" It was true. Damon had shared a great deal of the Master Plan with her, but even he didn't see the fulsome impact of his actions when and where it involved the Seals. He'd had multiple debates with her, Radin, Goldenbow, Kellen, and others trying to understand their impact on the whole and always came up with incomplete answers.

"The Seals are *supposed to be* hateful and terrible. They weren't meant to be opened until the end times justified it so. No one foresaw your petulant son opening them at the haste of your Master Plan because you've kept your plan so secret from us."

"I don't like your calling me 'petulant,'" Radin barked back in rebuke of the notorious Illirian Starfire, fully living up to her reputation. "The Seals had to be opened to summon the Creator *and* the Unmaking. Once the first was opened, they all had to be, and the quicker the better. I don't want to prolong this suffering any longer than necessary. I did what had to be done. You weren't there. You didn't see what I saw!"

"Just like you," she prosecuted, looking accusingly at Damon after her eyes again walked over every single facial feature of Radin. "Just like you." Approaching Radin carefully this time, with more regard, more uncertainty, and more fear, she looked him in the eyes. "This...," she said, sticking her right index finger directly into his chest and his crest, "...is a direct reflection of the Pillars of Creation you have just unmade, Son of the Dark Knight of Magic. I suggest you go see it—*while it still exists*." With that, she pivoted, storming out of Damon's study.

"A real piece of work—that one," Radin accused, his eyes watching her shapely body leave. "Did I screw up, Father? I did what I thought was right."

"You did *nothing* wrong. The fact that she's so disturbed has me wondering what I have miscalculated. What *I* have missed." His mind began running through everything he'd seen through *Durial's Eye* and every clue that had been dropped in his lap. He didn't know the full extent of future's impact on the present, or the past for that matter, but he knew there was a gap and he hoped it wouldn't unravel the Master Plan from the center outwards.

"And what did she mean, 'a reflection of the Pillars of Creation?'"

Damon wanted to answer his son—wanted to show him—but his mind was busy recalculating the future impact of the Third and Fourth Seals on Humanity, and Earth specifically. Till now, the Seals had been contained to mostly Perion. That would soon prove no longer the case.

(Stirling, Perion, Present Day)

Illirian's words still rang in his thoughts, indicting him the Dissident of Man he already thought himself to be. No longer merely the hand of Damon, he was beginning to see himself the harbinger of the Death of Men and all Mankind. *The Destroyer of Men* of prophecy from legend and myth on every world of Man. He couldn't let his burden become his father's, and he thought he knew where to look. The sign still swung from a heavy, wrought iron post, advertising his father's establishment as he walked into a world both familiar and distant—instantly recognizing a hand-carved chair here or a recently-repaired hardware there.

"My word." Mary Danvers gasped, looking upon the face she recognized but, in a form, and presence she had trouble placing. "Rowarc, get out here. It's—"

Charles W. McDonald Jr.

"My son," Rowarc interrupted her, the door to the kitchen still swinging behind him. Words weren't necessary as he moved out from behind the bar to greet his wayward son who was his no more. His hands clasping Radin's wrists, pulling him to his chest to hug him, Rowarc no longer held back the emotions he once doled out in droplets for Radin. *What's the point? Whoever his blood, Radin was a fine boy—a fine man. A good man.*

"Dad...," he paused at the familial term he still wasn't quite used to using, "...I thought we could talk."

"Mary, please bring us some cheese and fresh bread—as fresh as can be," Rowarc called out and then clarified, spinning a freshly-hewn chair to sit in it facing the back of the chair.

"I wasn't sure if I'd find you here. I half-expected you to be out and about doing your old job."

"I'm done with that. Besides, won't matter much with the Blood Night just about done. It's just been me and Mary running things. Not much business to speak of—what with everyone just trying to survive."

"That's kind of what I'm here to talk to you about," Radin offered, with his right hand extended palm-up, as if to proffer up some proposal.

"Oh. You look good." Rowarc didn't intentionally want to change the subject, but his gut was talking to him—loudly so.

"Dad. Stay with me."

"You've been learning a lot from that Damon fella." Not wanting to let this conversation go where it needed, Rowarc shunned the idea of the man before him being little more than a reminder of the boy he thought was once his.

"Dad. Please. Hear me out," Radin pleaded, seeing his father's eyebrows furrow as he retreated into silence with his elbows tucked into his chest—albeit now listening. "You didn't cause those men to die, Dad. I did. I can't let you live with that burden that belongs to me."

"Mary, where's that damn bread," Rowarc yelled out with his voice carrying well beyond and behind the bar.

"Okay. I'm just going to keep talking, and hopefully you'll keep listening." He paused, seeing the sheen of guilt washing over his father's eyes, clearly not letting go as he had hoped for Rowarc. "When Damon came to get me. When my son...," he paused at the thought of his unborn child being ripped from Elise's womb by his own actions. "…He led me back to Axum where he wielded some power like nothing I'd ever seen before."

"This isn't going to bring my men back," Rowarc interjected under his breath.

"No, it certainly won't. But, I'm telling you, Damon was able to wield this power using something I've never seen before, and I'm still trying to understand. Damon has many sources of power—not like most mages who only have one. One of those sources is souls. Before going into combat with a powerful foe, he—"

"He killed my men. So, don't you go taking the blame for Damon. That's not your new job. At least I hope it's not."

"He wouldn't have done it if I hadn't summoned the Chairman."

"Who?"

"Not important, Dad. I just wanted you to know that he couldn't have summoned the Chairman without me, and I freely chose to do it because of what happened to my son. It might have been the right choice, or it might have been the wrong choice, but either way your men are dead because of *my* choice."

Mary Danvers had snuck up on them quietly with a plate of bread and cheese. The bread looked right awful—shriveled up with no real whole grains to speak of and barely risen, but Radin assumed it was the work of the Blood Night—his curse upon the land he once loved. Seeing her look upon him with profound eyes of judgment told him everything he already knew. He was a monster—just like Damon.

"Sorry, you didn't need to hear that." Radin bowed his head to Mary, taking the plate from her. Tears in her eyes, she pivoted and practically ran back into the kitchen.

"I understand. Is that all you came to say?" It wasn't exactly a friendly tone, but Radin had dredged up some bile memories for him—memories he wasn't ready to relive.

"No, Dad. I wanted to tell you, I'm trying as hard as I can to fix what I've done wrong. It won't be much longer now," Radin suggested, tearing a meager piece from the meager loaf of bread. "I promise. It won't be much longer," he reiterated, getting up to leave and never return. "Goodbye, Dad." He never looked back, but he could feel Rowarc's eyes on him—no

Charles W. McDonald Jr.

longer judging, only wishing him well, blood son or not.

His *Portal* whooshed closed behind him. Radin needed to finish his conversation with Damon. There was something else he needed to understand, and it couldn't wait another moment. This time he knocked on the outer door casing of the decoy room to Damon's fourth-floor study.

"Come," Damon's familiar voice called out to him from beyond the veil as Radin's body slipped through into the space carved out of nothing from magic.

Seeing Damon had changed into what he knew to be Earth garb, he wondered where on Earth his father would be off to next. "What is Led Zeppelin, Father?"

"Not so much a what as a collection of who. Perhaps I'll introduce you to them some day," he offered from behind his massive, but functional, desk.

"Very good. If I can trouble you for something else before you leave for Earth."

"It needs to be fast. I'm on a tight timeline."

"I'm sure you are, Father. Why was an illustration of me in the book Elise used to find me? Did you put that illustration there? I'm speaking of the book that referenced the handcuffs that we discussed when you were teaching me *Damon's Rift*."

"I know what you speak of, and I remember the conversation."

"Did you put it there, Father?"

"No…," Damon lied—sort of. It was a rare thing for him—only done out of pure necessity, but he needed Radin, and answering this wouldn't help with that.

Radin squinted at Damon with scrutinous grey-blue eyes. Rarely did he question a word that came from Damon's lips, but something didn't set right with him. His instincts were rarely wrong, and his instincts told him Damon had left the breadcrumbs for Michelle, Lawna, and Elise to find him. *If not Damon, then who…?* "I believe you," Radin lied, closely examining his father's reaction. "If not you, then who?"

Charles W. McDonald Jr.

"Perhaps it was the *Eye*," Damon offered without elaborating.

"Perhaps. Thank you, Damon." The lack of the familial term threw Damon off, causing Damon's black gems to furrow as Radin walked out without so much as another word.

He had bigger fish to fry and Seals to hasten. A *Gate* swallowed him into the floorboards of his study, depositing him just outside Warwick, New York, where he had work to do.

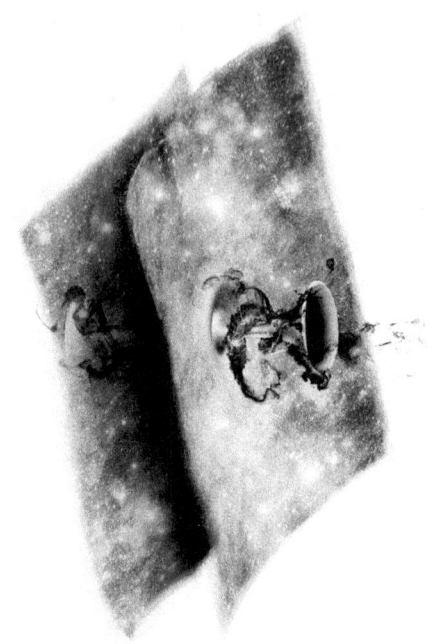

Chapter 34: Entanglement Broken

(The West Texas Plains, Earth, Present Day)

T's wife stared back at Mira in waves of contempt—layered by the body she knew her husband lusted after and the bullets the woman had used to steal her husband's body from her and her children. In every way, Mira was a home-wrecker, a slut, and deserving of death—Damon or no Damon. Besides, no one had seen nor heard from Damon in months. Out of sight, out of mind as far as she was concerned.

"I know it's a difficult concept to grasp," Howard offered, extending left hand outstretched palm-up in a gesture of explanation.

"Difficult," Kai postulated, his Asian accent cracking under his excitement as his dark eyes scrutinized and parsed every word coming out of Howard's mouth. They'd been warned this would be a highly technical defense, so they had their smartest people on the hastily-assembled jury that would determine Mira's fate. "What you're talking about is pure speculation that has NEVER been proven in any real-world application."

"That's not entirely true. Entanglement has been proven on an elemental level with momentum and rotation," Howard preempted what he
knew Mira would offer, motioning her to stay quiet with his left hand as he
stood as her defense just to her right before the nine-person jury.

"Yes, but not with any real information and certainly not on a system as large-scale as a human being," Kai quickly countered, staring down
Mira some ten feet away who stood near the opening of the tent.

"You don't think it possible, with everything we've all heard about
this Damon fella, that his interactions with Mira might have been powerful
enough to reach across time in a quantum wave method of communication,
causing Mira's mind to temporarily short circuit in what might have felt like
a very intense form of déjà vu to her? Think about what you've heard about
Damon—about what we've all heard about him, and tell me it isn't plausible, if not even likely." Howard paced to and fro between Kai and Mira, positioning himself, literally, in the jury's line of fire. Arranged along the back
wall of the tent, each member of the jury open-carried holstered sidearms
while two of the largest men Howard had ever seen guarded the only exit to
the administrative tent behind a seated Mira, each armed with M4s.

"I admit, from everything LT told me of Damon, that he might be
extraordinary beyond our understanding," Karren—LT's wife—postulated
while hatefully staring at Mira from across the tent, seated front and center
of the jury panel. "That doesn't make this science fiction defense of yours
any more plausible than aliens landing outside our tent."

Mira coughed into her braided-rope cuffed hand, apparently the
idea not all that far-fetched from her own experiences.

"If you'd already made up your mind to kill her, why even ask me
to present a defense," Howard protested, placing his hand flat against Mira's
back in a show of support and comfort.

"Because we are not animals, Howard. If this is your defense, then I
think we're ready to take a vote." Karren looked at the others down each end
of the jury panel who—to a person—nodded in agreement.

"I'm sorry...," Howard whispered into Mira's ear. As he stepped
away from her, the votes came in via written notes on little white slips of paper read by LT's wife before she announced the summary decision.

Charles W. McDonald Jr.

"By a vote of eight to one, Mira Castille, you are found guilty of two counts capital murder in the first degree and are hereby sentenced to *hang by the neck until you are **dead**. This sentence to be carried out immediately!*" With a nod, the two burly men in fatigues guarding the exit roughly grabbed Mira by each arm, picking her feet off the ground, carrying her to the exit flap of the tent as tears began streaming from her face.

She was ready to meet her maker. She'd been steeling herself for this moment. But that couldn't stop the relentless stream of tears escaping her beautiful, starlit, but mentally and physically exhausted, blue eyes.

Outside, a crude platform had been constructed with a trap door she was now being hastily positioned above. It felt solid under her feet, but as the heavy braided rope was quickly thrown around her neck and the noose tightened, she knew it was over. She just hoped her life had meant enough. Her brief life raced before her mind's eye, and she couldn't help but smile, but that smile quickly vanished as her thoughts drifted to Damon; she *still* couldn't comprehend how it had ended between them.

She could see Howard standing below the platform, trying to maintain eye contact with her, and then he suddenly disappeared just as the noose was being tightened around her neck and they were beginning to pull the slack out of the rope from the system of pulleys above. Without even asking if she had any last words, or offering her a priest, the trap door flipped down, letting her body fall through just as a single shot rang out from behind, severing the rope enough to let her fall feet-first, hitting the dirt below as she collapsed in a pile on the ground below the platform.

"COME ON," Howard urged, sliding to a stop just beneath the platform. "WE'VE GOTTA MOVE!" In a flash, he had her up on her feet, dragging her to his running Jeep® where he unceremoniously tossed her butt inside and jumped in after her, stomping on the gas as he nearly ran over six people tearing out of the encampment.

"Where are we going?" Mira coughed out the question, wishing she had a hand free to remove the severed rope from her neck.

"Remember my coordinates from the déjà vu I told you about…?" Howard motioned with his right hand toward the GPS position on the eight-inch UConnect® screen in the center console of the dash, reporting

Charles W. McDonald Jr.

they were still sixty-plus minutes out at current speed.

"I bet that's the first, and last, time broken entanglement theory will ever be used in a capital murder defense," Mira mused, still in coughing fits as she tried to pull the rope away from her now red-marked neck.

"Broken entanglement is how I knew to come find you, and it's the only reason you're still alive," Howard offered as food for thought as his engine screamed into the night, carrying them away from the preppers at well over 100MPH down dirt roads, cacti, and sweeping plains.

Turning to look behind them, she could see the headlights of two other vehicles chasing them down the dirt road. The 392-HEMI® engine already snarled like a pissed-off dragon from the dual three-inch exhaust, but as she pointed to the unwanted company behind them, Howard floored it, reaching over to toss open the glove compartment for her. "Let's see those deadly pistol skills of yours." Howard make a quick swipe with his tactical knife at the braided ropes tying Mira's hands. It wasn't enough to completely free her, but maybe enough for her to shoot.

The 9mm Glock® felt good and balanced in her hands, even if they were still loosely tied with a cumbersome, braided rope. The luminescent night sight helped, too, but hitting a moving target from another moving target, especially while the suspension was fighting the dirt road, it was going to take a miracle to hit anything but tumbleweed, dirt, or cacti. Briefly considering praying, instead she reached into her thoughts, calling out to the one deity she thought would care the most. She couldn't tell if the first round hit anything, nor the second, but the third had struck paydirt as one of the headlight beams burst out of existence, then another, then a strike through the windshield sent that 4x4 F-150 sideways down an embankment, crashing and sending its occupants through the windshield. The next shot fired must have struck the engine block of the trailing truck; a trail of steam shot out from the grill, and their chase was done too.

"Remind me not to piss you off," Howard jabbed with a nervous smile, but her face told him that her thoughts were a million miles away.

Still praying he would come to her in her hour of need, Mira's soul cried out to Damon—pleading.

Her RAM® HD pickup now disabled and leaking both oil and water all over the tumbleweed ground of the West Texas Plains, Karren watched Howard's Jeep® roar off into the distance to God knows where—taking that *whore* with him. Pulling her silver and grey model 92 Beretta® 9mm from her shoulder holster, she pivoted, pushing her body back for a clean shot, as she fired into the engine of her own vehicle—furious! "AHHHH! FUCK-ING BITCH!" Looking at her heavily-bearded driver, she thought about pointing the gun at him too, but instead muzzled it down to the dirt. "Get on the radio and get some more men out here. NOW!"

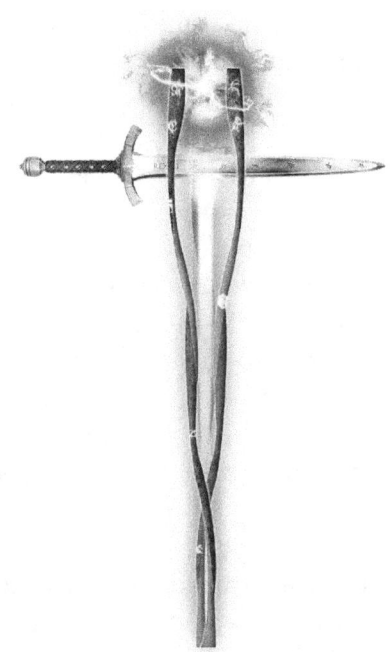

Chapter 35: Intractable Crossroads

(Osalin, Perion, Present Day)

The simplistic shelter was abandoned—not surprising given his last conversation with Daedrin. Still, there had been hope. May-be. *There is no hope for you. You'll just have to learn to live with it,* Talemar thought, looking into his mortifying reflection in a pool of dirty water, resting in a footprint he assumed belonging to Daedrin.

"Great Talemar, I barely recognized you." The ancient and famil-iar voice called from behind and to the rear, his boots being lapped by a Blood-Night-accosted ocean.

Pivoting to the middle-aged voice, who *would* be his natural enemy, Talemar's hand fell to Starfire at his hip, which began to glow instantaneous-ly at his touch and in recognition of the foe before him. "Castlin, I hope you brought help—for your sake."

"There's the old Talemar I know. That's the spirit!" Castlin's smile was caustic, bitter, and recognizable as more than the man he once knew.

Charles W. McDonald Jr.

"You can change your shell a million times, and I'll still be able to recognize you." Talemar's grip tightened on Starfire, unclipping its scabbard.

"And your appearance, Great Talemar.... My, how your path has vexed and rebuked thee." Castlin paused his approach toward Talemar, now only a few steps away. "You won't be needing Starfire. I'm not here for combat. I came to talk."

"I have nothing to say to you."

"Then listen. What harm would it do for you to listen?"

"Your words are poison. Your thoughts are...."

"Let us have a moment to bury the past, Great Talemar." Sitting cross-legged on the beach to reduce his own threat-level, Castlin tried to bring down the vitriolic hate and history between them. "I'm not here for Eldrac, nor Xarn, nor Anna, nor the Six. I'm here to see if there is an alignment.... For us."

"Alignment?!"

"Damon of Basrat means to bring about chaos untold—an ending no one has ever seen, nor experienced. None of us know what lay on the other side of it. Is that what you seek?"

A very long pause as Talemar tried to find his way in this. What was relatively certain before, was no more. He was rudderless and without sail—lost. "I.... I don't know."

Nodding his head in agreement, Castlin offered a moment of shared naked thought between them. "Neither do I. I thought I knew, but I no longer know where my services should fall or if I should just sit it out and see what happens."

"But you have your orders, Castlin. That much about you, I know."

"Indeed. I do."

"You need not tell me what they are. I know, for I know your allegiance."

"And have you ever disobeyed a direct order, Great Talemar?"

Talemar only nodded in reply. Indeed, he had—many times. Many times, he'd gone against conventional wisdom and conventional order to follow his gut. But his gut was currently in absentia ever since he'd been cursed by Damon. "I know you well enough to know you want to end up on the winning side, Castlin. So, what does your gut tell you about who will win this most-epic of battles?"

"What if I had something better to go on than my gut?"

"I'm listening, Castlin, but not for much longer."

"Hear me out, Talemar. I'm not talking about ordinary divination or witchcraft. I'm talking about genuine insight from a player you may not even recognize as on the board at all. Would you entertain an audience with her?"

It's a trap! His mind screamed at him from every corner of his consciousness.

"With the coming war and the players on *this* board, *any* outcome is possible. *ANY* outcome. It's important that we all know what we're getting into and where our influences should be leveraged. Surely the Great Talemar would agree…?"

"Set up your meeting, Castlin."

"You didn't even ask me *who she* was. That's not like you."

"Where I'm going to insist you set up this meeting, it won't matter who *she* is."

"Oh…. Do tell. This should be interesting," Castlin offered, clasping his hands together at their fingertips.

"The Halls of Aaramus. I will meet you and your key player in the Halls of Aaramus."

"Oooh. Wounded you are not. Disfigured, yes, but not wounded…? Neh. Very well, Talemar. I will set it up. Don't be late! *She* doesn't like to be kept waiting!"

(Damon's Manor, Eden, Present Day)

His stately room of three-stage crown and ornament-rich niches on the third floor had been more than accommodating, and being close to the spell test room had already proven useful, as he'd put it to far more frequent use than had Damon of late. Damon had been off, Creator only knows where, on an ever-frequent basis, but that was just Damon being Damon. Still, the handmade, four-post canopy bed was elegant enough for royalty with its slightly rosewood tint of stain over native wood—they called it Negi

Moss. It had similar grain properties to Earth maple but was as hard as dog-wood or walnut and as pretty as red oak but without the tint—making it a beautiful organic platform to receive the rosy-tinted stain.

Sitting up in bed, resting against a nest of pillows, he looked up at the underside of the cream and blood-red canopy, wondering about his counterpart on Perion. He hadn't seen or heard from Talemar in quite some time, and that was a powerful force of nature to be left in perpetual silence and unguided. He found himself thinking in ways akin to Illirian, Yksther-in, or Talemar himself, but strategy was important—especially now—and Talemar himself was a high-valued piece about the board of this immortal game they were playing. He needed to know and understand Talemar's role, for he felt as if he'd abandoned that piece to fate, and that was very likely the wrong thing to do. He had a lot on his plate for certain, but a lot was predicated on sequence, and that sequence had not yet fired in the precise order—yet. That had left him with time—time with which to consider and reconsider his mistakes and his own inactions.

Without pomp or pageantry, a silvery-blue flash of light announced the arrival of a small piece of torn parchment, gouged in the language of another world but gouged by powerful Arcane nonetheless. Exposure to Kaleion and its common tongue, as well as its old tongue, led him to imme-diately interpret the message for what it was and wasn't in all its simplicity. "Agreed.... M."

Snorting—not in derision, but more in his understanding of the sender, Radin thought aloud, "Chatty fellow." As he considered this other thread of proposal alongside his curiosity and concern over Talemar, Radin began assembling his arguments both for, and against, for surely Damon would press him for his critical thinking on the matter, and either way it went down, Damon would not be happy. Unfortunately, they were past making Damon happy; now it was only about the survival of Man.

Charles W. McDonald Jr.

Chapter 36: Problem Solved

(The South China Sea, Earth, Present Day)

Rena had been beyond tight-lipped about what this 'thing' of supreme value was that she was trying to retrieve—save that it had been stolen from her nearly sixty years ago. When asked, 'why go after it now, why not get it back immediately,' Rena's only reply was, 'because they would have expected that.' Possessing more secrets than the CIA, NSA, and MI-6 combined, Rena even ran her own intelligence agency—which hadn't surprised either Lawna or Michelle, but this mission didn't exactly dovetail with the rest of the mission parameters from JSOC leadership and the SEAL Team Lead. Sitting on the edge of her bunk, Michelle tried to close the gap between the two mission parameters, but she didn't like having divided loyalties for this very reason.

"Apple iWatch for your thoughts," Lawna jabbed with a pensive smile, knowing that troubled look on her wife's face all too well as she paced nonchalantly, from one end of their crew quarters to the other.

"Stop it. You're not giving that thing up, and you know it."

"True…but I know that look."

"What look?!"

"That brooding and conflicted look you have all over your face right now."

"Well, I'm conflicted, dammit!"

"Only because you're too much of a patriot," Lawna considered aloud.

"Pardon me?"

"Look, I love the stars and stripes as much as you—well, almost as

Charles W. McDonald Jr.

much. But, we're Rena's resources, and you need to get used to that. I've come to terms with it, but I don't think you have."

"You don't trust Rena one bit more than I do—maybe less even."

"That wasn't my point. We're in Rena's Immortal Army now—SEAL TEAMs or not. You need to come to terms with that."

"And she needs to come to terms with the fact that we can't always just blatantly break protocol for her whenever and wherever she feels like it. A double-agent is only useful if her cover isn't blown."

"Is that what we are...? Double-agents?"

"Not exactly, but kind of...yeah!"

"You really *are* conflicted!"

"FUCK YOU!"

"Promises. Promises." Lawna smiled broadly at that, pausing her pace right in front of Michelle, knowing it would dig at Michelle just a tad bit more. "You know you want to," she teased, making grinding motions with her butt in fatigues.

"*Real* attractive." Michelle reacted with raised eyebrows, apparently shocked at the depravity of her wife in this most tense situation where she was trying to work a serious problem that might prevent them from being shot or otherwise put in Leavenworth, Kansas. She'd never even been to Kansas before. Her random thought somehow led her full circle back to the original problem.... Their mission was to disable the Chinese Type 002 aircraft carrier—their flagship designated CV-18—not to abduct their flagship command flag officer, Rear Admiral Yin Yiping. Well, abducting him hadn't been their explicit order from Rena, but it had been all but authorized to get this 'thing' back—whatever the fuck it was. If Rena wasn't going to tell her or Lawna what this 'thing' was or at least give a description of it, abducting the alleged thief seemed the only reasonable outcome so Rena could interrogate him. That presented its own set of problems she wasn't sure how they were going to get around. She just wished Rena had given them some better guidance.

"You think they'll really do it," Michelle asked.

"Join up with their North Korean counterparts and protect a major above-ground test?" Lawna assumed she was referring to the Intel briefing they'd just received, but Michelle's mind always operated on multiple levels,

Charles W. McDonald Jr.

so it was always best to verify.

"Do you trust the intel? That was what I was really getting at."

"Your guess is as good as mine, but the direction they're currently sailing says a lot!"

"Yes, it does. North by northeast and in a big hurry too." Looking down at her watch—twenty mikes to feet wet. "Shit, we've gotta go. We'll have to figure the rest of this out on the fly."

"Situation normal—FUBAR! Mike. Charlie. Foxtrot." (Massive Cluster Fuck) Lawna smiled outwardly, but she was all pins and needles on the inside, and Michelle knew it as she put on her tactical vest over her body armor and slung *Bad Intentions* over her shoulder along with her gear, closing the bulkhead door behind her as they headed to the muster point in the hangar decks in the belly of the CVN Ronald Reagan.

*   *   *   *

After being transferred to the USS Seawolf and then to the Advanced SEAL Delivery System, which was basically a mini-stealth submarine designed for clandestine Operator delivery, the team reviewed blueprints of the all-new Chinese Type 002 Aircraft Carrier in total silence. Intel gave them confidence that the Advanced SEAL Delivery System 'should' still be stealthy enough not to be caught by passive sonar or other detection systems 'thought' to have been in service both on and around the brand-new flagship carrier, but those were all 'maybes' as far as Michelle was concerned.

A blonde bang snuck its way out from under her helmet as she blew at it, getting it out of her line-of-sight. Dressed in wet gear over light armor, she 'felt' ready, even though this was her first trip downrange as an Operator. Still, she didn't want to blow this. There was so much on the line. First female Operator deployed to the field. First mission for Rena. At least she had Lawna here by her side. She wasn't a bundle of nerves or anything, but she fidgeted silently with her scope, trying to get her mind right for what had to be done—hoping she'd be able to think fast enough on her feet to make this all work out.

Being a successful Operator was at least fifty percent in the head as she'd been told over and over and over as she reached out, in total silence, to that calm place in her mind's eye Rena's training had brought into focus after becoming an immortal soldier. It wasn't entirely unlike meditation, this technique of clearing the mind of cluttered thoughts and murky probabilities to visualize what success actually looked like. To clear a mental space for success to breathe and grow and flourish.

Her heart rate slowed as the visions crystalized in her mind.

Opening her eyes, she wasn't shocked to see a hard-pressed look from Commander Alvarez trying to tear through her immortal shell like sunlight would have done had it not been for Rena's advanced genomics project. But, another smile from Lawna made the world right as rain again as the Advanced SEAL Delivery System's pace suddenly slowed to a crawl beneath the 110,000-ton, skyscraper-sized target above.

EMCON (Emissions Control) had everyone using hand signals, as Commander Alvarez stood, waving the twelve-man team of Operators to the hatch where the chamber would be flooded, and pressure equalized, allowing the team to close the last bit of distance between themselves and their objective. Two-thirds of the team split off, making their way to the rudder and propeller assembly of the great carrier while the rest began scaling the exterior of the starboard aft hull in the dead of night.

There was no possible way four of them would make it through the throngs of sailors they would have encountered if they'd come in through the aft nest (fantail), but making their way quietly, silently, and efficiently along outside on the carrier deck, they quickly found themselves at the conning control tower where they'd find the flagship flag officer's quarters. With Alvarez riding point, Michelle right on his ass, and Lawna right on hers, Lieutenant Commander Ferguson brought up the rear in a trailing position since he was the most comfortable walking backwards, although Lawna probably had the best swivel hips of the group.

M4s at eye level—each looking through their scopes—they ascended the tight stairwell as a four-piece unit. The teenage, enlisted man in dark-blue navy fatigues didn't know what hit him as they rounded the platform to ascend to the next level up and the silenced NATO 5.56mm round from Alvarez's M4 made quick work of his chest, downing him on-the-spot as Michelle quickly dragged his body out of sight, tucking him behind some built-in storage units and ductwork. Less than a second later, she was back

Charles W. McDonald Jr.

behind Alvarez, ascending the remaining levels as a unit until reaching the command officer's deck. Michelle's left hand was on the door marked 'Flag Officer' in kanji, or Han, characters. Alvarez had his left hand on the door marked 'Captain.' On the hand countdown of three, they both opened the doors simultaneously, bursting inside with Ferguson backing up Michelle and Lawna backing up Alvarez.

The middle-aged, 5'9" man with a curved scar over his left brow had been leaning over oceanic cartography with navigational tools of the trade, but quickly shoved himself away from the table and began reaching for something at his desk. Before he could even get to his desk, Lawna was standing between the man and his desk with her duct-tape-laden hands completely covering his mouth, using a beefy zip tie on his hands as she smoothly shoved them behind his back and threw his body over her back like he was barely a sack of rice.

Michelle estimated the man in front of her to be at least in his early sixties, but she knew that didn't jive with his complicated story. The man Rena described had to be at least ninety; she had told Michelle that he shouldn't even still be an active line officer, but this man clearly was given his fitted-white uniform. *White was going to be a problem*, she considered as she rushed the man of exceedingly calm demeanor who didn't make any sudden moves. In an instant, Michelle was on him and Ferguson right behind him, tying him up with heavy zip-ties as Michelle calmly placed duct tape over his entire mouth. His eyes looked back at her knowingly, but none too happy about it as she pulled a black plastic bag from her gear and threw it over the top of him, tying off the bottom as she threw him over her shoulder to carry him out.

In EMCON, they couldn't radio back their status. JSOC command knew they'd be lights-out for at least two solid hours, and it had already been well over one so far as they began descending the slender stairwell the same way they'd come up—with M4s at eye level—ready to blast their way home if necessary. That's when it all went to shit! Alarms sounded, and red

Charles W. McDonald Jr.

lights were flashing everywhere as they hastened down the slender stairwell, rounding the platform where Michelle saw blood splattered on the platform's grated floor but couldn't sense the sailor's presence from where she knew she put him. He'd clearly been found, and that meant they would be expected as they came out of the stairwell. Stopping dead in her tracks with Lawna right behind her, Michelle hand-signaled Alvarez to toss two grenades from the lower part of the stairwell to the lower platform where it led to the gallery (flight deck). An instant later, the combined explosion burst the hatch from its hinges outward, killing several armed men that had been waiting for them both on the outside flight deck and base of the control tower. Gunfire erupting from behind, they raced their packages to the edge of the flight deck where Michelle and Lawna jumped one right behind the other, adjusting their packages on the way down to enter the water vertically with them as Alvarez and Ferguson splashed right behind.

*   *   *   *

He estimated the briefing room to be comparable to his own—about twelve feet by sixteen feet with two equally-sized tables hard-mounted to the painted steel floor and three rows of cushioned chairs with cascading, layered whiteboard, a projector screen that rolled up into the ceiling and an HD projector hung from the ceiling. It could have had a max occupancy of around twenty, but it was just the six of them—for now. "Hei Cheng. Captain. 410100197012189079." The brooding captain had little else to say to the four-person team that had abducted him plus one obvious intelligence officer staring them down through red bangs and green eyes of obvious Irish descent—her cute freckles ascending her creamy neckline belied her cruel intent.

"We heard you the first four times, Captain," the intelligence officer in dark-blue fatigues without a nametag countered with Michelle and Lawna standing right behind her. The trio of hard women apparently not having any effect on the forty-nine-year-old career naval officer. "Tell us about the plans you saw from the Norfolk Naval Shipyards. What did you see? We know you saw plans that included our EMALS (Electromagnetic Aircraft Launch System) system. What else was in those plans? What was the level of detail you saw?"

"Hei Cheng. Captain. 410100197012189079."

WHACK! The intelligence officer's right hand struck across his jaw so hard and so fast it knocked one of his incisor teeth loose, leaving a great red whelp across his jawline, causing curious looks from Alvarez and Ferguson and semi-knowing looks from Lawna and Michelle. "We can do this all day and well into the night, Captain!" Her green eyes grew forest-green dark, staring through those red bangs at him. "You don't want to dance with me!" That statement prompted a knowing nod from Michelle. Rena had planted another one of her Immortal Army soldiers into this to ensure an outcome acceptable to RR.

"You have committed an act of war," Captain Cheng coolly declared.

"So fucking what! We're already in a de facto state of war. That wasn't my question." WHACK! Another one of the captain's bloodied teeth was sent flying across the room.

Blood now rolling down the captain's chin, staining his uniform, he looked between the five of them, wondering what his superior would offer up to them and wondering why they hadn't started with him first. He'd barely seen half of what the Admiral had, if that much. If they were after the root and stem of the leak, they should have been talking to him. He had to give them something or he had to find a way to die that he could accept. "Let's talk about what you're really after," the captain calmly offered, spitting blood onto the perfectly painted flooring of the CVN Ronald Reagan.

"And, what do you think that is," Michelle interrupted, only to see the intelligence officer spin and give her a shut-the-fuck-up, right-goddamn-now look.

"You want the source of the leaks, and you want to know my orders," he countered with another spit of blood onto the floor as Michelle offered him her embroidered handkerchief.

"We're listening." The intelligence officer reasserted her position of command, getting in between Michelle and the captain.

"As far as I know, the leak came from the technical blueprint change control management team at the Norfolk Naval Shipyard. The codename

I've always heard associated with the source was 'Petunia.'" That had their attention even if it hadn't pointed a spotlight directly on any one particular person. Still, they'd be able to narrow it down from that, and it would end their flow of highly classified information for certain. So be it. They were pretty much on equal footing now—China and the US, but as far as he was concerned they had the upper hand on him—for the moment.

"And your orders, Captain," the intelligence officer pressed, leaning forward as if preparing to strike again.

"They'll probably launch from Kusŏng. We were to sail to NW of Guam (N 14° 10.751169' / E 144° 8.4375') to intercept any bombers taking off to respond to the test."

"You mean an above-ground test," the intelligence officer clarified.

"Above-ocean," the captain replied, adding, "EMP. Airburst."

"Thank you, Captain." The intelligence officer relaxed, handing him an ice-cold can of Coke®. "You did the right thing. For your country, and ours."

"And the world," Michelle added, motioning for him to keep her handkerchief.

"What will happen to my crew and my ship?"

"They will not be allowed to make it to Guam, Captain. That we cannot allow." The intelligence officer motioned for the others to follow her out of the briefing room where it had been secured by two MPs—from the outside—on either exit door. "Stay in there with him," she hissed at the MPs with her index finger pointed threateningly. "If he kills himself, I kill you!" Both MPs practically fell over each other trying to beat each other into the briefing room to ensure the prisoner was still alive. "Commander Alvarez. Lt. Commander Ferguson," addressing them both to get their attention. "I think between us and the MPs we have this under control. Could you relay to the command staff what we've learned and that they are to position the fleet between Guam and the Chinese Carrier Battlegroup and at a distance of at least one thousand nautical miles and keep their battlegroup out of aircraft strike range of any flightpath we might use to respond to any DPRK aggression?"

The captain and lieutenant commander looked between each other, and then the three women who formed a tight semi-circle as if operating as their own independent unit.

"I'll be along if we learn anything from the Admiral of consequence, but looking from that man, I doubt it will be much. The captain was the easier target, and that's why I wanted to start with him first." Her red hair tussled under her fatigue cap as she bristled her orders at them, still overtly asserting *her* control over the situation.

Raised eyebrows from Commander Alvarez at the none-too-polite blow-off from the intelligence officer as he mouthed something under his breath while pulling Ferguson away by his arm, "O.G.A."

"Love you too," she mouthed, pulling Michelle and Lawna with her to the other briefing room where the admiral was being held. "We've got maybe thirty mikes tops before someone barges in on us. Let *us* run this show. Got it?!"

Us, Michelle thought as her left hand turned the knob that opened the door to the briefing room next-door to the one they'd previously used, to see Rena standing there—smiling and the admiral sitting opposite her at the table still with that knowing, smug look on his face. Something told her he wouldn't be so smug for long.

"My sweet Darlings," Rena offered with her arms held wide to hug Lawna first, then Michelle, causing the admiral to frown.

"Don't start with that name, rank, and serial number bullshit," Michelle threatened, seeing right through him. "I know *what* you are."

The intelligence officer practically hissed at her in rebuke of failing to follow their agreement that was more akin to an order.

"Do you now," the admiral replied in perfect, unbroken English.

In perfect Russian, Rena countered, "Он шпион. Нет?" Translated, '*He's a spy. No?*' "Русский шпион." '*A Russian spy.*' "Trafficking both US and Chinese trade secrets back to Mother Russia. Isn't that right, Admiral Yin Yiping?" The last she didn't bother translating to Russian since his English was as good as his Chinese *and* his Russian—and many other languages he'd learned in his tradecraft.

"He should be at least ninety. How'd he do it," Michelle asked, throwing an index finger up at the intelligence officer to preempt any hateful comment or glower from her.

"Because of something he took from me. Something that doesn't belong to him." Rena's fingernails suddenly grew long and hard as her right index finger drove down with a smooth swipe, severing the admiral's left index finger at the last knuckle, causing him to cry out in pain as the distal phalanx rolled about the perfectly painted floor in a bloody, precision-cut mess.

"You CUNT," he hissed at her again in perfect English, grabbing at his finger to stop the hemorrhaging. "I don't have it anymore."

"You know how old I am. Don't you think I've learned how to see through the best liars on Earth?" Rena didn't pace or even appear agitated. She just calmly sat within striking distance of the admiral, clicking her long, hardened nails one against the other as if playing. She was the very large and very hungry cat, and he was the mouse.

His eyes darted between the four of them, calculating. He knew there to be at least several guards on the outside of those doors, and he presumed the other women in front of him Rena's progeny. He knew what she was capable of—or at least thought he knew—given what he'd read of her journal. *Was this the end for him?* If there was a way out of this for him, it would have to involve getting off this ship and away from the numbers. His tradecraft had saved him many times, but not from a handful of immortal creatures. "I don't have it with me. You know I'd never carry it on me. You know me better than that."

"I do, Admiral. I do...," Rena agreed, crawling her hand along the table toward him like a deadly spider about to strike.

"It's in a locker—in Vladivostok. I'll take you there."

"Mother, we don't have much more time for this. I'll have to create a diversion if we're to get him off the ship," the red-head intelligence officer offered, checking the doors behind them and in front of them.

"Before you take him anywhere, he needs to give us something we can use. The others won't believe he had nothing more to offer above the captain. It will compromise us if we don't have something useful to offer that could only have come from him." Bringing things back into perspective, Michelle tried to determine—given what she knew of him and his role in this, plus what she knew of what they were looking for at a strategic level—what information might be useful. "What were your orders, Admiral? You specifically. What were *your* orders?"

Charles W. McDonald Jr.

"From which government?" He played coy, then suddenly felt Rena sever the distal phalanx from his left middle finger as it rolled about the floor. "FUCK! YOU BITCH!"

Michelle smiled, but held back a nervousness as she knew time was running out; Lawna looked between the two doors with her M4 held at the ready, as if expecting a rude interruption any moment.

"Shall I take another," Rena asked sadistically. "I haven't had this much fun in a long, long time."

"I'm supposed to order the bombing of the US base on Guam in response to the shoot-down of our aircraft. The captain doesn't know, but my command code will authenticate with him. If you'll give me something to write on and a pencil, I'll write it down for you."

Pulling her pocket notepad and pencil from her dark-blue fatigues, the intelligence officer pushed it across the table toward Admiral Yiping where he took it up with his still-functioning right hand, beginning to write in Han.

" 晚上，中途岛，日德兰半岛 "Translated, 'Night, Midway, Jutland."

"What did you have in mind for a diversion?" Michelle turned to the beautiful red-head, whose smile was both sinful and deviant.

"Come with me." She romantically gripped Michelle's hand, interlacing their fingers, causing Lawna to frown.

As soon as the door facing Rena—to Lawna's back—closed, Rena frowned, too, adding, "I'm sorry, Darling." With a smooth motion, Rena sliced Lawna straight through her fatigues, deep across her mid-section with her elongated fingernails, causing Lawna to double-over in pain as she collapsed to the floor in a wounded heap.

"I've told you to keep your mouth shut, and I meant it. I'm running this interrogation," the beautiful intelligence officer berated Michelle directly in front of the MPs with her finger stuck right between Michelle's heavy breasts.

Michelle wasn't totally following the distraction concept just yet so the only thing that came to mind was, "Fuck you!"

"I bet you'd like that! Wouldn't you?! Well, let's see what you've got." Without warning, Michelle suddenly got the concept of the distraction as the red-head leaned in and began making out with her right in front of the two male MPs, who collectively responded with dropped jaws and bulging eyes.

The MPs didn't notice, and the intelligence officer barely did either, and she knew what to look for, but the blur that whooshed past them barely registered with Michelle's tongue probing the intelligence officer's mouth.

The corporate blacked-out Bell® 525 helicopter waiting on the flight deck already had the rotors turning when RR showed up in a blur with the wounded Admiral, still spurting blood all over his pretty dress-white navy uniform. A brunette in her early twenties, with pale-green eyes dressed in an all-black jumpsuit, threw a blanket over the soft, cream leather interior as she helped strap in the admiral while the helmeted pilot was already getting clearance from the control tower to leave.

*   *   *   *

Some twelve hours later at VVO (Vladivostok International Airport), a very long, double-stacked array of taupe-painted rental lockers with black combination dial windows low along the top rack and high along the bottom rack with a small silver pushbutton alongside, lay before Rena and Yin, who still clutched at what remained of his left hand—covered in a blood-soaked, white linen rag.

"Which one, Admiral?" Rena's eyes darted this way and that, keeping an eye out for trouble. Supremely confident in her own personal abilities, it was still her first time out alone without any of her immortal soldiers to aid if something went wrong.

"There." He pointed with his functional right hand. "Combination, 2370."

"Your birth year alongside your wife's. How sentimental of you…. Did you weep for her at her funeral?"

"What business is that of yours?"

Calmly opening the door since she sensed no traps and had his body in front of her in case of any shrapnel, she pushed him aside as she opened the slim, plain, and smooth silver box before her to reveal an ancient leather-bound journal with Cyrillic script on the front cover, "**Карастович**

Катарена Ректович." Translated, 'Carastovich Catarena Rectovich.' Flipping through the first fifty or so pages, she confirmed the account was still there in her original handwriting of her personal journal. "Very good, Admiral. Very good." In a whirl, they were outside the airport, slowing to a walk as the door to the locker swung at the vacuum of their absence. "We will settle this the old way. N'est-ce pas," she offered in French—his country of birth and the country where they'd met during the Great War. A smooth motion tore off his formerly functional right hand, leaving a crudely-torn stub behind for him to either bleed out or survive. Either way, she cared not. She had what she'd come for. Problem solved.

"And your wife," she dangled the dangerous thread, "Sweet Miriam. I killed her. Very, very slowly.... Goodbye, Admiral." In another darkened blur, she was gone, taking his severed hand with her as a future warning.

What Catarena wants, Catarena gets.... Always!

Charles W. McDonald Jr.

Part 5: The Symmetry of Hate

Charles W. McDonald Jr.

I am the immutable truth,
The key of Creation,
The key of Unmaking,
The Destroyer,
The I Am,
And the Eternal.
Know thee, and know thine Architect.

Charles W. McDonald Jr.

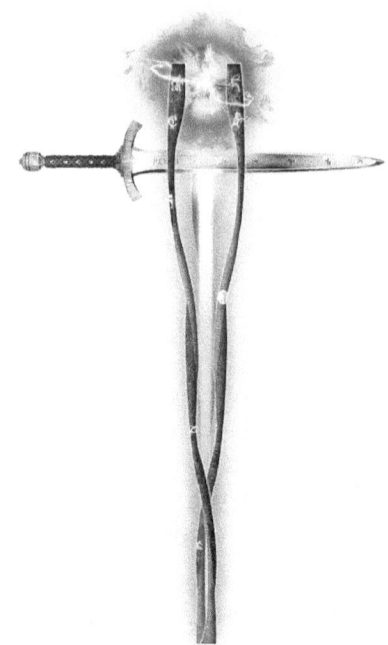

Chapter 37: A Witness to the Architect of Dallia's Death

(Wessex, England, A Long Time Ago)

"What more of this lovely land doth thou wish to see, my beloved Catarena," Knyaz Dragomir offered his beautiful wife, wanting only to please her—only to love her. They'd traveled so far and seen so much, following in the footsteps of the of the Knights Templar—never far enough behind to be targets for the rakes or brigands, but never so close to be a trouble or burden. *See the world together while they were still young*, that was their plan, but the world was a dangerous place.

Even with his title of Knyaz, which loosely translated to an English or French Duke, they were still strangers in a strange land. Strolling along the northern edge of Wessex with the sea-salt air filling their nostrils and the vistas of beautiful rolling green hills filling their souls, they were not alone.

Smelling the crisp and cool channel air and looking through long,

Charles W. McDonald Jr.

shiny, raven bangs with deep blue eyes, Catarena noticed the tall, dark-haired man walking side by side the magnificent, braided hair spilling down her back in radiant golden-blonde waves against powder-blue robes. They were the epitome of in-love—the way they walked in stride together, smiling at one another, loving each other with their eyes and shared energy. Even from a distance, they were beautiful together—meant for each other. "Look at them. This world was not meant for such love," Catarena suggested sardonically.

"I had no idea my wife's soul was so dark," Dragomir countered, drinking in her late-twenties, soft flesh dressed in a beautiful black dress with red, gold, and deep-blue accents that matched her eyes. "Why can't we let them be so in love?"

"*We can. This world* cannot." Just as the words escaped her lips, the tall man staggered in his own footsteps, as if his feet tangled with her own words—his face appearing to go blank from this distance.

Silvery-blue flashes of light rent the air between Dragomir, Catarena, and the lovely couple off in the distance as a magnificent, red-haired woman in a bright-red dress sauntered with supreme confidence out onto the Wessex rolling green grass. An instant later, the red-haired woman raised her hand toward the couple and the beautiful blonde's body was practically bent backwards as she was thrust into the arms of her man, explosively hemorrhaging all over him.

How could this be?

Catarena and Dragomir could hear him crying out to the heavens, stroking her blonde hair, searching, probing for something—they couldn't say what. Running to their aid, Dragomir didn't know what else to do.

Then she saw it; the ground splitting open, swallowing the beautiful blonde whole, and she was gone before Catarena's eyes as the tall, dark man lifted into the air on wings of ethereal hate, calling out to the woman in the bright-red dress in a language she didn't understand. Floating northwest toward the shoreline, the red-haired woman and Catarena, the man in charcoal-blue robes with silver and gold accents moved his hands with words unknown whilst his body floated some thirty spans above the ground.

A massive thunderclap from a misty, cold sky carved jagged craters of Earth where the red-haired woman stood, upending her body several spans into the air just as a violent hail of lightning exploded from the ground, searing her body, causing the red-haired woman to land in a violent, crushing thud. Even there, laying on the ground, her body was burned and bruised by bolt upon bolt of lightning from a sky rent by *hate*.

Surely the woman must have been dead, but Catarena saw her still moving, even whilst in a smoking heap on the ground, as she called out to her husband, "Stop, My Love. STOP! TURN AROUND!"

Just as the red-haired woman pointed her right index finger up at the man floating and looming threateningly above, the dark-haired man faltered and fell from the sky in a heap on the Wessex soil below. Catarena could hear others coming from behind her and to her left as the red-haired woman was up in a whirl of movement, with Dragomir's body broken and torn in half across her waist as she drank from what used to be her husband's body and feasted on his flesh. Before the dead husk of her husband's broken body could hit the ground, even before she could cry out, she felt teeth sinking into her neck and trachea. She could see beautiful strands of silken red hair being blown by the channel wind from behind her to just in front of her face as her body succumbed to the immortal venom—a victory meal for Chara to savor as Damon's body lay in a defeated and broken heap on the Wessex soil.

Consciousness came in small and slow doses, but as Catarena's young body tried to resist—in vain—the immortal venom injected into her neck, she couldn't be certain if what she was seeing was even real. So much of what she thought she knew had been challenged and upended, and yet here was even more....

All the people that she had heard coming to their aid stood silent and motionless on the rolling green grass of Wessex as the red-haired woman conversed with a magnificent *woman*...? Standing over the tall, dark and handsome man of many nations and none as if protecting him—or her interest in him, she appeared a woman in black iridescent skin, having the appearance of being wet with droplets of sweat, with beautiful platinum-blonde braids of hair down to the arched small of her back. And her eyes.... She'd never seen violet glowing eyes like that before. Nor her ears.

Charles W. McDonald Jr.

They were…pointed—as pointed as her black-skinned fingers pointing to the tall, dark man lying on the ground beneath her. Her and the red-haired victor looked to be arguing, and the dark, buxom woman with platinum hair was very emphatic, threatening the red-haired woman. Then the man and black-skinned female were gone, leaving only the red-haired woman, who ripped apart the air with silvery-blue flashes of light, walking through to somewhere else on the other side. Dark there whilst still light here. As the ovoid opening in the air whooshed to a close, everyone that had been held motionless suddenly came running to her, lifting her off the ground as her body still shook from the venom that made her lust for the blood of those coming to save her.

(Rena's Estate, Somewhere in the Carpathian Mountains, Earth, Present Day)

Seeing her hand-written notes and account in her personal journal, she relived the moment of the desecration of the man's love for his wife and the desecration of her own love for her own husband. She considered not only the fate of her own immortality brought to her that day but the value of the firsthand account to the strange man—should he still live. Though after all she had witnessed—both that day and since—that seemed far more likely than not. And with the knowledge she had acquired over the last thousand years, she knew of the other worlds from whence he had come and knew it was time to find him. The signs were upon them, and the missiles in the air. It was time to find the tall, dark-haired man with black eyes and a broken soul, for she felt the weight of this moment upon Humanity. She'd put two and two together with the handcuffs, the rod, the legends, the mythology, the coming of Excalibur, and reliving her firsthand account of this abomination and this fight brought to their world. It was time for her to share her witness and her account of the wrongs done upon him and see if he was their ally or their doom.

She flipped through scrolls of ancient parchment from all corners of the planet—especially Francia and England. In Latin, Old English, Old

Saxon, Frankish, and Old French—among many other medieval languages from across the world—she correlated the first and secondhand accounts of the powerful man she saw defeated and broken that day on the Wessex field. *Was he the Destroyer of Men—or Death of Men—she'd seen in some of those accounts? Or, was he the Dark Knight of Magic she'd read in other accounts? And, who was this man referred to as* **Resha** *by so many accounts?* He appeared to have returned a great many times and across the entire landscape of the planet, shaping this even or that, long after his defeat that day in which she had been forever changed. That meant he had to have lived a long, long time. Perhaps, he was just as immortal as her. She had traced the handcuffs and rod to him and his influence of William the Conqueror. He had both the answers and power she sought—that they all needed. The question was: *on which side would he stand, and if not hers, could he be persuaded?* This was the most delicate and dire mission imaginable, and it called for nothing less than her very best. So critical was this, she'd considered going herself, but this would be a mission of unknown duration and travel to unknown frontiers. She saw her role as holding things together here. With her resources, her planning, and her knowledge, she needed to be on the front lines to save all she had built and to save a vital resource for her and her army—Humanity as a food source. If Humanity was destroyed, so were they. Their blood banks would only last so long, and if Humanity were wiped out, likely most form of mammal would be too. The stakes couldn't be any higher.

As she assembled her thoughts of her mission for Michelle and Lawna, the biggest challenge—as she saw it—was bridging between the worlds as she had witnessed so long ago.

Charles W. McDonald Jr.

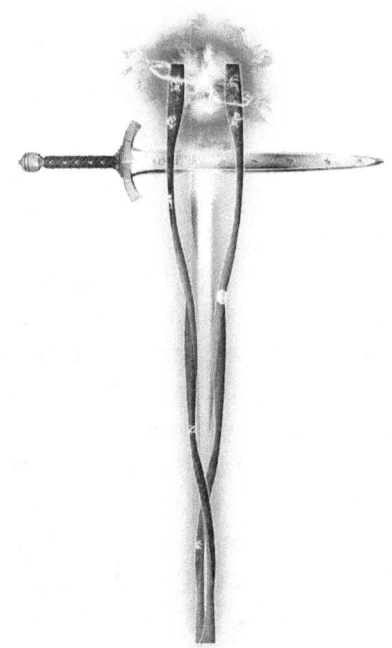

Chapter 38: The Entropy of Damon

(Damon's Manor, Eden, Present Day)

Illirian Starfire opened gold eyes to see Damon staring at her out of her peripheral vision as she rolled off her back to face him in his bed. "I could feel your eyes on me," she confessed, though it wasn't a creepy feeling—more akin to a sense of oneness across space and time as if his energy were living inside her flesh with her.

"I couldn't help myself. I'm sorry."

"Don't be." She reached out to hold his hand in hers, blinking as she felt in her the need for sleep more than ever. *The Starlight of Immortality* now in Damon's hands, she'd aged, and she wondered if he still lusted for and loved her the same as before. "Still think I'm beautiful," she asked, batting her eyes at him.

"Stop it! You know how I feel about you!"

"No, Damon. You should know when a woman asks such things of a man, it's because she doesn't. She *needs* to hear it. I feel time catching up

Charles W. McDonald Jr.

to me. You know that."

"Then, I should give it back to you." He didn't need to spell it out that he was referring to *The Starlight of Immortality*, but he knew her response before he even suggested it. Illirian could be very selfish about certain things, but very selfless about others, and this fell into the latter category.

"NO! I'll be able to concentrate my powers once we're done—if we live through this." A yawn forced its way through a hastily-formed fist that she quickly pulled up to her face to hide her fatigue.

"Yes," he replied enigmatically to a questioning look on her face. "Yes, I still think you're amazingly beautiful. I can see the toll it's taken on you, but if you appeared twice as old as you do now, you'd still be one of the most beautiful and talented women I've ever known." He thought about letting it lie there—hanging in the air between them like a misty cloud of reverence, but that didn't express everything he felt toward her—not even close. "I know everything about you, Illirian Starfire: the way you taste, the way you smell, the touch of your skin. If the whole world became a dark void, I could still find you—and believe me I would, even if it took the rest of eternity."

"That's how it's done, My Love." She smiled at him, reaching her hand out to stroke his long, black hair. Pulling herself into him so her body was laying just underneath his, she caressed his arms up to his shoulders underneath the blankets—feeling him pull back as her caress rose to the level of his scars. "I'm sorry. I had hoped we could get past that," she relented as she pulled back her fingertips and her caress. It angered her—the weight of the scars upon his soul. *Something has to be done!*

"Do you want to know what it's shown me," Damon deflected, referring to *The Starlight of Immortality* and *Durial's Eye*.

"Of course." Illirian smiled up at him as he rolled his body atop hers, pinning her down.

"It showed me that I have to find myself."

Furrowed eyebrows and forehead told Damon she was going to need more than that.

"I have to go back to Perion."

"Perion?! Why?"

"I'm not sure, but I recognized the vistas and the Blood Night. It

Charles W. McDonald Jr.

was unmistakably Perion. And, there was something else too…. Something strange….”

“Strange, like how? Do you know when or specifically where on Perion?”

“I think I recognized the locale. And, as far as the strange goes, how’s this? I saw the pieces of a shattered glass that had just struck the floor flying back together and re-assembling.”

“Okay, that qualifies as strange. That’s all I get from you—a broken glass flying back together and that you have to go to Perion…?”

“I was trying to share,” he offered, kissing her neck just below her earlobe.

“Try harder,” she countered and mused at the same time.

“I saw a message and a place and a specific time I had to be to receive it. I saw a swirling vortex of chaos around me, destroying all those who love me or ever loved me. I saw a long, tall, and dark shadow behind me. It was my shadow. It was me, and yet it wasn’t me.”

“Now you’re just talking in riddles.”

“Riddles are what *Durial’s Eye* shows you. It’s up to you to interpret them correctly.”

“Not from the accounts I’ve read. It’s supposed to be more precise and more certain than that, but it might require more practice with it before it does so.”

“Perhaps. Maybe it will be when I finish building it.”

“What are you building when you go out? I know you’re building it here on Eden, but what is it?” She’d seen him disappear, and her sense was that he was building something massive west of Warden’s Corridor, but she’d kept away—affording him his secrecy. “I heard you made that land off-limits.”

“Maybe I’ll show it you. Someday.”

“That was a polite blow-off, My Love.” She smiled at him—but only outwardly. “Just making it bigger won’t necessarily make it better,” she mused while caressing him under the sheets.

“You’re the one who suggested scaling it up,” he reminded, moving himself between her legs.

“Scaling up its power, Love—not necessarily its size,” she mused

Charles W. McDonald Jr.

for him again as she felt him swelling and beginning to throb in her grasp, wrapping her legs around him as she pulled him closer. Feeling this close to him still felt…odd. Not as if it wasn't meant to be, but more like it was still somehow wrong in some way she was unwilling to let get in between them. Yet, every time she was with him, that same strangeness was there between them whether allowed or not. "You mentioned a swirling vortex of chaos destroying all those you loved and all those who loved you. You didn't see my destruction, did you? I can take care of myself!"

"Yes, you can. Are you going to keep playing with me or are we going to make love?"

"Can't we do both," she mused again, smiling up at him.

It never felt like it had with any other woman when he was with Illirian. It felt both sinful and right—epic and domesticated—confusing and clarifying at the same time. He'd come close, in some ways, with the first Mira and thought her capable of handling herself, but the entropy of Damon destroyed even her as it had Dallia and future Mira Castille. The only ones durable enough to have survived the entropy of Damon had been Evanyil and Banthis—'til now. *What would Banthis think, and do, about Illirian?* Having mortal affairs with Leslie and Mira had been one thing, but Illirian Starfire was another entirely. Illirian was, in every way, Banthis' equal, and in many ways, more. He hadn't heard from Banthis in a very long time, and their next encounter weighed heavy on him as he sought to understand himself—to meet himself as *Durial's Eye* had foretold of him. The old maxim of fate versus free will came to him with each and every use of *Durial's Eye* and he felt would become even more so when the scaled-up version became operational.

(Holden, Perion, Present Day)

He caught them in the midst of packing just as he'd seen in *Durial's Eye*. *Was that a good sign or a bad sign?* "I take it your mission has come to an end," Damon offered an only-slightly off-taken Michelle, who pivoted instantaneously to his unannounced presence.

"Jesus, Damon," Michelle vamped, afraid of what might have

prompted this impromptu meeting as she examined him in blue jeans, a Led Zeppelin T-shirt, and what looked to be Brooks® shoes. "Are you going to Earth to wreak more havoc, or did you just come from there?"

"Why, do you need a ride," he offered in jest, feeling the awkwardness of the conversation growing between them. "Look, we haven't had that many one-on-one conversations…. And when we have, it usually hasn't gone well."

"You won't hear any argument from me," Michelle agreed, stuffing more clothing into her NAVY-issued duffle bag.

"Why did you lie to me," Damon asked. His eyes scrutinizing every part of the beautifully hard lines of her all-too serious face.

"Pardon me?"

"Well, a better question would be, why did you lie to Radin and everyone else?"

She was cornered. *How did he know?* Damon's sources of information were always both a problem and an asset for them historically. She had to be careful how she navigated this conversation as she sat on the edge of the four-post bed, looking away from him down at the floorboards. "It was never supposed to be about Radin," she began, pouring out the truth in small doses like droplets of medicine intended to sterilize the sour of a very big lie—or at least a very big omission. "Do you trust me, Damon?"

"Yes." He surprised her with that flat answer given how the conversation had started. Seeing her raised eyebrows, maybe that would allow her to open up to him.

"I have to say I'm surprised by that. I thought I had blown it with you."

"Well, I should have couched my answer. I trust you to do what you feel is right. I don't necessarily trust every word that escapes your pretty little lips."

"And that's my failure," Michelle admitted. "You were supposed to—at least when I figured out it was you."

"Go on," he added, seemingly satisfied he'd now come to the part he'd seen in *Durial's Eye* as he looked out the window over the Blood Night of the familiar Holden vista.

"When I was looking for you, I found myself looking for the Destroyer of Men—*Resha*—and that led me to Radin, instead of you. Rena sent us because we're critical thinkers, capable of adapting to whatever the landscape provides us. But, we were sent *for you*—not him. For the longest time, I questioned those orders. I questioned whether we should put one finger on the scales for Radin or for you and then we came to realize they were one and the same. So, here I am, coming clean with you. Asking you for your help."

"My help to do what, exactly?"

"Help us figure out the clues you left for us on Earth. Help us understand what all those trips back and forth between your homeworld and Earth were all about—long before there ever became a need for growing your powers. I think…," she paused, adding, "…I know we possess some information that you will find very useful and that might help you. I'm asking if there's an opportunity for us to help each other."

Damon nodded in consideration of her offer and her frankness, as he tried to think back to all the times he'd traveled between worlds and why. Sometimes he wished he'd never figured out how to do it. If he hadn't, Dallia might still be alive and here with him. There may never have been a need for the Master Plan, and he could have led a far simpler life, but this was seemingly the hand he'd been dealt and the destiny that had been chosen for him—*but by whom?* He thought he knew the answer to that question, but he couldn't be certain—not yet. Maybe Michelle's offer held merit and information that might shed light on that question. "You want me to talk to Rena…."

Damon followed probably faster than she had been expecting, but his experience was almost infinite compared to hers, and he was very sharp. It shouldn't have surprised her—his knowledge of Rena and her mission—but it did nonetheless. "I think a conversation between you and Rena is long overdue…," she smiled—tensely so—before adding, "…almost as long overdue as my need to see my girls—in person. But, I don't know if I want to go back to that Hell and see them in all that."

"Well…," Damon coughed into his hand knowingly, "…we might have a little time before all that."

"What?"

"Why don't you go get Lawna, and I'll show you?" It went against everything he knew to introduce anyone from another timeline to an already existing timeline with the same matter—the same people. But, this was a vital conversation that needed to take place, and he needed the Michelle that was before him now—not the one that would at this very moment be traipsing about the South China Sea, chasing his wake.

(Rena's Estate, Somewhere in the Carpathian Mountains, Earth, Present Day)

Barely back from the South China Sea and still in plenty of hot water with the Navy—that Rena would have to do her damnedest to smooth over—Michelle threw her duffle bag over her back as she walked underneath the canopy of hand-hewn Italian marble as the staff offered her and Lawna a seat in the golf cart to whisk them to Rena's offices.

"I can't wait to hear her explanation for this." Lawna pointed to her abdomen.

"I don't see anything but cuteness," her wife offered with a tense smile, definitely knowing where she was coming from. Rena had put them all on the line for this, so it had better have been damn well worth it.

"You're sweet, but I'm going to kick her ass."

"I'd like to see that," Michelle mused—not quite mockingly, but definitely dubiously.

"You don't think I could take her?"

"I know you could, Sweetie."

"Fuck you!"

"Promises. Promises," Michelle reminded to a tense but necessary laugh from her hard wife.

Many, many turns and several moments later, in the bowels of the Carpathian Mountains, they got off the golf cart that quickly sped away with their gear.

"HEY!" Lawna cried out, calling out after the driver.

"My Darlings." Rena flourished before them in a short, black chiffon dress with gold and white piping, very nearly bowing before them.

Charles W. McDonald Jr.

"Don't give me that *Darling* shit! You fucking cut me open, and it hurt! A LOT!!!" Lawna's eyes shot daggers at Rena from across the room.

In all the time they'd known and seen Rena and all her many emotions, they'd never seen her mood flop like that before. In an instant, her smile vanished to a thin, hard-pressed line, causing Michelle to grab Lawna by the elbow, pulling them closer together—nearly in a tactical defensive position.

Seeing Michelle's reaction, Rena used all her experience and skill to calm herself. She'd put them through a lot and was about to put them through a lot more. This was a sensitive mission, and she *needed* their buy-in. "You're right, My Dear. I hurt you. Please forgive me. Do you believe me when I tell you, I would never do such a thing if it were not completely necessary?"

A slow, solitary nod from Lawna provided her answer, but she still wasn't in the mood for anymore 'Darling shit.'

"Come. Sit." Rena clapped her hands once, and two beautiful serving maids appeared with lead crystal glasses of tea on scrolled pewter serving platters as she motioned for Michelle and Lawna to sit in a pair of elegant Christian Dior® wingback chairs sitting atop a twenty-by-twenty-four-foot plush Indian area rug. "Yes, it was absolutely necessary, and your diversions made all the difference in the world. I was able to retrieve what had been taken from me."

"Well, goodie for you," Lawna chided with a hard-lined smirk.

A sidelong sniped glare from her wife and another pensive-turning-nasty look from Rena said maybe she should cool it with the Rena bashing and let bygones be bygones.

"Please continue, Rena." It was the first time she'd addressed Rena by what she thought was her given name in forever, and it prompted a long-overdue moment of honesty between them.

"That isn't my name—really."

"Pardon me?" Michelle leaned forward—Lawna too—listening every word that followed.

"I was born, Carastovich Catarena Rectovich in what is now known as Saint Petersburg, Russia along the Gulf of Finland. Time came for Catarena to die, and well…Rena was born. When you've lived a thousand years, you assume many identities and many lives. You will come to know this."

"Why are you telling us this now," Michelle asked, leaning back in her chair as if to absorb the information. She knew Rena to have many secrets, so having many identities definitely fit her profile. Her senses and talents were becoming more well-tuned and refined, and they all said Rena was telling them the truth. The question was: *was it the whole truth?*

"Because I'm going to ask you to sacrifice for me again. I'm going to ask you to sacrifice a great deal. And, I hope you know that I wouldn't do this if I had a better option. There must be trust between us for there to be sacrifice among us. Wouldn't you agree?"

"Agreed." Lawna—still leaned forward—didn't bite her lip at all and clearly wasn't holding back either. "What are we to sacrifice for you this time, and why?"

Rena turned on the television, narrating over the top of the voice of Breaking News on CNN®: "While you were in the air, ballistic missiles have already responded to a DPRK atmospheric H-bomb test in the Pacific Ocean—the same test your battlegroup was going to intercept. The Chinese have made an effort to respond to the shoot-down of their aircraft, and the US has begun a response to their response. There is now a de facto state of global conflict."

"How did you manage to get us out of a wartime emergency like that," Michelle asked, still wondering and amazed how deep Rena's claws ran inside the US Government.

"Don't worry about that, Darling. Trust me when I tell you, we have even bigger problems on the horizon."

"Bigger than a nuclear holocaust," Lawna proffered, somewhat dubious.

"Yes…," Rena replied flatly, "…much bigger."

"Mother, what are you not telling us? What did you bring us here to do?" Falling back to her matriarchal title for Rena, Michelle was terrified—not for herself but for their children. She didn't want them to grow up in a broken society scrambling for crumbs and starving in the streets—just struggling to survive. She'd do anything to ensure that didn't become their reality. Anything!

"You are going to see one of these." Rena pulled an artist's colored illustration of a tall, dark-haired man walking through what could only be described as a doorway in the air itself—its edges defined by silvery-blue flashes of light.

"What am I looking at," Michelle asked, trying to wrap her brain around what appeared a violation of what she understood to be the laws of nature.

"Something driven by magic," Rena replied in a dead-pan serious and flat tone—her voice not wavering one bit.

Putting her hands on either side of her forehead, Lawna began shaking her head, trying to bring things back to a level of reality with which she could cope. "I can't be hearing you right. You said magic."

"We are creatures of magic, Dearheart. You've begun developing your talents. You know of what I speak. How is this any different?"

"It's extremely different, Mother," Michelle added.

"I brought you here because you're both analytical and adaptive. Did I make the wrong choice?"

A long pause preceded Michelle's consideration, "Please continue, Mother."

"Good. I don't know where or when you will see this phenomenon, but you must be prepared for it and you must jump through it before it disappears, regardless of where it may lead you."

"Do we know where it might take us or how we might get back," Lawna asked, her eyes welling with tears as she considered leaving their daughters.

"I'm not going to lie to you, Darling. I don't have those answers, save that this doorway—or whatever it is—is likely to take you to another world."

Raised eyebrows from both Michelle and Lawna as they considered the possibilities before them. It was a lot to take in, and their adaptability only traveled with them so far. Michelle began thinking about gunpowder and the laws of nature, considering even whether or not their weapons might work wherever the doorway led. "Mother, I'm guessing we can't be certain our firearms will work on the other side of the doorway."

"I've considered that a possibility as well. That's why it has to be one of our Immortal Army—someone capable of using virtually anything as a weapon or not needing weapons to survive."

"Why do we need to travel this great distance for you? What is our mission when we get on the other side of this doorway?" Michelle was still trying to process a lot, but mission parameters had to come first. She needed to understand if this was a mission that even had a chance of being successful and then she needed to bring the conversation back to why this was more important than protecting her children from a global holocaust. Or, at least understanding how this other mission could better protect her daughters instead of her being here with Lawna and all of Rena's resources at their disposal to directly protect their daughters.

"You're going to hear the term 'Resha,' or 'Destroyer of Men,' or 'The Dark Knight of Magic.'" Rena paused, letting that sink in before adding, "This global conflict, here on Earth, I believe is a cog in a greater wheel we cannot fully see. I've seen things that convince me that there is a conflict happening on a level above the level of this one planet. I need to understand more that only these off-world travelers can show us. How do we save what we can of this world and our food source? How can we work together with these powerful off-world travelers to secure a future either on this world, or theirs, or another world for us and our kind so that we can preserve as much as possible of what we have built?" Rena pulled from a small, cherrywood box a plain silver rod and digital handcuffs, showing them to both Michelle and Lawna, but not letting them hold them or examine them up-close before placing them back within the small, wooden box. "You might see reference to either or both of those objects. You will follow any leads associated with them. They *should* lead you to '*Resha*,' or the 'Destroyer of Men,' or 'The Dark Knight of Magic.'"

"I think I understand the mission parameters, Mother. Is there anything else you can tell us that might be helpful? Now is not the time to keep secrets between us," Michelle added, pointing her finger at Rena, though not accusingly. She wasn't aware of being seriously misled by Rena, but she knew there were blind spots when working with Rena and that just came with the territory.

"I don't know if these titles I've given you are of one man, or many, and I don't know if they'll lead you to him or not."

Charles W. McDonald Jr.

"Who's him?"

"The man of whom I speak is tall—very tall—probably 6'3" or a little taller. He has long, straight black hair with black eyes and looks like a man of experience beyond measure, but I know him to be a very wounded man—a very hurt man at his core. You'll never see this side of him without trust and friendship. If you find this man of whom I speak, your mission is to gain his trust and get him to come see me. Everything depends on it. Everything!"

"Mother—" Lawna started with tears in her eyes, before being interrupted by Michelle who was probably thinking along the same wavelength.

"We'll do it...," Michelle interjected, "...if you can look me in the eye and swear to me that this is the best use of our skills and capabilities to make the best possible outcome for our daughters, we'll do it. We'll find him. No matter what it takes."

Without blinking or hesitating even a second, Rena reached out to hold both Michelle's hand and Lawna's. "I swear it, and I swear that I will put my life on the line to save your girls—if need be. I'll sacrifice everything for them if I have to. I swear it!"

Nodding, Michelle only had one question before she went to go kiss her daughters *goodbye:* "Where do you think we'll find this doorway?"

"I don't know," Rena admitted. It was the biggest question she didn't have the answer to, but that was why she picked these two specifically. "I was counting on your judgment to find that. This is a hard man you're chasing. He's going to be in the thick of the action. He's going to be in the center of it. He's going to make it revolve around him if need be. I trust you to find him."

Michelle nodded, acknowledging at least internally that she felt like she was getting the unvarnished truth from Rena. Her gut told her she wasn't being totally used, but they needed to pack like they'd never packed before. An off-world mission required a totally different approach to preparedness, and they had work to do. But, they had daughters to kiss and spend time with first. Drinking the rest of her tea, she sat down the lead crystal glass. "Goodbye, Mother."

Lawna's face was a weighty wreck of mixed emotions, but she was trying to pull herself together as she straightened her pants and tucked in

Charles W. McDonald Jr.

her tank-top, getting up to follow Michelle out.

"I love you," Rena called out after them. "*Both* of you."

Michelle was already out the door, but she heard Rena. She just didn't have the words.

"Goodbye, Rena…," Lawna breathed aloud, "…I hope we see you again soon."

Rena stared down into her tea, wondering if she'd ever see them again. More importantly, she wondered if she'd ever meet the tall, dark-haired, dark-eyed man from so long ago.

The word came some hours later that both Lawna and Michelle had left for the US mainland. They hadn't indicated where specifically, but they were traceable with their implanted tracking devices. However, she was going to give them a very long leash. She either trusted them or she didn't, and she'd made a promise that she intended to keep. Their babies would be going down for a late afternoon nap soon, so she was pulling herself together to head to the nursery.

"Mother." The magnificent lithe blonde assistant, Alisa, stood just inside her office by the doorway.

"Yes, Dearheart."

"I think you're going to want to see this." Alisa's hand motioned to the long, sterile-but-functional hallway bore into the side of the mountain.

Rena never showed visible shock before, but peeking around the edge of the doorjamb, it took everything she had to keep herself together as she saw the tall, dark-haired, dark-eyed man walking down the hall toward her office, flanked by a travel-worn Lawna and Michelle, who appeared very different than those who'd just left her office only hours before. "My God…," she exclaimed under her breath, fully contemplating the possible tangled time before her.

"Mother?" Alisa had never heard RR utter such a thing before, so there was ample concern all around.

"Could you give us some privacy, Dearheart? Keep everyone out of the area. EVERYONE! The whole corridor."

"Of course, Mother." Alisa complied with a full bow.

A moment later, and she assumed him in earshot. "English will work

Charles W. McDonald Jr.

for our conversation, no…?" Rena's outstretched hand motioned for him to join her in her office.

The tall man looked around the office and its three chairs then mumbled something in a language she hadn't heard in nearly a thousand years. A subtle motion of his left hand produced a small vortex appearing beside the two wingback chairs, then another identical chair appeared beside them, making four now in total. "Yes, English will suffice," he added.

"Your English is better than mine," she offered, her accent a permanent reflection of her motherland as she motioned for Michelle and Lawna to join them. Hugging each one in turn as they came through the door, Rena gathered her thoughts for what she knew to be a *monumental* conversation. "You've blended in nicely," she added, motioning to his casual attire.

"What can I do for you, Rena?" The tall man cut straight to it, wasting little time as his patience appeared to be tested just by his being here.

"Mother…," Michelle interjected, "…this is Damon—The Dark Knight of Magic."

In a very rare move, Rena bowed to him completely, offering her hand to hold his. "I was there…," she paused, "…that day, when you lost your wife. I'm so very sorry for your loss, Damon."

His mouth twisted, but he recovered before it had become a full snarl. "What can I do for you, Rena?" He didn't enjoy repeating himself, and she could already tell doing so had bothered him.

How to proceed with this man…. She already knew so much about him—of how dangerous he was, but there was so much she didn't know. Clearly, he was at least as old as her, if not older—and she considered how little those who'd known her for only a brief portion of her life knew of her. That was how very little she knew of him.

She could see something behind those black eyes of his working at full speed as he made uncomfortable fidgeting moves in his chair.

"If you were there, then you are likely the seed of Chara," Damon added knowingly, completely uncomfortable at the thought of being this close to Chara's offspring.

"If Chara is the name of the one who murdered my husband and your wife, and changed me into who I am, then yes. I am her seed. Unwillingly or not."

Charles W. McDonald Jr.

Michelle and Lawna looked between each other at the word 'husband.' Rena was full of secrets—even now.

"My time is limited, Seed of Chara. What do you need?"

Catarena held back her instinct to show her spine and her skills to this 'wounded' man who was being beyond rude to her, instead moving to her bookshelf where she pulled from it a small six-inch-by-nine-inch, weathered, leather-bound journal. "Do you know Russian," she asked of him, pulling her chair around to sit beside him. "I can translate if needed."

He accepted the journal from her, beginning to read from the spot she'd marked with her left index finger. *Linguistics* helped, but it was written from such an emotional point of view that it was difficult to follow. Her emotions in her own handwriting bled into his own emotions as he read her description of his love for Dallia so prominent as to be disallowed by this world. Rena's description of his beautiful Dallia brought tears to his eyes as his stony, planed face twisted in knots over her firsthand account of her calculated murder. "The woman you describe standing over me.... You're completely certain of the accuracy of this description?"

"Very."

He'd considered Evanyil's involvement before. But just because she was involved didn't make her an accomplice. Evanyil had intervened on his behalf many times before, saving his life. This might just be another one of those times, but he wondered how she'd traveled to Earth. Evanyil of that era wouldn't have had that ability—not yet. And, Rena wouldn't have understood what was being said even if she had been in range to hear it and coherent enough to comprehend what she was hearing. She was bleeding out on the Wessex soil in the throes between death and undeath. He didn't know firsthand what that was like, but he could imagine it wouldn't produce the most cogent account of the events. He needed to be there himself to see what she had seen—to hear what she had heard—from her perspective. Before continuing another heartbeat, he invoked *Damon's Distorting Web* over the entire office to Rena's astonishment. "Could I probe your memories?"

He'd considered how general that sounded as soon as the question escaped his lips, but he wanted to gauge her response.

Batting her eyelashes at the proposal and the *Distorting Web* overhead, Rena considered all the knowledge she had locked away in her head. "I

Charles W. McDonald Jr.

don't think I would feel comfortable with that, Damon. Is there another way? What were you hoping to gain from that?"

"What you heard…. There's no way you could have made heads or tails of it unless you understood the language or had a translator. But, if I can see and hear those memories, I can make sense of it."

A long pause as she considered the trust matter. She'd ordered Michelle to earn Damon's trust, and now she was on the other end, having to trust Damon with every secret she'd ever possessed—and there were hundreds of them of tremendous value to her and everything she'd built. But, if she didn't let him do this, she could never ask anything of Michelle or Lawna as she'd done before and all their efforts to get him here would have been a waste. He'd never help her if she didn't give him this. She could sense it in him. It was put up or shut up time for the infamous RailRoad Rena. "Very well, Damon. Do what you must," she added as she turned her chair to face him.

As he turned his chair in kind, his hands reached out to touch each of her temples, as he mumbled something in a language she didn't understand. Both Michelle and Lawna looked to each other questioningly, as they turned back to watch Damon probe all of Rena's memories in search of the one he most feared.

Concentration on Damon's face begot a pulling back from him as he reached the moment of her fateful conversion—feeling her agony and remembering her torment as her body was ripped apart from the inside out in her becoming immortal. Then he looked through Catarena's eyes and heard through Catarena's ears the horror he'd considered but hoped untrue. He disengaged, letting Rena go. The whole process took less than a couple of minutes as Damon exhaled, "Thank you, Catarena. I am sorry for your loss." He stood to get up as if to leave.

"Damon, please." Rena reached out, grabbing his wrist, but not with her strength—instead with her compassion. "I want to help you make this right. But, to do that, I need to understand much more than I do now. Can you help us with that?"

"There's no making this right. There's only killing," Damon remonstrated, still considering what he'd seen and now heard.

"Michelle. Lawna," Rena addressed them for the first time in this conversation, thinking surely they knew Damon and his plans enough to offer some guidance. "What do you know of Damon and his plans? How can we best help him? Should we help him? Is there a way forward you can see us aiding each other?"

"Well, Rena...," Michelle started, foregoing the matriarchal title she once afforded Rena by default, "...there's much to tell you. As I understand it, Damon means to avenge the death of his wife. He means to unmake just about every part of the status quo we live in today. He's built another world and another society where Humanity can live outside of this status quo and hopefully survive this unmaking of his—although I don't claim to fully know the depth or extent of all that it entails. I do know he has, whether by his own hand or not, hastened the End Times across all worlds. I know he's coordinating with Resha—his son, Radin—to open the Seals that end Creation in an effort to both usurp the magistrates of the status quo and lead Humanity to the other side—whatever that may look like."

"WOW." That was probably the most impactful status report she'd ever received from one of her soldiers, but that's why she sent these two. "Damon, I have so very many questions for you. And, who knows, I might even have some answers. Won't you consider staying a little while? Please?"

Why hadn't The Starlight of Immortality shown me this? Was this meeting with Rena outside the continuum of scope for Durial's Eye? Am I forging a new timeline by way of this meeting? He needed to understand more. The level of magic afforded him here wouldn't allow for his use of *Durial's Eye*.... Not here. A single nod from Damon as he rested back into his chair to continue their knowledge sharing.

A nod from Rena preceded a smile. This man was every bit the challenge she'd expected, making his appearance here by way of her two soldiers that much more impressive. "I'd like to show you something. Something I'm sure you've likely seen before." Another trip back to the bookshelf returned a small cherrywood box, which she opened at a distance close enough to him so he could reach out and touch the handcuffs and rod within.

Rocking back and forth in acknowledgement, Damon considered the aid he'd given William the Conqueror so long ago. Reaching out, he grabbed the rod but explicitly avoided the handcuffs in how he grasped it, delicately pulling it out from underneath the plain, silver, digital handcuffs. The rod glowed with a familiar warmth in his hands as he acknowledged its genuine properties. *'Tis not a fake.*

"I noticed your avoidance of the handcuffs. Can you tell me what they do?" Rena was a shrewd individual, but she considered him not answering that specific question.

"They produce a distortion field that inhibits the use of magic—specifically one type of energy source most associated with nearly all vocation."

"Hmmm…," Rena considered, a very specific answer with a very specific repercussions. "…I take that to mean, they wouldn't work on you."

"They would not," Damon lied—sort of. They'd cut him off from Arcane, but not from Zero-Point—at least that was the theory. But, he didn't want to test it.

"And what of the rod?" Rena continued her probing, trying to understand the bigger picture.

"In the hands of the right individual, the rod gives the power to permanently destroy any mage while keeping them alive—removing their ability to cast—cutting them off from sourcing energy in any way that would allow them to form the energy into other forms of energy or matter."

"Essentially, it allows the right person to turn a mage into a regular person as if they'd never had the ability to cast. Is my summary correct," Rena clarified to a solitary nod from Damon in agreement. "So, who made these devices and why were they here? …On Earth, I mean…."

"I don't have all those answers, Rena, and believe me, I've been searching for those answers for a very long time. I do know that there are five worlds representing the Seeds of Humanity. Four Brothers were exiled from a world called Setinon—what we think might be the homeworld of Humanity. Each of these Four Brothers was given at least one set—some more—of these rod and cuffs. Why they were given these tools—and only given tools to restrain or destroy magic versus amplify it—speaks to a larger agenda that I think traces back to *The Eye of Time*. You can think of *The Eye of Time* as a sentient, general AI, and my belief is that it sees those who can cast as a serious threat to its survival." He wasn't about to reveal the fact that he thought the *Eye* did so because it, too, could cast. That knowledge needed to remain compartmentalized—for now.

Rena sat, closing the lid to the small wooden box. *Five worlds of Humanity. They were seeded here. They were aliens—colonists—sort of.* She'd considered, from all her research, the fact that they had been at least tampered with as a species—that homo erectus had been genetically modified to become the homo sapien sapiens we know today, but this was a new reality for her to absorb. Perhaps there were two forms of homo sapiens, each blending into one another's genetic code through procreation. She'd have to give that more thought in another conversation with Damon—hopefully one of many more to come.

"*The Eye of Time* is new information, Damon. When did you come by this knowledge," Michelle probed, going over each of their conversations in her head, one by one, trying to identify that phrase.

"It's closely held information. Radin knows. Talemar, I believe. Perhaps a handful of others."

"How does it change or adjust your Master Plan? Or, does it," Michelle continued her probe and line of questioning, not wanting to let it go until this thread had been fully run to ground.

"It's a fair question," Damon recognized, adding, "I don't fully know or understand the agenda of *The Eye of Time* as it exists today. I only understand—or think I understand—its intent from back then when the worlds were seeded. My Master Plan to unseat the magistrates of the status quo—as you so eloquently put it—hasn't changed all that much." His obfuscation was growing by the minute. It had changed drastically between the *Eye* and now what he knew and understood of Evanyil. His forthrightness had taken a back seat to necessity. Still, *he needed them*. They needed him more, but he *did* need them. Therefore, he had to give them niblets and only the smallest niblets possible to keep them around.

"Damon, who are the magistrates of the status quo as you see it?" Rena had registered that phrase when Michelle had offered it, but the meaning of that had eluded her.

"God the Creator and the Dragon of Darkness."

Rena gulped. Michelle and Lawna just looked at each other again—likely simultaneously having the same thought: *He's out of his goddamned mind.*

"Well, I'm glad we clarified that," Rena offered smugly, shifting in her chair. *This 'man' believes himself capable of destroying both the Creator and the Dragon of Darkness—whoever that is*, but she had a couple of guesses. "Tell me about this other world you've made—this haven for Humanity. I'd love to hear all about it—perhaps even see it if that's reasonable."

He paused a moment—thinking. Before, in the other continuum, he had specifically chosen not to save Rena and her kind—for good reason. He hated the undead. But he felt more certain by the moment they were forging new ground here and there were significant merits to saving Rena, and at least *some* of her kind. Plus, Rena had knowledge and resources that could be useful, but he'd have to find a solution for their food source. He couldn't allow their feeding on his children on Eden. *That cannot not happen!* "For lack of a better name, and for sentimental reasons, I called it 'Eden.' I terraformed it."

Rena nodded slowly. *He terraformed it—by himself.* It had been implied by himself, and the implication wasn't all that subtle. This meeting and this man was far beyond her expectations, and her expectations had been stratospheric. She'd been right about using Lawna and Michelle to go after him rather than keep them here dealing with the domestic issues of a global conflict when there was a conflict raging on a much grander scale. It had been a hunch, but an educated hunch nonetheless. "Does Eden fall outside the End Times you've hastened across these other worlds—these other Seeds of Humanity?"

"She's a smart cookie." Damon motioned to Rena while looking at Michelle and Lawna as if to compliment them on Rena's intellect. Seeing Rena smile—she was a beautiful woman, albeit darker in some ways than even he—made him want to help her. "I don't fully know to be honest. I think they're safely outside the operational effect of the Scrolls, but I can't say for certain. I know Eden—and everything else in this Universe—will definitely be impacted by my war with God the Creator and the Dragon of Darkness. It could unmake more than I intended." In his excitement to help, he'd opened his mouth too much.

Rena gulped again—hard. Michelle and Lawna too.

"Look," he started damage control, "I've put a tremendous amount of thought into this. I'm the only one in the Universe that can unmake what I have made. I'm the reason the *Throne of Souls* exists. The *Throne of Souls* gives her power she shouldn't have. I upset the balance of power. I mean to correct that. And, as for God the Creator.... Well, there are very old scores that must be settled. If he destroys me, the worst that should happen is a continuation of the status quo or some variant of it. If I win, then the hatred in those Scrolls will never be visited upon Man again. The meddling and the know-it-all interference will end. Fairness will matter. Balance will matter. A new equilibrium will settle things down, and chaos will have no asylum."

There was a very fine, thin line between genius and insanity, and she wasn't sure if Damon had crossed over it yet or not—but he was at the very least straddling it. Rena immediately began questioning the wisdom in helping him. But for Eden, and that's where he had them, she needed to get her people to safety. *Would he even care if he eliminated a parasitic race as ours? After all, Humans were a food source. Is Damon only interested in saving Humans or is he interested in saving the entire ecosystem?*

Then, an idea popped into her head—and a good one at that. "Damon, you've been so kind to us, and you've returned my two favorite girls to me safe and sound. I don't know if they told you, but they have triplet girls—babes really. Would you like to meet them? I'm certain they'd like to be with their loving parents again." Rena stood, motioning them to the hall that would take them to the nursery.

*   *   *   *

A beautiful black woman in her early thirties approached the nursery from the south hallway as they approached from the north. Her brown eyes flashed as she smiled at Rena and the unusual—even for Rena—company she was bringing to visit. Michelle and Lawna she immediately recognized with a smile, knowing how happy their girls would be to see them so soon after they'd left, but they—Michelle and Lawna—looked completely different than they had appeared just hours before.

"Back—" Chelsea was immediately interrupted by an index finger Rena threw in the air, which was a known signal of silence in the group. She frowned at being silenced, but with Rena there was always more going on than met the eye. So, hips swaying, she pushed the door to the nursery open—holding it open for the group and waiting for them to initiate any conversation.

The first through the door, Michelle fell to her knees just a couple of steps into the nursery where she found her beautiful Amanda pulling herself up from a seated lap position to a standing position against a standing Baby Einstein® toy that had large numbers of colors—blue, green, yellow, red, and purple. It appeared as if Amanda was still searching for her balance as her radiant, infant smile lit up the entire room at the sight of Mommy.

Tears streaked down Michelle's face in torrent waves of memory tinged with confusion as she struggled to understand how they could not be but hours older than when she remembered leaving them last. They hadn't aged but barely a nap time.

Lawna stood in the doorway with Damon and Rena standing behind her. Damon could see over Lawna's shoulder, but Rena could not. Instead, Rena opted to move to the large, rectangular Lexan® window that afforded a full view of the twenty-foot-by-thirty-foot nursery with but three vital, golden-haired occupants. Amanda, in a cream onesie that read, 'I Love Mommy… And Naps,' was pivoting from her standing Baby Einstein® toy to take slow but steady baby steps toward Michelle, who was sitting on the plush-carpeted floor. A series of padded mats sat atop the cushioned carpet with varying educational toys. Uniform, salad-bowl-stained maple toy chests with softened and rounded edges marched the perimeter of the room, attempting to organize the chaos of children at play. A bouncy sat in the middle of the mats, holding a pale-green-eyed Victoria, who bounced in it like there was no tomorrow, screaming, "Mommies, Mommies, Mommies!" A blue-eyed beauty currently being held by a brunette in a rocking-recliner appeared confused but just beginning to smile as Lawna approached her, clearing the doorway for Damon as she mouthed her name, "Alexandra."

Throwing her hands up in the air immediately as if to say, 'pick me up now, Mommy,' Alexandra beamed with boundless joy with a squeal that could be heard down the hallway as Lawna picked her up high into the air, whirling her around in joyful bliss.

Clearing her throat as she appeared in total stealth silence beside Damon, Catarena offered, "They are beautiful, no?"

"I…," he paused, thinking about and witnessing something first-hand he'd never before experienced. When each of his girls had been brought to him, they were fully grown. Radin he only had second-hand accounts of. This was what he'd been robbed of by Chara. This was the mis-

Charles W. McDonald Jr.

take in his timeline. "…I have children, but I never got to experience them as children."

"Then you were robbed." It was a bold declarative truth by Rena, but she offered it as if it were a total certainty.

He may have thought it, but hearing Catarena say it reinforced the reality of Chara's—and now Evanyil's—cruelty. As he watched Michelle and Lawna play with their beautiful progeny, three things flew into the cogs working inside his mind, causing his gears of calculus to grind to a halt until they became unstuck by grease of revelation. "Something vexes me, Catarena."

She looked at him in a way that acknowledged the wheels of thought grinding in his mind, sensing this man was about to figure it out. "Oh…. What is that?"

"Well, three things really are troubling me."

"Tell me, Damon. I will share with you everything I can."

"One: I knew Chara to only be able to operate at night and sometimes in twilight and dusk and only with the aid of magic—meaning her natural order of operations would be night-mode only. If you're her progeny and they yours…," he paused, motioning to the entire nursery, "…how is it that they can operate in full daylight?"

"I'm surprised *only* in the fact that you started with that one," she mused, turning to lead them outside into the hallway to get them out of earshot of the others. "We couldn't have done the genetic engineering required without those three little adorable girls in there. Their genetic code carries protein markers of the virus that Chara used to make me. Yet, they do not have the thirst. I don't know if they will develop it or not. I haven't seen abnormal strength from them yet, nor abnormal development. They're as close to homo sapien sapien Human as I believe possible while still carrying the protein makers of vampires. They're immune to the radiation emitted in daylight sun—UV-A and UV-B rays—so, we spliced our genetic code with theirs. Carefully. We'd been working on the gene therapy for decades, but the procedure wasn't possible until we had the right source code."

Processing the information as quickly as it was delivered to him, Damon countered, "Do Michelle and Lawna know that you used them to make your source code—in the form of those three beautiful girls?"

Charles W. McDonald Jr.

Rena's demeanor turned hard in an instant as her jawline tightened and her back stiffened like a viper's. "I came to them with a transparent offer: that I would help them where other IVF resources could not, to help them have offspring from both their DNA in exchange for their joining my Immortal Army, and they knew exactly what that meant."

"I bet they didn't know you were going to contaminate the DNA of their children with a virus from Chara before they agreed to do it."

She had been holding Damon's forearm the entire time during the exchange, but now she let go, taking a couple of steps back from him. *He was sharp. Cruel, dangerous, ruthless, and sharp.* He reminded her of herself and what she'd become, thanks to Chara. In Damon, she saw her own reflection, and it angered her deep within. How had she come to this point where seeing her own reflection made her ill and ashamed? "Harsh choices had to be made. Harsh choices I'm not proud of, but leadership requires sacrifice. Sometimes that sacrifice includes having to stomach our own actions."

Damon acknowledged both the reality of her statement and the honesty of it. He'd been there. He'd done that. He had no more grounds to judge Catarena than she had to judge him. Perhaps there was use in that fact—the idea of having an ally who couldn't judge you. "I can accept that," Damon agreed, continuing, "Two: I didn't save you or your kind before when I opened the *Portals* that led Mankind to Eden."

"I can't say I'm surprised by that admission. I can understand the logic of not wanting to save a parasite of Man."

"Perhaps that was a mistake on my part, but let's propose an idea."

"I'm listening, Damon."

"I have a problem on Eden—a problem your Immortal Army would be well-suited to mitigate."

Rena only responded with a knowing nod, motioning for him to keep going.

"Would it be feasible to either use the genetic code of these beautiful little girls to either remove to alter the thirst in such a way that the craving was no longer of Human blood?"

"Well, I too have already considered this, and I was surprised that the gene therapy we did didn't already solve that problem. That leads me to believe that they, too, will have the thirst after puberty, but I can understand where you're going with this. You'd be willing to take us to Eden with you if we could adjust our diet."

"Correct, and not feel like you were giving up steak for Spam®."

Rena coughed a small laugh into her fist at the remark. She rather enjoyed fried Spam® and eggs for breakfast, but nothing quenched her lust for Human blood—nothing she'd tried thus far any way. "The thirst is a very specific need. It fuels the talent side of the system of a vampire. The system of our physical bodies can be sustained by normal food sources— plant and protein. However, the system of the talent-driven side of who we are is fueled by the lifesource of mammalia. The higher up in the ecosystem that mammalia form of life, the more satisfying the meal. Dolphin and Human blood tastes better to us and fuels us for longer periods of time than that of horse or dog. Makes sense, no?"

Damon agreed with a single nod.

"So, I see several options. The most obvious is a short-term solution of a blood bank that could be contributed to by all forms of mammals and then categorized and made available for us like a menu. A longer-term solution could be gene therapy. A mid-term solution could be allowing us to hunt on Eden these problems of yours or to hunt mammalia-type life on other worlds. Surely, we both know and agree that the Universe is literally teeming with life. But, I could and would sign an agreement with you— a contract—that forbade Human hunting on Eden without your expressed permission. And, I would ensure forced compliance among my Immortal Army. Any member that violates the contract would be immediately put to death. No questions asked. I would take care of it personally."

"Agreed, but I have another condition." Damon held all the cards here, and he knew it.

Rena didn't blink nor shift her stance—merely a slight tightening of the focus of her gaze upon the Dark Knight of Magic.

"Third: If I do this, if I save your race, *your* army is *my* army. You will not subvert my agenda in any way, shape, or form. You'll have autonomy and decision making within your organization that you have built. But, when I say I need a problem solved and I need your resources to do it, I don't want to hear any argument or debate about it. I'm not going to save you only to be judged by you. Do I make myself clear?"

A hard man. He was every bit the challenge she thought he would be. *A hard man who is wounded is immeasurably dangerous.* "We have a deal, Damon." Catarena offered her hand, watching Damon extend his hand to shake hers without hesitation, forging a new alliance with the most dangerous entity she could possibly imagine. But, with nuclear holocaust upon them, it was the only play to be made and only possible by the outstanding work of her two best soldiers who right now delighted in the play of their beautiful girls. "Damon?"

"Yes, Catarena."

"You are familiar with many forms of Earth culture and knowledge, yes?"

"I am."

"Are you familiar with the Second Law of Thermodynamics?"

"I am."

"Its importance is that it clearly articulates and describes the natural flow of time. A glass that falls from a table to shatter on the floor does not have its pieces fly back together and reassemble itself. It illustrates a universal order of time of certain irreversible cascading actions that lead to further and accelerate or grow disorder in the Universe—described as entropy."

Like a bolt of déjà vu, the message of *Durial's Eye* rang in his ears at the mention of the pieces of glass flying back together. Damon smiled outwardly at first, but inwardly he was thinking the same thing as Catarena, and it bothered him from the moment he recognized the life he'd been robbed by Chara. *What is the natural order of my timeline? What was it supposed to look like? And, what was Durial's Eye trying to tell me?*

A cocked head from Damon perceptively reacted to the slightest twitch in Catarena's lips…. "I sense a pivotal question burgeoning in between those pretty ears of yours, Catarena."

"You're a handsome charmer, and I'm certain you're a big flirt with the ladies…," she paused, thinking about adding a statement that would quash any romantic possibilities between them, but then stopped herself short. "…My question for you, Darling Damon, is: have you figured out the natural order of your timeline, and does it allow for the agreement we have just forged?"

Charles W. McDonald Jr.

He needed to get back with his chief scientist and give it these new variables to add into the equation. It had been working on the very answers to this question, but from a very different perspective. He was about to make some very big and impactful decisions. Where he'd merely been shooting from the hip with the time manipulation before, he was trying to be more careful and calculated this time around. He wasn't sure how many more attempts at this he would get to get it right, and what did getting it right mean in his eyes? Things had changed for him, but that was the natural way of things. That was the *Entropy of Damon*.

Charles W. McDonald Jr.

Part 6: The Righted Continuum

Charles W. McDonald Jr.

Chapter 39: The Trident Gateway

(Damon's Manor, Eden, Present Day)

He didn't know if he was tampering with the temporal events or not by asking Michelle and Lawna how they knew to be in Warwick, but he found their answers...troubling. Neither of them could say—specifically—how they had got there. Lawna remembered seeing orders from official JSOC letterhead, and Michelle remembered getting a text on her proprietary comm-link from Rena, but neither remembered those messages with specificity. Just blurred images, as if a camera image taken out of focus. That led him to wonder.... He knew they had to go through the *Portal* of his wake to Perion, and now he had a commitment to save Rena's forces, which meant he had to make an adjustment to the *Portals* he'd soon be opening—or had already opened, depending on one's point of view. *Did he need to nudge things a bit more? Or, would they just fall into place?* If they just fell into place, that would suggest the Second Law of Thermodynamics doing its job. But, if they didn't, he'd have to be prepared to act in a timely manner that didn't shatter their reality on the spot.

Twisting Illirian's scroll in his hands, he considered his options.

Charles W. McDonald Jr.

Opening it, he appreciated both the delicateness of the feminine nature of her handwriting and the bold emphasis with which the message had been written. The Trident Gateway, she emphasized. A meeting of such importance, that nothing else was ever more important. He had to be there—precisely on time—and nothing could be allowed to stop him from making this meeting. Such weight to put on one meeting. He was both curious and skeptical, but Illirian had earned his complete trust. He knew her to be all-in at this point. There was no going back for Illirian. He had no reason to doubt her. None whatsoever.

A knock at the doorjamb of his private study brought him out of his deep thought.

"Come," he announced to what he sensed was his son on the other side.

"Can I bother you a moment," Radin asked, only taking a couple of steps into his father's study—no more than that, as if preparing to retreat.

"Come. Sit." Damon offered him one of his study chairs, to which Radin declined with a shake of the head, standing pat close by the exit. *Okay, that's odd*, Damon considered. "I'm almost afraid to ask. What's this about?"

"I need to know if you'll meet with me."

"Are we not meeting right now?"

"This time, tomorrow. On Kaleion. At the Hadron—specifically." Radin's grey-blue eyes darted around nervously from one bookshelf to the next, intentionally avoiding eye contact with Damon.

Damon began mulling over the specifics of the omissions and didn't like the outcome of that calculus in his thoughts. "With whom?"

"You're going to have to trust me on this one, Father. Please."

Shaking his head, Damon outwardly was telling his son, 'no way.' But seeing his only son's distressed reaction, picking at his own fingernails and looking down at the floor, clearly something was up. "Don't act like that. You're my son. Show some balls. Tell me what you want and why you want it."

Immediately stiffening his spine both literally and figuratively, Radin pulled himself together to give as much detail as he could without assuring Damon's disapproval. "Father, I *require* your attendance tomorrow this hour on Kaleion at the Hadron. I've already set up a meeting that I assure you, you'll want to attend. I set this meeting up without your knowledge because I knew you would not approve, but I can assure you that I know what I'm doing. I'm trying to tilt the odds in our favor that we can do this."

"Better, but I don't like the use of the word 'require.' You can use that word with others, but not me."

"Understood, Father. So, you'll be there then?"

"Yes. Yes. It seems as if everyone is setting up critical meetings that *require* my attendance."

Frowning at the not-so-polite blow-off comment, Radin retreated without further comment, yielding the study back to Damon and his privacy.

Damon frowned too. That had been an overly odd exchange between Radin and himself. *A meeting I surely would not have approved of.* That could entail lots of toxic possibilities he didn't want to entertain at the moment.

Holding Illirian's scroll up to his nose, his nostrils inhaled her scent, and as much as he delighted in the essence of being around all things Illirian, it still felt an anachronism to him and his being. He remembered when they first met, and how he responded to her when he found out she was the immortal Illirian Starfire, and how 'she was the fucking enemy.' How things had changed.

Still, the Trident Gateway of all places.... *Why there? Who could they be meeting with that would require such a meeting place?* Yes, he'd been there before, but that was a place of old magic and lore. Dallia had been fascinated by it and had begged him to go up there with her many times. Supposedly the dead branches of the gateway trees revealed unseen pathways of genealogy, housing the true history of the people of Kaleion. Damon baulked internally, shoeing away the idea as superstitious lore. Not that he didn't believe there to be old magic at work at the Trident Gateway. He did. But, he'd also seen with his own eyes a great deal of the true lineage of the planet and had been to the Trident Gateway many times. It had never revealed anything to him that would either confirm or disprove what he already knew to be fact.

Something inside Damon told him to prepare for this—to steel himself.

Then, he felt her naked presence before he smelled, or heard her

Charles W. McDonald Jr.

breathe. The moment he feared had come.

"Hello, My Husband," a practically nude Banthis lay on his study bed behind his desk, causing him to pivot in his chair.

In all her unholy glory, Banthis' eyes flashed pure gold as his preferred instantiation of her held his flesh captive with come-hither scents of arousal wafting over him.

"To what do I owe this pleasure?" Damon calculated on the fly what she might and might not already know. He could see her visible frustration at not being able to read his thoughts, as he'd already taken care of that problem.

"You chastened me for not coming to see you often enough.... Well, I'm here now. All for you." Batting her eyes at him, she pat the bed beside her expectantly.

Standing before her, Damon began removing his shirt in a slow and deliberate manner, never taking his eyes off hers. "Why are you really here?"

In a huff, she sat up straight, revealing the two strands of cloth that barely made an attempt to cover her nipples, descending downward in a V toward her naval. "I never thought you would fuck *her*."

"Oh.... So, *now* you're jealous." That caused her eyes to flash back at him in fire-rimmed gold.

"We all have feelings, Darling Love."

"I know that, My Lovely Wife." He sat beside her, letting her trace his chest as she snuggled in behind him with her legs wrapped around him from behind. He couldn't see it, but her blood-red, spear-tipped tail materialized behind her. He could sense the presence of her dark wings out to either side of him. "Did I hurt you," he asked, noticing her tracing stayed clear of his scars.

"I'm not the victim type," she whispered into his ear, seductively licking his earlobe, causing an immediate and complete erection, which quickly become the sole focus of her attention—tracing him through the outline of his slacks.

"No. I never saw you that way either."

"That's good," she replied softly, this time in his other ear, with her caress becoming more palpable to him.

"Did you know of Evanyil's betrayal of me?" As soon as he said it, he sensed everything inside her go dark. Really dark. Really fast.

Immediately her tracing of him through his slacks stopped and he could sense her wings expanding outwardly as her body tensed up behind him. "I didn't think it was my place to get in between you two. I know many things. About Evanyil. About Mira. About Illirian. About all the women you've...," she paused, having made her point as indelicately as intended, adding, "...But I've always made a point to stay out of your business unless and until it involves *our* business. I've always given you the latitude to operate as freely I promised. Is that not what you wanted?"

She always had this way of leveraging him against himself. Playing his words and wishes off of him. He did love her, but he often felt tied up in knots about it. "It is. I wasn't implicating you in any way. I was just curious what you knew and when you knew it."

"That sounds very implicative. Very accusatory."

He sighed heavily, leaning back into her body, signaling for her to keep caressing him. "I've never doubted you. And, I don't doubt you now. What you want and what I want are the same."

"And, tell me again what that is, Darling Love."

Damon's Distorting Web had been invoked over the bed all around them, pulsing and encrypting their conversation from the Dragon of Darkness and others who might be listening. "To slay the Dragon of Darkness, elevating you to your rightful position. To be free with you to do as we please forever and always and not be under the thumb of those who might want to influence and *use* us. To chart our own course in whatever way we mutually see fit. And, to ensure no one ever wrongs us again."

"*Yes*. That is what *we* want. Isn't it? It's what *we* discussed. But...," she paused, stopping her tracing of his erection again, "...it isn't what I think you have set in motion."

"I admit to expanding the scope of what we discussed." He didn't elaborate because he assumed she already knew.

"To what?"

"You know that I have to destroy *him* too." Damon's emphasis made obvious his intent to obliterate God the Creator and his lack of hesitation in how he said it delivered chills deep down inside Banthis, causing her wings to nearly shrivel involuntarily.

Charles W. McDonald Jr.

"That was *never* part of the bargain."

"Why should you care? I would think *that* would delight you."

"Upsetting the balance of power for a temporary coup is one thing. Blowing up the entire system is another entirely. I did *not* agree to that."

Rising from the bed to face Banthis in all her natural glory, he saw her lush, magnificently forged body shadow-cast by her own wings and tail whose venomous spear tip hung erect in the air nearly at her head's level. "I'm not asking your permission or your approval, Banthis. I mean to destroy God the Creator for what he didn't do—for the failure of his parentage—the failure of his own execution of his own value and belief system. For his insatiable and boundless hypocrisy."

"You've changed," Banthis finally noticed. In all her absentia of Damon—all her monitoring from afar—she'd allowed this change to go unchallenged and unmanaged, and now she was left to reap the harvest of seeds Damon had already sewn.

"You bet your sweet ass I've changed! I'm going to destroy him, and there's not one goddamned thing you can do to stop me. Either you're with me, or you're against me. So, which is it?" Now, he was forcing *her* to choose. She was going to have to agree to *his* part of the plan for him to execute *her* part of the plan. She needed him as much, and probably more, than he needed her, and he knew it.

"Careful, Damon."

"Don't threaten me." **This** was the moment he'd seen in *Durial's Eye* that caused him to fear the weight of this conversation in the first place. He knew what would come next, but *did that mean he should repeat what he'd seen or adjust?*

"You belong to me. You know that."

"Are you with me, or are you against me?" He stiffened his spine, towering over Banthis, the mighty *Staff of the Invoker* flying across the study into his right hand as he summoned enough Zero-Point energy with it to cause its shape to buckle before her. "ANSWER ME!" Damon's magic-laden voice shook his manor, causing the walls to vibrate his *hate,* as his scars flared and glowed hot amber.

In a rare move, not seen before and not a part of what he'd seen in *Durial's Eye*, Banthis fell to the floor before him. "Forgive me, My Husband.

Charles W. McDonald Jr.

I am yours as much as you are mine. I am with thee. Always." She paused, staring at the floor of Damon's study at his feet, not even considering looking up at him.

His breathing slowed as he calmed, and the *Staff of the Invoker* regained its shape beside him, still glowing and radiating its hemisphere of terror. "What did you know, and when did you know it," he repeated in a smooth, even, and expectant tone.

"I knew before Dallia's death. I could have stopped it, but I didn't because Dallia's death served me. It served all of us—including you."

Shaking his head, he couldn't break his thoughts free of the three little babes at play before him with their mothers. He couldn't square Dallia's death being anything that could ever have served him. Ever! "You need to leave."

"We need to talk through this, Damon." Daring to look at him, she could see his black eyes rimmed in a fiery hateful glow. *Was all that hate meant for her?*

"GET! OUT!" Again, the *Staff of the Invoker* flexed—brimming with enough power to obliterate Banthis where she knelt before him.

"I still control Chara's soul."

It was a threat from Banthis. An implied one, and one Damon immediately ran to ground in his internal thoughts. "And you'd set her free because of this...?"

"No. Never. I'd never hurt you like that, Darling Love of my life. You are everything to me. Everything. I want nothing but you. All I want, I want it for you and for us and for our daughters."

"Then why bring up Chara?"

"If you destroy me, you set her soul free. She will live again. In a manner of speaking."

He paused, thinking, though not letting down his guard. He had Banthis where he wanted her—submissive to *his* will—and he wasn't about to give up his leverage. "We will speak of this later. You, of all people, knew what Dallia meant to me, and this omission **will not go unpunished**. You will do *as I say, when I say, how I say* or even holding Chara's soul won't save you."

This was the Damon *she* had wanted—the Damon she had sought out only to find a wounded and broken man so long ago, weeks after Dal-

Charles W. McDonald Jr.

lia's death. Now that she had him, she wished she hadn't.

"Of course, My Husband. My Master."

"I will give you one Earth-hour for every year of your hideous omission to me to fill every single one of my manor's sublevels waist-deep in gold, silver, platinum, palladium, and diamonds. And, you better have made significant progress on it within the hour. You can lie, cheat, steal from anyone anywhere, but cannot take from anyone affiliated with me in any way. Tell me you understand, Banthis."

"I understand *completely*, My Husband. *My Master*. And, I will comply." Her form disintegrated before him, still kneeling at his feet—the dust of her essence filtering through cracks in the hardwood planks of the flooring of his study.

Financing this war and finding the right resources to fight alongside him had always been two of the biggest challenges of the Master Plan. Now, at least one of them could be removed from his plate, at the highest cost imaginable.

Releasing the energy he had held, he involuntarily let go of the *Staff of the Invoker*, letting it fall to the floor in a great clanging sound at his side as his body fell to a seated position on his bed. *She knew. She let it happen. Before they'd ever met. Did that mean, she'd used him to make the Throne of Souls she now held so dear? How did I benefit from Dallia's death?* It was a lot to process, and he needed to understand how it affected the Master Plan. *And, what of this meeting—shrouded in secrecy—at the Trident Gateway?* Looking at the rolled-up scroll from Illirian still sitting atop his desk, he wondered what could be so urgent a matter to be called at a place so shrouded in secrecy, mythology, and legacy. *Why there, and why now?*

Charles W. McDonald Jr.

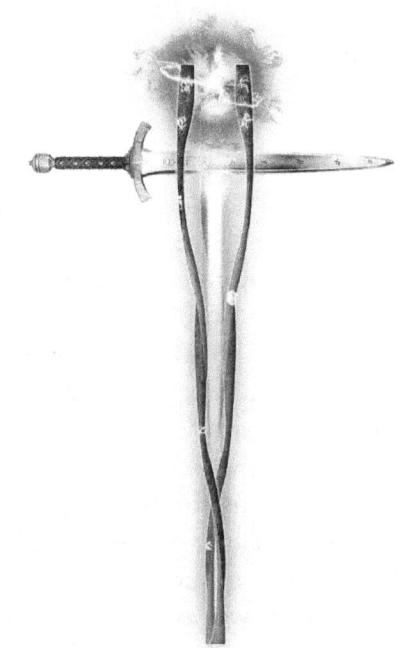

Chapter 40: The Fall of Hate

(The Trident Gateway, Kaleion, Present Day – Near Sunset)

The Kaleion star was still just above the mountain forming the Trident Falls that fed the Gateway Lake. Pulling the earbuds out of his ears as *Seether's – Against the Wall* ceased playing at just beyond full volume allowed by his Android® smartphone, Damon appeared pensive as the weight of the moment began to fall upon him in ocher veils of sunlit dust sprites floating waist high before him.

Releasing the Arcane that brought him here, the *Portal* whooshed close behind him, exiling him to the profound moment-in-waiting. Cagy was a woefully inadequate description of Illirian's behavior at her request to bring him here at this precise location at this exact moment. *Where is she*, he wondered. 'Bothered' wasn't the right word. Neither was 'troubled.' Vexed was the closest description he could come up with to describe his feelings of this moment as he took in the incredibly striking majesty of this place. No place on Eden could compare to the Trident Gateway, and Eden was one of the most picturesque worlds he'd ever seen.

Charles W. McDonald Jr.

Dressed in a long-sleeve, dark heather, tall-collared shirt with gold-scrolled accents and matching darker denim slacks, with his hair still cut shorter than normal from his mission to Graelon, Damon put his back to his home star as he leaned against the northernmost tree of the Trident Gateway, his head not quite coming up to the seemingly dead branches that arced across a dirt path, marking the Gateway itself. He'd been here before, of course, though not in centuries. Pivoting to look westward through the Gateway beneath its branches, he watched a trio of geese fly across the lake a few dozen yards to the north as a quartet of crows circled overhead in the valley of the Trident. One of them, making eye contact with Damon, broke formation, spiraling down without even a telepathic request of Damon. Shooting toward Damon with a purpose, its wings exploded open to brake and form a soft landing on the southernmost tree of the Gateway, now looking down at Damon as if awaiting his command.

"It's beautiful isn't it?" Illirian's voice shouldn't have startled him, but it did. She just had this knack of sneaking up on him, even though she knew how much he detested it. It was as if she was always trying to prove a point—not even the great Damon of Basrat could keep her out or contained or monitored.

Pivoting back to the east to address Illirian Starfire, Damon immediately fell to his knees in the tall grass, jasmine, and dust motes of sunset glory at the soft and radiant, red-haired apparition before him.

"My sweetest baby boy, how I have missed you," the beautifully pale, young, and red-haired female addressed a beloved son-in-disguise—distressed and encumbered by the Dark Knight of Magic.

All of his great atrocities struck home in an instant, preventing Damon's ability to look his mother in the eye. Naked, bare, and ashamed before the love and light of his mother's soul, all he could look at was her beautiful cream robes of stardust gold accents and royal-blue flutes.

"Please.... Rise, Kaylan. I am not here to judge you, my beautiful son stolen from me so long ago." Taking in the lost man before her in ocher highlights of the Kaleion star, she looked him up and down as he rose before her, Illirian Starfire taking his forearm in hand in both aid and comfort. A tear streaked down Seren's ethereal face as she looked her beloved Kaylan in the eyes for the first time in over a thousand solar years.

Charles W. McDonald Jr.

"It's okay, Damon," Illirian began, knowing the weight of this moment overwhelming the great Damon of Basrat. "I'm sorry I couldn't tell you. This meeting almost didn't take place. I had to do it in absolute secrecy. Even now, my strongest protections of this meeting are being heavily probed, and it won't be long before they are pierced, and this forbidden meeting known." Trying to comfort Damon yet emphasize the importance of every precious moment counting down to oblivion, Illirian needed Damon to understand...all that *she* could never convey.

"These...stems of *hate* you carry with you are not your doing, my precious boy. They are mine."

"NO," Damon protested vehemently before Seren, seeing the unconditional love in his mother's eyes for the first time in forever. All the memories of the unnamed one flooded to the front of his thoughts; the memory of running into the kitchen to see only his father standing there where a mother's voice had just been heard seemed the memory most paramount. "*HE* did this," Damon corrected her, leaning slightly forward as his scars throbbed in anguish most-surfaced at the thought of the *Cauldron of Hate* in which the great Damon of Basrat had been forged.

"Your father was a good man...once," Seren offered, trying to explain to *the man* who couldn't accept it because of the trauma *the boy* had suffered. "You don't know him. How could you? The man I knew was masked and marred by the *Instrument of Humanity's Hate*."

"Mother, forgive me. I don't understand." Shaking his head in confusion, memories of the unnamed one kept coming back wave upon wave, seeing, hearing, and feeling those relentless beatings again and again and again as Damon visibly cringed before Illirian and Seren, only to feel Illirian's grip tighten on his arm, trying to bring him back to the here and now. While the now was still possible....

"Listen to her, Damon...," Illirian paused, wanting not to interrupt but her heart desperate for her beloved Damon to hear what must be heard. "...Put down your *hate* of Keirill for just a moment to listen."

"It isn't just HIM," Damon fought back, "It's **HIM**." Damon pointed to the sky with his right index finger. "I was *abandoned* by this...this...*God the Creator. He's as much to blame as the hand he let strike me again and again.*"

"No, Damon." It was Seren's first time using his assumed name, and

Charles W. McDonald Jr.

it caught his immediate attention as he pulled his skyward, right hand back down by his side. "Your father was obsessed with being the best mage ever in all of Creation. Better than you. Better than any of the Four Brothers who seeded Humanity amidst the stars. Better than even the Great Durial. He did things…things you can't imagine or understand, and it wasn't enough for him. I see that trait—that obsession for greatness—in you."

"I'm nothing like him," Damon growled at Seren, then immediately cooled as her soothing presence and soft glare fought back with her own memories of the unnamed one.

"What I'm telling you is that, in his obsession he did something…. Something that went horribly wrong or something that became horribly misused. HE—Keirill—became the *Instrument* in a plan I cannot fully fathom, yet I know the intended outcome was this great man who stands before me…this great man hindered by this great weight of *hate* you carry with you everywhere."

Shaking his head in denial, Damon tried not to listen as the words of a powerful truth came flooding in one after the other in a staccato of release and relief most refused.

"*Your hate is my fault, for I was not there to be the buffer between you and the Instrument of Humanity's Hate your father had become as a result of his obsession.* It's my fault, Damon. Mine alone."

"NO. NO. NO. NOOOO," Damon growled. "HE KILLED YOU. I WAS THERE. HOW IS THIS POSSIBLE?!" Looking to Illirian to explain, yet his mother demanded his attention.

"He didn't kill me, Damon. The *Instrument of Humanity's Hate* killed him and then *it* killed me…and then *it forged you.*" Seren paused, seeing the precious boy turned hate-filled man before her, adding, "I wish you could have known your real father. He would have been so proud of you. I didn't want you to become a mage like us. And yet, here you are, and I realize I couldn't have been more wrong to want that. You were born to be this great man who stands before me now."

"How can you say that? I'm a MONSTER!" Damon's eyes glowed, burning hot with anger yet tear-sheen in shame.

"I see the greatness underneath all that hate you carry with you. Let me show you…." In the face of a majestic Kaleion sunset in amber repose, a

Charles W. McDonald Jr.

soft and pale blue glow grew brighter and stronger in Seren's masterful, yet delicate hands, turned palm-up, suddenly bursting towards Damon's chest, neck and shoulders.

Installing new memories inside Damon's consciousness, Seren's spell began filling in the blanks Damon—nor Kaylan—could not. Now seeing, for the first time—in his mind's eye, sides of Keirill he alone could not, Damon stretched out his hands towards his mother, feeling the unique energy of her spell that was beyond a spell working and tingling throughout his chest, shoulders, back, and neck. Seeing a tall raven-haired man with starry, bright-blue eyes and chiseled features lovingly caring for and even saving Seren's life time upon time so many centuries ago long before there was ever the nameless one, Damon's eyes weighed heavy with sadness as guilt began yielding to truth, bending like unto a reed in the wind and under the weight of Seren's magic. Now beginning to see the man before the *Instrument of Humanity's Hate*, Damon's shame broke before them in a transparent wave of energy cascading out in concentric circles like time-righting stones cast into the pond of Creation. A final and powerful blast from Seren's blue-energy spell shot into Damon in wave upon wave of Seren's forgiveness, showing Damon memories—from an adoring mother's perspective—of all the times she'd been right there by his side, only a breath away, for all his deeds both wondrous and malevolent. For every horrible deed delivering retribution for wrongs done upon him and those he loved, there was unconditional forgiveness of a mother's love in the face of the knowledge that these were not *his* deeds but the deeds of the *Instrument of Humanity's Hate*. For every one of Damon's greatest moments of doing what he knew was right, she was right there beaming with the pride of a mother's adoration in the face of the knowledge that she was wrong to ever to suppress her son's path of becoming what he must become and the burden he alone must carry.

Cascading into and throughout his body in a final blast of blue energy, Seren's powerful magic surged just before ending in the sound of a great and deep chord struck across the strings of time itself. Striking a mortal blow to *The Eye of Time*, Seren knew she had only but a moment, as she, too, felt the powerful forces probing at Illirian's protections shielding their actions and this profound moment.

Feeling the deep, in-perpetuity, scars upon his soul rising off his

Charles W. McDonald Jr.

body for the very first time, Damon's shame, hostility, and hate all gave way to a mother's undying love, falling to the ground in the ashes of the unmaking of the *Instrument of Humanity's Hate*.

Deafening silence preceded an earsplitting thunderclap from a cloudless sky as Seren's eyes reflected the knowledge her time was now fully spent.

"I love you, my sweet boy. I will always adore you. I have to go, but remember these words...*HE* is not who you think he is."

Yanked into the air before being shredded by a gust of wind, Seren's powerful apparition was obliterated before Damon as Illirian suddenly disappeared in a bright flash of light, which appeared to shock her as much as it did Damon.

"MOM!" Damon shouted at the sky some forty feet in the air where Seren's apparition was torn apart by the wind. "Mom," Damon breathed again just as the crow that had been sitting on the branches of the Trident Gateway now squatted before him as he collapsed to his knees in the anguish of an opportunity to express love unspoken now lost to forever. "Mom. I love you," he whispered to the air, hoping she was still there just like her memories shared with him that were now inextricably a part of him.

Three more crows swooped down out of the Kaleion sky to squat before Damon, who still knelt in the tall grass and dust sprites of a Kaleion sun retreating behind the Trident in amber trumpets of light that rent the sky with the full weight of the moment. In the four pairs of crows' eyes before him, Damon saw something he'd never before glimpsed—the reflection of his face and his own forgiveness of his own thoughts and deeds amidst a landscape of flesh uncontaminated by a programmed malevolence channeled through him.

He couldn't be sure they were asking him to do anything, but their presence spoke to him. Using the dead branches of the Gateway tree to pull himself up, the message struck him so hard he nearly let go of the branch as the truth revealed itself to him as never before. And this truth changed everything, or made everything more certain depending on one's perspective. He had mocked the Trident Gateway not for its beauty but for its lore, and its lore had proven accurate. Durial lived! Surely, as if he'd seen through Durial's own eyes. He lived. He needed to process this truth and this reve-

Charles W. McDonald Jr.

lation and all that it meant for him and the Master Plan.

Damon's hateful scars still sizzled on the ground around him, burning perpetual marks into the grass and soil of the Trident Gateway as the Kaleion crust now bore the full burden his great atrocities.

No longer the physical manifestation of the *Instrument of Humanity's Hate*, Damon rose free of the burden of a *hate* no longer his, ripping the air before him in super-heated, silvery-blue flashes of light. There was much work to be done and still a burden he alone must carry, but now freed of the burden of abandonment inexplicable, Damon dared to see the *hope* and *peace* that had been—until now—just outside his peripheral vision.

Charles W. McDonald Jr.

Part 7: The Distorted Continuum – Part III

Charles W. McDonald Jr.

My torment lifted,
My course set,
I know what must be,
And I know thou art with me.
Give me strength and let me, at last, find peace.

Charles W. McDonald Jr.

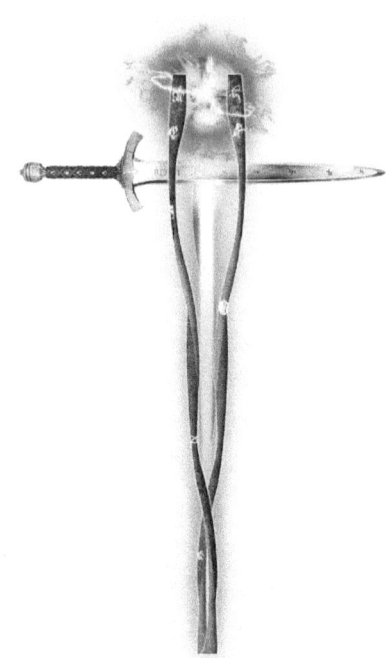

Chapter 41: Nonlocality and Retrocausality

(All That Was, Is, or Ever Will Be)

Events past, present, and future formed a cacophony of chaos within the slipstream of possibilities of Man and Universe. Seeing it all flash before him a nanosecond at a time, even his highly evolved cortex struggled to find the moment. He found the thread of the tall, dark-haired man with black eyes and hung on to it for dear life, experiencing the wreck and ruin and *hate* of his life and the entropy of the tentacles of his orbit, living through him and his great burden. Until that moment in a great field of nothingness amongst his friends with the great hall before them.... He reached out his hand, taking the tall, dark-haired man with him to the furthest reaches of this plane of existence.

His work now nearly done, a simple spell even against this greatest of mages of his caliber, and he was incapacitated, but of course, he had the advantage being hidden within the slipstream. Now, looking down upon the man in dark mage regalia of silver and gold piping, a thought snatched the mighty triple helix staff from Damon's iron grip into his own.

Charles W. McDonald Jr.

Tearing apart *both* space *and* time, he supposed the where and assumed he knew the when. Forming a second and third *Portal* within the *Portal* of his physical retreat, he created a fork in time, tossing the mighty *Staff of the Invoker* through one fork and his body through the other and it was done.

(The Halls of Aaramus, Time Neutral)

"I don't like it." Dallia's objection carried a soft intensity to it as she looked to her great and notorious husband, wondering how much more fame and fortune he sought.

"What's not to like," Damon jibed at the great and smoky void before them in all directions, remembering his research, 'there was no way to go in the wrong direction—here.' Or so it seemed, but in the moment—in this place of chaos of time and space—it very much seemed not only possible but probable.

"I'm glad you're so calm, Love." Her pensive smile tried to light the way but was quashed by the blackish-grey smoke curled and gnarled around their ankles in viperous vapors of promises of hate and animosity.

"Seems welcoming enough to me." The great and powerful Kellen the Destroyer smiled while throwing up yet another protection spell of magic unique to only him. Around himself only, of course.

"I don't think all this chit-chat is helpful," Goldenbow chided, his eyes darting all around them a grid at a time, even pivoting his body to walk backwards while he protected their flank. His eyes caught sight of something they thought should be in front of them. "Pssst," he hissed at the group, nodding for them to look behind.

"What the fuck," Kellen protested, seeing the outline of a great keep far off in the distance—what appeared to be some fifteen or more leagues away from their current position. But he knew, as well as Damon, distance and time were highly distorted here and senses couldn't always be trusted. In fact, they could almost never be trusted.

Damon's confused look said it all: 'how did we pass it?' That was the direction they had just come from over the last seemingly day and a half. And yet, there it was—The Halls of Aaramus. Blackness!

Charles W. McDonald Jr.

Snap, snap, snap. He heard a finger right in his left ear, and it immediately felt like he was laying down, but the surface felt...confusing. Not hard like brick or stone. Nor soft like a bed. More akin to laying upon the tips of thousands of fingers of air.

"Damon! Come back to me, Love," Dallia pleaded, attempting to shake her husband's massive body back to consciousness.

He recognized the voice of his beloved wife, Dallia, but something was wrong. Slowly he forced his eyes open, seeing Kellen leering down over him alongside his concerned wife while Goldenbow had a nocked arrow watching their backs. "What.... What happened?"

"Poof," Kellen answered. "You were there, and then you were gone. Just gone. Nice trick by the way. How'd you do it?" Kellen's magic worked in secret ringlets behind him, attempting to diagnose the hand at work and more importantly the how. Frowning, he could sense his diagnosis magic reporting back probabilities and data he didn't like, or moreover, could not explain, ruling out Damon as the possible root cause.

The last thing he remembered was gripping tight to his staff, and as he closed his right fist, he felt it laying down beside him—still in his hands. Trying to leverage it to right himself, he pressed the bottom of the *Staff of the Invoker* against the airy floor of the Halls of Aaramus, using it as a crutch to stabilize himself and put weight on his legs. "How long?"

"Hey, Day, you know as well as I do. Time doesn't mean shit here," Kellen chided with probing eyes. "We've had two meals in the time we've spent searching for you. So, it's been a while. What the fuck happened? What do you remember?"

"Nothing," he lied—sort of. His answer caused Goldenbow to pivot, looking directly at him. "I don't remember anything." It wasn't a total blank to him, but until he could make heads or tails of it; he didn't know what to say and felt they could have this discussion another time in another place that wasn't as lethal to their very existence as this. They had a job to do, and he wasn't the quitting type—especially not with this type of formidable team at his disposal.

"I can still see it in the distance. That way...." Goldenbow pointed

Charles W. McDonald Jr.

with his shortbow, adding, "If you're still up to it, let's move."

Moving his body wasn't the problem; he was quickly able to put one foot in front of the other as his wife walked with him side by side, holding his elbow as they often did when walking together.

"I love you." Dallia's smile of nerves couldn't hide her fears, and the look on her face said she could see through him as well as Goldenbow, but she respected and deferred to his judgment.

His right hand gently stroked the braided golden hair and ear of his beloved, falling and resting upon the nape of her neck. "And, I adore you, My Love." *The Staff of the Invoker* threw out its hemispherical aura of terror, predilection and protection both spans in front of Kellen and behind Goldenbow, and in it, his staff spoke to him in visions he did not understand. The tall and clearly powerful, middle-aged man of graying beard and hard-pressed dimple with stony planes of power about his face came out of the ether in waves unseen, akin to a mirage upon the desert, carrying him off to take his staff and whisper something in his ear, and yet the *Staff of the Invoker* was right there in the grip of his right hand. *Could the others not see this?* Looking to his lovely Dallia, she only smiled, looking back at him in curiosity as if clearly wondering if he was still all there after his disappearance from the group. It didn't make sense, but the gate to the Halls of Aaramus was upon them far faster than it should have been, and he had to focus.

(Warwick, New York, Earth, Present Day)

He could hear the fog of war in the near distance and see the awesome light of Excalibur upon Michael's tank. Even from this far away, it was unmistakable. From his waking dreams to his own direct handling of the immortal weapon of God the Creator, he knew this was the time; his whole body resonated with the energy and harmonics of the threads of destiny being struck by the great hand of a deity—however unseen but still felt.

His black gems radiated in the full moonlit night, seeing the two he had been expecting skulking about from his drone-operating position. Over the FLIR HD he could see just about the entire battlefield, but they couldn't see him. Operating inside his *Wall of Illusion*, all the outside world could see was a blonde-haired lieutenant of the Desert Rats doing his job.

Charles W. McDonald Jr.

He had but moments to act, and he had to be on top of the situation. *What better way to be on top of the situation than to literally be on top of it?* He smiled at his internal double entendre, straightening and hardening his gaze as Michael's Desert Rats scurried about all around him.

His mage regalia and staff hidden by his *Wall of Illusion*, he lost himself for a moment between the chaos of the war and shifting back and forth between reality, the monitor, and concentrating on the projected illusion. He thought he saw the *Staff of the Invoker* laying on the ground on his left side when he'd clearly remembered placing it on his right.

Then he took the moment needed, to tear his eyes from the drone screen, the battlefield, and his illusion to actually look down within the illusion itself and had to stop himself—rubbing his eyes and slapping his face to be sure. One *Staff of the Invoker* laying on his left and another laying on the ground by his right side.

The moment shook him, causing him to almost lose his balance as he knelt. Not the waking dream of God the Creator, but much akin to it in the way it blended and warped the reality around him, causing him to doubt what was real. Memories suddenly appeared in his mind that he hadn't ever remembered being there before, and yet he couldn't remember them ever not being there, as if their origin was completely unfathomable.

But in that moment, he knew and felt the time was *now*.

Tearing the air in front of him in silvery-blue flashes of light, Damon moved body and both instantiations of the *Staff of the Invoker* through the *Portal* to the Halls of Aaramus, dispelling his illusion from the other side of the *Portal*, watching from afar as the drone controls fell to the ground, causing the drone to spiral down out of the Earth-side sky.

Keeping the out-of-time *Staff of the Invoker* held in his left hand and the original in his right, it wasn't long before reality shifted again, and he found himself standing it the massive foyer of the great keep with the red-robed, decaying lich before him.

"You're late," his dead lips hissed over exposed jawline and teeth. "It's time to get to work." He reached out decaying flesh over dead bone— extending both left and right hands to accept the mighty *Staff of the Invoker* to put in its rightful place of honor.

Seemingly rogue memory upon rogue memory falling into place as if the corners of a great mosaic had now reduced probabilities enough for the rest to make sense, Damon handed him the original *Staff of the Invoker* from his right hand.

"Very good, Damon the Banished. Very, very good." If you could call it a smile, Aaramus did so with red glowing eyes under shadow of hood and veil of mystery.

"I think I finally understand," Damon proclaimed.

"Then you know you must move quickly. Go now! I will *deal* with the rest."

Without debate or discussion, Damon's form disintegrated along with the out-of-time *Staff of the Invoker*.

(Damon's House, Austin, Texas, Earth, Recent Past)

"It's time to come home, Damon," Banthis whispered in her deceased husband's ear as she knelt beside him, realizing not all of the plan was lost. They could still make it work.

The great room and kitchen began to hum and resonate with a warm energy like the coming of the morning. Witnessing the souls bursting through Damon's chest, circling him like a great toroidal energy field, Banthis' eyes squinted, throwing her left hand up to shield her face from the power and glory. Another moment of distraction caused Banthis to lose focus, looking down at the thousands of souls ensnarling Damon's broken and gaping chest as they circled Damon in torrent rings of energy, pushing back against Banthis' immortal *hate*.

Like unto flocks of wren, the thousands of souls captured by Damon's *Throne of Souls* moved in unison with two souls brighter than all the others seemingly coordinating with the ting of the microwave to cause Banthis to rock backward on her heels, crushing Illirian's tan, clay seal—summoning Illirian Starfire.

"But...," Banthis looked back at the seal's dust underneath her right heel, "...that's not right."

Charles W. McDonald Jr.

(Damon's Manor, Eden, Days from Now)

Like the torrent of inspiration that flowed to make the Zero-Point fundamental, his mind now worked on planes of past, present, and future as he began to see all possibilities. Before, he was a god. Now, he was beginning to feel like one as his mind began to see as if it had been blinded his entire life.

Flooding out of his right index finger, the fundamental practically gated itself as he worked shirtless and scarless at his desk—free of his hate and the *Instrument of Humanity's Hate*—the truth of reality and the nature of all things flowed from him in waves of knowledge immortal.

The smell of burned parchment perfumed his secret fourth-floor study as his light-orb moved with him, responding to his will.

Then.... *That was not the smell of burned parchment. It was something else.* Seeing the dark flash beneath his parchment, he moved the paper to see the numbers gated and burned into the marred surface of his desk as the smell of burned wood now overtook that of burned parchment. '31°35'40.2"N 99°48'41.2"W.'

Charles W. McDonald Jr.

Banchy and Demon of Bayeac

Charles W. McDonald Jr.

Chapter 42: The Hand of Fate – Part II

(Graelon Colonial Outpost, A Very Long Time Ago)

utomatic blue-green blaster fire erupted in from the vertically oblong Sentinel shimmering in its golden satin finish with matte-black barrels extended from programmable matter compartments on either side. One by one, Humans were mowed down with precision head shots—only the Humans who mattered, of course. Others—traitors to Mankind—flanked the dozens of Sentinels across a field of chaos and all-out war. Over hill and ravine, berm and trench, the AI Army had made their move.

The once-verdant valley of field and tree and flower now looked the part of a blasted and barren moon. Just inside the walls of the College of Invocation, Forkettès from throughout the entire outpost lined balustrade and battlement alike, casting with all their might across the field of the war for Man. Fireballs proved most ineffective, but they still flew from those of less skill, while forks of lightning from sky and Man alike disabled a Senti-nel hither and thither, but the hive-mind was very much alive and totally relentless.

Quarter-millimeter-wide lenses from the cavern high above provid-ed a bird's-eye view of the battlefield below for the hive-mind to coordinate both Human and AI assets.

"I.... We are the descendants of the four brothers: Durial, Alexe-

Charles W. McDonald Jr.

lio, Pierio, and Adamian. My name is Fondro. I am the Colonial Outpost President. If you're seeing this message, I, and likely the rest of those on this outpost, are the casualties of our own ingenuity." Fondro began his recording from behind his desk of millimeter-thick transparent aluminum flanked by infinity monitors where he observed their great losses. He took personal responsibility for letting it come to this. This was *his* outpost, *his* management, and *his* loss. It was all on him and his fateful decisions that he didn't have the guts to undo—instead leaving that for tailored others more capable and daring.

"It is important that you understand each brother was instructed to keep magic alive, but in their own way—eventually destined to bring a justice to their captures equal in measure to *their* sins. I don't know what happened to the other brothers, but Pierio, the brother banished to Graelon, kept magic alive with the intentions of merging it with the most powerful of technology. He instructed several outposts be built where the most extreme talent and possibilities could be tested. This was one such outpost." Fondro continued to speak the words of warning into the recording device he'd place into the plain, silver rod that would be biometrically encoded to only play for a direct descendant of the four brothers.

"Our experiment started to go wrong shortly after the college was built and the knowledge disseminated. The knowledge of building and replicating technology—at scale—through the use of magic. It built unforeseen pathways into the technology, creating an artificial intelligence unlike anything we'd ever seen before—unlike anything the brothers had seen before. On Setinon, there were accounts of AI carrying the brothers to the stars, but this new, general AI was infused and emboldened with the ability to control Arcane." He had to hurry; he could see from the monitors not only blaster fire, but heavy magic being thrown back at the Forkettès as his greatest fear came to life right before his eyes—*Portals* opening—everywhere. *Were they trying to escape or bringing reinforcements?* He had to move fast.

Encoding the plain silver rod with the message and the biometric print, he had to hide the message in a place where *they* wouldn't think to look.

He'd already tried the override for the Sentinels—several times, but that had been the first thing the general AI had hijacked. Frustrated, he

Charles W. McDonald Jr.

looked at the rate at which Humans were being mowed down and the AI holding their ground. It was all but done, save....

"You summoned me, Mr. President. I am here," Kirken's voice called out from behind a second and third tier of consoles and infinity monitors as he entered the Command Center. In a matte-black uniform of satin gold and aluminum gild with a brushed-finish aluminum belt did his friend appear ready for combat. Yet, combat was not his greatest ask of Kirken.

Pivoting his floating chair to face the mighty Forkettè school President, Fondro produced the encoded, plain silver rod for his friend to hide. "You said you had a place in mind for this. I presume it's ready."

"And the *Gate of Forseti*?" Fastidious and certain with hard lines about his weathered face, Kirken wasn't the assuming type. He would always rather verify. He recalled the last time he'd seen it, but that was so long ago. 'Twas far older than even *he* knew.

"It remains where we discussed, but I know that place is not secure enough. We cannot allow them to find it! We cannot risk the influence of *Eye*—even from this distance. It's possible they will succumb to its influence if they have not already. We must assume they already know of it."

"If I do not return to the battlements—alongside my people—all is lost. Every man, woman, and child that can cast is there, and it will not be enough."

"Then lose we will, Kirken. The *Gate of Forseti*—and this—is more important than our survival." Fondro paused, looking at his long-time friend who helped him build not only the college but the entire infrastructure of this colonial outpost and all its safety measures. "I wouldn't blame you; you know that." Pausing again, he considered leaving it unspoken, but this needed to be said. "...If you abandoned the fight after taking care of the Gate and the rod. You could always save yourself, and I wouldn't hold it against you. If the fight is lost, then let it be lost. It need not carry us *all* to oblivion."

His mouth worked in contemplation before considering the fate of his friend. "Where will you go?"

"Into the night, My Friend. Into the long, cold night."

A moment of silence between them as they watched the automated blaster fire obliterate another large section of the school's battlements, carry-

Charles W. McDonald Jr.

ing more student and faculty to their end in a heap of stone and satin metallic ruin.

Pulling his sidearm to head into the fight just outside, Fondro headed for the exit, placing a hand on his friend's shoulder. "Why are you still here, Old Friend? You have work to do. As do I…." Fondro heard the *Portal* seize the elements opening behind him as he knew Kirken would be off about the business of placing the *Gate of Forseti* into deeper hiding and the rod in the place where it would be found—but only by the right male and female descendants of the Four Brothers. The *Gate of Forseti,* he hoped, would never be found! As Kirken's *Portal* whooshed to a close behind him, the lift doors closed, carrying Fondro down to ground level in the valley below and the final fight for Man on his outpost.

The rod had been the easy part. In this cavern his magic prevented the entrance of all things not Human—and specifically all those not of the proper lineage. Not even their cunning enemy would find a way inside, but outside…that was another matter.

A whirl of energy unlike anything akin to a *Portal*, and he found himself in front of the other problem. And problem didn't begin to describe it. Not so small to easily move and far too permanent to destroy, the *Gate of Forseti* screamed with the echoes of Creation before him. Its ear-piercing cacophony made it impossible to stand here before it forever. Between black and translucent with a pitted surface that malleably transformed like unto waves off the pond of Creation, it howled back at him in forewarnings of doom in the voice of the Father of the Beginnings.

"I hear you, Great Gate. I hear you." Kirken paced about it like a bear stalking its prey. Roughly twice the size of a man with hundreds of times their density in mass, it wasn't going to be the easiest thing to hide. And, he didn't know Fondro's true intent. *Did he want it found by the right person, or hid so well it would never be discovered again…?*

Reading its three-word inscription in a language predating the seeding of Graelon, or any of the Seeds of Humanity, Kirken decided for himself—hoping Fondro would have approved. There was no time to consult the dead.

Looking around the volcanic spring water pool backdrop the great

Charles W. McDonald Jr.

slab of material unknown to Man, he needed to hide it where Man would fear to tread, and technology held no worth. A place created from nothingness—a place of nothing. And within that place, nothingness within. *The World Below and Between.*

His great magic struggled as tendrils of energy gripped at its sides, tugging and pulling at it toward the energy vortex that would carry it to the great void of its destination. The great *Gate* resisted Kirken's magic 'til he shoved at it with his bare hands, pushing it backward into the vortex that consumed it whole, then disintegrated as Kirken cried out in anguish at the immediate decay of both his hands—both flesh *and* bone—before his very eyes. Echoes of his screams permeated the volcanic cave from floor to ceiling long after they had been permanently imbued into that which would hasten God the Creator.

Charles W. McDonald Jr.

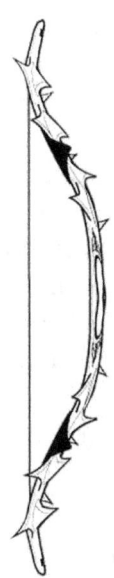

Chapter 43: Why He's a Living Legend

(The Crown of Spires, Perion, Present Day)

Edinaiel seemed peaceful enough as the magic and witchcraft of the Crown of Spires pushed back fiercely against the Blood Night Resha had brought upon the world. The divination tiles didn't play for him, but they did for Desindra. He'd dressed himself and ensured the cuffs were something he could easily break, as he floated inside his cage of branch and vine beside Desindra in the mid-morning light.

Being not even mid-day yet, he'd assumed Adena to be right where he left her—in her High Seat and Throne—albeit stained with the blood of her kind and her fortunes only brought to her by Desindra herself.

Desindra was coming about for some time now and beginning to function normally—even winking at him as they glided elegantly along the divination tile causeways toward the High Seat—and Adena. "Don't look too cute in that cage of yours," she mused with another wink.

"I'm only cute because I'm thinking of you." He toyed with her like a great spider plays with a grasshopper trapped in its web. "Don't forget about my confession."

Charles W. McDonald Jr.

"How could I forget about that?" Her fingertips ticked along the bars of vine of his cage as she smiled for him, thinking of the High Seat that would soon be hers, and hers alone. "But, Adena is very cunning. You'll have to be quick...and convincing."

His best wink had been reserved for this moment as he flashed that million-watt smile of his at her. "You do your job, and I'll do mine."

A giggle almost beget a snort akin to a child at play of hide-and-seek, nearly giving away her position. She was giddy and drunk with the possibilities shown to her just hours before by the divination tiles.

The moment had come—the arched and embossed doorway to Adena's Throne before them.

"You can do this," he coached with another smile as her magic opened the doorway for her to float him forward just slightly ahead of her.

Signing edicts and messages to be carried forth by her staff, Adena sat upon the High Seat of Edinaiel in figure-clinging robes made from diaphanous cream so sheer she was practically nude—her areolae erect and clearly visible through the delicate fabric. With cuffs that kissed the mirror-finished, diamond-shaped divination tile flooring, her arms did sway with magnitude and consequence. Drunk with power, obsessed with loyalty, and complacent in her position, did Adena function in her role. "What is HE doing here? Desindra, have you lost your ever-so-fragile mind?" She knew it rich and dripping with irony, her implying the insane actions of another, but....

Shooing her new assistant away with a swipe of her left hand and a look of derision, Adena wanted to know what would possess Desindra to bring *him* **here**.

"Mother, he has a confession to make, and I thought you'd like to hear it in person. Would you rather have me pull you from your important duties to come to him? If so, I can take him back to his cell." Only a few paces inside her throne chamber, the trap had been set. And, she hadn't even noticed yet.

"I confess," Goldenbow began from his still cross-legged seated position inside his cage of vine and branch. "Damon of Basrat sent me to kill you—to unseat you and to supplant you with someone he could trust—

Charles W. McDonald Jr.

someone he wanted to sit on your throne."

"Oh...," Adena leaned forward in her High Seat of ice crystal in perpetuity with the fluidic sound of water all around them echoing their conversation to the spire's peak.

"I told you, Mother, but he wouldn't tell me who he'd intended to put on your throne, so I brought him to you. Maybe we can work on him together to get the name." So carefully Desindra wove the lie and the spell, never having felt more alive than in this moment of risk-reward.

Rising from her High Seat, Adena began to close the distance to Goldenbow's floating cage—her nipples becoming even more erect with anticipation and her insatiable lust for both power and control. The elegant looseness of robes afforded both fluidic and wave-like movement in her reflection of the divination tiles that she didn't even consider consulting as the trap sprung. "Who is it, Outworlder? Who did Damon of Basrat wish to seat in my throne?"

"Me, Mother." It hadn't been easy weaving the spell with such subterfuge, but it was the simplest spell of all—playing on Adena's own confidence to not look down into the divination tiles that showed Adena's death as Goldenbow leapt from his cage and had his hands wrapped around Adena's throat.

The cuffs cut his wrists as he snapped them, but bursting through the vine-bar door of the cage was much easier as he felt the softness and feminine nature of Adena's pale skin in his mighty grip as he squeezed with all his might. His powerful biceps flexed as he felt her trachea giving way, her gold eyes relenting to original irises of blue—their veins bulging as they expelled out Adena's lifeforce before him.

In an instant, he flung her body upward while holding onto her by her robes, so he could slam Adena's body—back-first—down onto his bent and waiting knee where he broke her in half. A final gasp escaped Adena's lips as her soul fled her temporal shell. It was done.

Her body slumped down off of Goldenbow's bent knee, falling into the pool of water that surrounded the diamond-shaped divination tile flooring and bridge leading up to the Crystal Throne. With a slight plunk and splash of water did Adena's reign end and Desindra's begin.

"As we agreed, My Friend. As we agreed," Goldenbow reminded a

Charles W. McDonald Jr.

Desindra, somewhat alarmed by the ease with which he'd broken one of the most powerful forces on Perion.

A slow smile of long ambition now realized crept across Desindra's face as she recalled the outcome the divination tiles had shown her on her way to interrogate Goldenbow only hours before. "My friend," she replied repetitiously, still enamored with his scruffy cuteness and muscular power. "Of course, My Friend. As we agreed."

As Goldenbow began to melt his totem to carry him homeward, Desindra began to weave the spell of deceit that would explain her ascension to Adena's inner circle while eliminating them one by one. Her plans would take time to execute, but with Goldenbow's help—and Damon of Basrat—she'd clearly chosen sides and awaited the outcome of his great war with the status quo.

Charles W. McDonald Jr.

Chapter 44: Descendants of Destiny – Part II

(Just Outside *The Eye of Time*, Setinon, Near Future)

He saw the Sentinel's fiery gaze shift to its left—peering down the corridor—just as it was blown sideways by what he could only describe as a beam from some sort of energy weapon. Each consecutive beam had a hot, orange glow surrounding a starry-blue energy shell with rounded edges. Each round went completely through each Sentinel with the ease of Talemar's Starfire through flesh.

Through the walls and through the approaching Sentinel, the next energy rounds came, cutting through its neck, causing its severed alloy head to roll about the floor before them.

"WHAT'S HAPPENING," Kanet rang in his ear still buzzing from the seeming blaster fire, clutching to Radin's chest through his garment.

"You're asking ME?!" Radin's eyes shifted, moving Kanet out of his way so he could get a better look as he tried to pull himself upright with her.

"NO TIME," the command barked from around the doorjamb of the blown-open doorway to their room just as an unfamiliar, past-middle-aged face appeared, poking his head just barely inside the room. "There is no more time lest you come with me."

His accent was muddled and obfuscated by languages atop languages atop cultures and history profound as his whole body came into view. Taller than Radin and more akin to Damon, with hard and robust features, with black hair graying at its edges and a star-like dimple etched by fate into

Charles W. McDonald Jr.

in his chin, the man moved with a gruff nature and purpose but no longer with the smoothness of youth and good health. His grey and cream robes appeared tattered by time, tinged and soiled by great battle and travel alike with gold and silver gild piping frayed at their edges. "Are you hearing me, Radin? We have to move! NOW!"

The elderly robust figure addressing him by name caught him off guard just enough to snap him out of his funk as Radin nodded in realization. *Was this part of Damon's plan kept compartmentalized or something else entirely?* This man—he looked so much like Damon—minus the feature in his chin. Recalling his training for the mission, he addressed the stranger for the first time: "I have to get in there." Radin pointed through the wall toward what he assumed could only be containing what he'd come to destroy.

"Then come with me." The stranger's eyes merely acknowledged the presence of Kanet but said nothing of her as a threat to him, nor *his* plans. Lightning burst forth from his left hand as more blaster-like energy pulses erupted from his right as Sentinels were mowed down in smoking heaps of scarred, anodized alloy. Clearing the doorjamb and the hallway for Radin, he watched Radin running down the hallway. On Radin's left, the entire wall had a blue-green, shimmering, honeycomb-like appearance with no apparent door or entry.

Durial watched from some forty paces away as Radin skidded to a stop before the blue-green, shimmering wall.

"This is the way in." Radin's instincts and supposition ran at their peak under the duress and pressure of the moment.

Approaching Radin's location from behind, with Kanet loosely in tow of her own curiosity, Durial blasted the spot in the honeycomb-like wall before Radin, only to see his energy blasts absorbed into the wall in sheets of energy that looked akin to rats scurrying underneath a blanket. The wall remained intact and solid—denying them entry. "I'm assuming you had a plan to get in," he offered, expectantly looking at Radin.

"My plan didn't involve you. Who the hell are you anyway? And how is it you can cast inside the dampening field?"

"We don't have time for this, Radin. Do you have a plan to get in the room with the *Eye* or not?"

Just then, as if to answer, a hexagonal doorway opened just long enough for Radin to shoot through, and then it was shut before Durial in a whoosh and a hum of programmable matter.

*   *   *   *

(The Eye of Time, Setinon, Time Neutral)

Now inside the great hexagonal, technical cathedral room of dark carbon, nano-alloy, and programmable matter, energy from Setinon's home star poured like a great and colorful waterfall into *The Eye of Time* from above its platform. It took an immeasurable amount of energy to power the *Eye* as it now peered across the chasm of possible outcomes—seeing and all-knowing—like unto a god.

Honeycomb walls of programmable matter tried to contain the hum of all the power it took to run the *Eye* whilst sweeping arcs of alloy buttressed the hexagonal room of doom, forming the great technical medallion in the ceiling above from which the fountain of power from Setinon's star flowed. And, from that medallion of dark carbon, scarred by *hate* for Man, energy plumed in streams of brilliant colors highlighted by small bursts of elemental fusion contained within the energy waterfall's field boundaries. Down through the diaphanous, honeycomb, violet apertures did the fuel for the *hate* of Man flow into *The Eye of Time* below.

A great and deep chord, akin to the bowls of a great drum being struck, sounded as Radin approached the platform, surrounded by a moat of coolant, unimpeded by the Sentinels there to guard it. Oh…, they watched. Their digital eyes, behind glass, flashed with amber fire as they took up their defensive positions, but they did not attack.

"I'm here, *Great Eye*. This is what you wanted! *I am here*!"

Another great chord struck as a bolt of energy shot forth from the center of *The Eye of Time* out some twenty paces before Radin—not intended to harm, but to show….

Akin to a viewing window either he, or Damon, might form, it appeared with frayed edges of tattered energy formed by threads of magic he found familiar and yet very different, showing him a shirtless Damon with beads of sweat about his furrowed brow and down his scarred back, neck, and shoulders. Radin watched the *Eye* show him his father toiling in sweat

Charles W. McDonald Jr.

as he authored the spell that would send him to his torment by Voltor.

"Yea, I know thee," Radin proclaimed with his right fist pointed at the platform as he continued his approach to the *Eye*.

Again, the great chord struck the bowels of time/space in response to Radin's affirmation as the viewing window shifted to show him ever more....

Charles W. McDonald Jr.

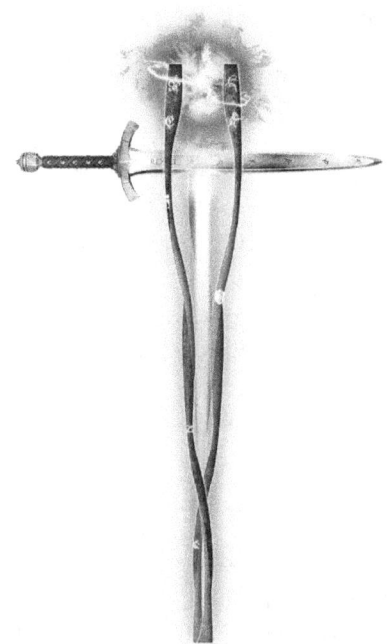

<u>Chapter 45: The Lord Thy God – Part II</u>

(Warwick, New York, Earth, Present Day)

Knowledge of what was coming didn't make it any less inevitable. She'd considered stopping it, of course. She'd do anything to save him, but something told her this was not that moment. However painful, she was going to go with her gut and observe. She was here to find Damon—not save Michael. Something told her that finding Damon would at least lead her to her children, and that was more important than anything else right now—certainly more important than Damon and his damnable plan.

Lead upon lead led to twisted knots of threads of ruin. She was tired of chasing the thunder and ready to catch the lightning of Damon. This was the one place and the one time she could count on Damon's being there to work his magic of misery and chaos.

Moments ago, she wept at the words of her beloved husband upon his tank as his spirit moved and inspired nations of Men to lay their lives on the line for all those who could not defend themselves. Moments ago, she saw the light of Excalibur disappear into the belly of a British Challenger II mainline battle tank, carrying her husband north to clash with the Chinese and North Korean armies.

With night vision goggles, she sat atop a nearby hillside until she saw Michael's tank take its fatal blow and the expected disturbance in the air forming the *Portal* she'd been waiting for, lighting the way in the stark dead of night, all the way to Damon.

"There you are," Elise declared, violently and hastily ripping the air in silvery-blue flashes of light to follow his other trail he'd hidden so well.

(Damon's Estate Grounds, Eden, Present Day)

The surprising warmth of the yellow dwarf just past its apex over cliff-side ocean-view made her gasp as the imposing shadow of a massive manor cast upon the soil of his terraformed world just clipped her right side, leaving her left side sun-cast by the light and dust sprites of the verdant grass all around. It was...*beautiful*.

For a moment she listened, as the white-capped waves crashed on the rocks far below and the massive double-door entryway of Damon's Manor called to her. She was here. It was time. And she wanted answers.

She actually had to force her left leg to move first, causing a slight stutter in her otherwise normal stride as the right followed—reluctantly so.

The door opened before she could even knock, revealing a well-past middle-aged man in amber shimmering vest over white long-sleeve shirt and black silk pants.

"Mrs. Day," he addressed her confidently, neither smiling nor frowning—just matter-of-fact. "You've been expected. Let me show you to him. Come this way, please," he prompted, motioning her sand-fatigued, feminine figure through a great foyer of three magnificent chandeliers, up a massive and elegant circular staircase.

Moments later, on the third floor, he showed her to the closed, double-door entrance of the spell test room.

"My name is Edgar, and I'll make sure you're taken care of while you're here. We have a full complement of staff to take care of your needs. Master Damon said to give you this," Edgar informed, handing her a scroll with Damon's seal in wax. "I don't know how it works, but he said you would."

Breaking the seal, she opened the rolled-up parchment, deciphering the minor spell that effectively summoned his staff at her will. "I've got it. When can I speak to him?"

"Right away. I'm going to go get him for you right now. I'll be right back with Master Damon in tow."

"You do that," she snarked, then caught herself, adding, "I'm sorry, Edgar. It's been a long journey, and I'm tired. That wasn't intended for you."

"No worries, Mrs. Day. We were told to make you comfortable and take care of your needs. You just use that scroll, and we'll help you any way we can."

"Thank you, Edgar," she managed, forcing a smile for him—if not for Damon.

Moments later, a jean-and-T-shirt-clad Damon poked his head around the corner—without Edgar. Neither smiling nor frowning—just expectant—he approached. His hair much shorter than the last time she'd seen him, though still long for a man as its raven tips rested upon the base of his neckline.

She'd considered what she'd say to him for quite some time, but now that she was here confronting him and obviously he'd been expecting her, she didn't know what to say or do. She was on uncomfortable and shifting footing.

"I can see the wheels turning in your thoughts," he proclaimed, stopping within arm's reach of her. "Nice gear," he jibed, looking over her battle fatigues and night-vision.

"Why were you expecting me? Why not just come find me?" Her eyes blinked at him expectantly, though she wasn't quite sure what to expect of Damon next. He was always so…unpredictable.

"Because you needed to believe."

"Believe what?"

"You're late…. We've got work to do, Elise."

Charles W. McDonald Jr.

"That's not an answer to my question, Damon."

"No, but this is." He pulled a small, torn piece of ink-jet-type paper, handing it to her. It was folded over a couple of times with his hand-writing inside in black ink.

Revealing its message, she wept, falling to her knees. Collapsing under the weight of her own knowledge of what cannot be.

"I want you to change into a dress—a proper dress of a beautiful lady. And, I want you to go to the New Georgia hospital. Then, go to the front desk outside main security and give them that message. You can hand it to them. They'll know my handwriting since my hand-written proclamations are on public display. They'll know it came directly from me. You need to do this now, Elise. We're kind of on the clock here; time matters."

"I…. I…."

"You'll be taken care of. You have important work to do. And, there's something else, but you'll see it when you get there."

"I don't have the words, Damon."

Smiling a million-watt smile for her, for he knew he'd mistreated her on many an occasion, Damon pulled her to his chest, holding her. "You can kick my ass later." Pushing her away, he turned and walked away without another word. The full weight of his scars removed it didn't feel awkward—his expression for her. More akin to long overdue. Elise was always a vital part of the Master Plan and she'd now found her way home to fulfill that role.

Will this make right at least some of my wrongs? He didn't know, but for the first time in a very long time, he was smiling again.

*   *   *   *

The white and grey multi-story building of sleek lines and sterile features would have screamed medical facilities even if it wasn't clearly marked as 'Hospital' in five languages—three of which she knew. Looking around at all the gleaming new construction, she realized this was Damon's Arc—his salvation of Man—and it, alongside the message in her hand, made her reconsider everything she thought she knew of him. Damon had proven himself a monster again and again and again, and yet, he was clearly a man

Charles W. McDonald Jr.

of purpose, profoundly clearing a path for his plan no matter the cost. Perhaps that was what made him appear a monster from time to time—his focus being so absolute. But the enigma of Damon had led her here; she approached the front reception desk, handing them the torn slip of paper Damon had given her.

Fidgeting her hands against her white summer dress, Elise hadn't bothered to hide her age again. Appearing the true mid-thirties version of herself, she pursed her lips in pensive wonder, looking at the strict biometric security double doors, which clearly led to many secrets beyond.

A slim brunette with brown eyes in white and grey scrubs with two badges hanging from her belt loop rose to take her torn slip of paper. As she opened it, she immediately snapped her finger, calling to attention the security guard at the front, signaling him with a twirling upward motion of her index finger. The brown-haired man in black uniform immediately pressed his thumb to the biometric pad, then pressed a red digital square on the pad, which apparently accepted his credentials, immediately turning green and opening the secured double doors.

"Ma'am…," he summed, motioning for Elise to follow. "…If you'll come with me."

Elise paused, her legs frozen in much the way they'd been in front of Damon's Manor. "You can do this," she coached herself, forcing one foot in front of the other as she fell in line behind the security guard armed with an automatic assault rifle akin to some she'd seen used by Special Operators in the past, but with some interesting modifications around the trigger that looked to be biometric-identity-related. Whatever Damon was building here, it was at least intended to be more advanced than Earth and perhaps not as much so as her homeworld, but then, she'd not been shown everything just yet.

"Where are we going," she asked, filing in behind the security guard whose name badge read, 'Schwartz.'

"I'm only supposed to escort you. If you'll just follow me. I'm sure they'll explain."

"But, who's they?"

As if to answer her question, a few turns later she found herself alongside a massive laboratory room that appeared to be more than one separate room unto itself, lined by computers and various electronic gear along the far wall and Lexan® glass along the hallway wall. Another biometric security pad challenged their entrance, but before Schwartz could enter his credentials, the door made a suction noise, immediately opening to reveal an almond-eyed, grey alien, whose four-fingered hand was held up as if to tell the guard he was dismissed as it slowly approached her.

The guard wasn't the least bit surprised nor in shock at the presence of the alien creature—making her wonder what other life might cohabitate this world.

"Your Majesty." She heard the words in her thoughts as if spoken aloud though its thin, pale lips that never moved below two oval ports similar to nostrils. Awkwardly, it made a gesture akin to a clumsy curtsy. "If you'll come with me." With one finger, it pointed the way as it slowly walked toward the lab, giving Elise time to follow. "Please. This way."

A right turn, away from the Lexan® and prying eyes, caused Elise to fall to her knees in tears and hope reborn.

Michael Anthony Day sipped hot Winter Wassail tea from a black and gold, tall ceramic mug as he shivered cold and nude underneath a heavy, brown wool blanket.

"My GOD, My Love! What happened? How is this possible? I saw you...." Weeping into closed hands before her face, her words were muffled, but he understood them as recognition, and memory came in slow and small doses.

"He's not fully himself again," the alien informed, adding, "It will take time for him to remember who he is, who you are, his purpose, and your role. But, this is your function now. This is your job. You are to be queen again and always, Your Majesty."

"Why is she crying," Michael asked, petting her beautiful strawberry-blonde hair in confused moments of recognition.

"She is confused, Your Majesty," the chief scientist—his only contact for the last two years—announced.

"Me too," Michael admitted, smiling at her, as his right hand lifted her chin. Her beautiful face stroked his heart with warmth of familiarity and profound emotions, but confusion reigned supreme as it had from the moment he'd been revived just minutes ago.

Charles W. McDonald Jr.

Looking up into hard, youthful lines of her once-deceased husband, seeing those scruffy short-brown tufts of hair against blue eyes, Elise wanted to kiss him, but so much had happened and so much was lost between them. Recovery would be an emotional process as much as it would be a physical one, but first she needed to understand how this was possible.... "How? How? HOW did this happen?"

Her face asked Michael, but her words asked the alien...and Damon!

"It wasn't easy," the alien informed, motioning toward the incubation chamber at the other end of the second-but-connected laboratory room. "Physically, it was a matter of cell manipulation to alter his normal growth rate and cap it. We still don't know if that was done correctly or not, but we can assume from the signs I've seen. In incubation, his new mind and neural network was educated and normalized. His brain was fed a steady stream of known memories—publicly available data. But, part of your role will be to help him fill in the gaps of private knowledge. He was only a public figure for a short period of time, and that meant there wasn't a lot of available data about his youth. Whatever he shared with you in the past, he's counting on you to help him restore those memories. They will be vital to restoring the character of who he once was and the greatness that made him king."

"I think I understand, but there was a lot he could never discuss with me. He worked in special forces on many clandestine missions that he could never speak of—not even with me."

"Then those memories may be lost." The alien realized perhaps this wouldn't be as complete a restoration as they had once hoped. They had been counting on Elise to restore most, if not all, of his private knowledge.

"I know something that might restore him," Elise realized, but it was something she no longer possessed, yet belonged to the confused man before her. For that, she'd have to talk to Damon. And, Damon had some serious explaining to do! "What of our children," she asked, seeing his eyes engage hers directly for the first time. She could see there was memory there, but still so much more confusion.

"Billings and your children are here. They don't know yet. We were waiting for you."

Charles W. McDonald Jr.

"Well, we're not waiting a moment more," she ordered, getting up off the white, sterile, smooth and contiguous medical flooring.

"I've been instructed to discharge him into your care. For you to take him home."

"Where's home?"

"I will summon Billings, and he'll show you to your new home where you can recover as a family."

"I still want to talk to Damon," Elise insisted, gathering up Michael, helping him stand and walk to the door.

"The Savior said as much."

"The WHAT!" She paused for a second, thinking. "Oh…. Yeah…. I suppose you would see him that way. Yes, tell the Savior, the queen wants to speak with him at his first available opportunity."

Michael's right arm wrapped around his wife, who still looked familiar to him and yet not, as she led them out of the secure medical facility. "My name is Michael Day." He surprised her at the recognition of his own identity.

"Yes, My Love. My Husband. You are my Michael, and I am your Elise. Your queen."

Raised eyebrows met with the last. "You don't look like a queen," he mused quietly with a scruffy but good-looking grin—albeit still dubious of her credentials and his, as they exited the main doors.

"And you don't look like a king, My Love, but we're going to fix that," as she sat him down curbside, naked save for the grey wool blanket he was wrapped inside, waiting for Billings.

Curious exchanged glances between the two scrubs-clad receptionists as the slender, Graelon-origin, brunette deciphered the message in what she now understood as Kaleion common-tongue, 'The Lord Thy God.' Shaking her head, she knew the handwriting, of course, but didn't get the reference to a god. Damon was the only deity she had ever known. She didn't know who the tall, good-looking man was, nor the strange woman who just escorted him out of the hospital against pretty much every patient protocol, but he sure was super cute wrapped up in that blanket!

Charles W. McDonald Jr.

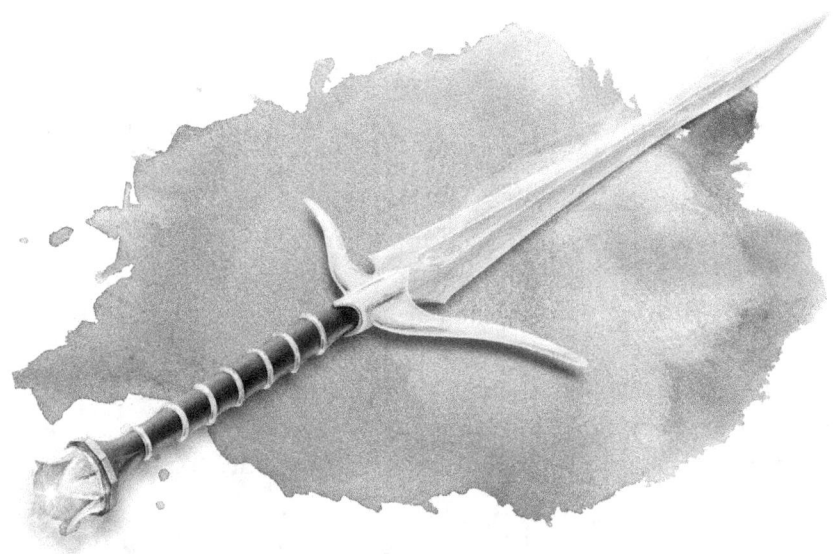

Chapter 46: Intractable Crossroads – Part II

(The Halls of Aaramus, Time Neutral)

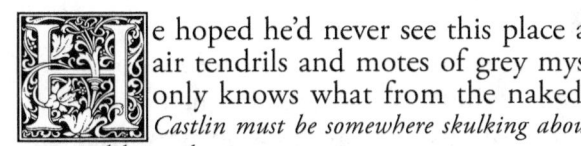e hoped he'd never see this place again, with its ground of black air tendrils and motes of grey mysterious smoke, hiding Creator only knows what from the naked eye. Yet, here he was…. *And Castlin must be somewhere skulking about.* Still, it wasn't Castlin that worried him the most.

His right hand instinctively went to Starfire's grip at his side as it's pommel glowed in the graying night that was the Halls of Aaramus. Every protection spell he possessed was up already, yet he still felt…naked and alone.

The closing whoosh of a *Portal* behind him, made him pivot just in time to see a robed Castlin walking toward him. Somewhat impressed at Castlin's skill level by the fact that he'd found Talemar so easily in a place where nothing was easy to find, Talemar wondered how far Castlin had progressed from the man he knew and battled so long ago. It also made him wonder what he was doing here in this crossroads of his life.

Holding Starfire's grip as Castlin approached, Talemar looked around, expecting the unexpected.

"I see you, Great Talemar. Do you see me?"

"Of course."

"One has to always ask. Especially here." Fire eyes through bangs of long silver hair against tall, slight-of-build warned of Castlin's intent, but it was already too late for Talemar.

"Where is this key player of yours? Where is she? You warned me to not to be late. I'm here…on time!"

"She is coming, Great Talemar, and she has instructed me to start without her."

"She's the reason I agreed to this meeting.… Because of her keen foresight. I wanted to see it in action."

"She hath shared with me her visions of you…for me to share with you."

No response from Talemar—only a stone-cold stare from withered and decayed, blackened, wart-covered flesh.

"She knows of the child most hidden with genitors most profound, and she knows you did not deserve this curse you bear for a death that you cheated."

His stance shifted in his consideration. *How could she know of that?!*

"She knows of the love given so much that it cost twenty years of her short and temporal existence, but twenty years is a nit in time for a great soul born of both gods and kings. In but twenty years, he shall be nothing but a youngling. But, what if he could live beyond those twenty years…?" Castlin paused now only a few paces from Talemar, gesturing outward as if to suggest…more. "You gave all this…," he motioned to encompass Talemar's now frail and disfigured body, "…for but twenty years of Ryker's life. What would you give for him to have a normal life?"

"No life is normal for the grandson of Damon. Besides, none of us might be around in a few years, let alone twenty."

"Indeed." He paused, considering all Talemar had done. "I understand why you hid his existence from Damon. Truly I do. And, you're not wrong to consider the possibility of annihilation, but…," Castlin paused again, his right index finger in the smoke-tendrilled air as if to make his point. "You *will* die in all this, Great Talemar."

Charles W. M\(^c\)Donald Jr.

"You're not telling me anything I don't already know."

"Is Damon's cause your cause?"

"I told you already. I don't know."

"Others may find difficulty in seeing what you stand for and what you care for, but I do not."

"Enlighten me!"

"You care for her. You care for Ryker—for his innocence. You care for those you've harmed and all you've broken."

"How is this helping anything?" A frustrated Talemar unclipped the clasp of Starfire's scabbard.

A sudden crack in Castlin's flesh about his cheeks and jaw grew wider as grey-cast light shone subcutaneously. What came next as flesh fell to smoke-tendrilled ground beget silver hair for long blonde curls of gnarled *hate* down to nude bottom as Castlin's robe burned away to ash, blown away by cold gale of decrepit wind.

The perfect nude flesh with serpent-like tail writhing out of the black-tendril ground of the Halls of Aaramus could only fit one description he knew—Lilith.

"Key player indeed. Your deceit is legendary, Great Queen."

"I thought you hearing this next part directly from me would carry more weight, Talemar...," she paused, her hair of golden gnarled locks nearly as erect as her viperous tail, leaning forward off her shoulder in cold gusts of wind that came from nowhere and everywhere. "I've seen your death, and it is certain."

"We all die. Even you."

"Our essence is immortal, but yours is not. I have seen its end if you go with Damon."

He paused. He didn't know what to say. He didn't know what that would even mean for him. His immortal soul robbed of its afterlife—to be totally obliterated from existence.

"Clearly, you wanted my service and my tools. Why? For what?"

"To stand fast. You need do nothing more."

"Surely if this is the war of all wars, I need to make a choice."

"Holding the ground of acquiescence is a choice, Talemar."

"You wouldn't ask my services for you, or your kind?"

Charles W. McDonald Jr.

"I wouldn't ask because you wouldn't offer. And even if you did...," Lilith paused in consideration. "...Well, even I could never see that. Hold fast. Stay out of it. That is but enough to tip the balance."

"And for this, you would give Ryker a fulsome life independent and not beholden to you or anyone...?"

"Agreed." Lilith's eyes of molten amber flashed at the bargain struck as her cape of flesh jostled about her perfect body.

"Agreed," Talemar offered with a nod, causing her serpentine tail to retreat below the cloudy forms of tendrils that made up the ground here.

With a gust and a whirlwind, did she disappear into the smoky tendrils of the Halls of Aaramus. Only the scent of her burned flesh still gave promise to her less-than-complete retreat.

A heavy sigh from Talemar as he exhaled heavy through his nostrils, trying to blow out her foul stench of death. A bargain struck anew, and yet he'd never felt more constrained nor bound. Never more troubled nor void of *hope*. What little hope remained now lived inside baby Ryker. Where he was and whomever he'd become, it was all on him.

Charles W. McDonald Jr.

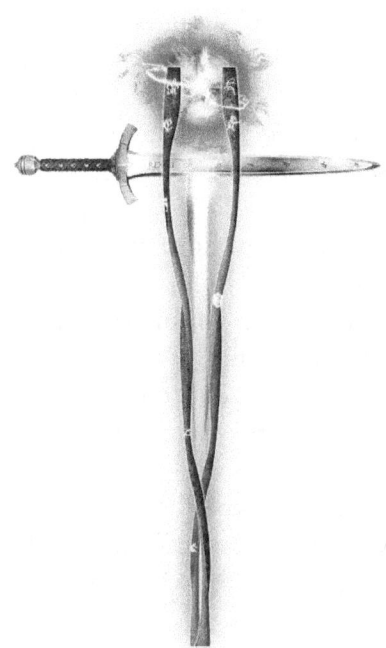

Chapter 47: Politics of the Status Quo

(The Hadron, Kaleion, Present day)

The great cleaved message of the Father of the Beginnings backdrop to a setting Kaleion sun, Damon and Radin arrived without *Portal*, *Gate*, or pomp in a materializing mist that Damon had used only once before in front of Radin, and that Radin had been too nascent to recognize the components then, but now that he'd seen and touched Zero-Point and many other great feats, he decoded Damon's spell in real time, cataloging it for future use.

"This had better be good," Damon prompted his son, motioning down the length of his own body where Radin had urged his father's wearing of full and most-elegant mage regalia.

Looking to the east, his back to the Kaleion sunset, Radin mouthed under his breath, "Don't make me look stupid." Nervously, he exchanged tense glares with his biological father, whose wall of morose abutted not only his physical shell, but his immortal soul of late. Yet, in looking upon

Charles W. McDonald Jr.

him now, this Damon—absent the weight of his scars—told him that wall wasn't a wall built of *hate*, but something else entirely, and it made Radin wonder exactly what it was.

"Who are you talking to?" Damon's right index finger was nearly in Radin's face when the *Portal* opened and stayed that way as Morden walked through.

Immediately, Damon began flooding himself and the *Staff of the Invoker* with all the Zero-Point it could hold as one defensive spell after another shot up around him, invoking layers of invisible shields.

"Father, stop. I invited him."

The look Damon shot his son could have cleaved again the great message of God the Creator behind them without spell or natural abilities— just on anger and mistrust alone.

Morden took no actions save holding his *Portal* open. Now, only looking between the two—taking his measure of the combined threat they posed yet striding confidently to meet with them—with his newly returned, familiar staff in hand.

"I see my son...," he paused for a moment, but the cat was already out of the bag with Radin's plea, adding, "...returned your staff, Morden. Why are we here?"

"We're here because we need each other," Radin posed to a Damon who now backed away from his son, head tilted in curiosity...or anger. It was sometimes hard to tell with Damon.

Stroking his black and gold-piped, forest-green robes with his left hand, Morden produced the product of his promise—a contract—handing it to Damon, who dubiously accepted it and began immediately scanning it top to bottom.

He considered burning it on the spot, of course. Morden couldn't be trusted with any agreement whether by contract or handshake, but perhaps by motives.... "Clearly, you two have been communicating. So.... Explain...." That clearly directed at Radin with a glare of finality just as a thought from Damon invoked *Distorting Web* overhead, encrypting the rest of their conversation.

"Father, we need the most talented resources on our side. It's that simple. This is a matter of the politics of the status quo, and I think Morden's wishes and ours are aligned. He's no fool. He sees the great message behind us, and I've shown him all the Seals. He's seen the hatred for Mankind firsthand. He's seen the same hypocrisy you and I have seen, and I think he's ready to accept a different outcome. I wanted to explore the possibilities of that with him in person."

Looking between the two and hearing the familial titles, Morden wondered why the son of Damon the Banished would be so cavalier about being known as such, or had Damon's reputation off-world become one of a totally different color than that of Kaleion? Clearly, the boy was his son. He could see the resemblance in hard-planed facial features and characteristics as well as mannerisms. They had spent much time together, and that meant a lot of what Damon knew, the boy now knew. But, still, he was just a boy, however much a man he tried to imitate.... "This son of yours has balls, Damon. I'll give him that. But...," Morden's left-hand index finger went in the air to make his point, "...I'm here to listen first. If we are in agreement at the end, I will sign the contract."

"If you're waiting for me to beg you for your help, you can go fuck yourself, Morden."

"Unhelpful, Father. Please. Let's talk the politics of the status quo and go from there."

"Fine. The politics of the status quo are this...," Damon rebuffed, still holding enough Zero-Point to cause the *Staff of the Invoker* to buckle and warp under its weight. "Four of the Seals have been spoken aloud in the voice of God the Creator. *The End* is upon all the worlds of Creation. What *The End* means is a mystery to us, but we can only assume that it means the subjugation of Man to deity or deities and that whatever war exists between God the Creator and the Dragon of Darkness, that they will continue to weaponize Man for whatever outcome they wish. *They* are not looking out for us, but for themselves. *They* represent the biggest threat to Man. They lie to us, abandon us in our hour of need. *They* are hypocrisy incarnate, and *we* can do better than them. Alone."

Damon's diatribe rang sallow in Morden's ears as if it had come from within himself. He hadn't considered—'til now—the similarity of their belief system. He'd never bothered to know or understand Damon on any level beyond his power. He knew Damon didn't lust for the same things as he, but he always thought Damon a dark light in search of the right place to shine. Perhaps, this was it. *Still, he was totally mad!* "I hear you seek to destroy not only God the Creator but the Dragon as well. When I heard this, I thought it was insane and could not have come from the Damon I knew. But, the more I thought about it and the more I hear you speak, I can see it is true. It is what you seek, and you have never been one to bite off more than you can chew."

"I hear a distinct, 'but,' coming," Damon finished Morden's thoughts.

"You're not wrong," Morden agreed. "Destroying the Dragon, I can see remotely possible, but God the Creator…? The Father of the Beginnings…." Morden just shook his head dubiously.

"We are all just matter and energy. Even him…," Damon postulated. "…Do you not think we could govern ourselves better than he?"

"No doubt," Morden concurred, adding, "…and I agree on the matter and energy statement. However, nine women can no more have a baby in a month than one hundred of the finest mages alive in existence could take out a deity one hundred times the strength of the strongest among them."

"You're not wrong." Damon tossed Morden's phrase back at him in tacit agreement.

"So, you agree this is not just about matching an aggregate level of power equivalent to our common foe…? This is about having a better plan. It's about having a winning strategy with contingency upon contingency."

The commonality of Morden's thinking to his own was both welcome and unsettling at the same time. Still, there was truth in the maxim, 'Great minds think alike.' Whatever he thought of Morden and his disgust for the man, he did consider Morden to have a great mind. "I have a plan many years in the making with parties—however duplicitous—deeply vested in the outcome we all seek."

The duplicitous comment apparently caught Radin off-guard enough to cause his eyes to shift from Morden to Damon in a questioning manner. Shifting his stance to balance more weight on his right side, Radin quickly returned his gaze upon Morden, holding enough source energy to blast him out of existence should he prove to be as untrustworthy as Damon thought.

"Very well, Damon the Banished," Morden acknowledged, adding, "Tell me more of this plan and where I fit in. When the dust settles after this greatest of all wars, what do I get and what do we even believe will be left of this Universe?"

Quickly thinking on his feet, Damon offered, "We will cede Kaleion to you—all of it. Do with it as you wish."

"Not good enough. Kaleion is already my possession, and from my understanding of the Scrolls, it may not be a possession worth having."

Morden was no fool. Damon recognized that. Long ago. "You may be correct, Morden. What is it you wish?"

Scratching graying and gnarled stubble about his heavily withered face, Morden considered the boundlessness of his ambition abutted the possible realm of whatever may remain when they are done. "Your wife will become the new Dragon of Darkness, no?"

However Morden had pieced that together, Damon couldn't say, but the look Radin shot him said that he neither knew, nor had he shared that information with Morden. Still, Morden had his sources just the same as Damon, and perhaps he had underestimated Morden, *and his sources*.... A simple affirming nod answered Morden's supposition as correct, causing Morden to inhale deeply in a protracted moment of consideration.

"Then, I want the Key to the Abyss to control her fate and keep her in check."

Damon's right hand immediately went to his chin in thought. The Key to the Abyss had been his, but he turned it down, assuming Kellen would assume that burden and that notoriety. Yet, notoriety and Morden went hand in hand. He couldn't promise what was not his, and surely he knew where the key resided today as much as either Morden or Kellen. That meant Morden also knew their need for the key—however temporary—to execute his plan. He had to assume Morden knew a great deal—that was best in negotiating with the man. Looking briefly to his son, whose raised eyebrows told of his misgivings about setting up this meeting in the first place, Damon had but one answer to give.... "When we are done with the key, it is yours to keep in perpetuity...Morden."

A lurid and twisted snarl-turned-smile told Damon the Banished

Charles W. McDonald Jr.

he had a deal as Morden's finger worked the air before him, causing the parchment of the contract to burn Morden's signature at the bottom. "Stay in touch, Damon the Banished. I'll be there when the time comes. Just be sure to hold up your end of the bargain." Morden's form transformed into shadow, then the shadow penetrated the wall of the *Distorting Web*, walking through his still-open *Portal*.

As soon as Morden's form left through his *Portal*, Damon turned to his precocious son and protégée-in-the-making, berating Radin with his glare.

"Did I do the wrong thing, Father?"

"Not telling me is **ALWAYS** the wrong thing!"

"If I had told you, would you have come?" Radin's hands outstretched, he pleaded with his biological father to see things from *his* perspective and that he was only trying to help because he agreed with Damon that this work *needed* to be done.

Radin is not wrong. But, Morden of all people! How am I going to give Morden something that isn't mine to offer...? Kellen would not be pleased, and he needed Kellen far more than he needed Morden. Trusted him more too. Of course, that wasn't saying much. *Who could ever trust Morden to do anything—contract or no?* He would have to discuss this new development with Kellen. Perhaps there was another bargain to be struck.... Perhaps.

Technically, he already knew the outcome of this. *Didn't he?* The Halls of Aaramus could be incredibly confusing—even to him. *But, how to reach that outcome...?* Those events were as fuzzy as one's peripheral vision, if not more so.

Charles W. McDonald Jr.

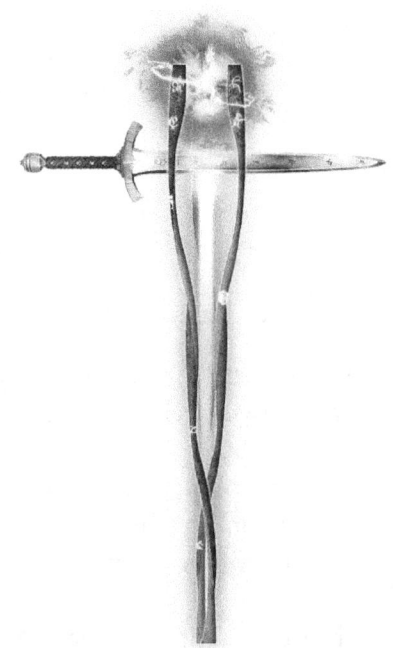

Chapter 48: A Mortal Toll – Part II

(The Kaleion Star System, Days Earlier)

Just outside the asteroid belt of celestial cloud of Creation debris, the massive Saline Comet roared through the solar system on its 3,600-year hyperbolic orbit of the Kaleion star. Orbiting both above and below the planetary ecliptic plane, its harbinger path had been hidden from crude mystics and astronomers for thousands of years.

The size of a small rogue planet—about a quarter of Kaleion's mass—it burst through the asteroid belt at hyper-ballistic speed, on course, on destiny, and on time to carry God the Creator's ancient message, from eras and epochs long forgotten, to Man.

Antiker—the fourth planet from the Kaleion star—passed just in front of the great comet, whose tail stretched all the way to the fifth planet in the star system, close enough for its mass to sway trajectory yet not capture it in its own orbit, causing a one-degree shift in the comet's path as it

Charles W. McDonald Jr.

made its way through the asteroid belt.

Like unto celestial billiards, the Saline Comet obliterated the first great rocky asteroid with which it collided, causing its cleaved-off pieces to strike another and another until many now formed into a linear shooting gallery on a cosmic scale.

(Morden's Manor, Diamond Head, Kaleion, Present Day)

A thirty-span, cream, grey, and tan stone wall alternated both arched and squared windows, revealing two oversized floors flanked by mural towers both east and west, north and south. A gatehouse connected to the main keep by way of arched stone and brick over smoothed cobblestone coach path. The same smoothed sandstone cobblestone formed the circular drive toward the east, with the back of the keep up against a canopy of trees that led to the western beachhead.

Pacing the full length of his upstairs hall, Morden considered the possibilities despite his contractual commitment. It wouldn't be the first time he'd broken one, and certainly wouldn't be the last either.

Damon was out of his mind, but he'd never known Damon not to do precisely what he said he would, and that meant all—as it had been known before—was coming to an end. Whatever would be, would be vastly different than it had been before, and whatever Morden was, he was a preservationist of his own life. He just had to decide, who had the likelier odds of winning this war. Damon might have been crazy beyond all recognition, but Damon rarely found himself on the losing side. Either fate was with him, or someone else was tilting the scales in his favor. And, that had always been the biggest mystery about Damon.... *Who, or what, was tilting the odds in his favor?*

A shimmering brown smoking robe broke up the gnarled mass of wet hair from his bath as he frowned at the burst of gulls overhead, shooting out away from each other in all directions, causing him to scratch his chin in concerned contemplation. The reflection of the contrail in the glass doors leading out to the cigar deck that overlooked the canopy of western trees and beachhead answered part of the why, and the glass-shattering sonic boom answered the other as he quickly found himself face down in the red and gold-gild, lush carpet of his hallway.

"FUCK!" Everything was prepared. All he had to do was execute the plan. Still, facing The End Times practically naked made him feel nonetheless ill-prepared and literally caught with his pants down. Rushing to his master suite, he grabbed everything he'd inventoried as necessary for the survival of his plans.

Another massive sonic boom shattered the atmosphere in sonnet rings of doom promised and not yet delivered.

"FUCK YOU, DAMON!" Hurried behavior now became flat-out rushed as items hither and thither flew from every corner of his keep into the last few containers he hadn't yet packed while other already-packed containers formed uniform lines marching on air toward already-opened *Portals*. Plural. Each the four times the size required to transport an adult Humanoid.

From the time the Seals had been spoken aloud, he'd wondered how much time they had. Now, he was left to wonder no more.

*   *   *   *

(Goldenbow's Cavern Fortress, Kaleion, Present Day)

The warning message—in the form of one of Damon's scrolls—had said it all. The End was upon them. However much they'd planned and prepared, it didn't remove the stinging shock Goldenbow felt returning to his homeworld being pelted by prophetic celestial ammunition. It was enough to make him wonder the accuracy of prophecies long foretold with fragments long since forgotten. In some cases, it had proven wrong, and in other cases, it had struck far too close to home—literally.

With fire blazing in his fireplace, did he melt the totem that would execute his evacuation plan as he gathered with him everything that truly mattered.

Looking around at the place he'd called home for centuries, he wasn't upset. He knew the end would come and it would be both abrupt and costly. He just hoped the reward was worth all this loss as his form disintegrated to another world—and safety. Or so he hoped....

Charles W. McDonald Jr.

*   *   *   *

(Kaleion, Present Day)

The Kaleion star dimmed in its great shadow as the main body of the vast and heavy comet shattered and blistered the atmosphere of the southern hemisphere with a concussive boom that could be heard in every corner of the world. Kaleion itself cried out in a heave of great relent as the thousand-league-radius rock of gravity-formed ice and stellar, iron-ferrite debris collected from the asteroid belt made its way toward the Hadron at twenty-six times the speed of sound.

Not a perfect sphere, with weight more heavily distributed at the northern and southern glacier-laden poles to cause a thirteen-degree axis tilt laying on its back to the Kaleion star from the perspective of the northern pole, the great life-bearing planet of Durial and magic collectively held its breath at the massive object now within a thousand meters of making contact with the Kaleion crust it would obliterate and instantly turn to magma upon contact.

Portal upon *Portal* upon *Portal* opening all over the majestic world of flower, tree, and life abundant—by the tens of thousands they came—shimmering beacons of *hope* to huddled masses of Man watching their doom obliterate the atmosphere and hastening their end.

From orbit, they appeared but tiny flashes of silvery-blue light, but from the ground they appeared as doorways of *hope*. From dark to light their eyes did see, with a deep male voice echoing on every part of the doomed world, each heard, in their native tongue, "Jump now…."

Some headed the call while others failed to act in the seconds they were afforded. Some looked to the sky in awe from continents away. Some blown to the ground by the concussive shockwave of the great comet shattering the atmosphere.

Like a great eclipse did the comet come to cleave off a great chunk of Kaleion as it struck the crust and core at a hard, oblique angle.

The whole process of extinction took only but an hour, but all life on what was Kaleion was obliterated and what remained in orbit around the Kaleion star was but two-thirds of what had been the beautiful home of the Great Durial and his progeny. The homeworld to Damon of Basrat, Illirian

Charles W. McDonald Jr.

Starfire, Kellen the Destroyer, Morden, Evanyil, Lorianus, Dallia, Daedrin, Keirill and Seren, Goldenbow, and so many other legends of time immemorial, was no more.

Now a dead and broken, fragmented rock in the dark void did the great world cast its progeny off into the coldness of space with their appendages flailing aimlessly, those bodies and souls not saved, hurled into a dark knight of oblivion by the fated collision of The Creator of Injustices' making. Great trails of cleaved off iron ferrite and still-hardening molten debris spun around the two-thirds Kaleion mass no longer remotely spherical and no longer rotating in a symmetrical way. Sputtering, coughing and jutting in its now-chaotic rotation the lifeless rock, bathed in the ocher rays of a weeping Kaleion star, the Father of the Beginnings' message had been delivered and ruin was the result. The once great world of dragon and mage was now but ashen rock orbiting a star in mourning....

Charles W. McDonald Jr.

Part 8: The Righted Continuum – Part II

Charles W. McDonald Jr.

The sword and great kingdom were mine,
As were its justice cavaliers of kind.
Verily, thy know my title, yet not my name.
I am yours if you'll but chance the game.

Charles W. McDonald Jr.

Chapter 49: A Kingdom Reborn

(Damon's Manor, Eden, Present Day)

Both the grounds and foyer bustled with activity as servants, groundskeepers, and tradesmen scurried about with pace in their steps as if their lives depended on it—albeit unclear their objective. With Damon's wishes and proclamations, there could only be educated guesses at best. For all the breadcrumb clues and slightest morsels of truth and information, her ledger with Damon was zeroed out now, and she wanted to start fresh—trying to understand him, if only she could.

Her children were safe—if a tad bit older—and their estate was every bit the grounds she once held as royalty on Earth. But, truly understanding her real role here, and in Damon's Master Plan, meant finally understanding his plan, and that was going to prove a much bigger challenge than merely chasing him down.

A tall, handsome, and familiar figure descended the foyer's circular staircase as her spine stiffened and her hands fell to the hem of her royal, blood-red dress, pushing it against her shapely legs.

"Father said you were here. It's good to see you again." Radin approached, with Damon slightly behind and to his left—still descending the staircase.

"Damon didn't tell me you were here, but I should have assumed. I should have just asked you to bring me here," she realized, her head down, staring at the massive tiles of the foyer floor.

Lifting her chin with his right hand, he kissed her cheek. "You look great! Different, but great! Should I address you as 'Your Majesty' now?"

"You better!" Shoving her closed fist into his side to playfully drive home her point, she pulled back, freshly reminded of how hard a young man Radin had become.

Charles W. McDonald Jr.

He jostled at the jab—if barely so—causing her to force a smile to match the awkward one he held for her. From lover to friend to ally were all hard transitions to make, and yet here they were.

"I imagine you have questions," Damon interrupted, now standing between the two and slightly to their side with his back to the main double-door entryway.

"You could say that," Elise cracked. "…Starting with Excalibur. Where is it?"

"You're welcome," Damon retorted—none too subtle about it either.

"He can't be king again without it. You know it, and I know it. He's still struggling to remember who he once was."

"I have a solution for that." A half-smile from Damon caused a firm and immediate furrowed brow from Elise as her light mood vanished in an instant.

"Of course, you do…," Elise sniped back. "…You seem to have a solution for everything, except letting those people around you critical to your success, and the success of your fucking plan, actually understand our real role in all this!" She made a sweeping gesture, metaphorically encompassing the room and all around them.

Looking down at his feet, not wanting to get any further in the middle of this, Radin tried to read between the lines. Saving Michael's DNA wouldn't have been enough for Damon. If he wanted to truly save Michael and who he really was, it would mean more than just saving his body or regenerating it. He knew that. Elise surely knew that, and that meant Damon, for sure, knew it.

Reading the tea leaves of Radin's gestures, she quickly pivoted her attention back onto her former lover. "What do you know that you're not telling me?"

"He knows the same as I've told you." Damon placed his hand in between Radin and Elise, drawing her fire on him.

"So, shit. He knows exactly shit," she countered.

Placing his thumb and forefinger together with about a millimeter separation between them, Radin made a small gesture suggesting more, only to have Damon's monster-sized hand grab Radin's mid-air, closing around Radin's gesture.

Charles W. McDonald Jr.

"Exactly. He knows even less than shit," Damon deflected. "Look. We can make the Excalibur thing work. Aaramus knew I'd be back for it. I'll handle it. Meanwhile, I need you to do your job."

"And, what the fuck is my job, Damon?" Her fists pressed against her dress-clad hips expectantly.

"Your job is to lead, along with your husband. Humanity is going to survive, and your job is to lead them. That means we need to have a ceremony where power is clearly transferred—or rather instantiated. The government I created here is a democratic monarchy not unlike the one you left on Earth, and it's been missing the monarchy component where I have been substitute. And this time, Michael will be more careful. You will see to it. This is also your job, and the job of a security detail I'm going to assign to you, and you're going to follow their instruction and their advice. Do I make myself clear on that?"

A solitary nod of the head said she understood—sort of. She understood his command—not the why.

"For my plan to work, I need Michael full and whole again—with Excalibur. I need him in his prime. I need him safe and sound—well cared for and with any of his major problems dealt with by his caring, loving wife. Do I make myself clear on that?"

"Okay, Damon, I get it. I hear you. I don't hear any explanation as to why or what's really going on, but I hear your commands."

"And...," Damon prompted her expectantly, motioning for her to continue with his right hand.

"And, I'll handle it," she complied, looking down again at the foyer flooring.

"We'll need a coronation similar in grandeur to the one he had at Westminster Abbey. Work with the president, Billings, and my chief of staff to make the necessary arrangements. If we're going to make Michael a king again, we're going to do it right. Everything depends on it."

Shaking her head at Damon in disgust she couldn't hold it in anymore, "What the fuck depends on it, Damon? What are you doing? Why is Michael so necessary to your plans?"

Clasping her hands together with his own, Radin shook his head at her discouraging pressing any further. "I'll tell you why. Damon has to go and speak with Aaramus, but I promise I'll tell you what I know—at least what I can of what I know, and you'll just have to trust me on the rest. Fair enough?"

With a knowing smile for his son, Damon disappeared, swallowed by a *Gate* in the floor of his foyer, causing a whoosh of air to be sucked into the *Gate* with him.

"He's gone. So, tell me," she prompted as she invoked a transparent ring of silence around them—shielding their conversation from the workers.

(The Halls of Aaramus, Time Neutral)

A seeming nanosecond from his prior instantiation—barely enough time for him to return, Aaramus was back in his main hall before the staves, swords, halberds, shields, and other weapons alike in their immortality. And, there again was Damon the Banished—obviously older by some days. He could always tell the difference, even if but a second since his last encounter with the lost, and yet found, Dark Knight of Magic.

Looking around, Damon the Banished had a confused look on his face. Expecting to see his staff in the place of honor it once held, but did not see.

"Something you seek, Damon the Banished?" His red eyes glowed with black halos of shadow, expectantly.

Damon's mind worked, trying to solve the problem before him, but this was not the problem for which he'd come. He needed to stay focused. With Aaramus, any and all great paradox was possible—even likely. And Aaramus always loved to invoke mystery over magic, but *mystery invoked by magic* was his favorite of all. "I'm here for Excalibur—as we discussed."

Aaramus pointed a gnarled finger of decayed flesh over graying bone to the Excalibur's place of honor among the swords, as if to tell him to fetch it himself.

With a thought, Excalibur flew toward Damon—scabbardless—stopping to float just in front of him and between himself and the mighty mage, Aaramus. "Is there anything I owe you? I never want to be in your debt, Aaramus."

Charles W. McDonald Jr.

"No, Damon the Banished. You do not."

It wasn't really an answer to his question, but he wasn't going to stand here—in his domain—debating the man. Or thing.... Or whatever.... With a thought, Damon's form disintegrated into nothingness, carrying the immortal weapon of Creation with him.

A hearty grunt akin to a snarl beget a knowingly twisted smile of decayed flesh behind the shadow of his blood-red hood as Aaramus went about his business of the doom of time itself and the greatest unmaking of all.

(Presidential Palace, New Georgia, Eden, Present Day)

Casey Williams escorted Damon into the president's offices where an armed Grant McCarthy immediately knelt before his god.

"You can leave us, Grant," Abel shooed away his security detail so as to have what he knew needed to be a private conversation between himself and Damon. They had much to discuss and much to catch up on. "You too, Casey."

Casey and Grant briefly looked between each other and decided distance was best, moving out of the presidential offices with some pace.

"I didn't take you for the type of mage to carry a sword," Abel quipped with a disarming smile, eying the gleaming sword of rune and fire that held a quiet hum of resonant energy in the room. "Did you only need to meet with me, or did you need me to summon Ron or anyone else?"

"I've told you about this sword in the past. It's a part of Earthen lore and has some matter of fact behind it."

"You have. So, this is Excalibur—The Sword of the First Kings. So, what's going on?"

"The constitutional government I provided you calls for a constitutional monarchy with checks and balances of power and elections for leaders in those checks of power."

"It does." No disagreement from President Abel—now some two years into his first term.

"I'm here to invoke the monarchy part of that government. His

Charles W. McDonald Jr.

name is Michael Anthony Day, and his heir will only be defined by the person who can make this weapon glow—which may, or may not, be his progeny. This weapon of Creation will determine our leadership that is not elected. Is that clear?"

"Perfectly. Did you wish a ceremony? To inform the public properly of the new part of government and its role in their daily lives?"

"I do wish it. In centuries past, there were coronation ceremonies held at a great church called Westminster Abbey. I wish for you to coordinate with Elise Day—your queen—a proper coronation equivalent to such."

"I have seen images of this church now destroyed. WE have no such facility here."

"Do what you can with what we have, Abel. We have to do this right. Talk to Elise. She'll give you the details of what we're trying to replicate."

"I'll handle it. May we talk other business?" Abel's eyes looked to Damon both guarded and troubled.

Sitting in one of the wingback chairs on the area rug before the president's desk, Damon placed Excalibur lengthwise across his lap, as if expecting this to take some time. He hadn't spent much time taking care of the business of taking care of this world, and it was a clear neglect on his part, but that was why he had people like Michael and Abel—to lead in his considerable absence.

"I updated you on the negotiations with the Negi."

"You did, and I approved those negotiations. Was there a problem or something else I needed to approve?" He thought about it for a moment. He might have approved them, but he hadn't acted up on those agreements yet. Too many irons in the fire. He still had yet to terraform their lands to their specifications, and that would take a feat of some engineering to do so.

"We have consulted with engineers and mages alike, and they concur that a shield of such magnitude as to greenhouse such a large part of the crust of the planet could only be done by the combination of both magic and technology—unless, of course, you have another answer."

"No, and I haven't had time to engineer a different solution. I've been busy on something else. You've instructed everyone that the great mountain island west of Warden's Corridor is completely off limits. It won't

Charles W. McDonald Jr.

be under the protection of this shield we're erecting, and I wouldn't want it to be friendly to the natives even if it were. I want it off-limits to everyone."

"May I ask why?"

"You can ask, Abel." Damon's black gems flashed with that statement as he tapped Excalibur's tip against his left knee cap.

"I have already made notice of that zone being off limits, but I will re-emphasize the matter and give it the proper weight it deserves."

Damon only nodded in acceptance, then his mind suddenly shifted to his other top priority. "How's Mira?"

Surprised and somewhat dubious of the question, President Abel looked at Damon curiously. "You should know. You took her. I assumed she was with you. Do you need me to do anything to help with Mira?"

"No, it was a silly question. I've got it. Forget I asked." That was the response he'd been expecting, but confirmation of it solidified his understanding of the continuum. That was a good thing. He hoped. "When we have a solution for the dome, let me know and I'll begin the terraforming process. Do you need me to speak with them? The Negi."

"At some point, I'm sure that would be helpful. They seemed to doubt my authority to make a treaty with them, and this introduction of a monarch may not exactly be helpful in their belief of my authority here."

"Your authority is temporary and constrained by both elections and term limits, Abel."

"Yes. Yes. I understand, but our treaties have permanence to them, and they need to believe in the perpetuity of those treaties lest they not agree to them."

"If a show of force and solidarity is necessary, you, me, and Michael, we can make that happen. However, I'm working on another solution to the Negi problem."

"Oh…? Can you read me in on it?" Damon's surprises often held with them far-reaching impact—for everyone. Being able to prepare the population was *his* responsibility, and preparedness meant foreknowledge—which with Damon was often a challenge.

He thought about it, of course. The less people knew, the better, but in this case, he was about to bring an army of thousands of immortals into a world of what would normally be their food source. They had a right to know. Still, he needed to be careful with what information got out into the public. He didn't want to create mass panic among his society. "What I'm going to share with you is presidential-level knowledge for now. You can discuss it with the royal couple, but it needs to remain compartmentalized to the upper echelon of government until I say otherwise. Are we clear on that?"

"Perfectly." *This ought to be good*, Abel considered.

"You're aware of a mythological race of immortals that feed on Human blood?"

"Ummm. Yes. They existed on our world, and on Earth as well."

"Yeah, well, I know how they propagated from Kaleion to Earth, but what I don't know is where they originally came from."

"Why are we discussing vampires?"

"Because I'm going to bring them here, numbering in the thousands."

"WHY?!!!"

"Because I need them. We need them. And if anyone can keep the Negi in check, they can."

"We can't have them using our society as a food source!"

"I have already negotiated those terms. They will not feed on any law-abiding citizen."

Raised eyebrows spoke of the president's doubtfulness of that. Blood lust was exactly that—lust. It was a burning and uncontrollable desire as far as he understood. *How can you ask someone to control that which cannot be controlled?*

"I know what you're thinking, Abel. And I've already considered it. They need us. We need them. They bring with them considerable abilities and technology we need—in gene therapy and genomics, in security forces, special operations forces, intelligence gathering, and so on. They will make us stronger."

"If they don't kill us all off." He didn't like this. Every one of his instincts said this was a bad idea. "How do you plan on keeping them separate from us? They can't integrate with us or their blood lust will get the better of them."

"They will integrate with us fully and completely, and I have confidence that we can find a solution to the blood lust."

Charles W. McDonald Jr.

A heavy sigh from Abel. *How am I going to make this work? First the Negi, then the monarchy, then Damon's quarantine, and now this.* He was beginning to question running for re-election. Sometimes the burden of responsibility just wasn't worth it. "I do wish you'd consult with me—or Michael—before making these society-altering decisions that affect us all."

"You forget your place, Abel!" Damon's black eyes flashed. "This is my society—not yours. It's only yours to govern and caretake. It is mine to forge as I see fit."

A simple nod from Abel said it all. *What else could he say?* He was a reed in Damon's wind. Sometimes Damon listened, and sometimes he led with an iron fist. That was just who he was. Either you trusted Damon, or you didn't, and many times over Damon had earned Abel's trust—going back decades—centuries even. "I need to let you know that I've been… compromised."

Immediately standing, with Excalibur at his right side, Damon's eyes flashed again with a shadow halo behind those black, swept blades of fine hair. "Compromised how?"

"The Negi placed a tracking device inside my bloodstream—something they said could not be removed. They warned it would kill me if I tried to have it removed, but it allows for direct and remote communication."

"And you thought to tell me this now?! After our sensitive conversation?!!! That should have been the first thing you told me!"

"They can't listen in on my conversations. And, even if they did, what are they going to be able to do about your plans? Nothing."

"Like a virus can remotely turn on a camera, or a microphone, I'm certain they can do far more with this remote capability than you're aware of. We will discuss this further, when I have a solution for this problem. Until then, you will delegate all your tasks to the Vice President. I will have no further compartmentalized conversations with you until this matter is resolved."

"Damon, if I'm seen to lose power, the treaty cannot move forward."

"You're still the president, and you can still negotiate the full terms of the treaty. All other matters will be handled by Michael and the vice president until I say otherwise. Clear?"

Charles W. McDonald Jr.

"Perfectly. I'll bring him up to speed."

"No, Abel…. You'll send the vice president to me, and Michael and I will bring him up to speed."

"As you wish it. I'm sorry."

"Me too, Abel." He looked upon the man who carried the name and likeness of his long-ago friend—the only friend he'd had as a child and killed with his incompetence. "I'll try to make this right."

Damon's face said he was angry—truly angry. Whether so at Abel's omission or Abel's condition, he couldn't say. But he knew he'd let Damon down, and that was never a good position to be in if you wanted to continue to live.

Charles W. McDonald Jr.

Chapter 50: Welcome to New York – Part II

(Warwick, New York, Earth, Late Spring, Moments Ago)

"Fire," Michael ordered, causing another 120mm sabot round to split open another Chinese VT-4 mainline battle tank. His hearing was mostly vibrational, but he sensed another round being loaded into the chamber as his HUD (Heads-Up Display) soon confirmed with a green flashing light on the left side of the screen. That had been kill shot number ten, and they were beginning to draw attention to themselves.

In the target-rich environment of a heavy battlefield, it didn't take long to find the next one as he called down to the driver to shift left ten degrees, swiveling the main turret around for the next kill shot.

A brilliant flash of white-hot light lit up the entire field of his scope.

Groggy waves of consciousness came back to him in small and slow doses. Now on the floor of the burning tank with his safety straps severed by shrapnel, dangling in front of his face, he could feel something was terribly wrong. He felt off—not just from a lack of total consciousness—he felt extremely light-headed and fragmented of thought.

Looking around and seeing but one survivor, in a raspy voice, Michael called out, "Jimmy, come on. We've gotta get outta here."

Propping himself up and reaching for the ladder, he felt the sudden pain shooting up into his chest from his right side. He could feel the blood coming out in rivers but could not see the wound when he looked down. The shrapnel must have come in through his back. He had to get them out of there, or they were as good as dead. They were sitting ducks in a burning tank. The gritty, oily smell of burning JP-4 fuel, spent gunpowder, and high explosives permeated the air—especially inside the tank. Perhaps it was best

Charles W. McDonald Jr.

that Michael could not see the large piece of shrapnel buried deep into his right flank and the deep-red blood gushing from around its edges.

*   *   *   *

(Two Hundred Yards Southwest, A Moment Ago)

"That's him. We've gotta move," Michelle called out to Lawna, who was in the process of lining up another TOW missile shot.

With a flash of light in the smoky night air, it tore through the barrel toward its VT4 target on a wire-guided line of death and mayhem, splitting the tank in half with an explosion dead center on the turret, right where it met the main body of the tank. Cleaving it open like a sharp knife through a can of SPAM®, the TOW projectile severed the turret from the main body of the Chinese tank, tossing the turret and its one occupant onto its side while the main body rolled slowly forward in a burning heap.

"Okay, now we can go." Lawna looked to where Michelle was still pointing, seeing the white-painted outline of a sword on the back of a burning Challenger II tank. "Shit! That's him!"

They hadn't seen him, of course, but the blood was still everywhere inside Michael's tank—or what remained of it. Protection spells kept the flames away from him while he worked, purple-top specimen tube in hand, he formed streams of Michael's blood into lines firm enough and narrow enough to pierce the top of the purple urethane as he collected small chunks of Michael's flesh as well. Hurrying, as he had but moments left, and the timing was crucial, he shoved the filled specimen tube into the interior pocket of his robes, disappearing in a silvery-blue flash as he moved his body with magic to a spot where he could work without being seen.

From behind the burning carcass of another tank, Damon was still close enough to work his casting of *Stasis* on Michael. The soul was a fleeting and amorphous thing at both the twilight of life and of death. Michael had signed his own death warrant with his reckless commitments and his careless actions. He had no business being on *this* battlefield—not now. Still, he could make it all work and perhaps…work better this way.

As the light of Excalibur winked out of existence, wispy tendrils of

Charles W. McDonald Jr.

Michael's soul—unseen to the naked eye—crossed smoke-filled terrain of destruction to the four-carat emerald gem that would house his immortal essence and everything he once was.

With but a thought, he rent the night air in silvery-blue flashes of light, leading the way, but not the moment, for the moment was not his alone. Disappearing into the *Portal*, he made sure to leave it open for them....

The starry night sky was the last place Damon of old would look as he looked down from on high to ensure the precise moment was not missed. With out-of-time *Staff of the Invoker* in his right hand, and the Amulet of the Five Gates in the other, doorways through time/space crossed over doorways within the *Portal* itself and the one trail hidden but buried not so deep as so she couldn't find it. One path to Eden of now, and one to Perion of the past.

Watching as Michelle and Lawna sneaked through one path and a sand-fatigued Elise through the other, he closed both paths via one *Portal*, and it was done.

It was odd...seeing himself operating in another timeline, but such was the path he'd woven, or the path that had been woven for him...depending on one's perspective.

One could drive oneself mad contemplating paradox upon paradox, but thusly, this was part of the plan.

Or was it...?

Damon's form disintegrated amidst the palette of stars forming the night sky above. The stars that had seemingly formed the outline of his face, and his staff, fell to the ground in stardust as the *Starlight of Immortality* lit the way for the Damon of the future to do his job and carry his burden alone.

Charles W. McDonald Jr.

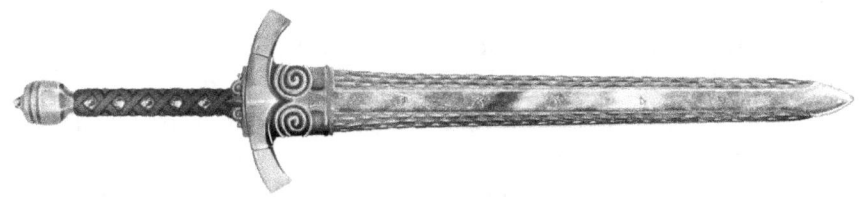

Chapter 51: Seven Grams

(Damon's Manor, Eden, Present Day)

"**F**adin suspected you might have done such a thing."

"What was I to do, Elise? What would you have done?"

"You could have stopped him from being killed!"

"So could you, and you didn't?"

He had her. *Dammit!* She hated when Damon was right!

Sitting across from him at his monstrosity of a dining table, she was only glad that Michael wasn't here for this conversation. *What was she to do?*

"There are no promises in this, Elise. Either you want the old Michael back, or you don't."

"But how do you know his *whole* soul lives in the *Stasis* gem?"

"Because I was there, and I very much knew what I was doing. There are few in this Universe more practiced in the magic of dealing with the essence of the soul than I. You know that as well as I do."

Accept Michael's *Stasis*, and the new Michael could be overwritten entirely. Like an operating system factory reset. Or, perhaps they could co-mingle and co-exist and be like water and vinegar together. Or, perhaps they could blend like a fine wine into a perfectly balanced sauce. Or, perhaps, they could both be destroyed in the struggle to capture the light of Michael's shell. It was a horrific choice, and it had fallen on her. It didn't seem right choosing Michael's fate without him even being there. But, she understood why. Too much was riding on this, and this needed to be a decision made with as much knowledge and objectivity as possible.

Still, she'd fallen deeply in love with the Michael she'd gone home with a few days ago, and he was perfect with her children—their children.

Charles W. McDonald Jr.

If he changed or was damaged in any measurable way from this process, she would be responsible for the death of their father, not once, but twice. A horrific choice indeed! "Damon, I don't know what to do."

"May I offer a suggestion," Radin chimed in from his seat beside Elise, taking her hand in his.

"Please…," she begged with teary-stained eyes, "…I need input to make this decision."

"I have researched many of the same source books that Father has used in his spells over the millennia, and those sources, along with sources on *Stasis*, suggest that not all of one's soul is captured by *Stasis*. Yes, it captures their essence, their memories, and is a good representation of who they once were, but I did not get the impression that it was absolute. Unless Father used a modified or customized version as he often does."

"I did not. I used the same *Stasis* spell we all learned," Damon informed, somewhat agitated at his abilities being called into question.

"I have heard the same thing growing up. I've never used *Stasis* in practicality, but I did learn the spell, and I felt it was incomplete. And…," she paused, looking between them, "…I have good reason to believe *it is incomplete*."

"Oh…," Damon countered, looking at her expectantly, "…do tell."

"This information comes from your chief scientist so if you don't believe it, go ask her. I mean it. I mean—"

"I get it," Damon cut her off, motioning his hand for her to continue.

"Your scientist told me that as Michael started the wake cycle process, his mass gained exactly seven grams." She paused, letting that hang in the air expectantly, only to see Damon scratching his two-day stubble.

"I don't get it," Radin prompted.

"It's an old wives' tale from Earth," Damon offered, still scratching his stubble in consideration of what it *might* mean.

"Not just Earth. We don't use the same metric measurement on Graelon, but there are similar experiences on Graelon where tiny measurable mass is lost at the precise time of death. We assume that to be the measurement of the immortal soul."

"I don't see how Michael's soul—the real one—could exist both in

Stasis and inside the Michael currently walking around on Eden." Damon looked even more agitated. This was steering dangerously in a direction he didn't like. He was supposed to have already restored Michael of old—with all his memories and who he once was intact. That was the plan! This new Michael didn't have the same experiences and couldn't possibly become who Michael had already become, and that brought Excalibur's acceptance into question, and that was unacceptable! Michael was who he was because of his experiences and his upbringing, and only the Michael in *Stasis* could fulfill that being.

"Father, I take it your biggest concern is Michael being able to wield Excalibur...."

"Not just that.... But yes, that is a *big* concern of mine. I don't know if Excalibur will reject this Michael or not. I don't know if he has the waking dreams or not, and if not now, will he? I don't know his connection to God the Creator, but the Michael in *Stasis* is a known quantity."

"If, and only if, Michael survives the re-integration," Elise pleaded with her hands outstretched. "There is a distinct possibility the two will struggle for the light of Michael's body and neither will survive it."

"Now, we're getting into unknown territory for me," Radin relented, throwing his hands up.

"Me too," Elise agreed.

"Me too." Damon surprised them in his agreement. "You were onto an idea...," Damon probed, motioning to Radin. "...Please finish it."

"My idea was to simply let Excalibur decide for us. If the Michael of now is good enough for Excalibur, then I think that speaks volumes of his character that none of us are qualified to veto."

"See...," Elise smiled at him, "...that's what made me fall in love with him. Not *your* genes!" Her eyes glowered at Damon in a somewhat-checked rebuke.

"Fair enough. We let Excalibur decide. Go get him and bring him here."

"For just one moment, you could stop being so damned bossy," Elise scolded Damon, getting up to tear the fabric of space/time with her *Portal*.

"Will you," Radin prompted his father.

"Will I what?"

Charles W. McDonald Jr.

"Let Excalibur decide? I know everything is riding on this, and it's not like you to relinquish control of the Master Plan to anyone's judgment save your own."

"This is different. This is a fork in the plan, for sure. But sometimes forks are meant to be there. They need to be there. It's *my* job to recognize those moments for *what* they are, *when* they are."

Radin nodded in acceptance. It was a fair answer, but Damon's aura that he wore about him like a suit of armor, said otherwise. "If Excalibur accepts this Michael, what's your biggest concern of not restoring him from *Stasis*?"

"Remembering who you are is a big thing. Who would you have become if not for the valuable lessons of Rowarc and later in life valuable lessons from me and from yourself and Talemar. Those are intangible but still measurable attributes. I'm trying to consider other ways of extracting those memories from the *Stasis* gem should Excalibur accept him."

"But you don't think Excalibur will accept him? This Michael, I mean."

Shaking his head at his son, Damon honestly did not know. But all of his experience with souls told him, '*no*.' There were not, and could not be, two immortal souls of Michael Anthony Day, and he held the only one in existence in his pocket. *If* this worked, it would undermine everything he thought he knew and understood of the immortal soul. Looking down at the far end of his massive dining room table, Excalibur's resonant hum filled the room expectantly as it lay on the surface of the table. Waiting.

A moment later, the air split with Elise's *Portal*, walking through hand in hand with her noble husband. He certainly didn't look like a king. From images Radin had seen of Michael the king, he had the hair, eyes, jaw-line, facial features, and body of Michael, but the aura wasn't there. In blue jeans and a blue-on-white plaid long-sleeve, button-down shirt, the tall, scruffy, brown-haired man approached.

Radin smiled at her happiness, but he still felt lost—in search of his new footing with her, and with himself. She was never his. He'd come to realize that. He'd come to terms with it.

Michael strode the ten steps between himself and Damon, stopping just a few steps from him as Damon rose to meet him for the first time—so to speak. "I understand I owe my existence to you." Michael extended his powerful grip to meet Damon's.

"You look well. My chief scientist does good work."

"I can't help but feel a bit like a lab rat," Michael chirped somewhat bitterly, looking around the room. "I've seen your statues, and I know the rules, but I will not worship, or kneel to you."

"Not required of you, Michael. I'd rather you be true to who you are, and who you're supposed to be, but that's why we are gathered here."

"My wife informed me. And, what happens to me if Excalibur does not accept me?"

"I suppose we'll find out."

"No…," Elise interrupted. "He needs to know the stakes. He needs to know what will happen in either occurrence. He needs to be involved in the decision. It's his life."

Damon tried, unsuccessfully, not to growl under his breath, causing Michael's gaze to turn hot upon him. There was definitely some of the old Michael in him. If he knew of Damon's power and still behaved so, then that was something. "Very well, my plan was to restore you completely and wholly from a spell called *Stasis*." Damon pulled the four-carat emerald gem from his pocket, which glowed with wispy tendrils of internal light—calling out to Michael's body from a few paces away.

"We don't know if it will even work," Elise countered. "It might, and likely would, erase everything you've become for what you once were. It might restore some memories, and it might destroy you. The smallest probability is that the two parts of you will integrate seamlessly and become one. I doubt that will happen, My Love. I do not want to even try the *Stasis* recovery—no matter what Excalibur's vote."

Michael looked down the length of the table at the immortal weapon of Creation, feeling its call from the distance between them. "Why do you need me? And, why do you specifically need *me* with *that*?" Michael looked at Damon but pointed down the length of the table toward the Sword of Kings.

"I can't tell you that. You're not ready for the answer."

"Do they know?" Michael pointed between Radin and Elise expectantly, his persona becoming agitated, and his stance becoming more aggressive.

"They can only guess...," Damon rebuffed, "...but I can tell you these people need a strong leader. They need the Michael of old. They need the Michael who commanded Excalibur—who wielded the Sword of Kings with authority, promise, and *hope*. They need that Michael, as do I. And, no matter which path we take to get to that version of you, one thing I can promise you is that you will listen to your wife and you will listen to my security detail because there will be no further recovery of your dead body from reckless and rash decisions. Do I make myself perfectly clear?"

That was the Damon he'd heard of. That was the Damon that Elise had very explicitly described to him. Still, he was no wallflower, and he was no reed to Damon's blusterous, blowhard wind. "I may owe you my existence, but that is where my debt with you is canceled. I am a free soul. A free and sovereign man. And a free spirit, Damon. I bow to no one. Do we understand each other?"

Another growl began to escape Damon's throat as Radin stepped in between them, putting some separation in the middle of their fire. "My Father went to great lengths to save you. He's only asking that you not put yourself into avoidable situations that would require those tremendous lengths again. We simply don't have time for it. The timeline in place won't allow for it. We need you. I need you. Elise needs you. Your children need you. And, your people need you."

Michael's mouth twisted as he accepted Radin's logic. Someone owed him answers, but right now, he felt like the only answers he was going to get were from Excalibur and from himself. "If Excalibur doesn't accept who I am, then you may proceed with the *Stasis* restoration, Damon."

Elise gasped and gulped at her husband's fateful decision made without her, but that act in and of itself was very Michael of old.

A rare smile from Damon as he afforded Michael, the candidate, the space to become Michael the king. One slow step in front of the other, with his hands pressed to the outside pockets of his jeans to wipe away the sweat of his palms, Michael answered the song of the Sword of the First Kings. Its hum began to fill the room in promise most profound as he closed the last few paces of distance to the immortal weapon of Creation—forged by The Father of the Beginnings himself. His right hand hovered over its grip as its

Charles W. McDonald Jr.

song filled the room from floor to ceiling and wall to wall. In a moment of haste and desperation to know, Michael grabbed Excalibur, lifting it off the table as it exploded like unto a molten, white-hot star in his hand, bathing his immortal soul and corporal body in the Love and Light of Creation.

Shifting his stance, and nearly falling against the side of the table, he couldn't help but lose his balance at the waking dream that was not a dream. Seeing the face of God the Creator on the other side of a great lake of crystal bathed in the light of the fire of the Creator's soul, he heard the booming voice of Creation calling to him, and reaching into his mind's eye with a message, "Pick it up, My Son." And, he knew.

His eyes shifted back as reality crept back in and the light of Excalibur still burned hot in his hands at his full command. With a thought, its light dimmed in utter obedience to him. Seeing now the fullness of the room, as if before it had been seen through glasses and now it was in high definition, he saw his lovely wife in all her past and future instantiations— all the way through to her immortal soul. To each in turn, he saw through Excalibur the light of each of their existences but when looking to Damon he saw...pain. Anguish. Torment. And, *hope*. His soul burned hotter and brighter than the others, but his burden was more stark and cast a great shadow over him and the entirety of the room. Damon carried with him a great weight. And, he knew.

"I think we have our answer," Damon acknowledged, seeing the man no longer candidate—but king. But, the answer brought with it more questions he didn't want to deal with right now—questions that made him doubt all he thought he knew of the immortal soul and the essence of Man. "But, do you remember?"

"I have no new memories. The Earthen kingdom I once led is gone. My only memories are those of public knowledge planted in my thoughts. For me, it is *a kingdom forgotten*."

Elise breathed into her hands as Excalibur still radiated waves of *hope* and promise profound. He was her Michael, and yet was not. She'd have to come to terms with that, but at least they had new footing and a place from which to move forward. It was the best possible outcome, she realized, running across the length of the room to Michael's one-armed embrace. "I love you," she whispered three times into his ear—each time more softly, more

Charles W. McDonald Jr.

slowly than the time before.

"What now," Michael asked, looking to Damon with understanding anew.

"What now is that we have a coronation, King Michael." Damon smiled at the title he afforded the broad, brute of a man before them. "And we introduce you to your kingdom reborn."

Seeing his father's plan fall into place before him was a sight unlike anything he'd ever seen before—even eclipsing his own rise to power with the Crystal Crown. So many years in the making with so many compartmentalized secrets and yet Damon was still finding ways to make it happen against all odds and all opposition. Damon was truly a force of nature, bending the will of the Universe with the power of his own consciousness. He had so much left to learn from Damon, but something told him he might not have much time left with Damon to learn. Damon's plan was closing in all around them and with great consequence everywhere he looked. The final moments were only a breath away, and it made him shudder inside as he watched the molten star quiesce in Michael's hand upon Michael's internal command.

*   *   *   *

(New Georgia, Eden, Days Later)

High Definition cameras captured every moment, from arrival by royal horse-drawn coach, to his walk up the stairs of the great entertainment amphitheater originally built for concerts and performing arts. 'Twas all being recorded for posterity, entertainment, and history in the making.

Blood-red tabard over grey pants and black leather boots gave way to Michael's crest of embroidered, pewter Celtic cross over cream, diagonally-opposing fields married with his wife's symbol of a simple cup on diagonally-opposing fields of royal blue and blood red. With blood-red cape golden-clasped to pewter and gold-gild chainmail underneath his tabard, Michael stood out like an imperial standard with stony planes of fierceness about his face as he ascended the stairs to his coronation hand in hand with Elise to one side and the Sword of Kings the other. In a full-length, fitted dress of pearl and pewter gild piping on a field of white with rope belt of

gold strands, she looked the part of queen, wife, mother, spouse, and part-
ner in leadership, ascending the stairs stride for elegant stride with her husband, her king.

Red carpet stretched from pedestal all the way out to the front of the
building where their coach had come to rest. Hand in hand they walked
the through a great open array of doors, following a seemingly endless pro-
cession of pomp and circumstance. Inside the amphitheater, a crowd of tens
of thousands erupted in cheers of *hope* immortal from wellsprings of promise
on air of dust motes that glint in the light of Damon's pale-yellow-dwarf sun
shining through the walls of glass, which comprised the amphitheater's new
construction.

Elise felt as if she was reliving a moment from years before, but
looking into the eyes of her husband, she could see the newness and the
weight of the moment falling upon his shoulders and wondered how he
would react. This was his moment—not hers—and she would yield to him
in it. She would guide him to it and support him through it. That was
her role, and she understood it now as she tightened her grip of his hand in
hers, walking the red carpet with him. There was no priest this time—no
Archbishop of Canterbury—only a finely dressed Damon, Radin, and President Abel.

On a red-carpeted stage they all now stood as Michael momentarily
looked up at the glass roof of the amphitheater some eight stories above and
to the well-dressed audience of nearly a hundred-thousand before them. He
was in awe and hoped the moment not too big for him to handle.

With a wave of Damon's hand and in full-mage regalia resembling
his statues throughout, Damon brought the audience to yield in total silence as he addressed them first with Radin at his right side and Michael
and Elise before him. "I'll need Excalibur momentarily to perform this, if
you would, Michael...." Holding out his hands expectantly toward Michael,
Damon motioned for him to kneel. Elise moved out of the way, standing
to Michael's left and behind him as Michael paused. He swore he'd never
kneel to Damon, but this didn't feel like abdicating authority to Damon—
more *accepting* authority *from* him. Just as Damon was about to afford him
a stern look of disapproval, Michael pulled Excalibur from its finely crafted
scabbard, telling it not to glow as he handed it to Damon, who grasped it

with both hands, then wielded it with his right.

It did not sing for Damon, nor afford him its full authority, but it hummed in Damon's hand expectantly as Damon spoke the words of old: "By the eternal song of Creation and all that is truth and justice, this soul is hereby recognized as King of Men by the Sword of Kings." Damon began touching Excalibur to Michael's left shoulder, then the right as he continued, "By the promise of *Hope*, will you wield it in honor of protecting Men. By profound wisdom, will you execute its full authority over Man in his judgment." As Damon concluded the process of knighthood, he touched Excalibur to Michael's head, closing, "By time immemorial, will you and your soul rule and guide Humanity through all that is *hate*. Swear it and become king."

"I swear it," Michael's mic'd-up voice boomed with confidence as the audience erupted in jubilation of *the rise of hope*.

A beautiful small girl—appearing maybe eight years of age—in a cream dress of hearts and palms—looking much like the Lis he had claimed so long ago—bore a crown upon a red pillow of gold-gild piping. Upon that pillow rested a king's authority in the form of metallic and jeweled beauty. With the symmetry of the golden ratio found in nature, its magnificent pewter scrollwork leapt from the center Celtic cross outwards—erupting in the same style of his scabbard by Gordon Russell. With its peak being some four inches in height, it wasn't tall and gaudy like the crowns of Tudor, Windsor, and the like. It held a series of smaller scrollwork peaks all the way around its perimeter, supporting small star sapphire stones with small pearls trailing away from each sapphire as well as creating a milgrain effect around the Celtic cross itself. Neither minimalist nor extravagant, the purpose-built crown felt perfectly balanced between the weight of its components and the weight of its authority as Damon lifted it off the pillow extended before him as he pivoted to place it atop Michael's brow.

"The floor is yours, Your Majesty," Damon proclaimed, handing the Sword of Kings to the soul who was its once-and-forever master.

Michael paused as the great amphitheater of throngs of his people fell wholly silent, taking Excalibur confidently into his right hand still holding back the molten-star within that threatened with each heartbeat to burst into flames of Creation before them. Little by little did he allow it to grow in its light and its fire as he began to address his kingdom.… "I am here for you now—both in whole and in memoriam. My old kingdom may have been forgotten, **but it is forgotten no more**. *I am here for you*. We have a hard road ahead of us all. There will be a time when your brother or sister falls, but I shall be your brother, *for I am here for you*."

Again, Excalibur's light grew as it began to sun-cast the stage and Michael with it. "There will be a time when your parents fall, but I will be your father, *for I am here for you*. There will be a time of light so bright it threatens to burn us all to cinder, but *I am here for you to pray over your ashes*."

Again, he paused, clearing his throat to continue as the light of Creation threatened to burn down the amphitheater, "There will be a time of both shadow and void, but I will be the one holding your hand in the darkness, *for I am here for you*. Yes, we have a hard road ahead, but *my* kingdom is **our** kingdom, and *our* kingdom is as immortal as our just souls. And for those of you who don't believe in an immortal soul, I will share with you the wise words of my wife. The moment a Human dies, there is an instantaneous loss of seven grams—this is the Earth metric weight of the immortal soul, and it's not just reserved for Humans. In interacting with our brothers from other worlds and other trees of life, we know they have a similar experience and knowledge of something greater than themselves and their mortal shell. This is a Universal truth of life immortal, however long or short our temporal lives may be. As we continue to interact with life outside our world, I have no doubt we will continue to grow and learn about what lies beyond and come to know more of what we do not yet know. Our job—our mission—is one of peace, exploration, and sharing. We will carry no weapons into space, but we will venture out into the dark and cold void. We will sow the seeds of life and prosperity on other worlds and with other worlds. We will carry Humanity to the farthest reaches of the known Universe. This is how we will survive the End Times. This is how Humanity and life here will go beyond and see a new day and a new dawn where we are not beholden to life immortal but a part of them and walk among them as equals amidst the dust of stars and their supernovae. This is our path that we must walk—and we shall walk it together—bravely and without hesitation. I call upon you to *know your brothers and sisters boldly*, to *love your spouses and your children boundlessly*, to *forgive your trespassers gently*, and to *prepare*. We have

Charles W. McDonald Jr.

much work in front of us. We have a hard road ahead of us, but we shall walk it. *Together*."

Michael's kingdom reborn, the molten-star that was Excalibur in his right hand, one by one, then tens by tens, then hundreds by hundreds did they all kneel before the light of the immortal weapon of Creation and the seven grams of Emrys Wledig's immortal soul renewed and integrated with the memories and knowledge of Michael Anthony Day.

Charles W. McDonald Jr.

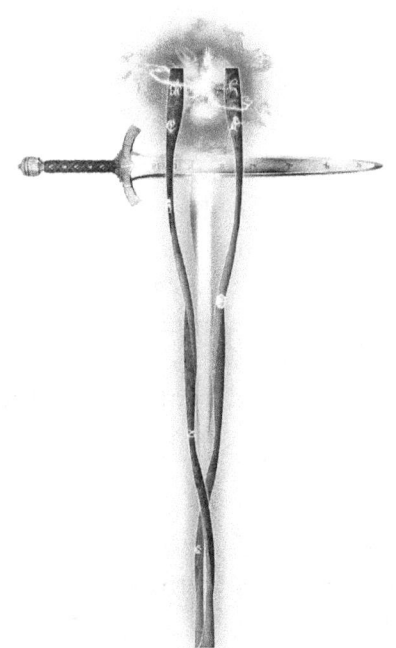

Chapter 52: Presentiment

(The Global Consciousness Project (GCP), Earth, Present Day)

REG (Random Even Generator) simulations caused flashing green lights across an array of enterprise solid-state drives across the 2,500-square-foot, glass-housed datacenter of the GCP. Real-time data mining across every social media account and platform globally fed decades-long enhanced algorithms that drove the ML (Machine Learning) view into retrocausality.

The keyboard warriors of truth the project sought so assiduously to protect hacked away at the data streaming in petabyte upon petabyte. One of them, with dirty brown bangs down well past the bridge of his wire-rimmed glasses, tapped away at his keyboard at well over 150 words per minute, collecting the latest dataset into a report he could hardly believe himself. "Fuck! The director needs to see this," Larry whispered to himself, though others around him clearly heard and tuned into his excitement.

Just the smallest of changes in electronic behavior globally and col-

Charles W. McDonald Jr.

lectively painted a picture in the form of a peak on a graph not seen since 9/11, as if the whole planet was holding its breath in aggregate anticipation of something…not good.

'Eggs' or 'nodes' hosted around the world, numbering around thirty-seven since the early 2000s, allowed for greater sampling of touchpoints around the world against the probability of chance or smooth-curvature envelopes. These 'eggs' continuously recorded events within their spheres of influences, reporting back their datasets in incremental micro batches that constantly fed the larger presentiment algorithms while the data hub scrubbed data spokes in real time for behaviors not captured by the 'eggs.' The bottom line was the recorded 'sentiment' represented by the jagged red line on each graph, especially when and where it greatly exceeded the smooth-curvature envelope of chance. This one massively exceeded anything seen in a very long time.

With nearly all of the jagged red line of data well beyond the curvature envelope of chance, Larry showed the stunning report to Director Nelson, now leaning over Larry's red and gold plaid-laden shoulder. "This will make for an interesting retirement…," Larry mused, as he subconsciously licked his lips.

"Hush with that retirement talk." Dr. Nelson smiled in mild rebuke. "Thirty-one eggs reporting, huh?"

"Yep. Pretty statistically significant for such an algorithmic response as that."

"Yes. Yes…." Nelson cooled dispassionately. He'd seen wild datasets before, but this was…*big.*

"Shall I publish it?"

"No. Not yet." He looked up at the room's monitors running CNN, FOX News, MSNBC, and Bloomberg constantly. *Nothing*, he thought. "What do you know that they don't," Nelson thought aloud, not necessarily trusting the bullhorn of the Deep State any further than he could throw them. Still…. Nothing. Looking down at the dataset, he knew this was not nothing.

"What's that, Professor?" Larry's eyes darted around, and he was short of breath as if he'd just got off the treadmill. He could feel his heart pounding through his chest, and he knew…. The professor might have

Charles W. McDonald Jr.

been calm and collected, but he knew.

"Nothing. Don't do anything with this yet. I need to make some phone calls." His heart sank in correlation to his furrowed brows as he considered the biggest tell-tale since 9/11, and this one dwarfed that one by a country mile. His first thought was to warn friends and family, *but warn them of what...?* This was merely a measurement of sentiment by a network of machines designed to probe at the way we look at data. It wasn't a specific precognitive predictor of specific events. It wasn't a window to a future event as much as it was a measurement of the world gasping in awe before a major gut punch. He didn't have the data to warn—only the data to cause him to worry, significantly, about the gut punch to come.

As he was walking away, to get some privacy, Dr. Nelson overheard the CNN Breaking News report missiles had been seen and heard by witnesses leaving their silos from the Minot Air Force Base in North Dakota. "No," Dr. Nelson mouthed as the report fell from his fingertips, floating in a see-saw manner down to his feet face-up, mocking him and his feeble attempts to see what could not be seen. "Get out," Nelson ordered to the room of young professional scientists, hungry to make their mark on society.

"Pardon me, Professor," a blonde-haired, green-eyed intern replied, just walking into the elevated command center from the double doors beyond that led to the hallway.

"Don't worry about shutting anything down. Just get out. Go home. Be with your loved ones...while you still can," Dr. Nelson ordered the command center, walking out as his right hand tossed open the double doors, making way toward the exit and his car.

The blonde-haired, twenty-something intern, Abby, reached down to pick up the damning report the director had left behind on the floor of the command center. "Shit!"

Theirs was the study of consciousness' interaction upon our Universe allowing things to operate outside laws that discretely describe the operation of a piece of our Universe. Meaning, either there was a larger set of operational laws of universal governance that our consciousness is a part of *or* that the laws of physics must catch up to the behavior in the Universe that our consciousness is describing and *creating* in our physical Universe in real time.

Charles W. McDonald Jr.

Clearly, the Universe had a big way of connecting and communicating with both living and non-living things if one had the tools with which to listen, and it had just spoken in a voice as loud as the Creator himself in a message that was petrifying. It was, perhaps, the collective gasp of Man held captive by the *End* he unconsciously knew was his, but was it only *his* alone, or an *End* to be shared by all…?

Charles W. McDonald Jr.

Chapter 53: Robbed of the Hidden Branch

(Exeter Manor, Perion, Months Before)

Softness and warmth pushed back against his knuckles as he brushed his hand against his home, feeling the comfort yet newness of everything around him. He liked the shape and function of his hands as he pulled it back in to suck on the thumb. That was the best. 'Twas comfort in much the way of Mommy's voice when she spoke to him. He loved Mommy's voice. He loved Mommy.

Jostling around, he spun his body with some effort, given how little room was left and having to move the thick cord of life out of his way so that he could lay sideways as Mommy got up to move again. Always moving was Mommy. *Why can't she just lay down for a while?*

He felt okay, but he knew something was wrong. Mommy didn't feel right, and he could sense it.

That's when he felt it. A sharp pain like nothing before as he felt something reaching around—grabbing at his legs and that cord thing—pulling so hard it hurt. Then again and again, causing him to scream, but

Charles W. McDonald Jr.

no sound came out.

Looking down at his legs, he could feel the hand crushing around his leg as it tugged at him, but he couldn't see anything, but he did see the cord break, and then the fluid all around him rushed out, and then he could hear his own scream—only for an instant. And, then it was over. Blackness!

*   *   *   *

(Hours Later)

Breath leapt into his lungs as he expelled death and breathed in life. Wherever he was, it felt very different. And she was different, too, as he opened his eyes outside Mommy for the first time—slowly—trying to understand his new surroundings.

He liked her and the way she looked at him, but it still didn't feel right. She didn't feel right. *Where's Mommy?*

Who's that? Another person who's definitely not Mommy…and what are they talking about…? This other person looks sad, but I like his eyes. He seems more like me.

Oh, we're moving again. What just happened?

(The Shoreline Northeast of Stirling, Perion, Present Day)

I'm gonna get this, he thought, pushing his little body off the sand where he'd fallen face-first into the gritty stuff he loved playing in so much. *PUSH!*

Finally! There. He sat himself back upright as New Mommy cheered and clapped on the sand just out of reach. He knew what she was trying to do. She was trying to get him to crawl, so she could watch this time. But he didn't like doing it when people were watching because he wasn't quite good at it yet. She had pretty eyes—New Mommy—and she squeezed him and kissed on him all the time. He loved her, but she wasn't Mommy. *Where did Mommy go?*

"Look, he's doing it," Leah squealed as she patted the sand in front of her to the sound of the Sea of Shirantal crashing against the coastline in white-capped waves. "Come here, Baby. Come here, Ryker. Come to Mommy." Again, patting the sand before her as she sat to be at eye level with her baby boy who was rapidly turning into a big boy, as he just said his first words the other day—'Dada.' Of course, it would be 'Dada' and not 'Momma!' It wasn't fair, but he knew the boy loved Pern more, and that was really fine with her as long as he was adored and returned such adoration.

"That's the first time I've seen him really crawl—like putting one knee in front of the other. Normally he just drags his body with his hands." Pern's smile beamed with brilliant fire of pride and joy at every new accomplishment because everything was new to a baby. He considered it fortunate the baby never knew what the world looked like before the Blood Night, lest it be concerned with The End that was just over the horizon and breathtakingly closer with each passing hour.

"Well, he's not dragging his body with his hands now, is he?" As soon as Baby Ryker was in arm's reach, she grabbed him off the sand, clutching him to her bosom as she held their precious gift as tight as she could, kissing him on his sprawling and thick, healthily-growing clump of black hair, which was such a stark and beautiful contrast to his beautiful starry-blue eyes. With full yet well-formed cheeks and great symmetry about his face and body, he was such a blessing, and they were so grateful. Yet, she was torn in her love for him at the knowledge he might not live. Lynn had told them—warned them. But, she couldn't stop herself from giving him everything she had. Her heart told her to hold back a little piece of herself, so she didn't lose everything—just in case. But, she just couldn't do it. "I love you, Baby Ryker," she whispered in adoration into his right ear as she held onto him tight as she prayed and believed that surely a life so bright and so brilliant wouldn't be—couldn't be—extinguished. "Mommy loves you."

*   *   *   *

So, this is what my brother had sought out...? He got it. He understood. Watching from a safe distance, Gareth's hard facial features picked up the stark attributes of both light and shadow of the Blood Night.

Family was everything. Luke had taught them both well, and Pern had finally found his. So be it.

It still wouldn't hurt for him to watch over his younger brother a while longer. Something about this babe was very different. Not that he didn't look like Pern's—he did. But, something wasn't right. Yes, it had been a long time since he'd seen his brother, and he wasn't even sure if news of Luke's passing had yet made it to him, but *how could this be the moment of Pern's great hour of need...?* That's what Luke had told him: "You will follow your heart and your soul and do what is right, and it WILL lead you to your brother in his greatest hour of need. I have seen it."

What was so wrong about this handsome baby boy as to bring about Pern's greatest hour of need? And yet, watching from afar, he knew it so. He felt it radiating from every fiber of that precious baby boy—that he would see them to their deaths.

(Damon's Manor, Eden, Present Day)

"I understand what you're saying, but we're not going to do this.... We're not going to dwell on the past," Damon emphasized to a clearly distraught young man who'd been in denial for some months now as the pain suddenly and finally had surfaced.

Staring up at the ornate copper and cream highlights of ceiling medallions and chandeliers of his great dining hall, Damon wanted to ease his son's pain, but this was a topic he'd prefer never to bring up again. Brushing the stubble of his chin, Damon exhaled a great sigh at the morose matter reborn. His hair starting to naturally grow back to that long, straight look he'd held for so many centuries as it was just now starting to grow beyond his shoulders.

"How do you deal with it, Father? Just tell me that much." His eyes welled as he forced it down ever deeper than before—the guilt, the pain, and Elise—swallowing it like a poison for his soul to deal with.

"How do I deal with what?"

"Well, you're the one who described it as being 'robbed.' I was wondering how you dealt with it?" Running his fingers through his auburn bangs, Radin pushed them out of the way to see the truth in Damon's eyes—if ever there was a truth on this.

"Wasn't my description, but...," he paused, sighing at Rena's description at the loss of raising children. All his children were adults when he met them for the first time. He really didn't have the proper compass to navigate this terrain—with his son, or anyone else for that matter.

Sitting across the width of his dining table from Radin, it might as well have been a thousand miles. For all their similarities, they were incredibly different from one another. But both were tormented in their own ways. Both were resilient in carrying their burdens and the burdens of others. But, Radin's childhood had made all the difference between them. Radin had one. Damon did not. It was a chasm of perspective. Not having a real childhood of his own, he couldn't relate to what he'd been robbed, but clearly Radin could, and it tormented him.

"I fear I may never have another chance at it," Radin grumbled into a fist clenched by rage—held shut by demons both literal and figurative.

"We're not going to do this," Damon growled, partly to give his son hope and partly himself. "The only way forward *is* forward! Do you want to make something of this new reality we're building or not?"

A simple nod said Radin was ready to listen—if not emotionally ready to act.

"You're not a boy anymore—and certainly not the boy I first met. You're a *man* now, and we're going to have to work on hardening your mind. The task before us is too great to be encumbered by the burden of prosaic thinking. You've shown me your critical thinking abilities at times, but that has to be more the rule than the exception. You're going to have to learn to build walls in your mind—walls and compartments—where this kind of distress can be prevented from providing others a doorway to destroy you and everything we're working to achieve." Damon understood. If ever anyone could understand what Radin had been through, it was him. Whatever their differences, they were more alike than not. "There is time for you, Radin. There *is always* time!"

Radin's steel-blue eyes glinted at the none-too-hidden meaning of the double entendre. "You know I'm ready to begin when you are, Father."

Charles W. McDonald Jr.

"It's not merely a matter of getting you ready," Damon pontificated, his right index finger in the air as if to draw attention to the point. "This is bigger than you or I."

"This is about Mira." It wasn't a guess or a question—more a realization of Radin's.

"It's always been about Mira…," Damon continued. "…And ever will be about Mira."

"How did you meet her, Father? You never told me."

For the first time since Michael's Coronation, Damon smiled as he remembered the moment fondly—tapping his feet to Zeppelin on campus and then boom, there she was. "That's another story for another time."

"I disagree. If I'm going to do this, I need to know everything about her. Everything!"

His black gems flashed at the realization that his son was right. If Mira were to be the payload, then Radin needed to know everything about her. It made him wonder—that realization—the hand that had to have guided him to her and her to him in the first place. There could never have been another. It was funny thinking of her that way when at first he'd only considered her a potential reincarnation of the Mira he once knew and loved and now could only see her uniqueness. Absolute. Still…there was something oddly familiar about her…. Something that mocked his great intellect and foresight from both near and far. Across the great chasm of time/space and space/time.

(Silverstring Manor, Yknyr, Perion, Present Day)

Betwixt the carved, stone pillars of his colonnade, Wraith cursed the Blood Night that killed the vegetation that used to fill and line every crevasse with flower and vine bursting with life, color, and scent that his sultry Silura so loved. She wasn't around much anymore. Gone Creator knows where—if he, or it, even existed at all. Wraith held more doubt than ever these days—especially after seeing everything he'd seen. Surely demons existed—he'd seen them firsthand as much as he'd seen that thing descend from the sky cutting it open with its sword of pure light. *But, did that mean the*

Charles W. McDonald Jr.

Creator himself had to exist, or was it all just myth and lore…?

Pacing the precision-laid paving stones of his colonnade, he pondered more than even his pensive facial expression led on. The Crystal Throne in benign and useless hands and the unmaking of all things upon them, he needed a plan that would succeed if Damon's failed. That had been his sole focus since leaving the Army of Hope—to the extent of pushing away the one he loved the most. She couldn't deal with him in his sour mood, but then she couldn't see what he could see either. *Could she?* If she could, then why leave when he needed her most?

"Fuck," he blurted to the open-air courtyard, causing a guard to turn his head Wraith's way from some two-hundred paces away at the guard tower. Noticing the guard's reaction, Wraith turned his head down again, focusing on the furiousness of his pace and the unevenness of the paving stones now that all the vegetation was dead and the ground beneath them cracked and blistered from heat. *They'd all die of starvation soon enough. There had to be another way.*

He'd considered leaving Perion entirely, but that was merely a patch covering a blinded eye of a problem. Damon's unmaking, if true in scope and scale, would reach every corner of every part of Creation. There was nowhere to hide from it. Not in this plane of existence anyway.

"That's some seriously brooding thought, My Love." Silura's soft and sensual tone cut through the cracked and hot night air of the Blood Night in pillowy waves of jasmine-scented sonnet.

"Where have you been," Wraith challenged accusingly.

"If that's going to be your tone, I'll leave." In diaphanous, knee-length dress of a forest-green palette, which echoed her eyes while its silver piping echoed the silver lock of her name, she stood bathed in the light of a large, waning moon whilst the other was just beyond the horizon. Her long, dark brown hair down to the small of her back in all-but-straight, shiny locks—only curving outward at their ends, did she remind him of his love, lust, and aching for her. "Shall I go," she reaffirmed.

"Stay…please," he offered, waving his hand downward as if to dismiss his own attitude as nothing when clearly it was more than that.

Taking a seat on the barren paving stones, Silura sat cross-legged before her husband and twin brother, directly in the path in which he was

Charles W. McDonald Jr.

walking, watching him frown at her in response. "Clearly, you have a lot on your mind. Want to talk about it? You haven't really talked to me in days. That's why I left, you know."

"Is it?" Wraith was no fool. His intellect and his gut were screaming at him inside. She had more secrets than a bard had tall tales. Still, this wasn't the hill he wanted to die on. "I'm sorry. That was uncalled for."

"It certainly was, My Love." She paused, carefully examining his demeanor. "I'm not fucking someone if that's your concern."

"Hardly," he countered with raised eyebrows at her lack of subtlety or tact. That was nothing new, but it always took him off guard. It was as off-putting to him as it was to others. "Does it not bother you," Wraith questioned with both outstretched hands and his words.

Silura only blinking in response.

"Damon's plan...," he added.

"Oh.... That!"

"Yes.... That!"

"Honey, we may have shared a womb, but when it comes to the way we think, we're not all that alike—you and I. You worry about and brood over things you can't control. I don't."

"Who said I couldn't control it?"

More raised eyebrows and blinking in response. "Surely, you're not going to try to stop him.... I mean, he's kinda got a point. I say let him have at it. Let's just deal with the fallout."

"That's just it, Honey. The fallout may be utterly devastating. Every corner of Creation is likely going to be affected, and who knows how bad it can get...? I've been reading...." He stopped, pointing over the open-air room with the massive stone map table lined from one end to the other with dusty scrolls—some of them on the edge of crumbling out of existence. "And, I think I know where the last Seal is.... Well, I think I know what it is—maybe not exactly where."

Her blinking immediately stopped—now fixated on her husband's every word. "Do you?"

That came across very...odd. As did her half-smile. As if she knew something he didn't—something very pertinent. "I'd really like to know where you've been. Not because I think you were cheating on me or anything. I just don't think it's like you to go off without me and be doing nothing. That's not like you. At all. You had a purpose in your absence. Talk to me. Please."

A small sigh escaped her pretty, thin, pursed lips. Marriage was a difficult thing. Give and take. Push and pull. And, what made it so hard was that the other—if they were intelligent—knew you as well as you knew yourself, especially if they paid attention, and Wraith always paid attention to the little details. It made it hard to get away with anything. And that... well, that was just no fun! Managing a smile, she offered, "I knew you were busy brooding and contemplating and whatnot. So.... I thought I'd do some homework. And...," she paused, whether for preamble or suspense, he couldn't say, "...I found something."

"Did you?" Turning the tables back on her, he threw her words back at her with the softness of a genuine smile.

"I did. I found Damon's little plaything world. I know exactly where he's keeping everyone. I thought it might be useful information if things go as south as you're thinking it will."

"Oh that." Clearly, he wasn't all that impressed, as his demeanor soured again before her.

"You're an ass, you know that," she huffed, getting up from the paving stones, dusting herself off to leave.

"I'm sorry," he lied, but he didn't want her to leave again. He needed her. For many reasons.

"That wasn't the only thing I was looking for while I was gone. That was just something I found along the way...."

"Oh...."

"Oh is right...," she paused, pacing around to the other side of her husband, watching his eyes following her lustfully, drinking in the power and intimate sway her body held powerful leverage over his needs. "I think Talemar has been turned. Which means he's playable. Which means we should be the ones playing him."

Wraith's jaw tightened at the possibilities she'd just presented. *How can we leverage that in conjunction with what we know of the final Seal?* He needed time to think, but first he needed his wife. Reaching out to grab her forcefully by the arm, he practically yanked her off the paving stones with but a tiny yelp

from her as he threw her over his slender frame, physically carrying her off
to their marital chambers.

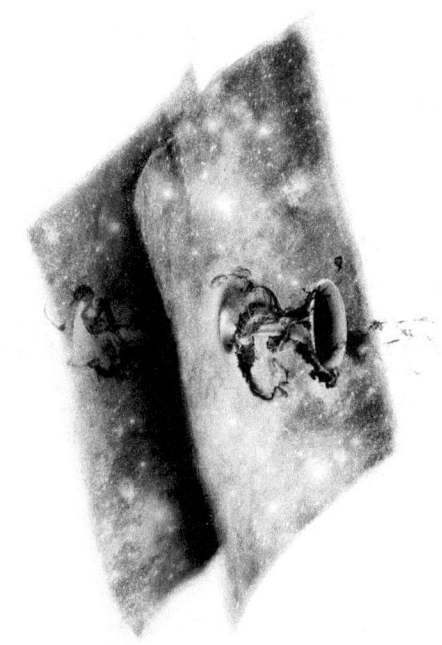

Chapter 54: Time Broken

(The North Central Texas Plains, Earth, Present Day)

The Coordinates on Howard's handheld GPS Plugger flashed in agreement with that of the UConnect in his Jeep®, '31°35'40.2"N 99°48'41.2"W'. This was the place in his déjà vu. *Now what...?*

"You look confused." Mira observed Howard's pensive pacing to and fro about the dirt road.

"This is the right place. I know it." His pacing stopped momentarily as he looked to the northeast, thinking he'd seen something out of the corner of his eye. *Your mind is playing tricks on you.*

"Your eyes say otherwise." She wasn't trying to be disagreeable, but her life was on the line here and they couldn't afford to just sit here much longer. The chatter on Howard's radio said they were going back to get more men—a lot more. They weren't going to simply let her go. She'd lopped off the head of their leadership, and there would be consequences. She'd come to realize that, no matter how hard she prayed for Damon to

Charles W. McDonald Jr.

come to her. Still praying to him, she tried to reach out to him across the great divide of spacetime, begging him to come for her. *Why had Damon abandoned her? Why?* It just made no sense to her, no matter how hard she tried—no matter what angle she examined it from.

Ground-based rockets streaked out into the vast Texas night sky some distance to the northeast right about where Dallas/Ft. Worth would have been. They couldn't see the DFW skyline, but those missiles were not a good sign.

"I've got a bad feeling about this," Howard quoted Star Wars® as his pacing once again came to an abrupt halt.

"How far behind us do you think they still are?" Mira wondered, between the doom on the horizon and the one hunting them, just how much time they had left.

"Ten more minutes. Tops." Howard's beady eyes furrowed in worry over things he could no longer control. This was the place. Supposedly, this was the time....

Mira gulped as her mind started playing back what little of her life had been lived. She'd gotten to see more things than just about anyone else alive on Earth thanks to Damon. He'd opened her eyes. For whatever reason, those memories had been extremely difficult to access, but access them she did, and again it brought a smile to her face.

"What...," Howard probed, looking at her. "You know we're about to die, right?"

"Quite probably," she agreed as the contrail streaked from the northwest toward the southeast, striking its DFW target to their northeast in a great release of energy and fire. Holding her breath in her seat, waiting the inevitable, she gulped again, closing her eyes to the intense light of the mushroom fireball, knowing they were not far enough away. Howard had driven them to within reach of the hydrogen bomb explosion that would kill them all.

"I don't get it!" Howard shook his head, wondering how his déjà vu had been so wrong just as silvery-blue flashes of light ripped the superheated air on the southern side of the Jeep® away from the blast. He heard—as did she—the distant male voice ordering them to 'jump now.'

"MOVE YOUR ASS," she called out to Howard, jumping from the

Jeep® in a flat-out run for Damon's *Portal*.

She could feel the heat and pressure of the shockwave at her back, but her feet felt like they were mired in quicksand and suddenly she couldn't move. She pivoted her torso to look at the light that was going to take her life only to see the tall, dark silhouette of Damon shielding her as the blast-wave hit—carrying Howard through Damon's *Portal* just before the blast scattered the magic of his *Portal* to dust and ash, closing it almost immediately.

Dirt turned to glass all around before her eyes as she watched pieces of metal from the Jeep® blown to bits, scattered on the winds of nuclear ruin.

Looking up, she saw the pulsating shield protecting her as Damon came forth from hydrogen-bomb-cast shadow, pulling her to his embrace as the world exploded in apocalyptic fire all around them. Kissing her like his life depended on it—like time itself depended on it—he then practically yelled in her ear to be heard over the chaos outside his protective shell, "I MADE A MISTAKE, THINKING I COULD LIVE WITHOUT YOU, BECAUSE I CAN'T."

Half expecting the time paradox to extinguish his life out of existence, Damon opened his black gems to see Mira Castille staring at him in wonder.

Earth was coming to an end all around her, and all she could think of was Damon as she passed out in his arms.

In a flash of light, they were gone...and Earth lay in nuclear-scarred ruin.

She opened her eyes to see somewhat familiar surroundings—Damon's bed. She looked at the view—definitely not Earth. Definitely not Kaleion. She assumed Eden given the smallness of the sunlight cast by Damon's yellow-dwarf star. She inhaled deeply in an attempt to confirm she was alive and smelled...perfume...*Illirian's* perfume. Slapping her cheeks, Mira tried again to make sure it wasn't a dream—that it was *indeed* real.

Her mind still tried to piece together the reasons for her separation from Damon, and it was like a fog atop a blurred layer of truth. She still couldn't access it as she had those beautiful memories. Sitting up in Damon's bed, wondering what was next, she saw Damon walking through the doorway crafted from nothingness that led to his secret study.

"Good morning, Sleepyhead," he offered, bringing Mira scratch-made French toast covered in blueberries to her bedside, carried on an ornate tray of pewter and gold.

"Where's Illirian," she asked rather hostilely, surprised at her own obtuse jealousy.

"Yes. Well. That's a different discussion," he offered, hoping his trademark disarming smile would get her to sheath her anger.

"Yes. Well. We'll have that fucking discussion right goddamn now."

Clearly that didn't work, he considered, pausing in his tracks where he laid her breakfast down in bed with her to take a few backward steps away from Mira's bedside and give her some space to vent.

"What the fuck happened, Damon?! I want some goddamned answers!"

Answers, answers, answers. I'm not the goddamned answer machine for the entire Universe. She had a right to be upset. And, as much as she needed answers, he needed to let her vent by listening more than talking. Looking into her beautiful eyes, he realized her preciousness and how badly he needed her—however short her lifespan might be. "I told you, I realized I couldn't live without you."

She sniffed at his honesty. His words were congruent his actions and mannerisms of the moment—if not his actions of the past. "Then why did you abandon me, Damon? I'm confused."

"Me too." He sniffed, rubbing his nostrils as he looked into her beautiful eyes wantonly.

"What do you mean, 'me too?'"

"I mean, I shouldn't be here having this conversation with you. I should be dead."

"Explain, Damon. Explain...."

"You're dead. Right now. You're not supposed to be here. I mean you are, but you're not."

"That's not fucking helpful," Mira barked, shaking her head as if trying to shake off a bad dream.

"What I mean is that you were supposed to go through my *Portal,* which would have brought you here—on Eden—years ago."

"And how did that lead me to be dead?" Then she realized the memory of herself shooting that *creature*, and it all came home to her in an instant. This time she saw the lower half of her body bleeding out all over Damon's floor in Austin, causing her to bite her wrist as she fought the reality hitting her in Damon's bed all at once.

Pulling her wrist from her teeth, Damon explained further, "I suppose that out-of-time version of you somehow hitched a ride back to Earth with me and it cost you your life in saving mine. I honestly don't know how I'm still here having this conversation with you. I fully expected that if I went back to save you the way I did just now that it would cost me the Master Plan, and my life."

He paused momentarily, looking into her eyes again. "You know me. I'd never do anything like this without a plan. I actually went to my chief scientist, asking for probability models of each continuum and each outcome down each path of each continuum, giving every detail I could. And, yet, I didn't even consult the output of that model before going to get you. I wholly ran on instinct. I did think that being a deity afforded me some level of immortality, but gods have been killed before."

"And, yet, you risked everything to come back for me the way you did...?" Realizing that for the first time, she sheathed her hostility instantly. Her tone had flipped on a dime to one of...compassion and recognition of her love immortal for him.

"Pretty brave of me, huh?" He tried to deflect from all the complexity of the time paradox conversation with another smile, but he knew it would be short-lived.

"Yeah. Pretty fucking brave." She sighed, relaxing her head and neck into Damon's pillows. "So, why can't I remember why we broke up?"

"Because I erased certain memories and augmented others before dropping you off in West Texas."

"That was pretty goddamned cruel of you."

"You have no idea how painful that was for me."

"Boo fucking hoo. *You* didn't hang from a gallows pole."

Charles W. McDonald Jr.

He deserved that. Actually, he had been hung before, but that was another story and entirely off-topic. Seeing how nervous she was by her toe-tapping fidgeting underneath his covers, he sought to calm her as he held her foot in place through the bedding linen. "It's okay. What else do you want to know?"

"So, if I saved your life…." She had to stop to correct herself—*goddamn this was confusing.* "…If future me saves you—or saved you, past-tense, sorry—then how the fuck are you still here?"

"That's a great question I wish I knew the answer to."

"Do they?" She paused, correcting her tense again. "…I mean, did they take an inventory of all people you brought to Eden?"

"They did," Damon realized, considering Mira's genius and observations he hadn't yet considered.

"Maybe you should check that inventory and see if my name is still on that list…? And, I'd like to see the output of those probability models too…."

Smiling, he realized why—beyond his love for her—he needed Mira so. She had a mind for this. She was the payload. "That's a good idea. I'll do that."

"And you'll share the answer with me immediately." It wasn't a question from Mira.

"And, I'll share the answer with you. Of course."

"And, now we can talk about you fucking Illirian."

Damon gulped, coughing into a hastily-made fist.

She thought about forcing him to undo all his mind-fucking of her but thought better of it. She didn't exactly trust Damon at the moment, and letting him traipse around in her mind again didn't make her feel safe. *But this Illirian Starfire shit was going to come to an end—toot sweet!*

"There is something else you should know," Damon deflected the conversation back away from Illirian again, hoping this would give her a bone to chew on more savory than Illirian.

She only squinted in her reply, pulling her head forward just slightly off of his pillows—meeting his gaze as she gauged him as perceptively as he did her.

"I have accelerated the timeline of this continuum slightly over that of the one you were previously in."

"Explain, Damon. I don't like this spaghettification you're doing with the timeline. Or, timelines. Jesus. What a mindfuck!"

"You shouldn't be here right now."

"We've covered this, Damon. I know that already. I got it."

"No. I mean you shouldn't be here...**NOW**. Even if you'd gone through the Portal, you shouldn't have gone through it until almost a year from now."

"Why did you speed things up?"

"To buy me more time."

Her head shook—trying to shake off the mindfuck of time manipulation.

Damon could see more explanation was required, but at least they were successfully off of Illirian. "Look, in the prior continuum, there was a break between the ground invasion of the US and the nuclear strike. This time that break was very small—almost non-existent."

"I don't see how that buys you more time."

"Because, I couldn't wait for you. I needed you **now**. In this continuum."

"Why?"

"That's another story. I need you to meet my son, and I'll explain. But, suffice it to say, you're one of the most talented and brilliant people I know. I need someone with a mind for mathematics, physics, *and* technology. If you don't know a solution to this problem, then I'm fucked. We're all fucked!"

Mira gulped again. *No pressure*, replying only with a head-nod.

Damon smiled, *successfully off Illirian Starfire—for the moment....*

*   *   *   *

Abel's office looked different than previously—more sparse and barren. He assumed having been stripped of some of his authority had something to do with it. New elections had already been arranged. Damon watched from the doorway as Abel observed crows outside the window flocking to announce Damon's impromptu arrival.

Charles W. McDonald Jr.

"I hadn't meant to defeat your spirit, Abel," Damon offered from the doorway in jeans and a T-shirt.

Turning to the enigma of his fortunes, Abel held no ill will. "Who said you had defeated me? I'm sure you could have if you had wished it so, but that is not who you are. That is not the man that I know." He paused, looking at Damon's all-black T-shirt with white lettering that read, '*Fear me for I am Death*.' "Should I be worried about that," he asked, pointing at Damon's shirt.

"It's nothing. Don't worry about it," he deflected, dismissing Abel's concerns. "And, you are correct, Abel. I do not wish it. Just the opposite, in fact. I hope it possible we can remove that method of their tracking of you, but if not, I'm prepared to use you."

Abel nodded. A similar strategy had occurred to him—use their own technology against them if necessary. He didn't know how feasible peace with the Negi would be, but he knew they had options now where little existed before. "How can I help you," Abel asked from behind his desk as he rose to shake Damon's hand upon his approach.

Taking Abel's hand, Damon shook it with a wink in his eye, offering perhaps more than his words, "The manifest I messaged you about. Do you have that ready for me?"

"I do, and I searched the database for the name you gave me. Mira Castille from Texas. She doesn't exist. No such person arrived from Earth. Only the woman you brought with you on a recent visit fits the description you provided, and she never entered the manifest since she didn't become a permanent resident."

A sigh from Damon confirmed his—and Mira's—suspicions. *How could he still be alive without her there to save him?!* "Well, enter her into the logs. She's here now. She's my wife and will be treated with the care and respect due her. Is that clear?" She wasn't really his wife—yet. He wasn't sure what would happen between him and Illirian, but it was all a perfect, hot mess now. He knew he truly could not live without Mira. He knew her purpose a profound one and her future inextricably linked to his. It was the only move that made sense—making her his wife, whatever Banthis or Illirian thought of that.

"Perfectly. I'll let the Vice President know, and he'll notify everyone.”

*   *   *   *

Damon's sudden disappearance hadn't come as a great shock. The man went where he wanted when he wanted as if he didn't have any strings attached. *Well, that's going to change,* she considered, sipping on a frothy cappuccino as she walked along cliff-side Damon's ocean-front property in a silken robe of cream and gold gild. Its knee-high length afforded a measure of coolness to legs that longed for freedom from harassment.

The ocean breeze hit her face head-on, whipping her beautiful brunette locks up against the back of her neckline, causing the collar of her robe to flutter.

“I heard I was the topic of some conversation.” Illirian's ultra-quiet presence nearly made Mira jump out of her own skin.

Pivoting to the sound of her voice and the now-familiar scent of her perfume, which shouldn't have been in her nostrils given Illirian's downwind appearance, Mira faced the bane of her love for Damon, shocked to see her not the youthful beauty he had described. Yes, she was beautiful, but she did not appear Mira's age as he had described her—maybe early-to-mid-thirties. Certainly, approaching middle-age. Perhaps, she wasn't the physical competition she had first thought. In a summer dress of peach pastel that perfectly matched the radiant hues in her red-gold hair, she found Illirian Starfire to be…majestic. Regal. And haughty. “I'm glad we got to meet,” Mira lied.

“Me too.” *Right back at ya,* Illirian thought with that certain special smile tailor-made just for Mira. Of course, they'd already met—sort of. Depending on one's perspective.

“I know you could kill me with a thought,” Mira offered, recognizing the truth of her situation.

“If barely that,” Illirian corrected.

“Look. This is more than love for me.”

“Me too.” It started out as a curiosity, then an obsession, then love…. Then something far more where words failed her. She'd risked everything for Damon. And would do it all again.

Charles W. McDonald Jr.

Mira paused, trying to think of a way to break through Illirian's shell. "What I mean to say is, this is more than about Damon and I or you and Damon."

"Correct," Illirian agreed without yielding so much as an inch.

"I've come to realize this is about something Damon calls a 'necessary unmaking' of a mistake he made long ago."

"Correct."

"How do we proceed, Illirian?" She didn't like yielding ground, but would if it meant Damon's unmaking of a critical mistake, and that mistake she was beginning to understand more and more with each passing hour, then so be it.

"I'm going to step aside," Illirian lied with a smile. "I've waited a millennia for Damon. I can wait 'til your bones are ash." *That* was not a lie.

Mira's smile vanished in the bat of a beautiful red-gold eyelash of Illirian Starfire. Advancing to within a hot breath of Illirian, with her right foot in full fidget mode, Mira showed the backbone of why Damon loved her so. "You listen to me, you haughty little cunt! Your job and mine is to ensure that Damon gets to fix his mistakes—that he is afforded the opportunity to unmake what should never have been made. I don't pretend to understand the full of Damon's Master Plan, but I do know this…. I know he needs me, and I know he needs you. I'm going to do my job, and I goddamned expect you to do yours. Do I make myself clear?"

"Perfectly." Illirian's form disintegrated in fine grains of peach-colored dust, carried on the ocean-front breeze off into the distance where Mira saw Damon's form returning to her—to them. In jeans and T-shirt. Wherever he was going dressed like that, she didn't think it appropriate for a deity to dress so—especially among people that were 'supposed' to worship him. She couldn't make out the lettering on his shirt, but she was certain it was inappropriate.

A moment later, Damon was in her grasp as she looped her right arm through his left to walk along the oceanside cliff beside him. Now getting a closer look, she could see his shirt read, *'Fear me for I am Death.'*

"I'm not going to ask how that conversation went," Damon smartly proffered.

"That would be wise." She winked at him in the pale-yellow glow of

Charles W. McDonald Jr.

his yellow-dwarf star. Poking his chest right in between the white lettering of his black shirt, she added, "So, what's up with that? Was there someone actually not afraid of you that should be?"

"I ran across it in a mall, and I liked it. It suited me."

"I don't know what I find more horrifying about that. That you were casually shopping for clothes in a mall like the rest of us or that you found *that* text suited you." She couldn't help but smile at him. He was always so full of surprises, she never knew quite what to expect from him, or of him.

The touch of her skin on his somehow made everything right. He wasn't beyond missing Dallia or loving Illirian, but *this* felt right. Somehow, in some way, and in some small measure of a righted continuum, he felt—for the first time in a long time—like he was doing the right thing at the right time.

With the stress of his *hate* gone and a somewhat clearer path before him, he felt a purpose beyond just the weight of the monster needed—beyond the burden he carried for everyone. Taking her hand in his, he caressed her, stopping her movement to look him head-on as his right hand began to brush back the hair over her ear. "Mira Castille." He paused, getting on one knee as her breath involuntarily halted and the ocean wind whipping her brunette locks around her face and neckline.

She wanted to say something. Anything. But her lips couldn't move. *She* couldn't move. It was as if time itself had broken and all her deepest dreams and fears both became real before her eyes.

Looking into her big, beautiful eyes—swollen with tears—he thought only of the now and the past robbed him. And, in a reckless abandon for *everything* else—even the Master Plan—Damon begged, "Marry me."

The beautiful blue-green pearl with puffy white swirls of weather and life abound now in sight of its terror, the black hole did come. Not much longer now and all of Humanity's children would be within its reach as the *Eye* collapsed spacetime before it, expanding spacetime behind it, guiding it towards the doom of Man.

Charles W. McDonald Jr.

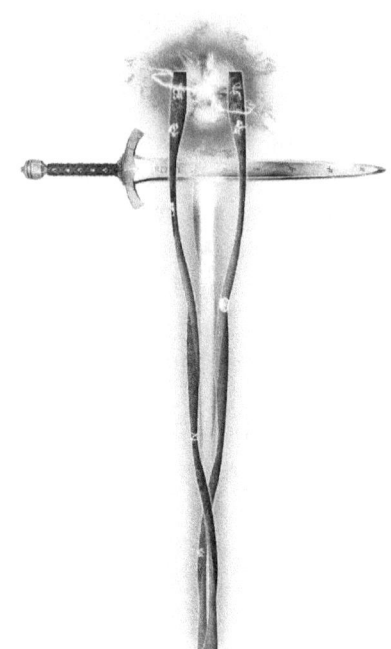

Epilogue: The Eye of Time

(The Eye of Time, Setinon, Time Neutral)

Frayed edges of the *Eye's* viewing window sizzled and hissed with its unique energy and threads of magic unseen and unexperienced by mortals. The image within shifted yet again, revealing this very room with these very Sentinels as a microscopic instrument came into being from nothingness right before the great lead Sentinel who worked its transparent console with alloy hands and genocidal intent.

Radin watched as they marched forth in a floating parade of death through a *Portal* akin to one of his own. He watched them obliterate the operating room and assassinate the doctor, and then he watched them place the *Instrument of Humanity's Hate* inside the great Keirill—genitor of his father, Damon the Banished.

Radin watched the viewing window shift yet again, seeing Keirill kick the womb of Seren, and the pre-cursor to Damon within. "Yea, I know thee!" Shaking his fist at the *Eye*, he continued his approach to the platform as the viewing window shifted yet again and moved with Radin—yielding

Charles W. McDonald Jr.

programmatically to his approach so as to always stay just before him.

Seeing Keirill obliterate Seren struck him deeply in waves of profound sadness as he saw the boy—Kaylan—destroyed in heart, broken in soul by *the cauldron of hate*. He watched that broken soul beaten and whipped beyond that which would break anyone and yet witnessed the framework of Keirill's integrity create the boundaries that would guide the man-become-Damon.

This forging of Damon begot the unmaking of Man. Struck by the immeasurable patience to erase Humanity, Radin realized—for the first time—exactly *what* he was dealing with and he knew his role.

"I have come for you, *Great Eye*. **Nothing** can save you now!" Reaching out to the source he knew the dampening field could not sever, Radin obliterated all three Sentinels in one mighty opening of his left hand as their alloy parts exploded apart from their centers. Outward, in quasi-uniform directions, their bits flew to the edges of the room where they disintegrated into the honeycomb walls housing *The Eye of Time*. Absorbed into the programmable matter of the octagonal room of Man's doom.

Again, the great chord struck across the multitude of outcomes of all the possible continuums as the viewing window shifted yet again akin to the mirage upon the desert's horizon—showing him once more.

Only a few feet from the platform, Radin watched the viewing window as it moved with him. He watched as *The Eye of Time* chased and exiled the Four Brothers to the four other worlds of Humanity for the purpose of meeting *him* here and now. He watched as the beautiful Lis was erased from existence and captured by *a throne of souls*—held by Banthis. He watched as those souls accumulated and all that was Damon's Master Plan executed, elevating Banthis to the great Dragon of Darkness—now seeing into the future.

His compass of thoughts and emotions—his knowledge of right and wrong fighting with him, he could tolerate seeing no more as he rushed the platform to kill the mighty *Eye*.

Now inside its energetic aura of *hate* and *genocide*, Radin looked into all of time and all possibilities—seeing the god-like, omnipotent nature of this thing for the first time. Colors flashed before him in translucent blue, green, red, orange, purple, and yellow inside the slipstream of a great multitude of governed continuums as he tried to discern the *one* coupled to the *agenda* of the *Eye*.

Looking down into the waterfall of time, Radin saw inside the womb of Elise, watching as God the Creator ruthlessly murdered his only son. These were not the actions of the *Eye*. That was clear to him now. They were separate and distinct from one another. They were at war with one another, with Humanity in the balance—each with their own agenda for Man—or what remained.

His actions froze at the horrific site of his child being crushed and yanked from Elise's womb in an abhorrent act of supposed Love for Man as he considered what he'd been sent to do.

He remembered Damon's coaching and his urging: "*The Eye* is the architect of lies and the father of our genocide—you *must* **not** hesitate."

"Yea, I *do* know thee," Radin proclaimed at last, reaching into both the waterfall of energy above and outwardly to all the power necessary to destroy the *Eye,* and in doing so—himself. With both his hands raised high overhead and palm up, the flash came across his mind's eye as the words escaped almost involuntarily so, "**Show** me, Great Eye.... Show me and **seal** your fate."

And so much more yet to come to pass....

End Book 3

of

A Throne of Souls

Charles W. McDonald Jr.

A Throne of Souls

Book 1: A Kingdom Forgotten Published September 2016
Book 2: Black Mirrors of the Soul Published April 2017
Book 3: The Fall of Hate Published June 2018
Book 4: The Rise of Hope Published December 2020

Look for *The Veil of White* 2017
The Epic Conclusion of
A Throne of Souls ®2016
Anticipated Late 2022

Charles W. McDonald Jr.

Thank you for reading *The Fall of Hate*. I hope you enjoyed it immensely, and I would be greatly honored for you to leave a review of your thoughts and impressions on either the channel of purchase and/or Goodreads. Self-published authors live and die by reviews. So, I would strongly encourage you to take a moment to leave an honest review and would greatly appreciate your time in doing so. I welcome any and all constructive, positive-intent feedback and would love to hear from you.

Please feel free to contact me at:
http://www.facebook.com/throneofsouls
https://www.facebook.com/royvanmiral/
https://www.athroneofsouls.com
Parler @CharlesMcDonald
Twitter @athroneofsouls
https://pilled.net/#/profile/2818 (@AThroneofSouls)
Email: royvanmiral@hotmail.com
Goodreads Author Page:
https://www.goodreads.com/author/show/16002346.Charles_W_McDonald_Jr_
Amazon Author Page:
https://www.amazon.com/-/e/B01MDPEUAW
https://itunes.apple.com/us/author/charles-w-mcdonald-jr/id1198345238?mt=11

Sincerely,

Charles W. McDonald Jr.

Charles W. McDonald Jr.

About the Author:

Charles W. McDonald Jr. was born in Oklahoma City, raised in Norman, Oklahoma, and is a graduate of the University of Oklahoma with a BBA in Management Information Systems and a Minor in Economics. He also has a background in Aerospace Engineering, High Availability Systems Engineering, Disaster Recovery, Cloud Architecture (Azure, AWS, and GCP), and DevOps. Honorably discharged from the United States Air Force Reserves, he also has a background in the armed forces and is a full member of both the AFIO (Association of Former Intelligence Officers) and NDIA (National Defense Industry Association) organizations. He lives in Roanoke, TX.

In the summer of 1995, Charles read every available book on the Wheel of Time by Robert Jordan in a couple of weeks, and later that same July awoke in the middle of the night from an incredibly immersive dream. Charles began writing, by hand, everything he could remember from that dream which became the outline for the story of A Throne of Souls. Very shortly afterwards, Charles wrote Robert Jordan directly, looking for advice and inspiration for his own work, and Robert Jordan personally responded in a three-page letter, encouraging Charles to tell his story in his way, in his voice, and in his time. The completion of A Throne of Souls is a deeply personal mission for Charles to thank the spirit of Robert Jordan.

Charles W. McDonald Jr.

Glossary of Terms

†¤‡- ˌÆ‡:ˇŒ – Earth, Graelon, Kaleion, Perion, Setinon, in that order precisely. Two icons per world.

Actual – Word used to describe the person with the actual call sign. Team members are associated with a call sign, but an individual specifically assigned that call sign is referred to as call-sign actual. This is typically, though not always, the team lead of that given unit.

APEX – 25mm high explosive round designed specifically for the J-35 Joint Strike Fighter.

ARV – Alien Reproduction Vehicle. As opposed to ETV (extraterrestrial vehicle).

AWR – Allah's Waiting Room. Squirters fleeing from a contact situation will typically gather in another structure to regroup. When an airstrike is called in on said location, it's typically referred to as AWR.

Balak – Typically a mid-to-high level demon, appearing part dragon, part man, with the head of a great wolf with a squared jaw.

BFT – Blue Force Tracker, a vitally important piece of electronic field equipment identifying friendlies (via IFF – Identify Friend or Foe) and hostiles on a battlefield.

Bigot List – A Military Industrial Complex term used to describe those who are authorized to be read into an Unacknowledged Special Access Program. Usually curated by what is called "The Watch Committee." What religious order has a periodical called "The Watch Tower?" In the Book of Enoch, what were the fallen 200 angels called? Coincidence…? Something for you to think about…

BUD/S – Basic Underwater Demolition/SEAL training.

CCP – Chinese Communist Party.

Contact – Usually a directional reference to making gunfire and/or explosive contact with hostiles.

Codenames of Presidents:
> **Eagle** – William Jefferson Clinton
> **Deacon** – Jimmy Carter
> **Lancer** – John F. Kennedy
> **Mogul** – 45

Charles W. McDonald Jr.

Passkey – Gerald R. Ford
Rawhide – Ronald W. Reagan
Renegade – Barack H. Obama
Searchlight – Richard M. Nixon
Scorecard – General Dwight D. Eisenhower
Supervise – Harry S. Truman
Timberwolf – George H. W. Bush (former DCI and VP)
Trailblazer – George W. Bush

Death Blossom – When a mujahid blindly sprays automatic gunfire in a contact situation.

DNA vs RNA – AGCU = RNA (adenine, guanine, cytosine, and uracil) while AGCT (adenine, guanine, cytosine, thymine) = DNA.

Durial's Eye – See the Starlight of Immortality for one of its two definitions. The other definition refers to a scaled-up model of the first definition of Durial's Eye using the crater lake atop a dormant volcano on Eden as the eye of the scaled-up divination tool itself. Illirian Starfire was the Guardian of *Durial's Eye* until she gave it to Damon in *The Fall of Hate*. She described it to Damon in this manner, "You, of all people, are the one most like Durial, Damon. You work closely with both magic and technology, and Durial's Eye requires equal talent in both. Magic sees the future while technology refines the vision like a great and polished lens to a telescope."

EBEN – Extraterrestrial Biological Entities. EBEN. This is not a reference to ALL extraterrestrials, but of a particular race of extraterrestrials thought to be generally benevolent to, and establishing a working relationship with, Earth Humans.

Elian – A mostly diaphanous exotic textile material manufactured only by cave elves in the World Below and Between. Its exact composition is unknown, though it is often sought after by witches for reasons not known to the general public.

Entropy – An element of the Second Law of Thermodynamics describing the linearity of time as it relates to irreversible processes and their increasing levels of entropy versus reversible processes and their constant entropy (aka isentropic processes).
https://www.grc.nasa.gov/www/k-12/airplane/thermo2.html
ETV – Extraterrestrial Vehicle.

EXFIL – Exfiltrate, to leave or exit/egress a hostile zone of action.

Ferian – A dead language on Perion derived from Aramaic and Latin.

Forkettè – A Perion equivalent of an invocation/elemental specialist on Kaleion.

GCP – Global Consciousness Project (http://noosphere.princeton.edu/). Research data leveraged in the chapter 'Presentiment.'

Goat Trail – A fucked-up road, usually dirt, gravel, or mostly rubble from being bombed to dust.

Intelligence Categories and Terms:

COMINT – Communications Intelligence

DCI – Director of Central Intelligence. Usually, but not always synonymous with MJ-1.

ELINT – Electronics Intelligence

FISINT – Foreign Instrumentation Signals Intelligence; FISINT is intelligence from the interception of foreign electromagnetic emissions.

GEOINT – Geospatial Intelligence

HUMINT – Human Intelligence

IMINT – Image(s) Intelligence; often inclusive of GEOINT.

INTSUM – Intelligence Summary

SIGINT – Signals Intelligence; often inclusive of COMINT and FISINT.

MASSINT – Measurement and Signatures Intelligence; often inclusive of TELINT, SIGINT, and IMINT.

OSINT – Open-Source Intelligence

TELINT – Telemetry Intelligence

Goyim – A term of derision used by the Jesuits Watchtower (the Elite of the Jesuits) and Khazarian Mafia (The New World Order / Illuminati / Luciferian Cabal) to refer to the 99+% of the population, whom they do not consider worthy of having progeny or owning property of any kind.

The Haedron – See map of Kaleion. This is a sacred place with a great stone in an immense crater, presumed to have fallen from the stars and yet did not shatter or explode upon impact, suggesting its structure is incredibly dense. Perhaps more so than even iron.

Charles W. McDonald Jr.

Lamean – A mage on Kaleion, Graelon, or Terran system. This word is commonly associated with the general ability to cast Arcane on Perion.

Looking Glass – The US Airborne Command and Control System in place 24-7-365, intended to provide a real-time, national backup to the NCA and NMCC should those ground-based systems be destroyed or rendered inoperable. In the event those ground-based systems are destroyed or rendered inoperable, the NCA would transition to the Looking Glass in real time and provide options for an immediate tactical or strategic response at the discretion of US Government Civilian Command and Control (POTUS and the National Security Team). There are actually several Looking Glass aircraft, but one is airborne at all times of the day and night protecting the United States of America and its interests around the world.

LZ – Landing Zone.

M-249/SAW – Fully-automatic-tactical-weapon-carrying member of the Teams.

MCCC - The MCCC is comprised of High-Altitude Electronic Pulse (HEMP) hardened tractor trailers enclosing a secure Command and Control (C2) network operations and communications center. The MCCC platform must be sustained to provide survivable and endurable C2 of strategic and space forces for situation monitoring, tactical warning, force management, force direction, and decision support. In addition, this contract will provide for internal integration among platform network and communication systems, as well as for external integration of these systems with other C2 systems (e.g., MILSATCOM, GCCS, and the like).(Sourced: https://www.fbo.gov/index?s=opportunity&mode=-form&id=562422c06e7019192fbe943ad51ecaf7&tab=core&_cview=1)

National Command Authority (NCA) – Within the US Government, the NCA represents the lawful and final source for any and all use of military orders, especially as they relate to the US nuclear arsenal.

National Institute of Discovery Sciences (NIDS) – A Robert Bigalow investigative unit (Est. 1994) of scientists and subject matter experts engaged in analyzing paranormal events and deriving hard, applied sciences from them. This unit dispenses with the minutiae of whether or not extraterrestrials exist. They know they do… Their (NIDS) focus is on gaining access to metamaterials and Close Encounters of the Second Kind artifacts from which to conduct real, applied sciences to them and gain a working knowledge of how these things work in the larger whole. They have produced real, tangible scientific data results, which have been purchased by the DIA and shared on the official, secured DIA file share system for internal use and further diagnosis.

National Military Command Center (NMCC) – Within the US Military, the NMCC has three primary missions: 1) generate Emergency Action Messages directed to the battlefield; 2) provide solution/response options to the Joint Chiefs of Staff in response to attacks on Americans/American interests/assets around the world; 3) provide a strategic watch component monitoring nuclear weaponized activity around the world in real time.

Nuclear Command and Control Systems (NCCS) – The collective infrastructure of assets, systems, resources, and agencies that supports the President of the United States and his military chain of command with the ability to accurately direct the nation's nuclear forces in real time. The NCCS includes within its infrastructure other components and systems (ground-based, sea-based, and air-based), which include, but are not limited to, the Looking Glass/NAOC, MCCC, NMCC, NCA, and USSSTRATCOM among others.

OGA – Other Government Agency (i.e. CIA).

Operator – An honored term for a special operations team member in the field.

OPORD – Operational Orders.

OSCAR MIKE – On the Move.

PCC – Pre-Combat Check.

PKM – A soviet-era general-purpose machine gun.

PLF – Programed Life Form. Typically, neutral in alignment (neither good nor evil), these semi-sentient, autonomous life forms operate similar to a cyborg but are more organic in nature.

PLUGGER – GPS Unit.

POTUS – President of the United States of America.

Raphael – Often depicted holding a staff, Raphael is considered by the three great Terran religions to be the archangel of healing but is also known to bring comfort to the dying and help transition their souls to the afterlife.

Charles W. M°Donald Jr.

Resha – Old Tongue Ferian for The Breaker of Seals, The Destroyer of Men, and thought to be, by some, the Son of God the Creator.

Resident Identity Code Checksum – This site is designed to provide valid checksum resident identity codes for Chinese male and females. https://code-complete.com/chinaid/validids.php

Retrocausality – The concept of influencing the past from the future through communication mechanisms that cut across timelines, usually by nonlocality principles or to explain nonlocality behaviors. https://phys.org/news/2017-07-physicists-retrocausal-quantum-theory-future.html

Rose Silk – On Perion, some silkworms feed only on the nectar of roses. Their silk is often referred to as rose silk.

RPG – Rocket Propelled Grenade.

Sandbox – Operating in a theater of war associated with the Middle East or Persian Empire lands.

Shofar – A ram's-horn trumpet used by ancient Jews in religious ceremonies and in combat.

Sorians – A malevolent race of extraterrestrials, originating from the Orion star cluster and having a great empire of conquest made up of several different races from many worlds. Considered possibly synonymous with Draco and Anunnaki.

Squirter – A hostile leaving the contact zone expeditiously to avoid certain death at the hands of an Operator.

SRR – British Special Reconnaissance Regiment.

Stasis Stone – A physical gemstone imbued with the abilities to capture and maintain the immortal soul of a mortal being and to house said soul for an indefinite period of time (for safe keeping).

Staff of the Invoker – This staff was about three's—three acid-etched metal triangular helical rods, twisted in exactly three revolutions each, in a triple helix masterpiece with a massive iolite gem at its tip where the helical assembly flowered open suspending the gem in mid-air. The metallic, triple helix framework was forged in Black-Dragon fire and shaped by a great Titan, then enchanted and imbued with great powers by Dallia (Kaleion arcmage of enchantment) over the period of several days roughly a thousand years ago as a wedding present for her husband, the infamous Damon of Basrat. Specifically, its powers greatly increase the amount of energy

Damon, and only Damon, can channel. The types of energy it can augment is universal. If anyone, other than Damon attempts to use it, the staff will obliterate them. It is a central artifact in this story and the story could not be told without it.

Starlight of Immortality – Small blue-green star sapphire made of supersolids materials, roughly the size of a human palm. Neither solid nor gas nor liquid, it holds many secrets, not the least of which is to incredible longevity.

Supersolids – Wikipedia defines supersolids as: "In condensed matter physics, a supersolid is a spatially ordered material with superfluid properties. In the case of helium-4, it has been conjectured since the 1960s that it might be possible to create a supersolid.[1] Starting from 2017, a definitive proof for the existence of this state was provided by several experiments using atomic Bose-Einstein condensates.[2] The general conditions required for supersolidity to emerge in a certain substance are a topic of ongoing research."

Telomere – A telomere is a region of repetitive nucleotide sequences at each end of a chromosome, which protects the end of the chromosome from deterioration or from fusion with neighboring chromosomes. Its name is derived from the Greek nouns telos (τέλος) 'end' and meros (μέρος, root: μερ-) 'part.' (Sourced: from www.wikipedia.org). Unsourced: The telomere essentially shrinks with age, thus providing a mechanism by which we can determine biological age. For more information, go to www.telo-years.com.

The Halls of Aaramus – Created by an immeasurably powerful lich known as Aaramus. This plane of existence is time neutral, and the normal laws of physics are suspended here, as it is created out of space that does not exist in the normal/known Universe; it is extra-dimensional. As such, travel here is incredibly dangerous, as one is held hostage to the rules of physics, magic, and technology allowed by Aaramus, which are dynamic to his will. *Portal / Gate* entry into the Halls of Aaramus is allowed, but *Portal / Gate* exit typically is not, at least not without the expressed permission of Aaramus himself.

The Seeds of Humanity:

Kaleion – The homeworld of Damon, Kellen, Illirian,

Charles W. McDonald Jr.

Goldenbow, and several other characters. This world is one of the Seeds of Humanity, with twin moons, developed into an agrarian and magical society.

Perion – The homeworld of Talemar, Radin, Brigance Fireheart, and several other characters. This world is one of the seeds of Humanity, with twin moons, developed into an agrarian and magical society.

The Terran System – Also known as Earth. This is the homeworld to Michelle, Lawna, Michael, and several other characters. This world developed into a mostly technological society, though some belief in magic and witchcraft still exists, allowing some operational and effective use of same.

Graelon – One of the five homeworlds of the seeds of Humanity, Graelon is a mostly technical society where magic and witchcraft still work to a limited degree. It is the homeworld most closely associated and comparable with the Terran system. Their technology allowed them to colonize outposts where magic was more freely accepted, to disastrous outcomes in some cases.

Setinon – Possibly the oldest home of Humanity and the original seed of the Human race, Setinon is an entirely technical and highly advanced society capable of controlling planetary weather, FTL travel, and using energy directly from a star—also known as Helium 3.

Pleiadian – Introduced as a possible source world for Man pre-dating even Setinon. This is a series of seven extraordinarily bright stars arranged in a unique constellation that folds back in on itself. It is not one given solar system but a great series of solar systems 444.2 light years from the Terran solar system (Sol). https://www.gaia.com/article/who-are-the-pleiadians

UNFPA – *United Nations Population Fund.* You will not believe the evil and disgusting things this organization is involved with and responsible for until you do your own research. And just remember that any time they talk about 'voluntary' *sterilization* and/or *termination/abortion* programs, they really mean 'compulsory.'

The Void – Also known as the Nether, no one knows who, when, or why the Void was created, but it is a highly dangerous place home to souls lost between death and destiny. Large asteroids perilously collide with one another on a regular basis, making the entire Void an unstable place to visit. *Portal /Gate* entry and exit is allowed, but strongly ill-advised.

The World Below and Between – Created by unknown entities, this gateway between worlds that house the seeds of Humanity allows those who understand its navigational systems to traverse great distances in a very short period of time. Those who do not understand are permanently lost. *Portal /Gate* entry into the World Below and Between is permitted, but *Portal / Gate* exit is not. This plane of existence is time neutral.

Throne of Souls – The first Throne of Souls was made by Damon of Basrat for his wife (Banthis). There have since been others made for other entities given the travel of Damon's first spell that made such an abomination (*Damnation*). Since that time, Damon has made a highly modified version of *Damnation*, called *A Throne of Souls* that allows the caster to grant the *Throne of Souls* to himself/herself. Literally speaking, it combines some characteristics of a *Stasis Stone* in that it can capture and hold inside itself the living immortal soul of a mortal being. However, unlike a *Stasis Stone*, it affords the holder of the *Throne of Souls* the living energy given off by that soul or a collection/aggregation of souls within the *Throne of Souls* itself. In other words, there is no theoretical limit to how many souls could be captured in a given Throne of Souls, so the energy output of such a device could become unfathomable. Soul energy is electromagnetic, so if one has a way to use such an energy type as a source/input, then the output of such a source could be fantastic in scale and scope.

Timeline – The timeline and location markers provided throughout the novel are intended to help the reader navigate the story. Here is a rough guideline to follow when reading these markers:

> **A Very Long Time Ago** – More than a thousand years in the past.

> **A Long Time Ago** – Up to one thousand years in the past.

> **Present Day** – Within a few months, weeks, and hours of the "now" in the timeline.

> **Near Future** – Within the next two to five years of the "now" in the timeline.

Charles W. McDonald Jr.

Uriel – The Book of Enoch declares the archangel Uriel is 'the Light of God.' Some traditions recognize Uriel as Patron Saint of the Sacrament of Confirmation. Some believe he guards the consciousness of Jesus Christ.

U.S. Strategic Command (USSTRATCOM) - USSTRATCOM combines the synergy of the U.S. legacy nuclear command and control mission with responsibility for space operations; global strike; global missile defense; and global command, control, communications, computers, intelligence, surveillance and reconnaissance (C4ISR), and combating weapons of mass destruction. This dynamic command gives national leadership a unified resource for greater understanding of specific threats around the world and the means to respond to those threats rapidly. (Sourced: http://www.stratcom.mil/About/)

Washington's Driver – A pseudo-derogatory and somewhat friendly term for a very senior Operator (i.e. He's old enough to be George Washington's driver).

Wave-Particle Duality – In experimental physics, and as evidenced by the two-slit experiment, the observation that photons behave as a wave when not observed and as a particle when observed. In other words, photon particles can behave both as a fermion and as a boson. This is the essence of the Uncertainty Principle.

Charles W. McDonald Jr.

Glossary of Characters

This is a 5+1-world story and as such has a plethora of characters. This glossary is my attempt to help you keep them all straight. Within this glossary, I'll show you a glimpse of the character development behind them. For example, I possess some seventy pages describing Damon of Basrat, but here you'll see a robust paragraph.

Aaramus – A lich of profound power, wealth, knowledge, and agenda. A Tier A character central to all things. Founder of The Halls of Aaramus and creator of new planes of existence that operate outside the limitations of spacetime and linear time. Allegiances unknown.

President Abel – A Tier B character and elected President of Eden's government. Has a rather extensive history with Damon and understands him better than most. He knows Damon's history—at least, as Damon has shared it with him—and is someone Damon would call a friend and ally. Whether Damon has befriended Abel because of the name and his likeness to the friend he accidentally killed so long ago is unknown, but it wasn't lost on Damon when Abel ran for and then won the presidency without his aid. Now, they work together as best they can with compartmentalized sharing of information more than occasionally getting in their way.

Armstead:

    Pern – Left Bouschè years ago for places and purposes unknown to his brother (Gareth). A Tier B character who finds himself in the middle of a maelstrom, raising the hidden grandson of Damon the Banished.

    Leah – Tier B character; wife of Pern. Adopted mother of baby Ryker.

    Gareth – A Tier B character whose purpose alludes him, but his belief in his grandfather's words and deeds carries the day for him, and it is in the simplicity of his guiding principles that he hopes to find the hour of his brother's greatest need and then the hour of his own.

    Luke – A Tier B character and a beautiful soul carried away by the archangel Raphael. His role was to teach and prepare both

Pern and Gareth and to hold true the most important truths: that Humanity is not the work of the random and that both science and history will prove that so.

Arturus Ambrosius Aurelianus – Welsh: Emrys Wledig or Romano-British: Riothamus/Supreme Leader. What fable pronounced as King Arthur.

Banthis – Once a modest succubus of unlimited ambition and intellect and now heir-apparent to the Dragon of Darkness. The holder of the oldest and original Throne of Souls with powers only rivaled by the Dragon of Darkness and Lilith. Current wife to Damon of Basrat. A Tier A character whose master-level manipulation is central to many parts of the storylines. The key thing to understand about Banthis is how greatly she has suffered and the lengths to which she would go to unleash and redirect that suffering upon others. The only thing or person she could ever claim she truly loved (via her own warped view of love) is Damon and, because of her love for Damon, their daughters.

Brigance Fireheart – A Tier A character of no real power save the one he makes through his sheer will. A brute of a man both broad and tall—more akin to a bear than a man in stature. Brigance is a pragmatic general of generals. Ever more scrutinizing of both Radin and especially Damon, Brigance only affords the light of realism to shine and show the way for him and his men as the Banner of Hope hangs on but a thread.

Chara – Both vampire and mage, Chara was one of the most powerful and lethal forces of Kaleion until obliterated by Damon of Basrat. Her seed and bloodline extend across multiple worlds and is considered to be the source of bloodlust across both Terran and Perion. She is the seed and fire of Damon's hate, though not the root cause.

Daedrin – Brother of Seren. Stripped Keirill of all his great powers. Allegiances unknown.

Dallia – A Tier A character of more consequence than any might understand, Dallia—The Enchantress of Winds—is the first wife and first love of Damon. His unconditional adoration of her broke his then-healing soul irreparably so. In a very short time, she wove her existence and her presence into every fiber of Damon's being. Whether a selfless act or a selfish one, she knew her time short and her love for him immortal. Her magic still lives and works itself upon Damon each and every day he draws breath. Her light and her promise are the most beautiful of all characters in the story, and her time is not yet done.

Damon of Basrat – Only child of the famed Keirill and Seren. Grandchild to Emry and Ersila, as well as Grant and Sala. Great-grandchild of Durial and Fara. Once known as Kaylan until the age of thirteen when he murdered his father. Also goes by the titles: Dark Knight of Magic, Wielder of the Staff of the Invoker, Author of Damnation, Maker and Destroyer of Worlds, and Damon the Banished. Likely the most central Tier A character in the story. A profound and prolific womanizer who has a monstrous past and has killed more than can be counted. He has an ethical compass that rarely allows him to lie and a heart tormented by being abandoned to the hate of his father as a child. For much of Damon's life, he has been wronged by others, and now he seeks to unmake his greatest mistakes afforded by his blind ambition of avenging the death of his first wife and most precious gift of love: Dallia.

Duron of Erden – Placeholder for this character.

Dylan – Placeholder for this character.

Elise Day – Tier A character born Farelise Camden on Graelon—mage registration number: 07874376Alpha221321. Elise has been manipulated and led to the point she finds herself by the Dark Knight of Magic for purposes she's only now beginning to understand. She knows she wasn't recruited for her powers, which are significant, yet nothing compared to those of Damon. Her assumption is Damon needed a fully registered mage to help execute some part of his Master Plan, but every time she solidifies the justification of her doubt of Damon, he puts forth actions that bring her squarely back into his fold. She considers Damon a complete enigma and keeps him at arm's distance, expecting the day will come when she will be forced to pick sides—permanently so. Wife to Michael Anthony Day and lover to Radin, she left Graelon to pursue Michael Anthony Day on Earth and then left Earth to pursue the reincarnation of Michael on Perion only to find herself intimately involved with Radin, whom she considered Michael's possible kindred soul.

Emrys Wledig – Arturus Ambrosius Aurelianus – Welsh: Emrys Wledig or Romano-British: Riothamus/Supreme Leader. What fable pronounced as King Arthur.

Evanyil – A dark/cave elf that is supremely capable at thievery, death, and deceit. This darkest of all pure dark elves, Evanyil is the personification of self-sustaining, self-interest. Her ever-present poisoned dagger about her right hip is one of her few constants in life, else she is as chaotic as the quantum particles Mira studies in college. Her compass is always and forever pointed in her own best interest, yet how she gets there is anything but a straight line. Straddling the fine line betwixt genius and insanity, Evanyil is just lucid enough to bring brilliant unconventional thinking to Damon's structure—making their partnership uniquely dangerous for any of their most unfortunate targets. At their peak, they pulled off some of the most legendary and atrocious acts in the history of Kaleion. Their adventures are the source of many biographical texts on Kaleion. Evanyil and Damon share a rich, passionate, and lethal history with one another and with Evanyil's sister, Lorianus. A living god now, Evanyil's ask of Damon some years back in the current continuum is the source of Damon's Master Plan and his need to grow his powers.

The Four Brothers:

Durial – Settled Kaleion with Fara. The leader of the Four Brothers. Maker and Wielder of The Starlight of Immortality, Father of Dragons, The Great Life-Bringer, and The Wellspring of Humanity.

Pierio – Settled Graelon with Ceres. The technologist and scientist of the Four Brothers, Pierio sought to recreate the conditions of Setinon where magic and technology collided, experimenting with how best to integrate and isolate the two where applicable. His foremost desire was to understand what conditions led Setinon down its path to create a more durable path for Graelon and Humanity as a whole, as well as to afford them the best opportunities to defeat the *Eye*.

Alexelio – Settled Perion with Elsa. Only second to Durial in his powers, Alexelio was the artist, the sculptor, and the creator of the Four Brothers. His bloodline created great and sweeping architectural elements inspired of wind, ocean, and starlight. He sought to keep magic, in its most powerful forms, alive at all costs—even if it meant the loss of the knowledge of science and technology. Is considered the most likely candidate for the architect of The World Below and Between.

Adamian – Settled Terran (Earth).

Goldenbow – Lineage unknown. Origin unknown. Kindred brother to Damon and long-time associate to Kellen the Destroyer. Tier A character whose compass and kinship closely aligns with Damon of Basrat. Professional assassin and living legend on Kaleion, Goldenbow holds a special and central place in the story, which—in time—will be revealed. He is often the source of special counsel to Damon and is Damon's most-trusted ally in all things.

Hadley Mason – Former SRI master Remote Viewer trained, like his father, by Military Intelligence before breaking away from the government's grip upon him and working alongside Ron Stencowsky after the Battle of Warwick. It should be noted Hadley is 6'1." His father, also in this story, in "The Looking Glass," is 6'2," so when you see that delta, I'm referring to the difference between father and son. These are not the same character.

Harrison – An alien hybrid son of one of the very first Men in Black and a deep black operative within one of the Secret Space Program(s).

Hersila – Placeholder for this character.

Herot – Placeholder for this character.

Iain Longbow – A Tier B character and a legendary archer on Perion and companion to Rowarc.

Illirian Starfire – Only child of Jorah and Hannah, grandchild of Grant and Sala, and great-grandchild of Durial and Fara. Born the daughter of a mariner, she often uses maritime idioms and analogies, even when not entirely appropriate. Illirian and Damon's history goes back a millennia or more as her affinity for Damon became far more dangerous over the centuries. Illirian holds many titles: 'Ruler of the Rod of the Nine,' 'Watcher of the Runes of Fate,' 'Guardian of *Durial's Eye*.' The Starlight of Immortality is synonymous with *Durial's Eye* (the original version used by the Great Durial himself), but also affords its master unlimited lifespan without the need for magic. Damon and Illirian's relationship is the definition of the word, 'complicated.' How they sort through that relationship is fundamental to the unmaking of *A Throne of Souls*. From none-too-far a distance, she both meddles and guides Damon's actions by manipulating and controlling his psyche. Some would say she keeps it on the frayed edges of sanity to keep Damon cold, calculated, and ruthless. Illirian's seal is that of a pale-pink rose with white leaves on a tan clay-cast circle. Illirian Starfire also sits on what used to be called Kaleion's Council of Mages.

Joran of Erden – A Tier B character and Royvan Miral's counterpart on Kaleion. A legend in his own right, he has a great, in-depth knowledge of both ancient and modern languages, history, lore, and relics. His power and influences come from his travels and the unearthing of secrets most profound affecting every major seat of power on Kaleion.

Keirill – One of the greatest and most powerful of all mages in history—second only to the Great Durial—Keirill tested the boundaries of what was safe and authorized to risk becoming the greatest of all. His heart was relatively pure and his compass modestly true until his greed and lust for power led him to a path of hate that would result in his hating of his own existence more than anything else. A Tier A character, Keirill's infection of the *Instrument of Humanity's Hate* both drives and vexes Damon into being. Kaylan may have been his physical progeny, but Damon was his most significant achievement for Man or Man's undoing—depending on your perspective.

Kellen the Destroyer – Child of Hersila and Herot, grandchild of Castlier and Freya, great grandchild of Durial and Fara, Kellen is a bane to all things female. There is no fouler misogynist that Kellen the Destroyer. His legendary hatred of women the only forerunner to his infamy. His actions are not entirely self-serving—at least, not on the surface—and his agenda is entirely veiled in mystery. If past is prologue, it won't be good. Like Damon, or because of Damon, he pays his debts and holds his word high in merit. Unlike Damon, he's incapable of seeing women as anything other than something to be used—usually as little more than his personal sex slaves. He has a tense but working relationship with Illirian Starfire only because of Damon's intermediary status between them. Before Damon they found themselves in combat with one another on more than one occasion but have dialed back the hostilities toward one another to see where the Master Plan is going and where they will fall on opposing sides of it. They may very well need each other, and Damon may very well need them both to work together to unmake *A Throne of Souls*. Kellen also sits on what was formerly called Kaleion's Council of Mages. A Tier A character, Kellen is one of Damon's oldest friends and allies, but the circle of his trust with Damon has found its limits on a few occasions. He is only afforded what information Damon must provide for him to serve his function within Damon's Master Plan, and that level of trust/distrust extends in both directions, as Kellen has a great secret of his own that greatly impacts Damon and the central storylines. Kellen the Destroyer holds many titles and monikers, 'The Hate of Mankind,' 'The Midnight Morning,' and 'The Flame of Hate.'

Lis – The Genesis input of *A Throne of Souls*, though the Genesis motive stems from Dallia's death. The theft and unjust condemnation of this beautiful soul forever altered the balance of power and became the first stone cast into the pond of Creation that would present and precipitate its unmaking.

Marshall:

Ethan – A Tier B character murdered in the first great battle for Man. Ethan's contributions to that war have yet to be fulfilled.

Lynn – A Tier B character, wife to the murdered Ethan Marshall, and now love of Talemar, Lynn has advanced and grown but has stumbled along the way in her love of a baby not her own. Now the balance of her life belongs to that baby boy. Her hopes and dreams now become his.

Michael Anthony Day – Tier A character and the first love of Elise. Michael is central to many—if not all—threads of the storyline. A great many characters in *A Throne of Souls* fall into categories that are very fluid between the spectrum of good and evil. Many characters in this story are quite far from either end of that spectrum, but Michael Anthony Day is an exception. He is the most extreme example of pure goodness available in this story. He is not without flaw and certainly not without internal conflict, but his compass is the truest (morally speaking) of any character in this story. There is no moral ambiguity in the character of his soul—whatsoever. And, quite possibly, the reincarnation of Emrys Wledig.

Mira Castille – Daughter of Charles and Elizabeth Castille. Dean's list sophomore physicist at the University of Texas at Austin. Intimately close to Damon of Basrat. Mira is a foul-mouthed, mouthy preacher's daughter of a Christian parentage, naughty by nature and rebellious by necessity of survival. Her far-reaching understanding of nature described through mathematics and the laws of physics are her most trusted guide to the new realities exposed to her through Damon and his Master Plan.

Mira (Original) – Long ago, after Dallia's death, he went through many loves and lovers, but the original Mira was special. She held the same passion and mage talents as Damon—though not holding all of his natural abilities. She specialized in the same categories of magic as Damon and was nearly his equal in all things and intellect. She was murdered shortly after her visit to the Graelon Colonial Outpost, as were many of Damon's loves whose orbit was too close for their own survival. Damon and this Mira never married, but they were as close as a couple could be, and her loss took Damon centuries to fully mourn.

Mora – A significantly powerful mage and member of the former Kaleion Council of Mages, this Tier B character held ties with Eldrac, though not by choice. More of a trophy to Eldrac, she once ran in circles close to Damon and now (via Talemar's great magic) finds herself in ever tighter circles with Radin. Mora longs to chart a path for herself of her own making, but fate may have other plans for her—as may *The Eye of Time*.

Morden – A Tier B character and arch nemesis to Damon the Banished. He served as court arcmage to many kings and stewards and had more than one run-in with Damon that didn't fare him well. But Morden is a powerful sorcerer, home to Kaleion, and one who has never found himself on the same side as Damon—until the latter stages of Damon's Master Plan, where Radin mended old fences of hate between the two and proposed their working together towards a common enemy. Or enemies common to the Master Plan...

Miss X – A Tier B character high up in the directorship chain of command for Continuity of Government and COG planning.

Quincy Arthur Billings – Once the head of Whitehall and formerly the superior of Michael Anthony Day, Billings was asked by Michael to be his Senior Advisor when elevated to the throne. Since that time and Michael's death, Billings has looked after his children as Elise went in search of

Michael's soul.

Quinn – A Tier B character and companion of Iain Longbow and Rowarc. A generic mage of modest-but-growing abilities and a good heart.

Radin d'Aguillon – Biological child of Damon of Basrat and Vosh. Raised by Rowarc (famed retired ranger) and Arella d'Aguillon. A Tier A character central to many threads of the storylines. Has rapidly developing powers and immeasurable potential with morals deeply conflicted by personal experiences and his proximity to Damon. The threads connecting him to his past with Rowarc fade on almost an hourly basis as he grows under Damon's wing but are more persistent than even he understands.

Rathemeer – Placeholder for this character.

Rena Rectovich – A Tier A character, born Carastovich Catarena Rectovich, she is one of a very select few surviving witnesses (other than Damon) to Dallia's death. She heads a massive corporate empire amassed over a thousand years of experience and investments. She has extensive reach—politically, influentially, and otherwise—into every major government on Earth and maintains an Immortal Army that can now operate in daylight, thanks to gene therapy of the genetic code belonging to three young babes (the Blade daughters). Catarena's agenda and Damon's may overlap at times and may conflict at others, but she has long sought out the man she saw robbed a life she thought might make him a totally different person than the man he is today.

Rena's Immortal Army:

Michelle Alexandra Blade – A Tier A character born in Denver, CO to Chase and Marie Blade, Michelle began a successful investigative firm that partnered closely with state and federal government officials. Discovered by and finding herself in reach of Rena's radar, Michelle was offered the opportunity to have something she'd only dreamed of before—but at an immortal price. Michelle's motives and drivers are relatively simple. She loves and adores her daughters, and that drives nearly all of her decisions. She has a healthy distrust for Rena and an even more robust distrust of Damon, but her gut and palpable instincts connect her to both and tell her to hold fast.

Lawna Blade – A Tier B character and wife to Michelle,

Lawna's mistrust of Rena is almost legendary. Like Michelle, her driving force is the daughters they share, but her love for Michelle is paramount and affords with it a lethal amount of jealousy. As far as capabilities go, Lawna is likely one of the most dangerous characters in the story.

Ryker – The only child of Elise and Radin, hidden from existence for sake of his own survival. Grandson of Damon the Banished.

Ron Stencowsky – Tier B character, former M1A2 Abrams tank personnel, and now master builder and security director on Eden. Runs in circles close to Damon and is extremely limited in his trust of Damon.

Rowarc d'Aguillon – A Tier B character, he raised Radin from a baby but was and is still conflicted over his absence in Radin's life and the absence of his wife—Arella d'Aguillon. Rowarc carries a great burden of guilt extending from his wife's death and what he now knows to be the death of his biological child lost some twenty years past.

Royvan Miral – Tier A character, legendary adventurer on Perion, and crucial to the Seals thread of the storylines. Many biographical novels have been written of his adventures and his findings. He has a mind for academia, languages, and cultures. He considers himself agnostic but cannot ignore what he has seen and experienced. He's trying—greatly so—to keep an open mind in operating this close to Radin and Damon, but his reservations of Damon's Master Plan run deep.

Royvan Miral's Crew:

Kerrich – Tier B character who grew up with Radin—a man he no longer recognizes due to his close proximity to Damon and Damon's agenda. Kerrich doesn't make pretense of an agenda that he doesn't understand, but in Royvan Miral, he found a man he believes he can trust and has ascribed himself to protégé to Royvan Miral as best he can. The End is upon them regardless, and the only way through this is through it. That much he agrees upon, but how we most safely get from here to the other side is a matter of the most urgent and delicate judgment, and that's where his mistrust of Damon leads him to defer to Royvan Miral—for now.

Levi – Tier B character and member of Royvan Miral's crew. Generally considered Royvan Miral's right-hand man and trusted advisor.

Ham – Tier B character and member of Royvan Miral's crew. A good and hearty soul, more in tune with the big picture than most afford him credit.

Seren – A beautiful soul compromised by hate's reach into her own life and the life of her progeny. A Tier A character whose role in this story changed everything. If not for her, there would be no Unmaking.

Silverstring:

Wraith – A Tier A mage of somewhat compromised values and mysterious background wed to his fraternal twin sister. Like many characters in the story, Wraith is neither good nor evil and wouldn't even fit solidly anywhere on that spectrum. His behaviors are more fluidly fitting to the dynamics of the situations before him. He's very much an agenda-driven character, but his agenda is shut to all but his sister and wife.

Silura – A Tier A very promiscuous character who is a mage and wife to her fraternal twin brother, Wraith. Even more complicated than her twin brother and husband, Silura shrouds herself in mystery and frivolity, masking intentions known only to her. With all the tact of a machine gun, Silura's brutal honesty is generally off-putting to others. As shut as Wraith is to the outside world, Silura is even more so and holds secrets, even from her husband—sometimes especially so. Both Silura and Wraith have silver locks of hair on opposing sides.

Sophia – Dean of the College of Invocation (Basrat, Kaleion). Potentially one of the incarnations of Mira Castille. One who imparted some vital information to Damon when he was but fifteen years of age and not yet a mage.

The Chairman – The right hand of God the Creator. From time immemorial, it was the Prince of Egypt until his immortal shell was slain in combat by Damon of Basrat. Now held by Illirian Starfire.

The Six:

Anna – One of the Six. A Tier B character converted by Lawna Blade into an immortal creature, Anna's history is one of a lust for both power and flesh, but her driving force now is the revenge of her affliction and it threatens to compromise her task that affords her newfound existence. As one of the Six, she has been given a mission that is expected to be carried out, and she knows herself not indispensable in that role.

Asmodeus – Prince of the Abyss. One of the Six.

Castlin – One of the Six. A Tier B character, careful and methodical and not entirely on-board or married to the role to which he was assigned. He has a long history with both Talemar and Eldrac and with Damon by reputation. His allegiances are his own, but which side he falls on may change the balance of power just enough.

Eldrac – One of the Six. Murdered by Damon the Banished.

Lilith – The Great Princess of the Abyss. One of the Six. A Tier A character, Lilith is known for an appearance so perfect and so abhorrent as to make those who look upon her physically ill. With a serpentine tail and flesh that is acidic to all living things, Lilith is a being most vile and with a contempt for Man only surpassed by her need to keep the status quo.

Xarn – One of the Six. A Tier B character, Xarn's lust for sex (with both men and women) is as legendary as her frivolity and volatility. She is quite mad and dangerously powerful with a unique gift for working massive-scale objects that will become apparent in later parts of the story. Her role is one pivotal in relation to the Monuments of Creation.

The Great Talemar – Once married with family, stranded and left behind to a fate unknown and only barely chronicled by books, half-buried by fiction, quarter-buried by time, Talemar is seeking new meaning to his life in a timeline not his own as he tries to leverage the best parts of his past to make better decisions in the future and tries to use the worst parts of his past as fuel to destroy those standing in his path. He knows himself *the One* yet is mystified by how Radin can wear his crown. He secretly seeks the answers to this question, but for now Radin has proven both powerful and useful, and he'll continue to leverage that situation for as long as need be— to buy time—as well as to understand Damon's role and Damon's Master Plan. Talemar has a great deal on his plate as he does all these things, while holding together Humanity on Perion, knowing that role will soon expand as the scrolls expound their reach throughout all the *Seeds of Humanity*. The time for his greatness may have to wait, but it *is* coming.

Terry Goodwin – A Tier B character and leader of Michael Anthony Day's SRR unit on Earth.

Toblain – A Tier B character and living gold dragon.

Voltor – Once a lesser demon, Voltor ascended to great power when allying with Eldrac (and others), who afforded Voltor souls he wouldn't have otherwise held claim over. Voltor's Throne of Souls was obliterated when his immortal shell was destroyed by Damon of Basrat. Voltor is most known for his capture and torment of Radin.

Vosh – Perion arcmage and lover to Damon of Basrat (Kaleion), who together are the biological parents of Radin.

Witches:

    Adena – A Tier A character, Adena is the Mother and High Seat of witches for over a thousand years. Adena ruled with the antithesis of her seemingly fragile and delicate frame. Feared by all who knew her, Adena is a formidable foe who demands utter loyalty, and one not to be taken lightly.

    Desindra – A Tier B character, Desindra is a legitimate threat to Adena, Desindra's burgeoning guile finds new life in the most unlikely of sources and newfound friendships.

    Silvaran – Character definitions forthcoming. As the witch thread becomes more integral in the story, you'll see many more of these characters and their development become front-and-center.

    Minna – Character definitions forthcoming. As the witch thread becomes more integral in the story, you'll see many more of these characters and their development become front-and-center.

    Sabine – Character definitions forthcoming. As the witch thread becomes more integral in the story, you'll see many more of these characters and their development become front and center.

Xaldran – A Tier B character and living legend of a mage on Perion though his true origins and fate were and still are unknown. Author to a great Tome of Power that articulates the history of Humanity as well as hinting to its fate, Xaldran's true purpose has yet to be fulfilled, but may yet come by that which (and who) have survived him.

Ykstherin – A Tier A character, counsel to both Radin and Talemar, whose history and future is veiled in mystery. This character hints at greatness yet yields the limelight, for it is fleeting, and he is not. Precisely who and what Ykstherin is will become known in time. Don't underestimate this character and his potential in the story.

Charles W. McDonald Jr.

www.ingramcontent.com/pod-product-compliance
Lightning Source LLC
Chambersburg PA
CBHW071342020726
47502CB00001B/213